LUCK AND PROBABILITY

MAP FELICIANO

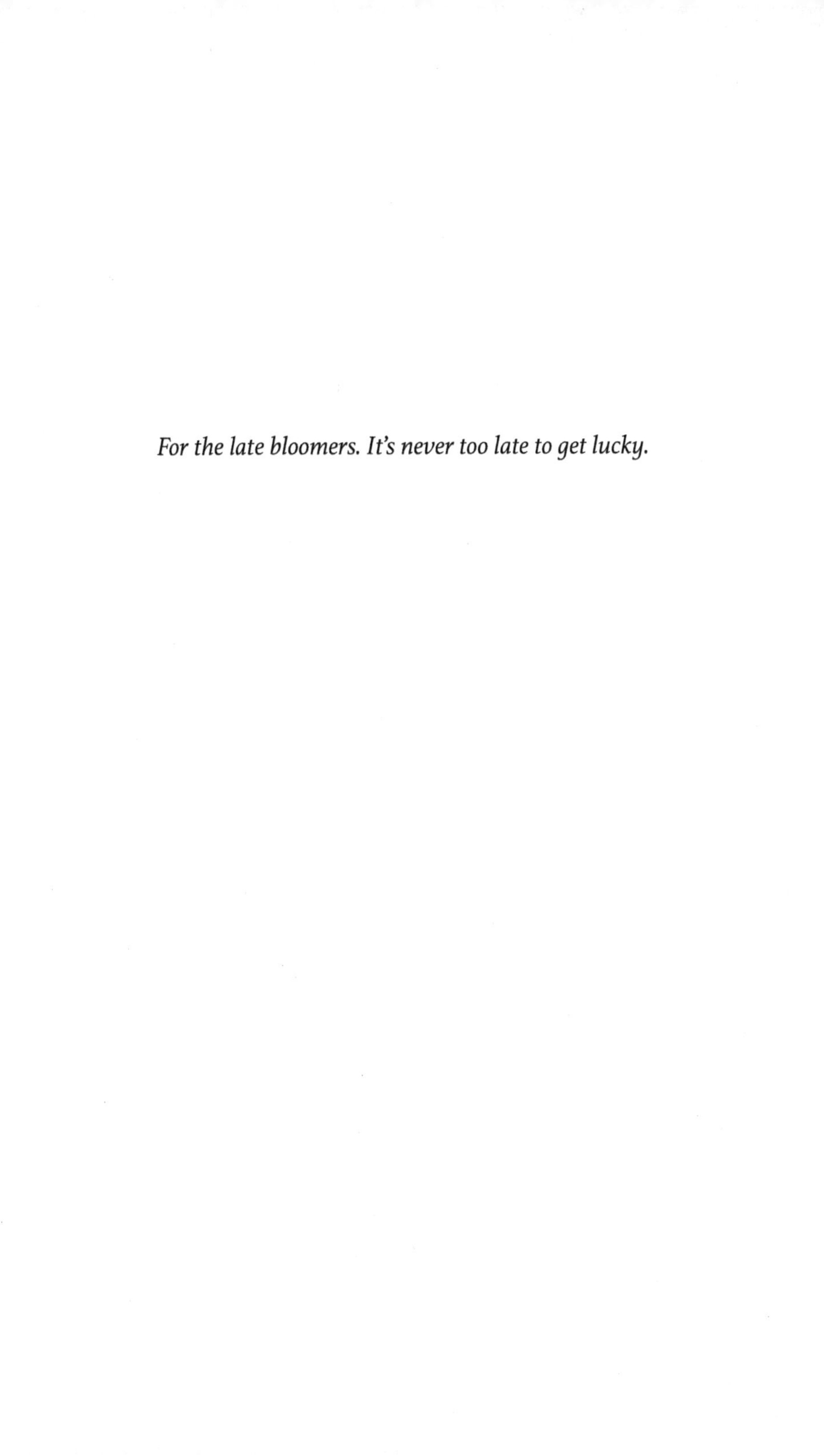

For the late bloomers. It's never too late to get lucky.

Luck and Probability

1

THE RIVER SPEAK

On a similar earth, with humans and civilizations quite like our own, Elaine Aquae prepares for the River Speak; and much like everything else in her life, her organization of said event is going exactly to plan.

The River Speak is a yearly tradition in her hometown, the population of Sigmut of the Alappan mountains. The town's children chatter amongst themselves in front of her before she claps her hands together. They startle into silence, and she smiles down at them. She's always had claps like thunder.

"You all are in charge of a very vital part of the River Speak today. As the youngest, it's your job to bring up barrels of wine from the foothills."

They all groan. They're small barrels, and it's just to tire them out by the time sundown hits so the adults can drink without worrying about the kids sneaking off.

"No complaining."

"But they're heavy."

She narrows her eyes. "Don't you want your wish?"

They straighten their spines. "Do you think we'll get ours this year?"

"Wishes come at the right time, not your time," Elaine says. It's what her mother told her as a child, and what her mother probably said before her. Elaine hadn't received her wish yet, so she knew it had to be true. "Now, get to work! We need you up here way before sundown."

They grumble and stagger to their feet. Elaine turns when she hears the call of her name and sees her brother Alan approaching.

She remembers the River Speak from the year she turned eight as she eyes the water critically. Her and her mother, Paola Aquae, steward of this river, looked into the water. Beneath, life flourishes: rocks, flora, and fish that swam by too quick for her to identify.

The Aquae family is one of the only families to live so freely in the wild mountains. And Elaine is the only sibling who stayed. Her brother Alan and sister Phoebe left twenty-four years ago to school and the wild respectively. Elaine never felt it was the right time to leave. At first, it had been the pollution from miners she'd had to help resolve. Then, her father had a broken foot one summer and she'd been in charge of spraying pesticides on the summer wyrms. One chore after another fell onto her, until the idea of setting out on her own became unfathomable.

"Just water?"

Her mother dipped her fingers into the water. They both watched it glide around her and noticed that nothing changed.

"Water is everything, Elaine. It's in the soup we boil, the trees that grow fruit, even our own two feet. Water is what makes Earth, Earth. Every biome and living creature depend on it somehow. Humans are especially attuned to it: the same moon that raises the tides, calls to the water beneath our skin. We're more than neighbors, we're cousins."

"Yeah, and cousins help cousins steal their baseball gloves back from ex best friends," her brother said. He popped up behind Elaine with sandy hair and a toothy grin. "That's what I'm asking for this year, for the river to steal my glove back."

The people of the town always gave, and continue to give, their finest crops, wine and other assorted gifts. In exchange, the river grants what all living things need: water and wishes.

"I thought you bought that together," Paola chided.

He pouted. "I did too. But he hasn't been sharing like he said he would, so I'm stealing it back."

"Stealing's not right," Elaine said. She crossed her arms. "It's not nice."

"It's not stealing if it's mine too," Alan replied.

His confidence made Elaine falter. Even then, Alan knew a lot more about the world than she and her sister Phoebe did, despite being born after Elaine. Mom and Dad wouldn't let them wander off alone at least until they turned twelve. Anything before then is a ripe age for young girls to be stolen by one of the creatures in the mountains. Boys only really have to worry about being stolen by the sea, and they're nowhere near an ocean.

In the present day, it's Elaine instilling her confidence into the kids in front of her instead of her mother.

"Bad news," he says. "The wood for the fire's wet, and the baker lost some pastries on the way here to something whispering his greatest desires from the trees. So, we've only got one sweet roll for everyone now."

Elaine rubs the bridge of her nose. "We can deal with less sweet rolls. The fire's going to be an issue. Maybe we can use some of the wine from the caskets to light the wood?"

"Where do you plan to get the caskets?"

"I just sent the kids off to get it. They should reach the foothills in an hour, then it'll take another hour and a half to get back up here. But it should be enough time." It might take even less. They'd taken her speech very seriously.

Alan tilts his head over her shoulder to look behind her. "Those kids?"

"What?" She whips her head around to see the children with their dress skirts in their hands and their pants rolled up to their knees, playing "catch the fish" with her sister, Phoebe. Phoebe, the fish in question, roils in one's grasp before escaping, causing the game to start all over again.

"What did I say," she yells.

The kids flinch and look back at her, guilty.

"Go on."

They run down the hill, and Phoebe, conveniently, swims away towards the house before she can be scolded by her older sister.

Alan puts an arm around her shoulder and guides her in the same direction, towards the Aquae family home.

"I don't have time."

"Family meeting. It won't take long, I promise."

They walk in, and there, her family has settled in. Phoebe swam up from the river and rests along the edge of the pond at their dinner table, elevated and at face level, while everyone else sits.

Her father looks at his son disappointingly. "Alan, your sister has been working all day. What is this?" Albert says. Albert Aquae, born Albertson Leatherforth, the father of the three Aquae's and husband of Paola, is a scruffy, rusty-haired man. Elaine goes to take a seat next to him, but not before giving him a warm side hug.

"Teacher's pet," Alan mutters as he walks past Elaine. She swats at his arm, and he smirks when she misses as he darts away.

To her dad, Elaine is as dutiful a daughter as they come

"Alan, you are in your sixties. Stop antagonizing your sister," Isabel says. She turns to address the whole table. "We have very exciting news."

Elaine smiles graciously at Alan's wife, Isabel. She was initially worried about the type of woman Alan would bring home but was grateful when he picked sensible, sensitive Isabel.

"You're moving back home." Paola claps.

"Well, not that."

"You've gotten a real job."

"Firefighting *is* a real job, Dad."

"Not one with money."

Phoebe's mouth gapes open then closes.

Isabel's smile grows tight, and Alan notices. He turns to his family, nostrils flared, and all the candles in the room light up in agitation.

"She's pregnant!"

Much like the people of our Earth, humans are born with magic in their body. But here, the magic is more than good parking karma or never stepping on a ladybug. It's the ability to read someone's mind or create light in a room full of darkness. Magic is dangerous, palpable, and a financially viable career path. Each living thing has a magical core, and each core has its own affinity. It's the same way each of us are born with our own strengths and passions. When you're a baby, your main passions are eating and sleeping. But as children grow and gain their own personalities, they learn to love soccer, or painting or —if a parent is especially unlucky—arson. Mage is as interchangeable a word as person here. Every living thing, with a certain amount of intelligence, is born with magic. Their cores, the spiritual well which they are born with, are different sizes, which affects their ability to use magic. The cores are different depending on the type of person a mage is. The core of a fire-affinity golem will have more in common with a telekinetic golem's core than it would with the core of a human with an affinity for fire, for example. Some cores, like Elaine's, are so weak that a mage can't use magic at all.

Alan was born a strong fire mage, like his father, and it had been a tumultuous few first decades of raising him. He is now sixty, Elaine seventy-three. To mages on this earth, who live well into their two hundreds, Elaine is a woman grown, filled with all the experiences and lessons over half a century has to offer. She is not so young as to be categorized as naive, and not so old to be viewed as feeble.

Elaine has an affinity for probability magic, which had been quite the shock. Her sister's affinity was water before she turned into a fish. Probability magic is on official record as being a rare affinity, and one that has been categorized by the world as impracticable, as those uncommon instances in history of other mages having it record it as being "not applicable to any occupations". In plain words: it can't be used at all. Like an empty lighter, except once upon a time, at least the lighter had a spark. On top of being practically unusable, Elaine's core has also given her silver eyes, set farther apart than usual, and silver hair. In the summer, when she lies next to the river, her hair glimmers like the scales of the salmon beneath the current.

"Pregnant," Paola and Elaine say.

"Congratulations," Paola cheers. "Oh, the first grandchild. Albert, a grandchild."

Albert grins from ear to ear and a misty film grows over his eyes. "I thought the day would never come."

Alan rolls his eyes, but his smile shows he's clearly happy about the antics. "She's far enough along now that it makes sense to tell you all. We wanted to keep it a surprise until the River Speak."

The chatter of her family fades into the background as she thinks about what this means. Alan, her baby brother, is having a baby. In the right fashion, too: marriage, then baby. Years ago, she was sure he would show up in his thirties with a pregnant woman and a 'what can you do' attitude. He hadn't lived his life by societal expectations: he'd dropped out of university, gone to work in the firefighter corps instead of coming home again, and lived a life of drinks and bachelordom for two decades. They'd all been surprised, but relieved, when he'd brought home Isabel. The fact that her brother is reaching this milestone before her leaves a bad, competitive feeling in Elaine's stomach.

She stands up and slams her hands on the table.

The room goes quiet as they all look towards her. Alan smiles nervously.

"I know you hate surprises, Elaine, especially when you're the one planning. But I figured this one could be excused?"

She exhales, trying to release the tension from her shoulders. Her parents watch her cautiously. "This calls for more wine," she says, breaking the tension, and her family smiles.

Paola rushes around the table to hug a still-sitting Isabel.

Albert takes Alan by the shoulder and careens him around the room, chanting, "Twice your weight in wine, twice your weight in wine!"

It's tradition in the mountains to drink for two when someone announces their pregnancy.

"I can't wait to tell those brats to go back and get another dozen barrels." Elaine cackles.

THE ADULT POPULATION of the town cheers when Alan announces it to all of them, and they giddily send their groaning children back down the hill for more wine. Everybody drinks heavily through the night, and the kids, as planned, are exhausted. Still, they are excited to have their homes to themselves while their parents drink the night away. Before heading home, they'd all gone and whispered their wishes to the river, dropping in their favorite meat or most treasured toy in exchange.

Most of the adults are gathered around the bonfire, so she

takes this opportunity to slip next to the river. She pulls out a rock she found earlier in the year, smooth and glittery, and drops it into the Aquae River. Drunk, she wishes for what she always does: "I wish for things to never change."

When she returns to the bonfire, Paola stands up to give a speech.

She stumbles a bit, but Albert places a firm hand on her leg to keep her stable.

"Thank you, all, for coming to another River Speak. I've known everyone here as long as I've known this river. With each year, our lives stay safe, full, and happy. We wish, and the wishes come when it is right, not when we want them. It's because we treat the river like family that our wishes come true. And speaking of family, it is time to talk about each of my beautiful children."

Alan and Elaine groan in dismay, but the rest of the crowd cheers and whistles, in no small part, due to the wine.

"My sweet Phoebe, my youngest. She never told me her wish, but I imagine it had something to do with escape: to be free and live life according to her own means. And now, she lives her days as an exceptionally healthy salmon, of whom we all love and cherish. I remember when she was born, and she could hardly speak a word without stuttering."

She turns to Alan, whose wife places a comforting hand on his. "My sweet Alan. My only boy. And soon to be a father."

The crowd cheers.

"We didn't know what to do with you when you were born. Elaine was so easy, and then you came, loud and brash and on fire. I remember the time you lit all the crop silos on fire. We were banned from the foothills until you worked it all off! You were so angry as a child. I am so glad you came around and calmed down." Alan grimaces and clenches Isabel's hand hard. Elaine braces herself when Paola turns to her.

"Elaine. Sweet, sensible, Elaine. I always wondered how I

got a child like you. I was wild when I met your father, and he was just the same."

She nods politely, and Albert looks at his wife, bemused. Still, he smiles before making eye contact with Elaine. They both know she got her temperament from Albert—who had never been wild a day in his life.

"I was so nervous when you were born. I didn't think I was ready to be a mom. But when I became pregnant with you, I knew Albert was the one for me. Some people would call that night in the woods a mistake, but I call it a blessing: destiny. Because it brought me you, a natural steward of the mountains."

There's polite clapping.

Paola laughs and spins in a circle, enjoying the attention. Wary of her speeches, Elaine can still appreciate how free her mother looks. It's the kind of freedom she envies, why she sometimes wishes she was more like her siblings and mother, less practical. It makes them look like they know the secret to being happy.

"Why, if I hadn't slept with someone other than Albert, you wouldn't be here at all."

Silence at the bonfire. Some guests chuckle nervously, but most whisper between one another. Elaine feels like the world has just been ripped out from under her feet.

"What?" The question comes from Albert.

Paola's face pales. "Wait. Did I..." She drops her cup and clasps both hands to her mouth, looking in anguish between Elaine and Albert. Albert looks at Elaine with the same look she must carry: horror. Alan and Isabel thank everyone for coming and ask them to start descending down the mountainside.

Elaine does not speak. It feels like her ears have been filled with water. Her body sways side to side, drunk, shocked, and hurt—like the river has just swallowed her whole.

Chaos ensues. Albert goes into the house, her brother accidentally sets fire to the banquet tablecloth, and Elaine, in a rare moment of weakness, runs to the river and wishes for something new, something she didn't even realize she wanted: she wishes for the adventure of a lifetime.

2

BLACKOUT IN THE GARDEN

Elaine is seventy-two when her dad decides he doesn't love her anymore. "Carry me, Papa." She giggles, holding her hands up to the father-shaped blur above her.

"Look at her, Albert. She's drunk."

"Well, we know she didn't get her alcoholism from me, don't we?"

"It was one summer."

Elaine groans, pressing her fists into her eyes. They're arguing too loudly.

"Elaine, get up," Paola says.

She pouts and turns her back to the shape she's fairly sure belongs to her mother. "Get out of my room." It's very rude of them to argue in the only place in the house that's all hers.

"You're lying in Dad's garden."

"What used to be my garden, actually," her father says.

Her mother hisses something back, and they start talking over each other and making her head hurt even more. She lifts her head up and takes in the torn-up dirt around her. This was terrible. Dad's already upset about the question of her lineage, and now his prized garden's been ransacked by pests.

"Did gnomes get past the wards?"

Her father pinches the bridge of his nose, sighs, and walks off back into the house. The garden is truly wrecked.

Petunias are strewn across the yard and the carrots have one bite taken out of each of them. There's a cartoon genitalia-shaped hole where the lettuce heads used to be, and she's currently lying in its left scrotum. She vaguely remembers resetting the gnome wards the night before, but her inability to recall is disconcerting.

"What happened?" she asks. "I drew the wards, said the incantation, and then there was a..." Her face goes slack. "Oh, no."

Her mom, Paola, grimaces. "You blew up the mango tree, then destroyed the rest of the garden."

"Why did you destroy it all?" her father yells, sticking his beet-red head out of the kitchen window just to scold her.

Her neck shrinks into her shoulders. Her memory is hazy. "I thought...well, that maybe it would be less noticeable if it was all gone."

Her maybe-not-father's garden is all torn up, and the only household pest for miles is standing in a penis-shaped hole of her own creation.

To her dad, Elaine was once as dutiful a daughter as they come. She's not addicted to drugs, she cleans up around the house, and hasn't married a mage her parents hate. When her mother let slip her infidelity a few nights before, in that moment, her father stood between her and her mother, chest heaving and eyes wild. His large, cloak-covered back obscured her view of her mom and her wine-stained lips.

"Look at her, Paola." Her father turned to look at her. "She's no child of mine."

For seventy-two years, she'd known and loved her father, and not once had he questioned her heritage.

"Even if that's true, you raised me," she'd said. He didn't respond, and Elaine had taken that as a sign she was getting to him. "Mom's drunk. She doesn't know what she's saying."

She brushed her fingertips against the rough material of his cloak, but Albertson Aquae jerked his arm away from her touch.

"Tell him it's my magic that makes me look different, Mom." She turned towards her mother.

The wine in her mother's hand had spilled about five minutes ago, and now the red tendrils of wine dried sticky against her fingers. She leaned back against the sink, white knuckling the porcelain.

Dad opened their old, wooden door, and sticky August filled the cottage with its humid air. "I'm going to go for a hike."

Paola smiles nervously at her daughter. "Your brother is still here for breakfast. If you'd like to come in."

She brushes past Paola, muttering about her headache. When she enters, Alan is there, but Isabel and Phoebe are gone.

"Isabel was getting homesick, and Phoebe, well, y'know Phoebe. Not one for conflict," Alan says.

Elaine sits down across from her brother. The last few decades of her life play out in front of her like an old movie: how she stayed when her siblings left and the fact that she's never gone against her mother's desire to keep her close.

Her (possibly soon-to-be single) mother has a water affinity. The strength of a mage's magic, and thus the specific powers of their affinity, are still a mystery to researchers. Learning she had a water affinity meant her powers could have included being able to tell when it's about to rain, or being so strong she could bring tsunamis into creation. And while many believe you cannot control the strength of your magical core, Mom controlled what she could, and chose to love a river. It has many names—Colonel Green, medicine, Jack and Blue—none that any could claim have superiority over another. She was the middle child of a family of miners, too weak to work the grueling pace, and too tall to crawl through the smaller shafts like her younger siblings. So, she spent many days by the water, playing with the river. She was a ghost, disappearing into the woods with a full day of meals and a hairbrush.

Over time, a joke became a nickname, and a nickname became a legend, and the unnameable river became Aquae's River.

"It changes too much to name it." She winks. "But if they have to name it, it should be after me."

Her magic became the river's magic, and the river gave her some of its own in return. Many mages find themselves destroyed or consumed by external magics that meld with their own core—but Mom is lucky all the river demands is her constant presence.

The Aquae family is one of the only families to live so freely in the wild mountains, and Elaine is the only one of her siblings who stayed. Her brother, Alan, and sister, Phillipa (Phil for short), left twenty-four years ago to school and the wild respectively. Elaine never felt it was the right time to leave. At first, it had been the pollution from miners she'd had to help resolve. Then, her father had a broken foot one summer, and she'd been in charge of spraying pesticides on the summer wyrms. One chore after another fell onto her, until the idea of setting out on her own became unfathomable.

Her mom believes Elaine will be the next steward of the river, despite having a different affinity and a younger daughter who is a literal fish. Every so often, while washing the dishes, or cleaning, or skipping rocks, she'll grab Elaine's hand and remind her, "It's your fate. Just like mine. When you stay, so can our legacy."

"I'm going to leave for college. Apply to Lock University in Garriver," Elaine says.

There's silence, for a moment. Alan's pancake slides off his fork and slips back onto the plate with a light *plap.*

"But you're 72!" Her mother exclaims.

"You're never too old to learn."

"What will you study?"

"Accounting."

"She's always been good with numbers," Alan chimes in.

"Not helpful."

"Thanks, Alan."

"I just always thought you'd be here. With us."

"I need to make my own way, Mom. I'm already late." Here, her eyes become misty. It feels like she's been late to a lot of things.

Her mother pats her arm as tears already fall freely from her eyes. "Oh, Elaine. It's never too late."

"I know."

Elaine is not one to make last-minute decisions, and this, in a way, isn't one either. She's a woman, looking for her place in a world that has suddenly ousted her. She might not know her parentage, but she knows that, above all, she loves to learn.

"It's not easy to get in. Acceptance rates are less than one percent."

Elaine doesn't interrupt while her family discusses logistics. She doesn't tell them the acceptance rate is 0.26 percent, and 0.22 percent for applicants over fifty-five. That athletes had their odds raised to 1.3 percent, and they were shoe-ins if they were nationally ranked. That housing has increased thirteen percent in the last thirty years since she first applied, and she'd need to win the Sesame Scholarship, which accepts nine in 10,000 applicants every seven years. What her family is saying isn't meant to teach her something new; they're exhausting their own fears by speaking them aloud, then letting them go.

They need to talk through their fears, but all Elaine needs is her binder, with tabs categorized by urgency and color-coded for visual recognition and pleasure.

Alan eventually departs, giving Elaine a longer-than-usual hug before taking off for home. Once her brother leaves, it's just her and her mom.

A MONTH PASSES.

Her mother knocks on the door and opens it. "Breakfast," she says.

Elaine waits to hear her feet move away from the door.

"Your dad's eating with us," her mother chirps. Then, quickly, as if it will wipe away Elaine's horror at that statement, "I made your favorite: pumpkin waffles with gold calf cream."

The door closes with a thick *clunk.*

Elaine weighs the appeal of breakfast. On one hand, each day her dad spends away from home, Mom creates more and more delicious and elaborate apology meals. The waffles are a guaranteed delight.

On the other hand, her dad is eating those waffles.

She rolls onto her back with her long legs stretching off the twin bed and her mustard sheets slipping off her feet. She creeps towards her closet on the balls of her feet, then slips on a green gown. She crawls out her window, scaled the ivy-covered side of her home, and heads into the forest.

It is a welcoming sight. As she slips into the tree line, she can hear the song of the silverhoppers. They've come back from the northern mines, full, and ready to sing through the coming winter. They're a curious form of insect that was once closely related to the grasshopper, but who developed a taste for metal somewhere along the evolutionary chain. They hunt north of the mountain valley, where the Aquae home is tucked, and are the bane of many miners' existence. For those who don't live off the silver under the peaks, they're a welcome contrast to the silence of the winter woods. Not only do these strange creatures collect and consume silver, but they wear it like armor. In the summer, their silver legs rub together but don't make a sound. When the winds change and the weather cools, they move south towards the Aquae's, and strum their metallic limbs. and the sound of music fills the air. In their neck of the woods, the silverhoppers play one of the four notes in C major 7. Elaine's mom claims an old boyfriend taught them the chords to make her winters less lonely.

"Don't tell your dad," she'd said with a wink. "He gets jealous."

Elaine rubs a cool hand against her stomach when it growls. She sighs. Waffles do sound nice. She trudges back home and opens the front door. The smell of fresh food wafts through the air. The end of summer is nearing, and with it, a cool morning breeze. The warmth of the kitchen is a welcome feeling. She brushes a hand against her blue cloak that rests across the back of the door, ignoring the heavy beat of her heart when she sees her dad's hanging next to it. She takes off her shoes and enters the kitchen, wondering how they'll play this.

Dad is facing the front door when she walks into their kitchen. His eyes flick away from her when she enters.

"Elaine, come sit. I just made some more waffles." Mom sets a plate at the table for her.

It seems they're pretending it never happened. She sits as far away as she can from Dad at the table.

Her mom is humming a tune and brings another plate out before sitting down herself. "Dig in!"

Sitting with her parents, Elaine wishes this had happened when she was fifteen. If Dad had left then, she would have dyed her hair red and pierced her nipples. Seventy-two is a terrible age to be abandoned because, technically, she is an adult, and adults don't get tantrums. If she dyes her hair and pierces her nipples now, her mom will say it looks "punk rock" and her dad won't say anything, if this breakfast is anything to go by.

Her mother is uncharacteristically quiet and sneaks glances at Elaine and her father when she thinks they're not looking. Both have found particularly fascinating shapes in the oak table in between fast bites of their meal.

"I'm going to college," Elaine finally blurts out.

Dad slices a knife across his waffle with a passionate ferocity.

Mom laughs nervously. "Sweetheart, you haven't applied."

Mom looks to Dad for support, but he's busy glaring at a chunk of butter on his plate.

SHE GETS a letter in the mail the first week of July. Her dad still spends most of his days avoiding her and leaves the mail he used to bring her on the dining room table. She breaks the seal on an envelope with the words Locke University scripted across the front.

Her eyes flit across the first sentence, "Dear Elaine, we regret to inform you..." before she sets it down. Her mom comes in from the river, still damp from a swim session.

"Oh, perfect," she says, unaware of her daughter's distress. "I need your help fixing your father's cloak. Looks like he ripped it again. Third time this month!"

She doesn't look away from the letter, proof she failed. But patience is the friend of success, and she knows she has to try again.

THE NEXT NIGHT she huffs out a humid breath as she reached a second false peak. The Allapan Mountain range was covered in the sticky sweet air of midsummer. To escape that all-encompassing wetness, Elaine had decided to climb up Mt. Sheep. That was not its true name, but the rock stuck in the middle of the river flow looked like a sheep if you squinted your eyes after a few bottles of SmoothSilk.

The peaks of mountains were where she felt most at home. The flair in her lungs reminded her of the stuttered, heaving breaths she'd inhale from her brother's cob pipe, a nasty habit she left behind in her forties when Alan moved away.

She sat cross-legged in her dress, alone, deep in the wilds. In the distance, the silver peaks of the mines glinted reflections of the setting sun. Soon enough, they'd be the only light on earth, the full moon glinting off their metallic sides. She wished she'd inherited her brother's fire affinity or her sister's knack for cobbling. If she was strong, she could stay out as late as she liked.

Instead, she was stuck with probability magic, theoretical at best, as rare as it is useless, and she is the only mage alive who has it, according to the official affinity registry. If she was strong, she'd also probably have money to make her own decisions, like Alan. She could follow her dreams regardless of the demands and wants of her town and family. She loves them dearly, but her mother's betrayal was selfish, and she wants the opportunity to do the same. Money can't give her everything, but it will give her options.

The last glint of sun dipped beneath the forest, and she stood, brushing off her dress before stumbling off the boulder.

"Hm?" She mumbled to the air, placing a hand against the rock to steady her feet. There might have been more SmoothSilk in her body than she thought. Giggling, she stepped back towards the Aquae River, ready to follow it home.

"Smooth as silk. Right as rain, all will be merry if you don't abstain," she sang.

Her body and mind felt lighter under alcohol's influence, and that might be why she decided to take the long way home.

"I've got luck, faith, trust, and a little-oh, SmoothSilk!"

She dove towards her travel bag (when had she put that down?) when she saw the telltale red cap sticking out from the carrier.

"I'll climb down after one more sip." She promised to no one.

SHE WAKES up when she felt a breeze curl around her shivering body. Her hands slap against her cheeks, stinging them as her brain beats against her skull like a heartbeat.

A whimper falls out of her when she sits up, and her hangover makes the world around her spin. She's lucky to be alive after being foolish enough to fall asleep alone in the mountains. Then, with the confidence of a woman alone, she screams at the top of her lungs, high and loud and guttural. The forest quiets for a second before the silverhoppers sing again, and the leaves rustle in the wind.

Is this all I'll ever be?

A week later, she applies for university again.

IN THE MONTHS following her second application, things at home don't change. She often holes herself up in her room, and her dad is almost never home before the sun goes down. On a cool August morning, while she yawns and shuffles through her mail, another letter from Locke University comes in. She drops all the other letters in a harried flurry as she flips the creamy envelope over and tears at the deep purple seal.

Dear Ms. Elaine,

We are happy to invite you into our curriculum this fall. Out of our many applications, we chose you and your fellow classmates off of excellence, both in and out of the classroom. To join the class year, please adhere to the following instructions...

A grin, larger than any smile she's had in months, spreads across her face. She holds the letter close to her chest, careful not to wrinkle it as she runs out the front door to find where her mom is along the river.

"Mom," she shouts. "I got it. I did it!"

She leaves in August, just before the River Speak, for the first time in her life.

After the initial excitement, the days pass in a silent and tense atmosphere until the morning she's set to leave; the poisoned truth of her paternity hanging around like a dark cloud. Her mother knocks against her door.

"Come in," Elaine calls as she folds up another dress.

The heavy steps of a much larger person come up behind her. A rough, familiar hand claps her on the shoulder twice before the same footsteps turn around and leave. The door closes and she's alone once more.

She takes a deep breath and puts another gown in her suitcase.

When she finishes packing, she heads down to the kitchen, where her mother drops a stack of papers in front of her. The top page has an address in Garriver city listed.

"What is this?"

"You'll stay with your Uncle Neil. He can keep you safe and show you city magic."

"Uncle Neil? Uncle Neil lives across the Atlantic. He's studying legless lizards."

Mom shakes her head. She smooths down Elaine's hair, and

Elaine moves her head out of her touch. Mom sighs but moves her hand away anyways.

"He got a job at a private potioneering company in need of a wizard. He lives close to campus, so don't worry about paying for a dorm."

Wizard is the highest ranking a mage can earn through high-level mastery of their craft. This is great news. Elaine had been prepared to go into a lot of debt to make the housing fees.

"And what if I want to live on my own?"

"You'll be safer, Elaine. The city is not like the mountains. We never taught you how to defend yourself in that environment." She steps closer to Elaine, and whispers, "and they're not always kind to those that aren't like them. Neil will keep you safe."

She sighs, even as the weight of decade-long payment installations is taken off her shoulders. "It will be good to see my favorite uncle again."

She'd always liked him because he was so grumpy compared to her dad. Where Dad is tall and passionate, Neil Leatherforth is stout and cynical. He has a soft spot for Elaine, and she was delighted when they were the same height by the time she turned eleven and she could finally explore the tiny caverns under the mountain with adult supervision.

She looks up at her mother, who gnaws her lip with her teeth. Elaine wonders if she'll bring up the fact that she ruined their lives, and if she'll apologize for pushing Dad away. Does she feel bad?

She's glad you're leaving, a voice whispers. *Now she can fix her marriage without the problem sticking around and ruining it.*

For a moment, it looks as though Mom might say something. But she shakes her head and smiles wetly at Elaine. "You will write, won't you?"

"Of course, Mom."

"And if it doesn't work out, you can come back here. Your

room will be just as you left it." Paola looks around before leaning in and whispering, "Just give him some time. Everything will be back to normal, like nothing's changed."

A pit settles in her stomach at the thought of coming back home, the same way it used to when she thought about leaving.

"I know, Mom."

Elaine was seventy-two when her father decided he didn't love her anymore, and she is seventy-three when she leaves him alone to reckon with it.

3

IT'S RAINING RATS

She could get over the glares, the thieves, and the devastating lack of mountains. But that is all, of course, if it was not for the rats.

Elaine moves leisurely through the crowded streets of downtown Garriver on her third day in the city, ignoring the glares of those around her who might be late for work or late for lunch—they move like they're always late for something. The sun gleams off the modern skyscrapers wrapped around the river, all made entirely of glass paneling and steel. She meanders through the middle of the city, bobbing left and right, just as the miserable droves of office workers file out of the trains. She knows they're all going off to work for more powerful mages, likely doing mundane tasks like bottling brews and labeling brooms. Many of them don't use their own magic at all, but an apprentice vow from Locke University is mandatory if you want to work an office job with any chance of becoming something more.

Wrapped in her cerulean cloak patterned with pink fish, silver hair pinned tightly to her head, she takes confident strides towards Locke at the heart of the city.

A wizard bumps against her shoulder, knocking her back. "Watch it." He sneers, long clawed hands reaching out to her neck. Thinking better of touching her, he pulls them back inside his cloak and disappears into the wave of city goers.

She looks around in disbelief, but her fellow commuters avoid her bid for camaraderie.

Elaine pushes her hair back against her skull. It suffocates under her hair gel, making escape impossible for a single strand. Her six silver pins sit snug against her scalp, lovingly crafted by the hands of her mother. They're shaped like the salmon that so often spawn outside of her family's home.

She'd left herself plenty of time to get to the school registrar early. At Locke, you are assigned professors instead of classes. Students who want to get ahead as soon as possible make appointments to choose an instructor based on the affinity of their magic. Having a weak core and an affinity with very few in-field benefits, it is essential for Elaine to pick a professor with an affinity for something compatible with her own, someone specializing in something like statistics or mathematics. Here, a good professor is the difference between becoming a financial advisor at a large firm or an underpaid barista who happens to have an apprentice's degree. Being late today would mean the promise of a boring, undervalued life.

A large swath of brown collides with her chest, and scrambling hands startle Elaine out of her reverie and into a panicked, roiling mash of blue and brown cloaks on the ground. Her body buzzes, crackling like a thousand static shocks all over.

"I'm so sorry! Are you alright?" a baritone voice slurs out.

Elaine pushes the heavy body off her. Bristly fur scratches the palms of her hands. The man beside her grunts, folding to the ground and away from her arms. Elaine takes in the shape of her attacker: his vacant brown eyes are muddled by half-moon glasses and the stench of stale alcohol falls from his breath, intermingled with the smell of a tantalizing magic, foreign yet familiar. His long face is filled with a long nose and a wide, sheepish mouth. He smiles, showing a pair of gapped teeth, through which a tongue piercing can be seen. Homeless and drunk, she concludes. Elaine finds herself attracted to his broad, hunching shoulders and the Adam's apple prominently sticking from his neck. Despite his ruffled state, she can see that his face is a handsome one, one that reminds her of *The Dishonored Wanderer,* an old story about a knight, forever banished from his home. The reason for his banishment changes between storytellers. Sometimes the knight is guilty, in others, he takes the blame to protect his kingdom from war. It was her dad's favorite story to read on stormy nights. But instead of fine and shining silver, this man wears a pelt cloak, with tufted, curved ears sticking up off the top of the hood.

"Fine," Elaine says. She makes a silent promise to herself to go on more dates. While this man has a draw to him, it's jarring to have strong desires for a stranger. While there had been a few men before, the first three had been enough to convince her that sex wasn't as great as the build up and hardly worth the effort. She'd laid with a fourth, just to confirm her hypothesis, and was relieved (and disappointed) to find that she was right. She dismisses the urge to wrap her cloak closer around her like a blanket. She did not enjoy touching the felted, scratchy wool of his brown cloak. His cloak feels stale and his magic beyond that initially delicious whiff smells of mothballs and polite disdain. Smelling magic is a unique trait of hers that no one else in her family has, and she's very jealous of those that never have to bother with mystical odors.

Large fingers push a gold coin into her palm, closing her fingers around it. His hands feel like sandpaper against hers. She takes note of the stately gold signet ring wrapped around his knuckles, sporting a prominent "G." Perhaps an heir playing starving artist, then.

"For your troubles." The man nods to the coin before disappearing around the corner.

Elaine thumbs the pink fish swirling around her cloak, taking comfort in their cool, scaly bodies. The magic woven into the cloak has them pooling around her hand, tails swishing as she feeds more of her own magic into the fabric. Her heart beats fast against her chest. She pats her pockets, but nothing feels amiss. Her hip satchel still holds her money.

Her shaking hands clutch at the gold coin, and she decides to move away from the crowd to take a closer look. She smooths out the now-disheveled stray hairs on her scalp.

Her first step forward is halted by a slight tug on the back of her cloak. A brown rat clutches her cloak with bald, wrinkled fingers. Its eyes peer up: wet and black. She'd heard rumors about rats addicted to cigarettes who run *towards* mages instead of away from them, looking for another hit. Her heart prickles with pity.

"I don't have any tobacco," she says.

She tugs hard to dislodge her cloak from its claws. The rat stands on its tiptoes, nails clinging to her garment. It tugs back, beady eyes staring straight into her own. She cocks her head to the left and it mirrors her. She cocks it to the right, and it follows. She raises a trembling hand, and watches with rising horror as the rat wiggles its dexterous fingers in sync with her own wave. She grimaces. It makes a low grumbling noise like it's trying to clear something lodged in its throat.

Did the rat just snarl?

She thought they chittered, squealed at most. But no, this rat had most definitely snarled. The loose cigarettes littering the city's sidewalk must have made this one extra twitchy.

She hears scratches along the gray concrete as another rat scampers towards them and also grabs hold of her cloak. The three of them now block the steady flow of the crowd, and mages bump against her in passive-aggressive attempts to get her to move.

"Whoever's prank this is, it's not very funny," she announces to the crowd around her.

They barely glance her way as she struggles to free her cloak from the clingy mongrels. Tears fill her eyes, and her throat closes. It's barely been a week, and she's being singled out by the city itself as an outsider. The rats must cling to her because they can smell the un-belonging in her sweat.

"Mom, it's biting me!" a child cries.

A horrified relief fills Elaine as she watches a child adorned in the latest city fashion be nibbled on by a terrier-sized rodent.

Soon enough, Elaine isn't the only person experiencing the plague. Rats filter into the street, from sewer grates, dumpsters, rain pipes, and shadows. They converge, their scampering feet unleashing a cacophony of quick and light pitter-patter, like rain hitting the pavement. Weaving in between the legs of the citizens, it's clear their target is on the sidewalk, and the office workers do their best to save themselves, darting into the street and cursing at the cars that honk and swerve to avoid hitting them.

A pair of rats sweep under the legs of an elderly man who tries to offer them a loaf of bread, tripping him over and knocking him unconscious, stampeding over and passing him. Elaine's heart rises into her throat at the sight. Not even the rat sympathizers are safe.

A group of pixies laugh at the old man, until a rat nibbles and tears away at the end of a shimmering wing. Their mischievous snickering melts into shrieks of anger. Hundreds of pairs of shrewd black eyes home in on Elaine, as the rats squeeze past everyone in their passionate flood towards her.

She feels a pull in her stomach and acid build up at the base of her throat. She swallows, refusing to die because she threw up in fear. She takes a step forward, her legs jelly beneath her as she stumbles forward, wrought with fear. She feels the vomit press up against her throat, knees quaking and unsteady. Her head feels light, and as she puts her right foot forward, another bout of nausea knocks her to her knees.

Spitefully, she knows her mother will be croaking a teary "I told you so" at her funeral, when she reads the paper's headline: *Elaine Aquae Killed in City's First Magical Attempt at Reverse-Extermination.*

A water pipe in front of her rumbles, groans, and wrenches free of the wall, shooting a pressurized gush of water at the path in front of her. The rats scurry and hiss, dispersing as the water washes a sudden, impossible river in front of her, clearing a rodent-less escape into the alley ahead. The bottoms of her feet cool as the water soaks into her slippers.

A rat leaps forward and claws into the thin skin of her ankle. She hisses and beads of blood trickle down her heels.

The scrambling sound of the rat feet changes, turning into a heavy *thump, thump, thump*. She looks behind her and sees rats of an outrageously large size. Their screeches sound off at a haunting octave below their brethren like wheezing trumpets of her impending doom. At this size, she can see each strand of wiry hair and the wrinkle on each pink toe, their pearly nails scratching the brick below them. They've run her into the outskirts of downtown, where the bricks are cracked, sprouting vibrant green garlic underfoot. Her silver slippers turn a mutated shade of that same green as she careens down an alley full of dumpsters and day-drinkers.

"Control your rats, idiot!" yells one man.

She clips his shoulder before he leans back in to continue throwing up.

More dreary heads pop up, and seeing their irate friend, the drunks begin to throw things into her path. Filled with a new rage, she grabs a snickering drunk as she passes, throwing him back into the rats.

"Not mine," Elaine clarifies.

As she continues to run, their feet patter like the rain after her. Rats nip at her ankles, having finally gotten close enough to her to topple over each other and take grand leaps off their kins' backs. They latch successfully onto her before being beaten off by the heavy ends of her cloak.

She hears the snapping clack of their front teeth, narrowly missing her calves, her thighs, even her ears. As she pumps her fists again, keeping them curled tight against her body, she screams out in pain as one bites her hand. She lets loose the coin she had clutched so tightly to her palm.

Flinging from her elbow another rat, who leapt valiantly off a triple stack of its fellows, she runs towards the light at the end of the alley. There has to be a police station somewhere, anywhere.

But it seems she's worried for no reason, as the rats who once held her by the skin of their teeth fall behind and stay in the alley. The flood fades into a slow trickle, until there are no more rats following her.

Elaine breathes a sigh of relief when she reaches the break of light.

When she looks back into the alley, she sees them dispersing, freed from whatever spell they'd been under. She wonders morbidly if their appetites were sated by the people she toppled on her way. Onlookers gawk at her disheveled form. She's sure she looks as though she's fought a tweaker and lost.

"You should see the other guy," she says to a man who can't seem to stop staring.

His eyes dart away, and his steps quicken when he realizes he has her full attention. She heaves in breaths of air, placing her hands on her knees for stability. She hadn't run like that since she was a child in Allapan, and her heart's heavy pump fills her head with memories of running so fast it felt like flying.

Elaine kicks the sides of her slippers free of dirt to no avail.

They squelch with every step she takes, a wet mix of rain and alley debris. The red tries to soak into her silver slippers but fails as the fabric is already completely soaked through with water. She reaches up to tidy her hair, shoulders relaxing when she feels no strand is out of its place.

Over the next hour, Elaine's shoes dry enough for the loud squishing to quiet into a faint quack, like ducks, every other step. Her mind plays the attack over and over, promising herself that she'd find another way to get to school from her uncle's house. Despite being walking distance from campus, she might have to walk twenty minutes in the wrong direction before heading to Locke. It'll be a burden, but if there's rats like that all over Main Street, she's prepared to leave her house an hour early. Her feet pick up the pace, and the other passersby stop glaring at her as she starts to match their speed. She keeps her eyes locked on the ground in front of her, suspiciously eyeing the loose grates and pipes.

Finally, Locke rises in front of her: a collection of old, cobbled buildings, Gothic stone, and green, green grass. In the early years of the city's formation, mages came and settled in the town and offered apprenticeship and work to travelers who stayed to help the town grow. Too big of a population led to outward growth, and the original heart became an intimate academic hub for those wanting to learn. Each awkwardly-shaped turret and poorly-placed shed was a piece of protected history, making it one of the most confusing yet well-loved artifacts she has ever seen.

She brushes a fond hand across a building, excited to learn its secrets.

Her heart stops when her eyes land on the clock across the quad from her; she's late to her mage assignment.

She breaks into another run, but this time her muscles protest at the sudden jolt. The adrenaline that pushed her when the rats were chasing her is used up and gone. She limp-runs the rest of the way to the admissions office, where she finds the front desk manned by an older mage, hair twisted up in two gray knots.

"Ms. Aquae, I presume." She eyes the clock. "Late."

"Yes, but I—" she heaves a gasping breath, "—I—"

"Locke has strict rules about being on time."

I know, she wants to scream. *It's why I came here. I love time. Being* on *time!*

"Rats," she wheezes.

"Rats, darn, shucks." The secretary shrugs. "Regret doesn't change the fact that late is late, Ms. Aquae. Your professor will now be whoever is left after the students who arrived on time made their choice. Your name's already been placed on the waitlist."

Her heart sinks, which she thinks is just as well, because her agitated lungs expand two sizes in her ribcage. "Where on the list?"

"You were a whole five minutes late, Ms. Aquae! You're at the very bottom."

4

UNCLE NEIL

"And the rats tried to eat me." Elaine gesticulates with her hands as she tells the story a few hours after returning from registration. She paces across the clay-tiled floor of her uncle's kitchen. The gleam of midafternoon light washes through their river-facing windows, catching on the rim of the copper cauldron that takes up most of the sink. They are inside Neil's place, which they fondly call the watchtower. It had once been a clocktower and defense post along the river, but time domesticated the land, and it turned into something softer: a home.

Uncle Neil hums while his hands move back and forth against the cauldron, scrubbing away at a lone, green stain. He'd been at it for five years now, always in the first thirty minutes he gets home from work. While her father had turned his back to her, her uncle doesn't see family in blood, but in history.

"And the stupid mage who ran into me...there was this—" she mimics a buzzing sound, "—and I'd never felt anything like it before. Like some kind of...kind of..."

"Magic?"

She huffs. "Very funny, Uncle."

Uncle Neil is a broad man, with an evergreen scowl and deep black hair. His body is short and stocky like a bull, the likeness only exacerbated by his nose ring. Like much of Elaine's family, his proportion magic—the ability to discern exact proportions without the use of a measuring tool—is practically nonexistent. But he loves this city, and it introduced him to the complicated and precise world of potion making. While his magical core isn't the strongest, he's found success in a nine to five. His wizard potioneer badge shines with every aggressive rub against the forever stain.

"Plus, now my palm smells like his magic. See?" She holds her hand inches from his nose.

He pushes her away. The scrubbing intensifies. He doesn't look up from the stain.

Her frown grows deeper. "I was late to my mentor assignment because of it."

That gets his attention. She winces when his head snaps to her, disappointment clear on his weathered face. "Nellie!"

"I didn't mean to! I was chased!"

"You need to be wearing protective spells, Nellie. Your mother's cloak will protect you, but not against everything the city throws at you." He points a rubber-gloved finger at her. "If you can't handle impromptu vermin attacks, I'll find someone to escort you to and from school."

"I'm not a child," she says.

"You might as well be," he snaps.

The sound of his wire sponge grates against the cauldron. She breathes deeply for five, out for three, until her hand unclenches from the fist it's in.

She curls her body against the kitchen counter. "What do you have to do today?"

"The usual: supervise my coworkers, file a few things, might meet up with a client for drinks." Neil sighs, placing the pan down in the sink. He turns and braces his palms behind him against the sink, eyes softening when he catches her glare. More gently, he says, "I'm just worried, Nellie. You're not part of this world. I know you and your dad didn't end on the best of terms, and I'm happy to have you here, but I can't take care of you."

She didn't come here because she needed him. "I'm going upstairs to read over my supplies list."

He grumbles, smacking a soapy palm against her back. "You *can* do this, Nellie." He turns red, swivels back to the pot, and barks, "Go up and finish setting up your room."

"Yes, Uncle," she says.

"And tell me if the window is drafty," he yells after her. "I can't tell if I fully sealed it after taking out the clock face."

Elaine takes in a deep breath of relief when she's alone in her room. Its tall, exposed-beam ceiling allows for every step she takes to echo, and today, the sun beams through and heats the floorboards where the light touches. She moves until her bare feet lay flat against those boards, looking out into the city beyond. Everything downtown, save for a few ancient constructs, is new. Glassy skyscrapers and residential buildings reflect the cyan blue sky, and the clouds paint a warped picture across their semi-transparent panels. Locke, and the bridges that weave across the river, are older than them all, and they are all feats of architecture from different periods of time, long before she was ever born.

A pigeon flaps and flutters against her window, distracting her from her contemplation. She sees the carrier pack attached to its back and opens her window, allowing it to stoop on the carrier pigeon ledge. It bends its grey neck low, and she takes the parcel. She breaks open the green Locke seal as the messenger flutters away, devouring the words before her. It's class assignment, just hours after registering.

Elaine Aquae

Affinity—Probability (Rare)

Core—Human

Priority—Rolling Application

The words ‘rolling application’ make her heart pump faster. “I didn’t mean to be late,” she mutters.

Assigned Room—111

5

INTERLUDE: ROGER

Roger, the rat, has a very important mission today. Sniffing the air, he searches for the smell that came off the gold coin. The Ivan's magic smells off, like it always does, filled with sickness. Cursed. Hard to track.

He twitches his nose, following the scent in the wind as it carries him to his mark. If he pulls this off, the master promised he could sleep in the middle of the rat pile tonight. He sniffs the air again as the scent gets tangled in another. Magic swirls and trails together, like smoke and air. It's easy enough to pick out which one is Ivan—the smell of a river, and copper, and scales.

He skirts along the edge of the cement curve, close to the sewer grates. He hangs left past Galdor Bridge and ducks back into the sewage system when the foot traffic picks up again. The sewer is familiar and dewy, all sorts of fungi zinging with an electric hum. His ears twitch, their frequency jarring compared to the loud cacophony of the city above. Here, the chaos is a constant hum in the background, rather than the arrhythmic circus the street offers.

The scent grows stronger as he nears the city center. There's a peek of sunlight through metal bars, the scent mere feet away, and Roger heaves himself back into the sunlit world of the overlanders.

He can't wait to be in the middle of the pile tonight.

6

AN AMPUTATED TOE

A week later, Elaine is on her way to an introductory, pre-school year meeting with her professor when a rat bites off her pinky toe. A yell of disbelief screeches its way out of her throat and blood spurts freely from her right foot. She howls in pain, dropping to her back. The pain is acute, rippling all the way up her spine. The brown, raggedy rodent scampers off, toe in mouth, heading right towards a sewer grate.

"No, you don't," she snarls, tearing the bottom of her white corseted dress and stuffing it against her amputated toe before limping after the rat.

Was it her? Was she, somehow, the spitting image of the city exterminator, who they promised their rat-mother to avenge upon her death via rubber-gloved hands?

Her nine toes curl. The perpetrator slips into the sewer grate just as her hand reaches out for the end of its wormy tail—slippery, rubbery, and gone.

Elaine is stretched out against the lawn, hand grasping at the metal gates of the sewer, onlookers giving her bleeding foot a wide berth.

"Come back," she cries.

Gods, it hurts. She curls her foot upward, pressing a hand against the bloodied cloth. The pain sharpens for a moment before dulling into a blunt throb. She collapses, defeated, against the sidewalk.

A rat, she thinks. *What kind of rat bites toes off in the middle of the day?*

"Hello?" A shadow overtakes the warmth of the midday sun.

A *rabid* rat. She groans in dismay. A rabid, awful little creature, who is munching on her best pinky toe. An original too! It will take months to save up for a new one.

"Hello." The sun-blocking menace nudges her with his foot. With all five of his toes, she bets. He'd never understand her, the one-toe-less. A little bit worse at hopscotch, never to receive a ten percent discount on a pedicure, despite the obvious.

"Go away," she says.

The shadow above her is silent.

She finally opens her eyes and gasps. "*You.*"

"Me," the brown-cloaked man cheers. He has the same wide smile, but today he wears round glasses, so black she can't see through them. "Ivan. It looks like you have a bit of a rodent problem."

"A bit?" She points to her foot. "This is more than a *bit.* Not that it's any of your... Wait. The rats." She gasps, pointing at him. She fumbles with the deep pocket of her cloak, feeling around until she finds a round metallic disc. She tugs his coin out and thrusts it forward in accusation. "The *rats.* You set the rats on me."

He shakes his head. "Negatory."

"You've taken my toe."

"I briefly put their attention on you a week ago. The spell should've worn off by now."

"I'll never double Dutch again."

"What's your affinity?"

"Only three places for a pinky ring, now," she continues, ignoring his question.

He pokes her foot, and she flinches away.

She hisses at him when he tries to grab it again.

He puts a long finger to his chin, as if in thought. "Anything animal related can get tricky."

Elaine stares. Perhaps she could take *his* toe, see how he likes it. Could she be overreacting?

The man, Ivan, pushes a finger against her forehead. "No animal magic? Maybe something to do with dairy? The rats got a taste for Brie after their raid at the *fromagerie*—"

"Probability," she interrupts. He likes his own voice too much for her taste. "It's probability magic."

His eyebrows raise all the way up his forehead, shock and confusion spread across his face before he seems to make some sort of decision.

He pushes those glasses up and across his forehead, revealing brown eyes and a slight widow's peak. He grabs her hand, and she finds her palm dwarfed by his own. His fingers are calloused, with tiny scars and scratches all alongside the back. Her own are strong from years of hiking and climbing, but the mountain is a beast of nature, not of combat, so her hands are merely rough, where his are riddled with silver scars.

They stare at their joined hands. He shifts his weight from side to side, and his big brown eyes watch with rapt attention. It's like he's waiting for something to happen between them, some shift, some significant change. Under his warm touch, she begins to expect it too.

Elaine snatches her hand back. This is not a friend, but a stranger. Trepidation floods her as she eyes the bear-cloaked man for signs of insanity. His eyes are sober, though she's not sure if that works in her favor yet. He looks no less tired than the first time she'd met him, large purple shadows are bruised across his eyelids. It makes him unfairly sexy, she decides.

Both his hands twitch, fiddling with his smattering of gold and silver rings, the occasional lightning zap of magic stretching and breaking between the movement of his forefinger and thumb. She eyes the mixed metals with dismay. She prefers silver herself. Mismatched metals are a sign of indecision. His glasses are connected to a gold chain draped around his neck, reminiscent of a librarian she had a dream about once.

She places her hands on either side of her. Her neck stretches to the side, eyeing her distance to a populated area, just in case—

"I can help you," he blurts. "With the toe."

She raises an eyebrow. "I don't think the rat is planning to keep my toe on display." She speaks slowly, making sure he understands. Not completely sober, then.

She sits forward, and Ivan bends into a crouch in front of her. His knees crack on the way down, as does his left hip. As if to assert dominance over his creaky bones, he cracks his knuckles on purpose, the magic no longer physically sparking between his fingers. He grabs her knee, and she yelps when it sends a jolt of pain to her foot. He's either oblivious to her pain or doesn't care. Eyeing his ugly, bearskin cloak, she's guessing it's the latter.

While he's distracted, she sniffs her palm. The smell of his magic is strong—wet laundry, wine, hot pretzels with cheese. She wipes her palm against the grass, though she knows the stench of his magic won't go away so easily.

His eyes are unfocused, even as he crouches mere feet away, his brows wrinkled in thought. "The rats are controlled by the rat king. The spell on the coin didn't wear off because of our compatible magic."

She growled at him. "You tried to kill me!"

"I tried to *save* you. Besides, who keeps a coin from a strange mage? You were supposed to *drop* the coin, not keep it in your grip." He pushes a hand through his hair, mussing it further towards the sky. "I'm in a dicey situation with the rat king."

"The rat *king*? There has to be more than one mage that works with rats." With such little wildlife, surely at least a third of the animal mages in this city used rats.

"He's the only rat mage that matters. Most mages can only communicate with one, maybe two rats at a time. He controls thousands, if not hundreds of thousands. They're his eyes, ears, and employees. He meant to steal something of mine to lure me into the sewers. Looks like the rat thought you were me."

"We are nothing alike," she says. "That rat should be fired!"

Ivan shrugs, hands held up in surrender. "Interns. What can you do?"

He spins around, gaze roaming until it lands on the sewer plate. He pushes it to the side, the grating sound of rusty metal on cement rings in her ears.

"Come on. We'll get your toe, take the rat king, then collect some gold for our efforts. Think of it as an...apprenticeship."

She stands, foot wrapped in a tight hold. The way she's balanced probably makes her look like an indignant flamingo amongst the college's non-indigenous grass. She sneers. "And why would I ever be anything resembling a student to *you*?"

He's waist deep down the ladder when he pauses at her words. His head perks up, mouth open to spare his nose from the sewer smell. His eyes light with recognition when he sees her. "Ha! Forgot you were there." He places a fingertip against his chin in mock thought. "That's an easy one: I'm the only other probability mage alive."

Her heart twinges in shock, but outwardly she scoffs.

He grins at her. "It's true. You know it."

"Impossible." She winces when she stamps her foot. "Not possible! There hasn't been a probability mage in—"

"Improbable. Not impossible."

She tears off the bottom of her dress and wraps it around her wound. Even Locke, for all its resources, doesn't have a professor whose magic compliments her own; but no one can compliment probability, a magic so theoretical and weak that it's not worth the effort to study. His voice shrinks further away, and after looking around to see if anyone's watching, she hastens down the ladder after him.

The dirty, brick lining of the sewer entrance ends, and her vision is filled with a green glow from crystals sticking out of the cement wall, bathing the sewer in a cool glow. The light casts an ominous hue across the stale, opaque water. To her right, a gush of water fills the unnatural river from a pipe; the sound of a flush ringing through the metal echoes around them.

Elaine's eyes water and her nostrils burn. She retches, her gag reflex lit by the collective waste of the city. When she reaches the bottom, Ivan is there waiting.

"Left up ahead. We'll be heading towards cleaner air, but there will be eyes on us almost immediately. So—" his eyes twinkle, "—stay on your toes."

It would be so easy, Elaine thinks, *to push him into this river of shit.* "Who even are you?"

He hums, playing with his hands like her questions lay between them. "You used a fancy word. Probability? I prefer something more debonair. Like 'intuitive genius.'"

"I'm the *only* probability mage," she argues, quietly. The registry is international—something everyone has to enter into once they present their affinity. She remembers squeezing her mother's hand tight, hoping there would be someone who could teach her to do something incredible. Instead, the teller looked at her with pity and said she was the first probability mage born in two hundred years, and the last one was fatally mutilated seventy-five years ago.

"You being the only one on the records, I can believe. But there's plenty of mages who never register and slip through the cracks."

"So, you've met others."

He grimaces, shaking his head no. "You're the only other mage with my affinity I've ever met. I'm glad I found you first." He turns and bows at the waist, taking her hand. "Ivan Gray, at your service."

Her cheeks feel warm, and she breaks the eye contact he's making. It's ridiculous how pleased she is by the fact that his entire hand encompasses hers. She shakes out of his hold. "Every working mage has to be registered. If they aren't, job assignments would be impossible to dish out."

"That's only if you're working boring jobs, like accounting or marketing. If you work underground, experience is all you need."

Trying to get work with no degree? No accolades? No connections? She places a hand over her heart. "But that's a huge disadvantage."

"Not always. You'd be surprised at how many old families stay off the registry, as well. If they can't avoid it, some will even register a false affinity."

She's embarrassed that, in all her years, she hadn't even considered that people would *lie*. Something like that has to be a crime no matter how rich they are. It's not easy to evade a system so old. She lived in the middle of nowhere and was informed of her registration window the day after her magic flowered.

They turn a corner, and both the water and smells run clean. Her shoulders drop with the relief to her senses, save for the dull throb of her foot.

"Why my toe?" she asks, voice ricocheting off the wet, stony tunnel. She fiddles with the fish pins in her hair, smoothing out nonexistent bumps and ridges in her tight bun.

"The rat king kept going on about taking something I'd be sure to miss if I didn't bring back his crown." He waves a dismissive hand. "If I fail, then he'd hang me by my toes, have rats eat my eyes, something, something, blah blah—'eunuch!'—I'm dead. Pretty standard threats."

"Are all city mages so…" She struggles to find the word.

"Handsome? No. Dramatic to a Shakespearean degree? Yes. You get used to it, and then you become a part of it. Strong mages all have our...proclivities."

"*Our*," she scoffs.

He swivels, walking backwards. He pouts. His brown eyes peer into hers over the rims of his glasses. "You don't think I'm strong?"

"I know you're not. Just like I'm not. Probability magic is useless."

"No wonder they were so quick to steal from you. Not believing in yourself can have some pretty gnarly consequences for us, y'know."

There's silence, save for the echo of their feet against the cement, hers uneven as she limps along on her now deformed foot, the wound stopped by a makeshift bandage she's wrapped tightly around it. Deeper and deeper still they descend, not only inwards but down. The city is built upon layers and layers—swamp, then magic, then swamp again. Layers and layers of cement, dragon skulls, pewter, fallen towers of arcane magic, gravel, oil, everything piling up until it's the city they stand on today. There are gaps like the sewers that allow for entire ecosystems in between the layers, for people like the rat king to reign over.

"No wonder they were so quick to steal from you. Not believing in yourself can have some pretty gnarly consequences for us, y'know."

She changes the subject. "If you're so powerful, what's your baggage?"

She thinks she sees his shoulders stiffen for a moment, but by the next step, he returns to walking with a relaxed confidence.

"Terrible hay fever."

She rolls her eyes, and they move through the rest of the tunnels in silence. The water runs clear now, so clear that Elaine can see her reflection warped and wavering in clear ripples. The salmon swim lazily on her cloak, and she imagines them as pink minnows in the real world, thriving in this underground haven. It's easy for her mind to sail back to her home's coursing river. The salmon break through frothy currents, snapping, jumping, and shining against the sunlight. If she were home, her mother would step into the river with her, and the salmon would circle her, let her and Elaine enter their sacred movement for as long as they could walk upstream.

Her chest bumps into Ivan's back. He's stopped in the tunnel. He turns to the side and wraps a long arm around her shoulder, bringing her right up next to him. She gasps, then rearranges her face into a scowl, unable to escape from his warm grasp. This close, she can smell his musk, and the undercurrent of his magic is just like the one stuck to her hand. Here, the underground river is quiet, save for the dripping of pipes, trickling out of all the odds and ends of the ceiling. They are fully stopped now, and she looks around for the reason why.

"We're at the edge of the rat king's throne room."

The entrance is an eroded piece of sewer wall. If it hadn't been pointed out to her, Elaine would have assumed it was just another monument to poor infrastructure. What she thought were the drips of leaky pipes is now clearly the scratching of tiny nails, the squeaking of tiny maws. She hears the phantom of her previous chase and rubs at her elbows, feeling their phantom claws.

"Should we hide?"

He waves her concern away with all the confidence of a mage with luck on their side. "Oh, no. They already know you're here. There's a hoard of rats making their way here to kidnap you."

"Oh." Her voice does *not* go up an octave. "Why not you?"

"All ten toes," he says. He presses himself against the wall, winks at her, then leaps across the twenty feet of water to the other side of the sewer. "Don't worry," he shouts, "I'm a master of luck, and I know exactly what I'm doing. I've been gambling and winning at the game of life for seventy years."

Elaine's jaw drops. That should've been impossible. Undoable. The odds of someone making such a leap would be—

"Thief!" shrieks a rat on the floor in front of her.

"Thief!" comes another from behind.

Squawks of accusation fill the air from rats that speak English, and nipping teeth force her to move forward, nearly toppling over her own feet when she stumbles through a gap in the wall.

She flashes a horrified look at Ivan as rats skitter above her, nipping and snuffing at her head. Flashes of silver are plucked from her slicked hair, the only reminder that she's here, she has herself. Her second time stuffed amongst the rats.

For some reason, she feels how easy it would be to disappear within them. A simpler life, with simple solutions and predictable ends.

She flinches as fur bristles brush her cheek. When it happens again, she shudders softly. It soon becomes a welcome touch—that of a lover, a friend, certainly not a stranger. A sleepy smile crosses her face when she realizes they're not so bad.

The rats move her across splintered brick into a dim room, a hundred feet or so away from the sewer channel and Ivan.

The mob she'd considered joining just moments before leaves her behind on the cobbled floor as it moves in amorphous chunks, circling a shadowed tower in the middle of the room, with ceilings so high she can't see the top in this darkness. They squeak and whine as they use each other to reach a peak hidden from her eyes.

One close to her squeaks in pain, its left eye now closed in the relentless pursuit upwards. Why up? She clenches her fist, resisting the urge to reach out and grab the injured rat as it's lost in the midst of others. She doesn't want the answer to her question, doesn't want to be a part of it anymore. There's a sick, codependent magic in the air, and it burns her nostrils. She knows now how he controls so many rats—he's honed his affinity for animal magic, and his core must be one of the strongest she's encountered.

"The prodigal son of luck returns," hisses out a rat from the top of the hoard.

Rats scamper above Elaine, bodies parting to reveal a beam of light across the face of the rat king. His humanity is missing. His clawed, furry hands and feet and his face are just like that of a rat. One of his hands scratches incessantly across his scalp. He's poking and plucking at the few fine hairs left on his mostly bald head.

He takes a step forward and sinks into the other rats. He descends like smoke, each step cushioned by the plump bodies of his underlings, until he's a few feet away from Elaine and her pounding heart. The rats surrounding her snuffle and hiss before moving past her to sit at the feet of their master.

He squints at her. "You're shorter, Ivan. Did the family curse take away a couple vertebrae?"

"I..." She clears her throat. Her voice shakes. "I'm not Ivan." Her mother had been worried about her coming to the city, but neither of them could've predicted this. Being led into a death-trap by some deranged probability mage, her story cut short by a sewer king with a rat head. Her heart grows heavy with resentment; she knows that if she dies, she will haunt Ivan Gray for the rest of his miserable life. Her lips curl at the thought. Yes, she'll wail every other hour, and whisper horrible things whenever he thinks he's alone.

She flinches when the rat king snaps closer to her.

"Not going to work, Ivan. Even if you're in a silly new body, I have the toe to prove it." The rat king holds Elaine's pinky toe in the air.

She stumbles when she sees it, returning her eyes back to the rat king. She didn't realize how queasy she'd get about bits of severed people.

"Please," she begs. "I'll give you whatever you want. Just... my toe." She reaches out for it, but the mage pulls it away.

He hisses and snaps at her through bright, buck teeth. "You know the deal, Ivan. A toe for my crown back."

"I'm not Ivan," her voice cracks.

He lets out a high-pitched squeal again, and Elaine realizes it's his laugh.

"Take another toe!" something screeches behind her.

She reflexively shrinks back, curling her remaining toes as if that will save them.

He replies, "Yes, perhaps I should," and the rats are sent into another flurry, moving across each other in wretched, hairy waves.

"Give her the toe back, rat king," a voice echoes from the shadows of the throne room.

The large rat hand clenches harder against the scruff of her neck, nails digging into her skin. "Ventriloquism has no use, Ivan. Drop the illusions."

The real Ivan prowls out from a dark corner and up to the rat king, heavy steps forcing the rats to move if they don't wish to be squished. Now, she sees how tall he is. Before he'd been hunched over, spacey, and unserious. Now his glasses are perched on top of his head, and he stands like he's ready for battle.

Was it to make himself look smaller so he didn't scare me? she wonders. *In this light, he looks like he might be someone dangerous.*

The rat king's huge right eye moves back into Elaine's field of vision. The bulbous thing is watery and looks as though she could pop it with a single finger. A pimple, ready and waiting. And her nails are in need of a cut. *Maybe*, she reaches out a hand, *I could just—*

"What is this thing, then?" the rat king snarls. He shakes her, the "thing." "Another foolish lady you've tricked into helping you?" He laughs. "Bet he didn't tell you the cost of taking on his tracking spell."

"No, he didn't." She glares at Ivan.

"I don't 'trick ladies,'" Ivan says. "I trick my equals. Feminism, so on and so forth."

"And the cause is *so* grateful to have you," Elaine says.

Ivan ignores her, pulling off his sunglasses and placing them on the tip of her nose. They really are opaque, and she raises her eyes in an attempt to see over the rim.

"She's my apprentice. The only other luck mage in the city. I've heard rumors of your... lover's quarrel, Titon. That *is* why you're looking for me? Trouble in—" Ivan's lip curls in disdain, sneering at the dark throne room, "—paradise?"

I am far from lucky, she thinks with disdain. He mislabels their shared probability affinity, and moreover their relationship, as she'd have to be crazy to follow Ivan in any capacity. He assumes she'll agree to working under a madman who's proven oblivious at best, and consciously suicidal at worst. Presumptuous, cocky, impulsive: Ivan doesn't just put the cart before the horse, he buys the materials, plops them in front of onlookers, and expects them to see a wagon instead of a pile of wood and steel.

The rat king—Titon, apparently—snarls. "I need your luck to get the crown. Without it, my face is returned to *this*."

Elaine eyes his furry, scarred head from the side of her eye. Is this not his true form? It must be a consequence of overusing his magic. She knows that, when particularly attuned mages lose too much of themselves to the affinity of their magical core, the physical body transforms as well. Titon, this rat king lurking in the cobbled shadows of the city's sewers, is a victim of his own power.

The rats scuttle over each other, and she remembers with a shudder how she had, even if briefly, yearned for the company.

"That's a two-man job, Titon. Me and Lainey here will take care of that for you."

Elaine scrunches her nose. *Lainey?*

"She'll probably need her toe back, though. Nimble feet for sneaking, y'know." Ivan holds out a hand.

Titon clutches the toe closer to his chest. "The toe stays. Leverage. Toe for a crown."

"Toe for a crown," the rats cheer, "Toe for a crown."

"Unless you'd like to give up yours, instead?"

Elaine brightens.

Ivan crosses his arms to make a large X. "That's gonna be a no from me."

She frowns.

"We'll get your crown from Ophelia, don't worry. Just don't let the toe go bad. And don't blame us if we get caught because she has a lame foot!"

Grabbing her other shoulder, Ivan hauls Elaine away from the rat king's clutches. The salmon swim in an agitated rhythm against her blue cloak as they hurry out away.

Elaine reels away from Ivan when they leave the throne room. "Like hell I'm helping you. I need my toe back."

He looks at the crown of her head. "You've got a gray hair."

She slaps his hand away and sticks an agitated finger back towards the throne room. "Go give him *your* toe and get mine!"

"And what good would a severed toe do you now? You have no way to put it back on, and then we'd both be limping through the thievery. What kind of caper would that be?"

She huffs, curling her fists together, but she doesn't disagree.

"I'll handle the big stuff. Do you have any, y'know, special moves? I, for example, am extraordinarily good at getting myself out of near-death situations, with the wind in my hair and enemies right behind me."

"My magic isn't useful." She'd tried using it her whole life and had nothing to show for it. "That's why I'm going to school for math, not magic." Her eyes widen. "Class! I'm going to be late to class again."

Ivan waves her concern away. "Class will always be there. But adventure is a hard to find in a life as dull as yours."

She shakes her head. There are about five different reasons why what he said is wrong and incredibly short-sighted, but there's no way she can find her way back without him. She'll have to see this through if she wants to get home. "Who exactly would be stupid enough to steal from *that* guy?"

If he notices her changing the subject, he doesn't let on.

"Ophelia, the water mage. She and the rat king are long-time lovers, but they've been known to get into some mutually destructive spats every now and again."

His feet echo against the wet brick as he stalks away.

She follows after him. "It's a bid for attention, then."

He scrunches his face up. "A bib? Like at a smokehouse?"

She rolls her eyes. "I should just stay here while you do whatever—" she gestures to all of him, "—heisting you're apparently so known for."

Ivan puts a long arm over her shoulder. "Oh, really? I'm doing this for you, y'know."

She scrunches her face up as his hot breath skims over the cuff of her ear.

"I do get so lonely as the only luck mage around. But if you're willing to *abandon* me, I might as well find the next ladder and leave you to your remaining appendages."

He enunciates "abandon" in the way her mother does when she's left something in town and wants Dad to get it. When she looks up into his dingy face, his mouth is in a grim line, and his eyes are drawn together.

"Are you...pouting?"

His head snaps away. Her skin prickles with sick satisfaction, happy to have ruined his day, even just a little.

"Leave it to me to run across the first luck mage the city's seen in a few centuries, and you want nothing to do with me," he says.

"Luck," she scoffs. She takes offense at the vagueness of the descriptor. All magic can be studied, broken down into facts: statistics and study. "Probability," she corrects.

He waves his hand in a "so-so" gesture. "Same magic, different fonts." A loose brick topples to the ground and Ivan avoids it with a smooth slide of his foot. "See?"

She eyes him shrewdly, before turning back to her own hands. Nothing about their magic was lucky. "You can't expect me to follow you, Ivan."

His body shrinks further into itself. Looking at his slumped form, something tugs on the string of her heart. He looks more like the sad lecher she first thought he was, all hunched and cloaked and covered in grime. He has no one, given the state of his cloak's magic. The fur is dull, and the runes on it are at least fifty years old. The way he talks and acts makes her think he's all about leaving caution to the wind, the ultimate glory of being a free agent; but on closer inspection, the poor guy looks lonely. How could he, of all people, believe the two of them were lucky?

Traitor, she berates herself for her empathy. *He took your toe.*

He could be useful, though. Elaine has never practiced her probability with a self-proclaimed master, and it seems as though he's the only one who's at least good enough with their "luck" for other mages to abduct. If Ivan's been doing this as long as he claims, she could learn a thing or two.

As though he can sense her change of heart, he squeezes her closer to him. This close, she can see a tongue piercing swipe against his teeth. Her face warms, gut slithering like a pleased snake brushing against the hands that fed her the mouse. He smells good, she realizes with horror. And his arm feels strong along her shoulders.

Her own magic purrs with satisfaction at his proximity, seeping out of her with the intent of joining his own.

7

OPHELIA

"You're clever," he says. Fifteen minutes later they're still walking down the sewer path, him leading her in the direction of what's hopefully the crown and the end to this misadventure. "I think you should try to talk the crown out of Ophelia. I never could reason with her. Elementals are *so* temperamental." He pauses, mouth still open, eyeing her up and down. "You'll get on like bees and honey."

She ignores how warm he is compared to the damp sewer as she takes deliberate steps away from him. "Maybe you should've given your whole *foot* to the rat king. That way you could've kept it out of your mouth."

A laugh escapes him, and a traitorous laugh escapes her as well. Her eyes home in on his, so deep and brown.

Elementals, or element mages, are people with the ability to manipulate the external world with their knowledge of the periodic table. Like her parents and siblings, their magic is connected to the elements of earth, fire, air and water. These are, of course, separate from creatures *of* the elements, such as sirens, golems, nymphs, and dragons. All have subsets spread across the world and are considered dangerous due to their unpredictable natures. Human elementals do tend to be temperamental, but nymphs are known for it; creatures of pure nature with personalities that are as unpredictable and inflexible as their origin.

The line drawn between mage and creature is usually determined by their likeness to the human form. Academics, a human invention, has only recently opened to non-human mages, after unflattering and apt comparisons were made to Garriver's long history of racial segregation.

"Why won't they just fight each other," she asks.

He turns around to grin at her. "Curious? Getting into the mission at hand?"

Her face pinches. "Just wondering why they aren't fighting their own battles."

"Titon and Ophelia have a strange relationship. They're all mood swings and violence, but Titon never goes into her domain when she's truly angry. He knows he won't get the crown back, and that there's a very good chance she'd never speak to him again. He probably did something to violate her boundaries, and she stole the crown to show him how it felt."

"That's wildly immature."

He shrugs. "Yes, but I've never met two people more meant for each other. Something about terrible people is they always have extraordinary luck in love. Same with the strange ones."

Her steps slow as she ponders this. "You must have a wonderful partner, then."

His jaw clenches, his eyes slightly narrowing. "Har-har. Focus on the task ahead. Jokes aren't your thing." He whips back around, shoulders rising next to his ears as he mutters under his breath.

She will never admit to Ivan that she is actually incredibly equipped to deal with Ophelia. She's been dealing with the attitude of the entire Aquae family since she was born. And water mages are her specialty. Though Ivan doesn't seem too worried, she is wary of a temperamental water mage. Her mother was as consistent as the river, but if Ophelia is as powerful as they claim, then she is connected to water in a way Elaine has yet to encounter.

She hurries her steps to stand next to him. Her body relaxes, warmer now that she's standing arm to arm with Ivan. She sneaks a glance up at him to see he's already looking, and she whips her head away. There's static between them, a tension different than what she felt in the presence of the rat king.

"How did you do that before, the jump," she asks before her thoughts get away from her.

He smiles. "Would you like another demonstration?" His hand gestures to the other side of the sewers again.

"Please," she says. This jump is wider. If she's lucky, he'll fall in.

"Luck magic is a lot like how dogs know it's about to rain, or birds learn to fly. So, when I look across this sewer, and see a nice, dry walkway on the other side, I can imagine myself being on the other side. I jump and I'm there."

"But you shouldn't be able to."

"And human babies shouldn't breathe fire. But some are born with the ability, in spite of their very average lungs."

"Probability is uncertain by nature. You can't bend the world around you on a whim."

The implication that the world can be changed in its entirety for one man's desire to jump farther is daunting. Does that mean he can have anything he wants with no consequence? In another part of the world, is a long jumper falling flat at the exact moment of his tremendous leap?

"You think you can teach me how to use magic like you do," she says.

"I know it."

She thumbs the edge of her cloak and bites her lip. Being confident about a situation he's never encountered before is arrogant. And the fact that he uses their affinity so seamlessly means he probably has a much stronger core than she does. But to have a willing teacher with clear talent isn't something she should overlook. There'd hardly be time for both accounting and magic. Children in her town didn't start schooling until they were eight, just so they'd have time to acquaint themselves with their magic. She'd never been strong enough to need that time.

"I can see you thinking too hard," he says.

Her attention is drawn back to him standing at the edge of the walkway, arms swinging as he prepares to leap again. He jumps out towards the water, legs stretched and arms not bracing for a fall. His face twitches, and the arms that were once spread out in freedom curl around his stomach as his legs kick frantically while the luck magic seems to fail him. He barely makes it across, body clipping against the edge of the opposite walkway before tumbling back against the wall with a low and solid thump.

Elaine gasps, getting as close to the edge as she can without falling in. "Are you all right?"

From her view, he's a clump of groaning brown cloak.

"Yep. Hereditary charley horses, a nasty and unpredictable demon of mine."

She eyes the distance between them. "Are you going to jump back?"

His eyes tiredly sweep the gap between them. "I'll meet you ahead. It all connects back together the further down you go."

And they walk with the water between them, silent, until an echoing splash hits their ears just beyond the bounds of the sewer gate now in front of them, paths finally converging.

The tension seeps from them like an open wound, soon

filled with a bloom of anxiety. Ahead, she sees a garden of alabaster pillars behind a gate with a milky-white sheen, swirling like glitter in water. He must see her uncertainty, but he merely slaps a hand against her back, pushing her forward into the waiting light.

"Let's go, Lainey. We've got an elemental to appease."

The pearly gate swings open under his dexterous touch. He sweeps an arm across the entry of the door, bowing in deference, and Elaine takes the invitation to enter the water garden first. The sounds of steady water pour into their ears from the ravines, waterfalls, and cracks on the flowered walls around them. Unlike the dingy lair of the rat king, Ophelia's chambers are scrubbed free of any imperfection.

Elaine drags a finger across the wet, white, cobbled walls and pulls it back, a thin watery sheen now stuck to her fingertip. The dry area of the wall is quickly submerged in water again. Though it's made of the same stone as the rest of the sewer, the walls here gleam like they're made of pure marble. The room is lit in a warm glow from hovering orbs, and it's empty, save for a large chaise in the middle of the room. Elaine stops at the precipice of the chamber where the water is deeper and would flow over her injured foot.

Large hands scoop her up, and Elaine's vision is full of brown.

"Don't want my sidekick getting a staph infection on her first day," Ivan says.

"I am not your sidekick," she replies.

Her heart beats faster and she holds back a smile at the word "sidekick." It had been a very long time since anyone had partnered with her in, well, anything. The more he mentioned it, the more the idea of studying under a man as powerful as Ivan seemed less and less crazy. She feels weightless in his arms, not a grunt or a strain in his body or voice as he wades further into the water towards the chaise in the middle. Much like the walls around them, it's a pure marbled white, with pools of water swirling around and out of the center. It's unnatural, the way it moves from the center of the room, reminiscent of a pulse, an errant heart. Elaine feels cool magic wash over her, gentle against her skin. She sighs, content.

Suddenly, the cool becomes warm, her pores fill with globs of sticky water, so close to her flesh that she can feel it clogging and trapping her sweat. *It's too much,* she thinks. She wipes a hand against her nose, but the humidity hugs her skin no matter how many times she rubs her face.

A large thumb comes into her vision, and her crossed eyes try to focus on it before it presses onto the ridge of her nose before pulling away again. She follows its path upward towards Ivan's mouth, sucked between his lips.

"Tastes like you."

Her forehead creases in distress. "What the—"

"Who dares enter my chamber?" a voice hisses.

Their heads snap towards the chaise; Ivan's hands tighten around her arms and hips.

"Ophelia." He bows, dripping his own sweat into Elaine's silver hair and the clear water below as he does so. "We humbly request a meeting with you."

Ophelia is more of a watery apparition than woman, Elaine decides. She rises and molds herself together from the water they were just walking through, slithering onto the chaise until she's lying back. Her face is light blue, and her body looks solid, but it swirls, sweeps, and sways in a pattern that cannot be confused with a completely corporeal form. She has the telltale signs of a nymph—eyes far apart, nose too delicate to really be hiding any cartilage. And her blue hair lacks frizz, all coiffed and couture, despite the way she rolls it back and forth across the dewy, bed cushions. She lifts her head to get a better look at the pair of them, nose wrinkling after sniffing the air.

"On your own behalf, Gray?"

He adjusts, pulling Elaine's body closer to his. Ophelia's eyes flit to Elaine. Unimpressed, she focuses on Ivan again.

"I am here on behalf of your ever-loyal admirer," he says.

The humidity increases.

I'm going to faint, Elaine bemoans. *I am going to faint, wake up to vomit, then die of dehydration.* Her foot pangs. *And blood loss.*

It has to be Ophelia's magic sucking the water out of her skin, like thousands of leeches, gnawing her life away. She misses the rat pack. At least they tricked her and eased her into compliance.

This was a demand for her shallow drowning.

Ophelia's leeches push something odious in, spitting malicious magic into Elaine's immune system. Her body heat increases, and all the sweat that pours out of her feeds Ophelia's magic. She can feel when her own magic abandons her, in its desperate attempt to breathe, clinging to Ivan.

"Ophelia, the rat king merely wants his crown."

She grunts, flipping over to show them her back. "He can stay an ugly rat head for all I care, because he's shown he couldn't care less about me!"

Elaine doesn't understand how Ivan can still speak. She feels as though the magic is washing her empty.

"Ophelia, stop putting pressure on my apprentice. She's already had her toe stolen today."

Indignation grants her a moment of energy. "An original, too," she pipes up.

As the pressure ceases, Elaine takes a deep breath. She's still warm, but her body no longer feels as though it's being sucked dry through a plastic straw. Has she always been able to breathe through her nose and mouth at the same time? It's fantastic.

"You smell awful, Ivan."

"That's you, Lainey."

"Oh." The mixture of dry mouth, open wound, and extreme

sweating causes a nasty cocktail of human odors that made even Ivan's eyes water, she can see now.

She rearranges her arm over his, and he winces when her sweat seeps into his cloak.

"Have pity, Ophelia. My sidekick here is—let me see—two *hours* into the business. She's not used to magic pressure, and she's starting to get heat stroke. I can fetch anything you want from the city: clothes, food, antiques from the museum." He shifts nervously.

Magical pressure, or pressurized magic, is an advanced skill not every mage is capable of. It manifests differently depending on the affinity, but in Ophelia's case, she's changing the temperature of the water in the air, clogging Elaine's pores and making it impossible for her body to regulate through her sweat. Skilled mages like Ivan can reinforce their bodies with their own magic, creating a shield from outside influence. For someone like Elaine, long exposure will lead to her body having no room for its own magic, and ultimately, death. It's a disease that her body isn't strong enough to fight.

Ophelia's eyes stray to Elaine. She wiggles her fingers in greeting. "How about a snack?"

"No," Ivan shakes his head. "I told you, she's an apprentice."

Elaine's woozy tolerance is fading. Where she once felt delirious, pain and a great thirst overtakes her. Her body shakes, feeling too cold and too hot all at once. She grips Ivan's arm, weakly. Her tongue tries to form the words for help, but it feels swollen and dry in her mouth.

"How boring." Ophelia snaps her fingers, and the water behind them rises and writhes in the pool around them. "Throw these two into the dungeon. They smell of unpursued dreams and it's ruining my appetite."

Yes, Elaine thinks. *Anything to get away from her.*

"She needs medical attention." Ivan raises his voice. "She's not like us, Ophelia. Her body can't find this on its own. She'll die."

She lolls her head to look up at Ivan. Die? She hears the words, but it's so hard to think about them when her head feels so full.

The rising water pushes them forward, and Ivan has no choice but to follow it, lest they be drowned.

8

JAILHOUSE ROCK

"I can't go to jail. What will my parents think?" Elaine says.

"Your parents?" Ivan says. "Lainey, you are nearly a *century old*. And dying."

Her jaw ticks. The dampness sticks to their feet, but the magic clogging her cheeks finally leaves her skin. She slumps willingly against the dungeon wall, sliding down it. A full-body chill rakes her body. There's no expiration date on wanting your parents to not be disappointed in you, the same way that growing older doesn't mean you hate ice cream, nor does it make broccoli taste any better.

"Not dying anymore." It felt like a lie. She could feel the foreign magic leaving her body, but her own was failing to fill in the blank spaces. "Why do you look fine?"

He chews his lip, and she knows she must look truly awful to inspire such a piteous glance. "I'm used to pressurized magic. Your body is trying to replenish your magical core, while also supporting your immune system. This is bad, Lainey. We might have to share magic."

"Hah," she laughs, but it's weak and dissolves into a wheeze. "Sure, Ivan."

"I'm not joking," his tone is tighter. "You can barely even lift your eyes to look at me."

"I just love the cracks in these stones. You can find shapes in them if you look long enough."

She'd heard of sharing magic before, her and everyone else over the age of thirteen. Mages with the same affinity multiplying their energy with touch. With *intimacy*.

It takes all her strength to lift her lashes to make eye contact with him. He couldn't care less what happens to her. But she notices the way he looks at her, eyes glowing with interest, the gap between his fingers once again sparking with magic as he eyes the curve of her collarbone, the glint of the sweat sliding across it.

She's conflicted between needing to have sex in order to survive, and if she really wants to. Her body has been drawn to him since the first moment they met, and she does wonder, would this time be different than all the men before? Was what was missing in her previous amorous affairs the compatibility between affinities? Death and sex are strangely connected activities of human life. One can't exist without the other, and it's fitting that an act of lust could save her life.

"I know you feel the magic too. You already know what our best bet is to get you out of here alive. But I won't—not without your permission."

Warmth pools in her groin. "I smell horrible," she whispers.

Seemingly subconsciously, he widens the distance between his legs. "Once we start, you'll just smell like magic."

She inches towards him, panting in exhaustion from the effort. "You're lucky I've been having a dry spell."

Ivan looks up from the floor as her blue cloak catches his eye while she moves closer. She sinks down onto his lap and holds back a moan at the connection. His hands brush aside her cloak, grasping onto her waist. He gives an experimental squeeze that finally draws a moan from her lips.

His hands are so big, she thinks.

Her hips shift instinctually against his, reveling in the friction wetting her core.

Ivan grunts in approval, thrusting up into her willing touch. She responds in kind, and his shoulders relax as if he feels her magic's enthusiasm at his lap. He grins, smugly flicking his tongue against his lips.

"They say compatible magic increases pleasurability. Is that why you're so eager to grind on me?"

"Shut up and get me off," she says. "And use your hands."

"Shutting up." Ivan rolls his hips upwards, drawing a gasp from Elaine's lips. When she tries to grind down again, he holds her hips captive. "You told me to use my hands."

She frowns at him. He raises his eyebrows, as if daring her to say a word about it. She places a hand against his erection and applies pressure with her open palm, reveling in the roll of his eyes, and the *thunk* of his head against the floor.

"You're going to regret that."

She laughs. Oh, she sincerely doubts it.

Time slows down; each of them looking at the other, paying attention to their quickening breaths and admiring glances. The damp, low ceiling cell they've been placed in paints the entire world in gray, the smell of rust and the dew of humidity filling their senses. There's a smell of familiar things filling the air as well: copper and water, spices and longing.

He flips her, her back hitting cool brick as his hands feather down her throat. He tenses his hand around her neck, gently squeezing. She takes in a deep breath as the magic makes her lungs feel like they're working again.

He snatches his hand back, eyes widening. "Sorry, too much."

She pushes her hand into his neck, squeezing back harder than he did. "It's working."

Her neck tilts to the side, and he skims further down to unclip her cloak. Her neck free, Ivan leans over, breath huffing before his pierced tongue trails down the side. He spends several minutes pressing soft kisses against her throat. When she grabs his hair and presses him harder into her neck, he groans, drawing a long, flat stripe before nipping at an artery.

Elaine is surprised by her willingness, but the combination of his physical attention and the way his every touch breathes life back into her magical core makes her lean towards him in the moments he pulls back. It's not ideal, sharing an affinity with a man this impulsive and rash. But her head is clouded with lust and survival, and Ivan looks at her as if her touch can save him; she's always had a thing for men in need of rescue.

"So pretty," he mutters to himself, before moving his hands down onto her waist, placing a kiss just above her corseted breast.

With no purchase behind her, she grasps onto his biceps, muscles flexing under her hands as his arms flutter across her body. His thumbs stroke the side of her hip before pulling her underwear off, left taut between her outstretched ankles. Her mind is unusually foggy, and she frowns in confusion when a finger is brought up in front of her lips.

"Suck," he says.

She obliges, twirling the digit around in her mouth. His pupils dilate. Even now, as magic replenishes in her, she can feel that she needs to be touched closer, harder.

"Next time," he mutters to himself. Before she can ask him what next time means, he's sliding a gentle finger inside her center.

She shudders, feeling the relief that only comes with being filled, and she can feel her magic being made stronger at its very core. The contact, both because of the surface touches and his fingers moving skillfully inside her, is drawing on Ivan's probability magic to refuel her own. Still, she wishes he'd move more, add something.

He continues to stroke with admitted skill, but she grows tired of it. It won't be enough.

"Forget that," she scolds. "Ninety percent of women can't come from penetration alone, idiot. Think *higher.*"

"You're so bossy." He frowns. His thumb moves outward and upward, though, rubbing her clit in smooth, heavy motions that bring a smile to her face.

Her next sigh is heavenly, light, and sweet. A smug smile comes over Ivan's face, and she can feel him growing harder against her. He continues to rub his clothed erection against her thigh.

"Let me inside," he begs.

"Make me come," she demands.

He rubs faster against her clit, clearly spurred on by her growing moans.

"Yes," she says. "Yes, Ivan."

Her body uncoils, hips rotating up towards him like rolling waves. She hears the latch of a buckle, but he stays clothed, clearly too impatient to deal with buttons, snaps, or zippers. He hurries to place himself between her legs but still outside of her, thumb steady as he tries to push them both frantically towards a shared orgasm.

"Can't...undo your own pants?" she says, even as she feels another orgasm building.

"They're my—ah—tactical gear. Usually doesn't get in the way."

Ivan's eyes scrunch closed, but he doesn't take things further, like he's satisfied just being against her.

Elaine's magic is stabilizing. She can feel it. "Ivan, I—"

"Come," he says.

She unravels again. Warm and tight and closer than she's ever let anyone else.

When she calms again, she realizes he's staring. She rolls her eyes and pushes his face away.

"You're so mean," he sighs, light and forlorn.

She can tell that his orgasm follows when he shudders and his shoulders relax, his thick pants the only reason it doesn't leak and stain both their bodies.

9

HOT AND COLD

Elaine rubs her feet together to keep warm in the aftermath of their coupling. Ivan lays back, cloak covering any evidence of his pleasure. Elaine feels his eyes roving across the white corseted dress she wears, her cloak splayed around her like a halo.

"That was—I mean—" he runs a hand through his hair, "—we really, *wow.*"

If she sits a little straighter, arches her back a little more, he doesn't point it out. He shuffles closer to her on his knees, settling and grasping both her hands in his. She lets him kiss her knuckles and feels the heat of a blush rising in her cheekbones. Her carefully done up hair has loosened from its tight bun, and Ivan pulls out a strand, letting a curl at the end twine around his finger. His eyes don't leave her face. Elaine keeps her gaze steady too. She feels physically stronger, and as though her day's taken a turn for the better. Her magical core, which she'd never trained enough to know when it was empty and when it was full, is no longer aching from the pressurized magic. It's like the first day she can breathe through her nose again after a weeklong cold. He looks stronger too, and his eyes are sparkling. He smells less of mothballs, and more like burnt wood, or a beloved memory.

"I'd always heard that mages with the same affinity could have...explosive interactions."

She bats her eyes. "Does this mean you'll get me a new toe?"

"Baby, I'll get you ten. A whole new set."

His kisses move up her arm, from her wrists to her shoulders to her neck.

Is this what sharing an affinity is like? she wonders, as she generously lets him lavish her with affection. Maybe this wouldn't be so bad.

"Let them go," a voice states.

Ivan's head rises from her shoulder, eyeing their intruder with disdain. When Ophelia appears, he moves in front of Elaine. Elaine peers around him at the intruder.

Ophelia's face is soft, eyes wide and misted over with unfiltered emotion. Quiet, like glass, she says, "I didn't know they were *lovers.*"

Elementals are, above reason and logic, temperamental, and this time the untamable magic of water works in Elaine's favor.

Ophelia walks away as a mist settles over the latch and unlocks the door, and they are left in the jail cell alone. Ivan springs to his feet as soon as the door opens, but Elaine sits there for a moment longer. When she feels like it won't wind her, she stands and walks through the open, prison cell door.

Exhaustion replaces adrenaline as they make their way out of the sewer prison and into the city. She's sure they look crazy, crawling out of a manhole covered in blood, dirt, and smelling of rot.

The post-orgasmic spell is broken—if Ivan's new mood is anything to go by. His moony-eyed look turns into a glare, and Elaine, after a moment of confusion, sticks her tongue out. Still, even with his edgy looks, he hovers around her like a moon, orbiting so quickly it makes her head spin.

"I'll take you to get a new toe. I know a mage with a growth affinity and extensive knowledge of the human body."

"A new toe won't be as good as my first."

"Well, clearly it will be a while until we get yours back. And we should. It's not safe to have bits of you lying around, waiting for an enemy to buy and use against you."

Elaine tries to make eye contact, but despite his hovering, he continues to look everywhere but at her. She trips over a wayward rock, and his hand grabs her before she falls. She puffs out a breath in relief. The relief comes too soon, however, as that same hand snaps away and she falls face-first into the ground.

Lovers is too passionate a word for what they just did. It was a practical exchange of energies; one she hadn't experienced before. It's a common curiosity that mages with shared affinities explore at some point in their lives but one she hadn't thought she'd get to. She's still tired but her soul feels full, and she can feel the magic circulating her body once more.

Blood drips into her palms, from where, she's not sure yet, but her face is buzzing in pain. He doesn't offer to help her up, clutching his hands tightly to his chest, so she uses one hand to heave herself up from the cement while the other cups the blood coming from her face.

"Ow!"

"He does noses, too," he says.

Her fist clenches, but she forces herself to take a deep breath. He did, technically, save her life. If a person is drained of all magic, it kills as quick as a heart attack. This is a man who runs on impulse and very little remorse, so to blame him for being callous would be illogical. Near death experiences are like a morning run to him. He's not off the hook, and she certainly won't be doing anything like that with him again. It was practical magic, not a declaration of love. And besides, why would she ever fall for a basket case like Ivan Gray?

By the time they reach Ivan's growth mage, she has a broken nose and one black eye (from the nose), a reek of death and—despite her brave misadventure—only has nine toes. The store is tight, with dark wood stretching across the floor, walls, and ceiling. A myriad of curios spill over from shelves and tables. In one corner, stands a coffin with foot-long spikes sticking out of the velvet lining.

She looks around for the mage Ivan promised would help her, but it's a small shop. There's only an imp, clacking with clawed hands at the brass keys of the till.

"Excuse me, sir. We're looking for the doctor?" she asks.

Ivan stiffens next to her.

The imp turns his slow gaze onto her. "I am the doctor."

She eyes him, confused. "The growth doctor?"

The imp's nose twitches in the air. His mouth pulls back into an evil smile, his teeth sharp like a shark. "You and I both know humans aren't the only mages."

She rubs a hand against her nose. Her eyes flick to Ivan once, then twice.

"Put her on the table," the imp demands, donning bulky spectacles with about twenty alternative lenses. Once Ivan does so, the imp ducks into the back of the store, where clanging and jingles ring out as he shuffles through supplies.

"You'll be busy tomorrow," Ivan says, breaking the silence between them.

"Will I?" She asks, bewildered.

"You have to head to the Locke office and tell them you're withdrawing, at some point, so you can work full time with me. Might as well get it over with." He finally looks at her again, shooting her a shy uncertain smile.

Elaine laughs. But when he doesn't follow suit, that

laughter turns into a horrified gasp. "What, and just follow you around like a crazed lemming?"

He seems to ponder what she said for a moment, forehead scrunching in thought. "That's really saying something, since the regular ones are famous for throwing themselves off cliffs."

In what world would she change her life on a whim? Months of planning, years of studying. The promise of security and stability thrown away for a stranger? A sense of adventure? And to throw it away on someone so dodgy, so unpredictable, so impulsive. Adventure can never replace the sanctity of peace of mind.

"You're asking me to abandon my careful planning for—for —" she struggles to find the words, "for a career in urban piracy!"

HE SCOFFS. "The jobs aren't always going to be in the sewer. Besides, you need a boat to be a pirate."

It seems to dawn on Ivan that she's serious much in the same way it had for her: with righteous indignation. "You're serious. I'm the only other luck mage in the world!"

But she is no fool, and she's certainly not a luck mage. Despite recent circumstances, she is not a woman of quick decisions. Every locked door may have its key, but she will not even try to jiggle the handle unless expressly given the permission. And if her sound judgement wasn't enough to dissuade her from this decision, the fact that it's coming from Ivan—the man who orchestrated what was the second most traumatic event of her life—is.

"It's preposterous, Ivan," she says. "I won't do it." Straight to the point, no room for interpretation or niceties.

Ivan gestures for her to sit down. She looks for any sign of that previous warmth, of nerves. Instead, his eyes are cold, mouth only pulling upwards when talking to the imp. Shame rises up in her cheeks, but it's quickly replaced by the flush of anger.

"I should have your head for this," she says. The blue tone of her cloak deepens and the loose waves of the river move faster and faster. The fish are gone, leaving only dark waters that reflect Elaine's mood.

Ivan has the gall to look confused by her comment.

She's happy to explain. "You cursed me, got my toe amputated, and then forced me into some weird lovers spat between sewer dwellers where I almost—" Her breath hitches. Quieter, she says, "I don't want to ever see you again after this."

"The good doctor will fix you up," he replies. His brows furrow as his eyes flit over her, clearly looking for something. She senses he's nervous now, the emotion drawn out by her ire. "I'll get you a new toe. A better toe."

"I want *my* toe," she cries.

"My god, you're mercurial."

"*I'm* mercurial?"

Before she can push him into the spiked coffin at his back, the imp returns.

"Lay back," he barks. "It'll be seventy for the nose, two-fifty for sewing up the foot, and five hundred and fifty-five if you want it regrown."

Elaine's heart clenches. She's sure she doesn't have any money on her.

"It's three-fifty for a new toe, Delius," Ivan says.

Delius looks at him through one magnified eye. "City voted to tax more for public schools. It's five hundred and fifty-five." His eyes turn to Elaine. "And I don't like her."

What did I ever do to him? she wonders indignantly.

"C'mon, what about as a favor to me?" Ivan flutters his lashes.

The good doctor takes this into consideration. "Six hundred."

Ivan's foot taps incessantly against the tiled floor. He runs his tense fingers through his mussed hair, fluffing it up further. Elaine has moved from anger, to grief, to acceptance. She'd dry-humped a neurotic, penniless, wraith of a mage. Maybe she didn't deserve a whole foot.

"I'll do a job for you," Ivan finally concedes. "The impossible one."

The imp looks at him, before going back to assessing her nose. He skims a hand over the bridge. "These employers aren't kidding around, Ivan. Besides, I thought you weren't accepting the big jobs anymore. Just sticking to petty theft and walking old ladies across the street."

An idea of what Ivan does forms in her mind. He must be a marketmage. Much like a sellsword, who will fight in your name, they're for-hire mages that use their affinities to complete a job, for a price. Most of them operate outside of the law, and the jobs range from being a bodyguard to making counterfeit coins. Ivan must be a thief for-hire.

"That was before inflation increased the price of a good right pinky toe."

Elaine breaks into a sob.

"Don't worry, Lainey, you pull it off far better than I could."

"All right, I'll give you the job, Gray," the imp replies, never moving from his work.

Ivan nods, lips pursed tightly. And he had the nerve to call her mercurial.

Fixing her ends up only taking ten minutes, four seconds, and one bottle of whiskey.

"For the pain," is all Delius said before her nose straightens and a new flesh-covered bone grows out of her foot.

"Ow," she yelps in pain.

Ivan motions for her to follow, and she does so without argument, feeling more balanced now that she's got all five right toes even as she rubs the remaining tears from her eyes.

"Careful in the dungeon, Ivan," the imp calls. "There's been a man working on the same puzzle, seeking refuge with lonely widows on the north end. He's been leaving them to be found sucked dry. To the bone."

The luck mage hums, rubbing a hand across his chin. "Vampire?" Ivan asks.

"Or worse."

Ivan waves, not bothering to look back as he closes the door tightly behind them.

He takes a deep breath, as if he's going to speak, but instead strides into the street without another word. Elaine follows his sweeping figure all the way to the main roads before losing him in the crowd.

10

SNAKE EYES

The tailor shop commissioned by the university to make the school cloaks is large, with black and white tile and fluorescent lights hanging from a popcorn ceiling. It used to be a diner, if the unplugged jukebox in the corner is anything to go by. Uncle Neil scrutinizes the sticking spell of the aforementioned jukebox, muttering and tapping along the chipped paint as Elaine's poked and measured by the seamstress.

Elaine's school cloak fitting makes it clear how painfully inefficient Locke fashion is. The material itself is a jeweled green and purple, with leather buttons and clasps along the front.

"Is this for a child?" Elaine asks. It only reaches her ribs.

The seamstress raises an unimpressed eyebrow. "It's meant to be this short. Long robes are out of fashion."

"But there's hardly any magic in it!"

Her own cloak, added on to year after year as she grew taller and taller, had all her family's protection within each thread. Her mother had picked the colors from the river, the tint of blue dependent on the color of the water that day. It resulted in a monochromatic swirl of blues, so fond of Elaine and her magic, and her, so used to its presence, that not having it on felt like she might as well be naked. Now, fingering the slippery and easily stained spider's silk school robe she'd once been excited to wear, she promises herself she'll only leave her own cloak behind for school ceremonies.

"Uncle Neil, is this right?"

Neil drops a coat hanger he's fumbling with, cursing when it lets out a low moan of dismay. He hobbles over and scrutinizes the cloak. His lips thin, and she knows he agrees with her. The fabric is blank of any sort of writing, and the strongest spell on it is an anti-theft ward that will come off once they purchase it from the store.

"Extra enchantments are available for an add-on price," the seamstress explains. "Would you like to add a seasonal protection spell for just two hundred more gold?"

Such terms spark another round of questions in Elaine—what kind of protection? What makes it seasonal? "Who would add them on?" Surely, she couldn't be suggesting a stranger do it.

"We have spellcasters in the back, just for Locke students." The seamstress says it as if it's something Elaine should be impressed by.

"But those would only last a year, at most. Six months if they're not concentrating."

"That's how spellcasters work," she says. "This is Garriver. You'd be hard pressed to find someone who makes enough money to fund a year-long project like that. Especially when the trends will have changed by the time fall comes around again."

A surge of appreciation for her mother takes hold of Elaine. Twenty years of threads, plus thirty more of protective runes and incantations, is turning out to be priceless.

"It has all of our magic," her mother had said. "And you

won't grow any taller. Now you can collect the protection of anyone you choose, but the cloak itself is done. The details are up to you."

It's the next day at Locke, and Elaine itches to rip the slippery school robe straight off, but she can't afford to be late to the assembly speech or her first mentor meeting. She'd rushed to campus after missing her initial professor meeting only to find the door locked and lights off. The administrator had rolled her eyes and just told her to meet her mentor on the first day of class.

At Locke, the words "professor" and "mentor" are interchangeable. For undergraduate programs, the degree you earn is an apprenticeship. From there, you can get an entry-level job at a company, though that's often only obtainable if your mentor knows someone there. Elaine's first choice had been Professor Rigor Mortis, who is notoriously as boring as he is well connected. Her affinity for probability is negligible, and wouldn't negatively affect work in finance, accounting, or other math. With a neutral affinity like Elaine's, she's certain to get a stable job if she proves herself good with numbers at an intellectual level.

Locke University's history is tangled up with that of the human colonies that first settled on the river back when it was wetlands, and garlic made of silver and gold still grew along its bank. Young human mages took it upon themselves to build a college, and for years, it had been human-only. Non-human mages have only been allowed to attend for the last 200 years. Humans claimed that because different species have different cores, that academic systems couldn't support inter-species disciplines. In response, many non-human mages decided to create their own schools near the same location as the fairy ring, the greatest well of magical power in the region and the one that amplifies the magic of individuals. Through a series of wards, illusions, traps, and protections, it became hidden from the public. Eventually, when the success of those non-human schools became too much to ignore, and the profits too enticing, Locke absorbed those colleges and become one of the largest campuses in the nation. There have been a few changes to the structure to accommodate non-human students, but the system itself still heavily reflects the original Locke code of conduct.

She looks at the frayed yellow paper in her hand, with the words "Professor Sap, Rm III" scrawled across it. Where her stomach once jumped in excitement at the thought of her first day, it was now weighed down with dread. Being late that first day had meant Professor Mortis was taken and she got whatever mentor was left over, and she knows nothing about Professor Sap. What if he's mean? Or worse, lazy?

She sighs and makes her way towards the assigned room. Her bottom half feels exposed, and the silk school cloak flutters with the slightest breeze, flying up and into her face. Her hands end up holding each flap down as she walks across the vast green courtyard.

The building for STEM apprentices is a historic limestone building that looked better suited to the romantic nature of English majors, who are trapped in a building whose architecture can only be described as "riot proof." The inside courtyard is filled with lush green grass that would never grow naturally in a marsh environment, but Locke could afford to prune, plump, and garner Bermuda grass, whether it makes sense or not.

Her slippers pad along the stone floor as the numbers along the outdoor hallway grow larger, and she stops and enters through the weathered door marked "III."

At the front of the lecture hall sits a large potted plant. She takes a seat in the row second from the front as a frog croak signals the start of class.

Silence fills the hall outside, and she looks around. Late mages get late mentors apparently. She sticks her hand under her chin, watching the clock tick by.

When it reaches fifteen minutes, she gets up to explore the classroom. Her curiosity leads her to the potted plant in the front of the room. When she reaches out to touch a leaf, the lime-green bottom half sprouts forward, unfurling and revealing a little green man. He yawns, handlebar mustache wiggling and made entirely out of leaves.

Elaine takes a hurried step back, horrified at her attempt to fondle what she now knows to be this man's head.

"Oh, is it that time already?" he grumbles. "Another year, another late student." His voice echoes clearly throughout the wooden hall, springing cleanly against the empty chairs and tables. "Our first probability student in two hundred years! And the first one *I've* seen in fifty. I hope you won't make a habit of running late."

Elaine smiles weakly. "I'll try not to."

He hums suspiciously before tugging himself out of the plant with a loud grunt. He makes his way behind the desk, heaving himself onto the chair and turning his attention to the papers in front of him. "Now, we'll need to discuss your curriculum. Since your affinity has nothing to do with your accounting goals, the school saw fit to assign me."

She stands up straighter. "You're an accountant."

"Goodness, no! I'm a gardener." He shakes his head in disbelief. "How boring. No. But we'll stick to the basics of using your magic. It'll be good for you to learn."

"I didn't come here to learn magic," she says. "I came here to take classes to get a degree in accounting."

That's what she wants a professor for, to guide her through her studies and help her make connections in her field.

He smiles up at her. "We'll start with an easy assignment: "The Inherent Magics" essay."

It's a remedial essay. And nothing to do with her degree. She's overcome with a strange, paradoxical feeling of desire for Ivan: as a guide and also a willing conduit for her rage. It's Ivan's fault she's stuck with Sap, and yet, he's the only one willing to teach her about probability, magically or mathematically. Even if he does call it luck.

UNCLE NEIL ASKS her to meet him at his downtown office, Potioneers Inc., after her mentor meeting, so they can head home together. He wants to show her around the city...with guided supervision this time.

His office is situated on the river, and the excess ingredients flow into the water source from a series of pipes. The glass-plated building is shaped like a potion bottle, with a wide round base and long, tube-like neck. Its green-tinted windows reflect the city. She's not sure why they're meeting at his office with how much he complains about his job.

"If I won the lotto," he laments, "you'd never see me in another office again."

As much as her uncle bemoans corporations, he's in sore need of a pension, health insurance, and forced socialization.

She approaches the receptionist seated behind a white alabaster desk. The man wears a crown of cranberries, incredibly wide and high. He has sharp cheekbones and eyes that are a dull black, sclera and all.

"I'm here to see Neil Leatherforth?"

"Relation?"

"Niece."

He eyes Elaine's tall body. He purses his lips but reaches under his desk for a guest pass.

"First door on the left. The password for the elevator is 'shroom dust.'" He hands her a lanyard. "Keep that on you at all times. If the fellytusks see you without it, they'll eat you."

She doesn't know what a fellytusk is but is sure she never wants to meet one. She clenches the lanyard tight in her fist as she makes her way up to her uncle's office. She arrives without encountering a single wayward fellytusk and wanders past the low walls of cubicles towards the more private, though transparent, wizards' offices.

"Come in." He waves her in, easily seeing her through his walls.

"These are new." She nods to the floor-to-ceiling glass.

"New boss came in with fresh ideas: new glass walls and no quarterly bonuses."

Elaine feels the press of commonplace horror on her chest. She initially worried Neil had left his legless lizard research to take care of her at his brother's request, but he assured her he needed to come back to the city this year anyways, so he'd returned to his job with Potioneers Inc. as a contractor. Even still, his descriptions of his job sound horrible.

He'd told her about it over a dirty cauldron. "When I first joined the workforce, there were pensions, an eight-hour workday, and plenty of time to finish everything you needed to at the day's end. Then they started laying off the potioneers' apprentices and replaced them with interns. Then the interns went away, and the warlock candidates had to do the work of two. Then half the warlock candidates got laid off, and the ones left had to do the work of four. Now we're all overworked and underpaid, and if I didn't have a consultation contract from before we were bought out, you can bet your silver pins I'd be gone too."

She wishes, for the first time since she learned her affinity, to find something so incredible in her magic, so unreplicable, that she never has to work this hard. Ivan surely didn't have to deal with any of this nonsense.

"Lucky," she mumbles.

Uncle Neil rises from his seat. "Be right back," he says. "Take my chair."

She sits down, eyeing her uncle's documents. *Potioncon, Recipe patents, Reform non-magic certifications, Uses of potions and liquor licenses.*

She pulls the pins from her bun, placing them between her teeth before she redoes the top of her hair into a half bun. The loose hair rolls down her back in a smooth wave and tensions of the day leak away with the change. Minutes tick by, and a few curious potioneers eye the stranger sitting in a wizard's office. She presses her feet into the carpet, pushing away from the desk in slow, smooth circles.

This isn't so bad, she thinks. *At least the chairs are ergonomic.*

She stops swiveling in his chair and leans in further when a particular file catches her eye—a violet-shaded envelope labeled *DO NOT TOUCH*. Workers mill slower outside the office, occasionally glancing at her, doomed to a terrible fate for sitting in Leatherforth's chair.

How she wishes for the folder to open and give her the tiniest peek as to what could warrant a capitalized "do not touch."

The crowd outside the office scatters as the office door swings open, and Elaine quickly slouches back into the chair, the back squeaking. Uncle Neil storms back in, his eyes flicking to hers, then to his desk. He hobbles over, leaning heavily on his staff, swipes the folders up in his pudgy fingers, and sticks them under his arm.

"Let's get moving," he says. "I've got someone I'd like to see before dinner."

He holds open the door, and she steps back out into the hallway.

"What about?"

"Locke University's fairy ring is in need of some more defensive spells."

Her nose wrinkles. Circles of power have many names. Also called fairy rings, circles of power are location-based sources of magic, a powerful happenstance of nature that places them across tectonic plates that sit just so under constellations. Some places, like California, have mobile rings that shift every few years. But Garriver's rings are steady, connected not only by stars but by the swampland a few layers below the surface. Before they rolled the swamplands over with concrete, it is said the land itself would speak to those who lived within it. Elaine —who once spent an entire month in the woods before realizing she hadn't spoken in thirty days—doesn't believe it. If land could speak, she would be able to hear it.

The murmurs speculating about the tall woman's relation to Wizard Leatherforth in the hallway cease, and the lights flicker overhead. Someone, wearing a deep gray cloak, steps out of the elevator like a wraith, and it feels as though the floor beneath Elaine might rot and drop her straight through it.

She steps behind Neil, whose own legs wobble. He stays upright with the help of his staff, entwined with runes, both familiar and strange to her.

The being moves like any normal man. But people scatter out of his way like pigeons out of oncoming traffic. As he draws closer, she thinks he walks handsomely, but her body screams at her that something about him is wrong. Murky. It makes her want to lotion her legs, clear her face of blackheads, and redo her hair over and over until it's perfect.

He strides down the carpeted hall without looking at anyone, but his feet hesitate in front of Neil and Elaine. He looks down at her, assessing. Her stomach clenches, and her throat fills with bile as she swallows against what feels like the remnants of her lunch. His hood holds unnatural shadows, obscuring everything but the very bottom of his chin in a way that must be magic. Her brain begs her to stand with her shoulders back and chest forward, lips slightly agape.

The Someone turns his head forward to continue his walk, never turning to look her way again.

When he turns the corner, Elaine sags against the wall and takes a deep breath. "Who was that?"

The office lights up in conversation, employees asking the same shaky question. They clutch their cloaks, the lower-quality ones now fraying at the edges like they've been eaten away by moths.

"Never you mind." Uncle Neil grasps her elbow with a shaky hand. "Quick bathroom break. Then dinner."

The further that Someone walks away, the better she's able to change the subject to something more pleasant. "What's the purple folder?"

"Special project for the mayor. *Classified.*"

Elaine bets the mayor wants a love potion. Or, better yet, Uncle Neil must cover up a scandal involving a legless lizard, twenty DMV employees, and a particularly irate hobgoblin.

For her entire life, Elaine believed she was the sole probability mage. And now, it seems as though she'll never meet another one again. It had been two weeks since her horrifying adventure, and no sign of Ivan.

She rolls onto her stomach and groans into her pillow when she thinks of the useless damsel she had so excellently played in that misadventure. The beginning and end had been horrible, but in between, there'd been tension. A quest where she'd mattered, with twists and shake ups to her belief in reality that left her breathless.

She lays across her four-poster queen bed, wiggling the

right toe she'd painted black, while the rest of them are painted a coral pink. She was in her mourning period after all.

Life must carry on, and school stops for no mage. The past two weeks have been a cycle of studying, eating, and sleeping. The monotony leaves her plenty of time to think, and so her mind oscillates between thoughts of Ivan and how much she misses Sigmut. She misses the clear air, the familiar faces, the home cooked meals. Neil's talent for formulas starts and ends with potions, and she misses having company in the kitchen as she makes her meals. Every meal tastes a little duller when it's cooked alone. She hasn't reached out to her parents yet. Thinking about writing to her dad makes her feel like throwing up, so communication with him is a definitive no. She'd been planning on writing to mom as soon as she got her professor, so she could tell her about all the wonderful lessons ahead. But with her academic plans being ruined not even a month into her big move, it feels like admitting defeat to write out "I don't know how I'm going to fix this." Part of her has also grown to resent her mother for her father's choices. If she hadn't lied and cheated Elaine wouldn't exist. She can't rationally blame her for the cheating without wishing for her own extinction. But if Paola had kept her mouth shut after making her mistakes, then Elaine would still exist, and she'd still have her dad.

She searches for a distraction to avoid her dread. Her eyes move to her unfinished theory homework. She flops forward, stretching out her arm to grasp the textbook, pulling it to her side to continue reading.

The Inherent Magics

While a person's magical core always has a unique quality, there are a series of basic magics almost everyone can achieve. These include simple tasks, like connecting with others with compatible magic through purposeful exudence; and the ability to bottle and store their own magic in conduits, such as staffs, wands, weapons, and household runes. Runes are particularly helpful in protecting blood relatives and having a property with several generations worth of sealing and protective charms. While magic can also become stronger stacked with similar cores, it is unlikely to be as useful as those linked by ancestry.

She groans, falling back in her bed. This is so *boring*. Still, the thought of going downstairs to Uncle Neil seems worse.

He hadn't taken the story about her toe too well.

"Are you mad? Your body, Nellie, is not something to lose. You know the kinds of things mages can do with just a toe." His eyes shift around their kitchen, clearly paranoid. "What *dark* mages will do? Mind possession, body manipulation. Not to mention the potential for Staph infection. You are much too old to be making these kinds of mistakes. Maybe you aren't ready to live in the city."

"No!" she says. "No. Please, I know I haven't had a great start, but this is it."

Her uncle grunts. It's one of his "I'm listening" grunts, so she keeps going.

"This is my best chance at a better life. You know what it's like to have a bad affinity."

Her uncle, unlike her parents, would not give her a speech on how that wasn't true, how there's value in every affinity. He was honest to a fault, but it also made him incredibly easy to convince.

"And the stars only know how long it will take me to get a good job without this degree. It could be another century."

"If university really means that much to you..."

She jumps on the slight approval before he can take it back. "Thank you! I promise I'll be more careful."

"Speaking of that." He eyes her hair. "Hair's another way to take control. Y'ever considered...?" He mimics buzzing his hair off.

"I'd sooner choose mind possession."

She knows for certain other students who share affinities also share professors and are at least able to practice with one another. With a plant mage as her teacher, her entire education will be stuck at multiple choice and two-person Socratic seminars. Thoughts of Ivan fill her head before she can help it.

I bet he's out there, using magic like it's as easy as breathing.

She wants to wring his neck. She hadn't allowed herself to be treated as expendable by a man since she was nineteen and didn't know better, and to do so in her seventies? She should wring her own neck, not his.

She strides to her wardrobe and pulls out a pink corset to lace across her white, knee-length flowing dress. No more brain matter would be wasted on that shriveling wreck of a thief. It's a hot September day, even hotter than the week she'd first moved here in August. Uncle Neil said this always happens right before the plunging cold Garriver is notorious for.

Fastening her cloak over her shoulders, she feels more comfortable stepping back into the wind. Since her abduction, Uncle Neil whispered his own magical intent into it. He insisted on sewing silvery runes onto the nape of the hood. For having such thick hands, he's well versed in tiny, delicate lettering. She's never seen letters like these before. They hold everything but a straight line: all soft triangles and ovals. The triangles are not all equilateral, which bothers her immensely.

"My father taught me," he says. "It's old family magic. I should've done this the moment you stepped foot into this city."

It was an open secret that her dad and Neil had different fathers. Their magic, skills and looks were too different, but it never came between the bond they had. In the small hours of the morning, when even the city's quiet, it gives her rubbed-raw heart hope that Dad might come back around to seeing her as his again.

She wraps her hair in a bun, but she can't get it quite right.

This way is too tight, the other lifts her hair into unsightly bumps. She gives up and lets it fall into silvery rivulets behind her, clipping her salmon pins in to pull back the frontmost strands. In the mirror, she cocks her head to the left and admires the way her hair falls against her dress. The corset accentuates the slight curves on her tall, lithe body.

"Huh," she says. She looks beautiful with her hair down.

She descends the wooden staircase to the kitchen looking for a basket in the closet. It was impractical, she knew, but it was a superstition of hers: a good basket guarantees a delightful day. She finds her uncle in the kitchen counting beans.

He raises a brow. "Someone's looking spiffy."

She grins. "Thank you."

"Hot date?"

Unbidden, Ivan flashes through her mind. "Just a trip through the farmers' market."

"Wear your hood up over your head. Did you pack the bear spray?"

She holds up the can, shaking it for effect. Neil believes that everything bad that can happen, will. So, when she's "inevitably attacked", she's to run as fast as she can, and keep her cloak around her head. The wards will keep her safer than most and make her a harder target. The bear spray is for anything or anyone that decides to step too close. She'd spent many seasons slipping through trees and caves with her uncle, but it's much harder to navigate a moving, breathing crowd than a still winter forest to avoid a migrating banshee. The bear on the can does make her think of Ivan. She shakes it, fantasizing about the opportunity to spray him in the face.

"Bring back any purple maize you find. I need to restock our allergy tonics before fall's in full swing." He scrutinizes her face. "And stop smiling like that. You're thinking of something awful, and I don't want to hear it."

Garriver is so removed from the process of growing, hunting, and eating their own food, that the city folk all come together on the weekend to buy all of their groceries at once in a market. Their minds must be constantly running on that quick-fix-it high, she reasons—it explains the pace of their walk, the minute-by-minute planning. All perfectly reasonable impulses when you have farmers driving hours and hours to get a moment of your attention and a portion of your pocket.

She walks straight into the midst of the Saturday morning hullabaloo. Unlike her parents, she doesn't mind crowds. Despite the lack of space, people aren't keen to touch strangers. Elaine's always been lucky when it came to crowds, usually no one would brush against her—the other day with Ivan being a notable exception.

The stalls are manned by all sorts of people: goblins, pixies, orcs. There's a spider who was cursed to be human, and a human cursed to be a spider running a booth together called Topsy-Turvy's Partial Curse Remedies. Currently, Elaine is perusing all sorts of oil lamps by a stall called Wish Wares.

"Of all the djinn joints," says a low voice behind her.

Her toe twitches in annoyance. She walks away and towards an orc selling extraordinarily large grapes, ignoring the previous merchant's shouted promises of half-off oil lamps.

Ivan follows close behind, cloak fluttering behind him. His hood is pulled up, and she thinks he looks unfairly innocent with those tufted bear ears on the top of the brown cloak. Her hand reaches out for her bear spray, but she thinks better of it. She turns her head away and gives her rapt attention to the watermelon sized grapes in front of her.

"Come on, Lainey. Don't be like that."

"Are the grapes magically enhanced?" she asks the vendor, hoping that Ivan will get the hint and just go away.

The orc eyes Ivan with suspicion. "No, miss, harvested from giant's soil. Right on the clouds overlooking Pompeii."

Ivan places his hand on her shoulder. "We've always wanted to go there, haven't we, darling?"

She stomps on his foot, only to wince herself when she feels the steel-toed boot under her heel. His grin fractures, and he takes his hand off her shoulder. Rolling her eyes, she deigns to turn to him.

His smile reappears with her attention. "Is the idea of people thinking your heart belongs to a sickly man too much to bear?"

Sickly? she thinks, confused.

"I was under the impression we'd never see each other again." She strides away, nose in the air, and he follows soon after.

"What gave you that idea?"

She glares.

He rubs the back of his neck. "Alright, I admit I left coldly. But it wasn't because of you."

"Oh really." Her voice grows louder. "Because, from my end, you coerced me through drainpipes, humped at my leg like an ill-mannered goat, then left me alone in a strange part of town smelling of sewage and sweat. *After* I started crying."

The other marketeers shoot them horrified glances. An old man tuts at Ivan.

He pulls her around the corner to a less populated section entirely dedicated to miniature wooden figurines. "I am truly sorry, Elaine. Let me make it up to you. Let me teach you something."

He does look truly sorry, fiddling with the edge of his cloak and gazing down at her with pitiful eyes. She thinks of that wretchedly boring textbook back home, and she glances down at her cloak. The salmon swim calmly. She takes it as a sign.

"Alright, Ivan. Lead the way."

He takes her to his apartment in the old meat-packing district. Its architecture is strictly brick. During the mob era, golems figured out how to work the native red clay into the magic of the bricks they laid. The buildings are so sturdy that new developers were unable to destroy them to make room for skyscrapers no matter the skill of the wizard they brought to take them down.

"It's believed that the dozens of factories will outlast civilization itself. At least, that's what my landlord told me when she upped my rent." He smiles at her when her hand grazes the horseshoe above his door. "Keeps witches away."

She wrinkles her nose, pulling away from the brass. His apartment is unfinished; bricks line all four walls. The floor plan is open: his kitchen against the left wall, with a second door on the right wall, a large window right between them. The only saving grace of the place is the large bay window with a bench across it. The mattress (she is not so generous that she would call it a bed) is only inches off the ground. Her feet lead her to his frustratingly unorganized cabinet of potion ingredients. A shiver of delight runs through her spine when she thinks about how it would look all organized and lightly dusted. Would she order by name, expiration date, color?

"Make yourself at home." He gestures to the table in the middle of the room.

Elaine hesitates. For seating, there are a few painfully thin pillows, and the edge of the mattress, set off the ground upon upside down pots.

"What are we, twenty? Where's your bed frame?"

He straightens his spine when her attention is drawn back to him. His eyes twinkle when she points out his bed. He lays back on it, arms beneath his head. "Care to test out the formidability?"

She makes sure he's far enough back before sitting on it in front of the table. She bounces on the edge. "Very sturdy."

He scoots forward, legs on either side of her. "Then don't question my methods."

Stupid, she scolds herself when she leans back into his warm embrace. She's never felt so much like a cliché, a puzzle piece snapping into place. Is this how her brother felt when he met his wife? Was this how everyone with common magic affinity felt? Like meeting an old friend, like an escape into a childhood she hadn't had.

She shakes herself out of her reverie. "Weren't you going to teach me magic?"

"Right." He clears his throat, scooting away from her to swing his legs over the mattress and sit next to her. "I'll be starting with my greatest trick, Snake Eyes." He moves around her and off the bed, sitting at a square wooden table, and she follows suit. His legs sit high up from his seat on the floor, extending right up past his shoulders. He holds a pair of dice up.

He looks ridiculous, she thinks fondly.

"There's a one in thirty-six chance of getting snake eyes. With luck magic—" he rolls the dice, each landing with the one face up, "—I can get it 100 percent of the time."

He does it again and again and again. After the fifth roll, he hands them to her. "You try."

Real, actual magic. She screws her eyes shut, searching for something, anything that feels like magic. Elaine rolls the dice, heart beating fast. Her hope wanes when she rolls a three and a five. She tries again and rolls a two and a four.

"No luck."

"Try thinking that you *know* it's what you'll get. You have to be confident, or else all the numbers get jumbled together."

"That's not how probability works," she insists. "You can't just believe in yourself. There's logic to magic. Numbers."

He doesn't look like he believes her. "Sure, core size factors in—"

She shakes her head. "Even then, let's say we have two fire mages of equal core strength. If one is six foot five and the other five foot six, they're going to have completely different physical capabilities. The large one might be stronger and able to withstand heat longer, while the shorter one could be quicker and have better endurance. The large one will most likely use fire in large, overpowering moves, specializing in being a heavy hitter whose body can handle high heat that packs a punch. The smaller will focus on quick blasts, careful not to overwhelm their body temperature. Because of the necessity of keeping temperatures under a certain threshold, five foot six will be able to fight for longer periods."

"But what if the taller one wants to use short bursts as well?"

"That would be impractical. So many fire mages are under five foot five, that a tall one would be destined to make tons of money with employers who need a specialized worker."

"You're assuming this fire mage cares about that sort of thing."

"A job?" she clarifies. "Yes, I did assume that."

"What if they don't want the cushy job? They could just want enough to live off of, and maybe they find the high temperatures unbearable. They even give him eczema!"

"You don't know that."

"Neither do you."

At some point, he'd rounded the table, knees knocking against hers and passion lighting up his eyes. "You're thinking about this as if magic is a get-rich-quick scheme. For most, it's synonymous with being alive."

"I know magic is more than money. But you need money to live the life you want. Money means security, and security means freedom."

Elaine looks up at Ivan once she finishes her rant. He has a look of surprise on his face. She mistakes it for confusion and hastens to explain herself further.

"It's not a perfect example. I'd need secondary sources of course, but the logic will be backed by any half-decent book you read."

"I agree," he says. "You like magic, don't you? I thought you hated it from the way you talked about it in the sewers, but it's just ours you can't stand."

A hot flush covers her face. As a child, she had high hopes of getting some sort of physical magic, then surviving in the woods. She'd studied night and day, sure she'd get elemental magic, because that's what both her parents had. When that didn't happen, she came to terms with settling for a mind affinity and poured over old tomes from the library in town. She had to start trading fish for knowledge with local merchants when she ran out of written material, hungry for stories of their adventures. Her brother had nearly burned the house down when his affinity appeared, and her sister had to dive into the water when she found breathing air was no longer an option. The day magic came for her, she got something that was worse than she could have imagined—hardly studied, never funded, and fiscally useless.

"I used to hate magic too," he admits, "when I learned I was born with a family curse."

The admission startles Elaine out of her reverie. "Born cursed?"

"That's all you're getting out of me," he says. "That's for me to know. But once I learned that magic was more than curses, a whole new world of opportunity opened up to me. It's why my magic stops sometimes. Like when we were in the sewers, and I almost didn't make the jump. My core is a well, and there's a drain that unplugs without my permission or warning and takes the luck right out of me."

A curse. This man has fought mages, bartered and stolen

with his probability magic, and all while dealing with a curse. She's always been a tactile and visual learner, and his life is more than anything she could've imagined on her own.

"I didn't know someone like you existed," she admits.

"What, devastatingly handsome?"

"Someone like me who's worth something."

His eyes widen and pink dusts his cheeks. He furrows his brow and sits back, crossing his arms. "You're worth something because you're alive, Elaine. Doesn't matter how useful other people deem you. They can love you, regardless of your affinity."

Her heart swells with a feeling she thought long dead. Stomped under the boot of expectation, and held closely by her parents, she'd not thought of her sense of worth with such a sharp lens in a long time. But that's what happens when someone you love leaves you; it carves out a cavern in your heart, and the bits left are forced to listen to the echoes. She had worried over her place in the world since society labeled her affinity as useless. It drove her to excel in her studies to make up for that absence of power. The events of the River Speak made questions that had stayed deep in her wounds since childhood bubble up to the surface again: Would her father have stayed if she was useful? If, despite her parentage, she'd been a fire mage like her brother? She crosses her arms over her stomach, the thoughts twisting around in her gut like thick, gnarled thorns.

Her throat tightens. She clears it, shaking a bit of hair in front of her face as she blinks away the sudden wetness in her eyes. "Alright. Let me try this again. A feeling, you said."

He nods, eyes stuck on her face. "A feeling."

ELAINE IS UP VERY LATE one night, rolling the dice.

"Come on," she whispers to them. "Just once. I can do it, just once."

She rolls two sevens. Groaning, she throws herself back on her bed. She's been trying to make it happen for nearly two hours, but she still can't roll the dice that she wants, more than once in a row, at least not with magic. Tonight, she chose a three and a two. And there was no magic-based exhaustion, just regular old I-should-be-asleep-right-now tired.

She takes a deep breath, rises from her bed, and stares at the dice in front of her.

I can do this, she thinks. *Magic is like walking. It's a feeling in my gut.*

She closes her eyes, takes the dice into her hands, and rolls them forward. The moment they leave her palm that twinging feeling in her stomach isn't so strong, and she feels a new pressure in her forehead. And when she opens her eyes, she sees a three and a two in front of her. She picks them up and, feeling that same pressure against her skull, she rolls again.

She leaps into the air, silently cheering. It's 2 a.m.: she's a bastard, she has a useless affinity, an even more useless professor, one fake toe, and she's finally done magic.

I have to tell someone, she thinks. Then, *Ivan's only a twenty-minute walk away.*

Their relationship has changed since they talked about what magic means to them. She pulls on her cloak and shuts the door behind her. It's a silent Tuesday night in Garriver, but her heart is racing. Elaine Aquae has just performed magic.

Time flashes quickly on her walk, and she rings incessantly on the doorbell to Ivan's apartment. After a few moments, it comes alive with a buzz.

"Hello." His voice is scratchy.

"Ivan. I've done it."

A pause. "Elaine? It's two in the morning."

"I did magic."

His voice gets stronger. "When?"

She bites her lip, smiling ear to ear. "Now. With the dice. I just closed my eyes, thought about doing it, and it happened. I can do it, Ivan. I'm a lu—probability mage."

The intercom turns off. She taps on it, but he doesn't start speaking again. The thud of feet coming down the stairs sounds through the door, and Ivan appears, smiling wide as he shoves his arms into his cloak. His eyes are still heavy, and he slumps a bit against the archway before pushing off it and lumbering towards her, the spitting image of a hibernating bear with the tufts as his cloak's ears are pulled up atop his head.

"This calls for celebration." He wraps an arm around her shoulder. "My treat."

Her eyebrows draw together. "Where are you taking me?"

She falls into step beside him, and their footfalls sync as he guides her through the city night.

"The only place open at this time."

The only place open at three in the morning is a place called Shark Tank. The street is well lit and empty of anyone other than a few drunk college students and a large, clean tent, with books lining a bookshelf that simply reads "mine". Ivan pushes the diner door open, allowing her to enter first. It's a diner with walls lined with large aquariums. She looks at it all with wide eyes. She's never seen an ocean before.

"Shark Tank is a 24/7 diner. All the creatures here like the dark, and so do the patrons." He guides her by the small of her back to two empty barstools, and she sits there for a while, soaking it in. There are all sorts of people here, but she notices most of them are golems, which is strange for an ocean bar, she thinks.

"What'll it be?" The waitress asks. She's short, with tired eyes and walrus tusks coming out of her mouth.

Ivan gestures to the table in front of them where the menus are stuck under a plate of glass. Elaine hums in contemplation.

"I'll take the Garriver Breakfast," Ivan says.

Elaine's eyes dart over the colorful menu in front of her. There are twenty different names for variations of what seems to just be meat, eggs, and wheat products. The waitress taps her foot impatiently.

"I'll get the same," she says.

Ivan whistles as the waitress walks away. "I had no idea you loved tarantula legs that much."

Her head snaps to him in horror. He laughs, and she pouts when she realizes he's joking. Her heart flutters at the comfort of being teased by a friend, and she smiles, cheeks warm. His brown eyes stare at her with unrestrained warmth and mouth agape. Clearing his throat, he looks down at the table before looking back at her, broad grin back across his face.

"So, you've gotta show me."

"Show you what?" she feigns ignorance, taking a sip of her cold water.

He rolls his eyes good naturedly. "The magic. C'mon, show me what you did."

Elaine smiles. "I don't have the dice."

"Now, I know that's not true," Ivan says. "I have a feeling you bring a whole arsenal of 'just in case' items with you everywhere you go."

She laughs, the comment making her ridiculously happy. Slowly, for dramatic effect, she pulls the dice out from the inside of her cloak.

He leans back, putting his arms behind his head. Elaine ignores his deliberately raised eyebrow as she focuses on the dice in front of her.

"Let's do a seven and a four."

Her stomach churns, and her face goes ashen as she rolls the dice. They land on a seven and four, and she smiles in triumph at Ivan.

He eyes her face critically. "You look a little green in the gills."

"It's probably a side effect of using my magic. I get nauseous and woozy sometimes." her cheeks warm as she explains her inadequacy.

Ivan doesn't critique her, only nodded his head in understanding. "It can be hard to connect with magic after so many years of not using it. It's like trying to run a race when all you've eaten that morning are leftover meatballs. But the human body is flexible. You'd be surprised how quickly it'll adapt to your new lifestyle."

"I wasn't aware I had a new lifestyle."

He leans forward, arms crossed in front of him. This close, she can see the dilation of his pupil in his dark eyes. He reaches out his hand to her own, fingers skimming across hers as he pulls the dice from her hands. Her heart beats faster as he turns his attention to the dice in his palm when he continues to speak. "You're not planning on leaving me all alone, are you?" The tone is teasing, but a tension lies beneath the words.

"You can't really think between the two of us, I'd be the one to run away." It comes out sharper than she meant it to, and she winces when his eyes snap to hers.

They've both become cagey, their bodies rigid like feral cats crossing paths. Ivan sighs, slumping forward in his seat. Her heart pounds against her chest, watching as he fiddles with the dice in front of him, chin resting on his forearm. "I've got nowhere to run to, Lainey." He turns to her, smiling cautiously. "You're the one with a family off in the east."

Maybe, she thinks, chest tightening as she thinks about going home.

In an attempt to push the conversation to something more lighthearted, she puts a hand on her stomach. "Is using magic always going to feel like I've eaten something rotten, and I have to get it out?"

His shoulders loosen at the change in subject. "It'll get better with time. You just have to trust that you'll get there with practice. Then you'll get to work as freely as I do. It's easier once you do it the first time. After you figure out it's possible, what's the point of doubting yourself again?"

The kitchen door swings open and shuts behind her stool as she watches Ivan fool with the dice between his deft fingers.

"Being free to take the work you like does sound nice. But I'm willing to trade that sort of freedom for a steady paycheck."

His eyes alight at something behind her.

"We'll see if you feel that way after I show you *my* payday." He slides off his stool, and strides towards the part of the bar that flips up. He lifts it up and motions for her to follow him. She looks warily to the waitress, but she's looking off at the clock, bored and unbothered by two customers entering the staff space.

She follows Ivan into the diner's kitchen. Ivan leads her beyond the kitchen, the dishwashing station, and the freezer, until they're in front of a steel-enforced door. It's guarded by two large men, who look far too mean to be guarding a diner pantry. He walks up to them confidently, and they look down at him with a sneer.

"Boss expecting you?" The one on the left asks.

"I'm early, actually. But Jerome will want this as soon as possible." Ivan pulls out a brown pouch, shaking it lightly in the face of the guards.

The men step aside for Ivan and Elaine, one opening the door to let them through. "He's in there. Make it quick, he's busy."

The room is spartan, save for the back wall being a large pane of glass with ultraviolet light shining down on sea creatures, some of which Elaine hasn't even seen in books. There's what looks to be a seahorse, but it has the head of a hippo and a long, flowing mane made of seaweed, and seems capable of only swimming backwards. At the center of the room is a large wooden desk, behind which sits a large man, otherwise plain except for the fact that he's got blue scales all over his body. He stands and circles in front of his own desk, leaning back against the front of it as he gives Elaine an appraising once over.

"You brought someone nice for a change, Ivan. Who might you be?"

Elaine smiles politely. "His apprentice."

Jerome waves away her answer, eyebrow ticking up. "Not just that. You have a bit of water about you. Someone loves you deeply—if the smell of the cloak is anything to go by." He grins and taps his nose. "Got a good sense of smell. I'm a quarter siren. It's where I got these scales."

She smiles nervously, which makes the man's eyebrow drop and a grin grow on his face, pleased.

Sharp, she thinks, regarding the man's pointed teeth. *And temperamental.* The books always describe sirens as beautiful, mysterious creatures. But this man's magic smells jagged and blunt and of salt brine.

"I got the Mother Pearls, like you asked."

Jerome's greedy eyes move back onto Ivan, now sparkling at the sight of the brown pouch Ivan has taken out of his cloak. "They told me you were good, let me see." Jerome goes to reach for the bag, but Ivan lifts it higher.

"Show me the coin, first."

Jerome laughs, hand lowering to his desk drawer. Ivan's shoulders loosen, but Elaine tenses. It's the same laugh her mother has after someone tracks mud in the house or lets sourdough burn. It sounds pretty, but there is danger laced in it. It's too pointed to be kind.

"Your diner is beautiful," she blurts. Jerome pauses in his reach for the drawer. She continues, "I've never seen the ocean before. But you're right, I've lived next to a river my whole life."

Jerome's eyes are still stormy as they pass between the two

mages in front of him. They linger on her, looking as though he's weighing something. "You did, did you?"

"I was in charge of the River Speak."

His hand removes itself from the drawer entirely. It lays flat on the desk as he leans forward, a wide grin on his face. This one is conspiratorial, softer. "That's real magic. There used to be one in this city every year, but now, it's all done privately. No one gathers like that in downtown anymore."

He looks calmer when he finishes talking. His eyes flick between his desk and Elaine, seemingly thinking something over. He reaches for a different drawer and pulls out a pouch. He throws it at Ivan, and it jingles when he catches it. Ivan puts forward the pearls.

"Good doing business with you, Gray. I'll keep you in mind for the future." He smiles at Elaine. "And I'll keep her in mind, too."

She shivers, very much ready to leave this place.

"Pleasure," Ivan says. His tone is light, but he places a hand at the small of her back to guide her out, looking over his shoulder as he pushes her back out of the kitchen and into the diner. The touch sears through her cloak, and she shivers as they exit the café. Ivan removes his hand to open the bag from Jerome, sighing in relief as he looks at the gold inside.

"Why do you look so tense, Elaine? That couldn't have gone better."

She shakes her head. "He was seconds away from biting off your head, Ivan."

He waves his hand at her comment. "He would never. Besides, he took a liking to you, eh?"

She turns and points an accusing finger against his chest. "You're lucky he did. You have to be careful when you talk to people, Ivan. Read the room, guide the conversation to safer waters."

He grabs her finger but doesn't remove it from his chest. He smiles at her, lashes low. "I've been doing this for a while. I know how to handle clients just fine."

She steps closer, pushing her finger harder against his chest. "You catch more flies with honey. And if they find you not only likeable, but dependable, people will call you back for more jobs."

She can see his brain chugging along behind his eyes, absorbing, and thinking over her words. She knows she's right, and the sooner he realizes it, the easier his life is going to get.

He squeezes her hand before dropping it, and it falls back to her side.

"I have had issues with getting repeat clients. My people skills could use some work. Perhaps," he says.

"Perhaps," she mocks.

It feels good to have her social skills acknowledged as a skill she has over him. It's not magic, but there's power in reputation and charm. It makes her feel as though they're on more equal ground than she previously thought.

She raises her chin and grins. Yes, her magic is coming along slowly and surely, but her tongue? It's always been as silver as her hair.

THERE'S a spring in her step as Elaine heads back home, despite her brush with diner danger. The hair on the back of her neck prickles when she feels a pair of eyes on the back of her head. She sniffs the air, but Ivan's scent is nowhere near her. Whoever this is, they're a stranger.

She keeps track of how close she is to Uncle Neil's house. His violent protection wards make sure no intruders can steal his recipes, and they'll keep her safe too. She's almost home when the stalker reveals himself, stumbling out from the bare city underbrush.

"You," she snarls.

Before her is a brown sewer rat. It sits on its haunches, sniffing the air.

"I'm quite unwilling to see your master." She shoos it. "So, it's best if you go home."

It sits still in front of her. She doesn't relax when she passes it, but she breathes a sigh of relief when it merely follows behind her instead of attacking. When she reaches the watch-tower, she's pleased when it cannot pass her uncle's wards.

"I'm onto you," she warns, before running into the house and up to her room.

An hour later, the rat is sitting just outside the wards, staring up at her from her seat at the windowsill. It cocks its head.

You've got another thing coming, she thinks, *if you think I'll let you in.*

11

MONARCH MIGRATION

School is dreadful the next morning, as all the students are in a bad mood with the new security regulations. Someone tried to break in the night before, and of course, law-abiding citizens are the ones to pay for it. Now, no one can enter campus unless they have an ID, and guest passes have to be approved by the Dean of Students. Professor Sap has her going over commonplace uses of magic for finding friends —insisting even she can do it—when there's a tap on the window. It's Ivan, and he waves a cheerful hand at her. He shouldn't be able to circumvent the security measures, but he also shouldn't be as lucky as he is, or given his history and impulsivity, alive. He signals for her to exit the class. She glances at the professor, who has now turned to an empty desk, asking if it knows the five senses. She slips out just as he begins his speech on "When I could hear out of both ears..."

When she closes the door behind her, Ivan is already waiting.

"Hi," she says.

"Hi."

Ivan doesn't speak, and he looks like he's about to hurl, so she asks him, "Is there a reason you pulled me out of class?"

A panicked look crosses his face. "We need to talk about this." He gestures between them.

"This," she repeats.

He looks uncomfortable. He hunches a little more, as if to be smaller. Elaine's confused at the sight of him so unsure.

He grimaces. "I think it's best if we—don't? I'm not really the settling type, and you're..." He waves a hand up and down her body.

"What, too ugly to kiss?"

His eyes widen in panic. "No, no—actually I find you rather —Elaine, I..." He takes a deep breath. "I really, really like you. And I *really* liked it when you—that's to say I'd never—" he shakes his head as if to rid himself of the memory, "—but I often get carried away in these things, and then leave at the first sign of..." His face scrunches up. "Emotion."

She can't help it, she laughs. He looks at her with wide eyes, straightening up for a moment, before seeming to think better of it and hunching back over again.

"Ivan, I think you made that very clear when you turned to ice after we left that prison. I wasn't looking to *date* you." She spits the word "date" out of her mouth like it's a particularly soggy fry. "It was fun, but you don't have to worry about me getting attached."

He puts a hand to his chest and opens his mouth to respond before shutting it again. He combs his hand once, then twice, through his hair, before nodding to himself. "Partners in crime?"

She laughs, more kindly this time. A tiny part of her, the youngest, most romantic part she thought she shoved away, is crestfallen. But all the older parts, layered and hardened atop that nubile seed, are assured by the fact that, even as Garriver tries to prove her discernment wrong at every other turn, her instincts with men are as keen as ever. "Partners in crime."

Elaine goes to class after her talk with Ivan. It takes thirty more minutes after that for Sap to redirect his lesson to the "whole class"—meaning just her—and not just an empty chair. By that time, she's been back for fifteen, still laughing to herself about Ivan thinking she'd ever want to date him. He's charming in the way a street dog is—you'll throw them some food and water, but you'd never let them into your house.

"Elaine, we'll be putting away theory for something far more fun," Sap says.

Her head perks up.

"It's time for the school showcase! Oh, the first probability mage to come here in decades. It'll be a treat."

Professor Sap seems to have forgotten that she's not been able to do any magic for him so far. He must be tenured, she decides. She places her chin on her hand, watching as he rambles on about the job scouts that attend.

"You might be given the chance to become an accountant." His eyes sparkle as he goes into the non-magical jobs she could apply for.

Once upon a time, Elaine felt that was all she could hope for. But seeing Ivan talk to Delius about getting *paid* for his luck magic ignited a hope she hadn't had since the doctor told her about her affinity. In secret, she practices on her own dice every night before bed. It hardly ever works, but in the small hours of the morning two nights ago, when she succeeded in using magic for the seventh time in her life, she could've sworn she felt something old and familiar in her come alive.

"Will you be showing off as well, professor?" she asks.

He puts a stumpy hand to his green mustache. "Me? No. No use in me doing magic anymore."

"Plants mages are rare in cities," she remarks.

Although Garriver beats New York by a mile in terms of green space, it's hardly plant friendly. Some mages, who live so far from human invention that they've never breathed in a whiff of coal in the air, can't even visit without getting sick from the air pollution. Poison mages have the most polarized opinions about it of any affinity group. Those that are drawn to natural toxins hate the city. Others find immense pleasure and power in using landfills and improperly disposed polluters to create deadly sludge that kills both humans and non-humans alike. They call it People Poison.

He chortles as though she's told a particularly hilarious joke. "Plant mage? No, I'm not a plant mage. My magic is, well..." He pauses, brow furrowing. His eyes glaze over for a moment before returning to Elaine. "Great news, Elaine! You'll be putting away theory today. It's time for the school's showcase."

Definitely tenure, she thinks.

She glances at the clock, despite lecture having at least another hour left. Ivan would meet her after class, he said. She couldn't wait to try magic again.

NEIL WAKES Elaine up early next Saturday morning and drags her to a grassy field far from the city center. It's windy, and far warmer than it was the day before.

"It's the weekend," she groans.

"You're just being lazy. Get up, I have something to show you."

Elaine pulls the duvet cover from her eyes, squinting at the lantern Neil's shoved on her bedside table. "It's barely daybreak."

"And that means we won't be late." He pats her knee. "Come on, you wanted an adventure, I'll give you an adventure."

She shoos him out of her room to change, head still full of her dreams. She'd been a pirate atop a giant whale. She trudges downstairs, snagging a basket and pulling her cloak from the entryway cloak rack, and follows her uncle outside, her blue hood pulled tight around her head, ignoring the rodent sleeping beneath a nearby tree.

They travel by foot for well over an hour, the skyline glowing in the light of the sunrise and casting a blue hue over the city as the cement under their feet turns into grass, and they find themselves standing on the precipice of a marsh. The marsh is alive with the chirping of birds, crickets, and all sorts of creatures that thrive in the humid, wet marshlands. Around them are other mages, who she's sure are here for the same reason Neil is keeping a surprise. They congregate in small circles, talking quietly in the morning light. She notices they're all wearing the same plum-colored cloaks and are looking upwards expectantly in between chatter. Everything goes silent when a muted thumping sound fills the air. The steady *thum thum* continues, and as it does, the sky is covered in a clementine orange hue. All over the field, monarch butterflies' wings spread, leaving sparse gaps between their bodies where true sunshine can seep through. The world is blanketed in an orange hue, making the glass skyscrapers surrounding the field light up like bottles of amber, and the river's reflection of light flickers like fire.

"Why doesn't the city slay them?" she asks her uncle.

"Because of what their wings and the fog bring." His eyes stay trained on the sky.

There's a flash and the roll of thunder. All around them,

mages dressed in purple redirect the lightning—some with their hands, some with their feet, some with their voice—into the wet ground. Up from the strikes sprout tiny caps.

"Mushrooms," she gasps.

"Electric mushrooms," Neil confirms.

They come in all sorts of colors, all zinging with leftover electricity. Uncle Neil works quickly, pulling them from the ground rapidly, looking at the next shroom before he even finishes plucking the first.

"What are they for?" she asks.

"They're good for potions that need a zap, and keeping you awake when coffee isn't doing it anymore. Some mind mages are using them in clinical trials to see if they can adjust mental states."

She eyes them distrustfully, "what, like a shock?"

"Collect as many as you can. Maybe if they zap you a bit, you'll finally perk up."

She eyes her scarred uncle with trepidation. He motions purposefully at the ground. She bends to grasp at an electric mushroom, wincing when she feels the static. She waits for more pain. But the shock is tiny, just like her uncle said, and so she continues to pluck them straight from the ground. They pick silently, and as she works up a rhythm, her mind clear, like she can finally sort through her thoughts.

Ivan jumbles her usually organized mind. He wants to teach her, yet he pushes her away. She's embarrassed that he doesn't want to be intimate again. Was it something she did?

She eyes her hands, remembering the way he'd trembled against her touch. She's sure she performed adequately. So, it must be her personality. She admits she's...headstrong. And that she'd been useless and sweaty through most of the sewer system. But they'd reconciled during his lessons, hadn't they?

And despite his words, he still reaches for her touch,

wanting to be close, demanding she keep her eyes on him, always on him. He is arrogant, an insecure child that strides around like he has nothing to fear, who speaks like a friend, then pulls away when she shows him affection. She's glad she told the truth, that she didn't want to date a man like him. They're always more trouble than they're worth.

Uncle Neil interrupts her thoughts. "Once a migration, a great lightning mushroom forms. It's rare, once a year."

She hums, her attention drawn back to her mud-covered uncle. He'd waded into a murky pond that the mages were redirecting most of the lightning into, something about it being "less of a fire hazard." Where the mud comes up to her knees, he wades through what comes up only to his ankles, collecting as quickly as possible and covering his legs and arms entirely in mud in the process. He curses every once in a while, when his beard catches on a mushroom, and a jolt travels up into his face.

"What's the lightning mushroom used for?"

Uncle's hands dig a bright, yellow fungi from tree bark. "All kinds of things. Most people who find it sell it to the highest bidder. It's less about what it can do, but rather how few there are. A rare thing is a valuable thing."

"But there's more value in practical use," she argues. "Is it really that weak?"

"It can't do much that a wizard-rank potioneer can't do with a few replacement ingredients," he concedes. "If I ever found one, I'd put it in a jar, on display above the kitchen window." His eyes are far off, a rare grin on his face. He turns it on her. "Of course, I'd invite people over just to tell them 'no' when they ask to buy it. Then kick them out for the trouble."

She laughs a real, bright one. This is why she's here, she decides. If she'd never left the Allapan Mountains, she wouldn't be watching a giant monarch migration or seeing mushrooms sprout from lightning. She concentrates on what she's learned from her magic lessons with Ivan, trying to feel the luck in her gut.

The blue sky turns into a yellow ocher as the sick feeling she associates with using her magic grows stronger. Her head starts to throb, and she closes her eyes, thinking of the mushroom, brain focused on the lightning fungi her imagination comes up with.

"What's it look like?" she asks Uncle Neil, without opening her eyes.

"It's made entirely of lightning. All the kinetic energy zaps a mushroom, toasting it to a crisp, and knocks it out of the ground. The lightning holds an echo of the mushroom's form, the constant electrical circuit keeping it in that cap head shape. You just can't touch it with your hands. It would be like a real lightning strike."

She pictures it, zapped and rooted in the ground, lightning scars forming a circumference around it in the soil. She's about to pass out from the nausea when she reaches out and feels something in her hands. Her eyes flit open in triumph.

Uncle Neil pokes her in the stomach with the walking stick she's grasping, and she throws up all over it.

The great gust of the butterflies' wings grow faint, as does her magic, her world turning from yellow to orange to blue. Cicadas begin to sing again, the skies turn a clear blue, and the mushrooms begin to dissipate, a lightning mushroom nowhere to be found.

LATER, she rides home on the above-ground subway with an "I <3 Garriver" t-shirt over her now ruined dress. Neil hums a happy tune, bag stuffed to the brim with electric mushrooms, and a few photos of the monarchs eclipsing Garriver with the breadth of their wings.

When they arrive home, the rat waits on the border, never approaching, but keeping a weathered eye on them.

"Uncle Neil, can't you do something to make it leave?"

Neil turns and scrutinizes the rat. It glances at him briefly, before returning its attention to Elaine.

"I could." He turns and makes his way past the wards, and into the house.

"Don't you get tired?" she scolds. "Shoo, shoo."

He yawns before curling up in front of their home.

Her steps are heavy on the creaky spiral steps, and she heads straight to the shower to rid herself of her vomit-covered dress. She returns to her room in a large, fluffy towel and her hair hanging loose, ready to dive into bed until Uncle calls her down for dinner. Lunch is for the conscious.

That's ruined by the mass of brown sitting in her corner chair.

"Ivan!" she yelps, drawing the towel closer. "How did you get past the wards?"

Obediently, he smacks a large hand over his eyes. He does turn a bit pink, though he never stops smiling. Today, he's wearing red, heart-shaped sunglasses that scrunch up above his now covered eyes. He moves his fingers apart to make eye contact with her again. "Lucky, remember?"

She glares at him until he closes his fingers over his eyes again.

"Want to practice snake eyes?"

She moves to her dresser and grabs a nightgown before disappearing behind a changing screen. "I definitely need to practice. My professor signed me up for the school showcase this year."

"A showcase!" The legs of the chair squeak against the floorboard. "We'll come up with something much more exciting than boring dice."

She hears his feet stop just on the other side of the divider.

"How comfortable are you with flaming swords?"

She comes out once she's dressed and walks past him to her vanity. She sits down and pulls out her brush, dragging it through the still-wet waves of her hair. "Be serious: other than it being well above my skills, I don't want to do anything flashy. I want to stick to something practical. They're expecting me to fail, I'm sure. So, succeeding at this, no matter how small, is going above and beyond."

He whistles, wagging his eyebrows. "Look at you, taking risks."

She smiles at him in the mirror. "Will you come?"

"To Locke? I had to sneak past security to see you on campus the other day."

She averts her eyes to the floor. "It's open to the public for the presentations. But you don't have to."

He looks deep in thought, then nods. "I'll be there. I have to support my worst student."

"I'm your only student."

"Tomatoes, potatoes. Now, finish braiding your pretty hair so we can get started on your practice."

THE FUNNY THING about academics is that they often think others are too dumb to outsmart them, despite history showing otherwise. If they have the best security systems, the tightest protocols, all brought together by the world's most applauded minds, then surely nothing could go wrong.

Luckily for Ivan, the Bullitzer Prize is not awarded to the brightest. And the security measures here were not created by the legendary Ko-Akal Banti, but by Nelson Meeks, the third-generation spawn of Meeks Security, whose grandmother had a longstanding relationship with Locke University's financial aid department.

All of that to say, the wards were intricate, yet incredibly shallow, like spider webs. Meeks set them up during his first and only visit to the campus, and the spells clearly lacked the familiarity that a local master could've produced. The holes in the entrance are many, as the spellcaster had not accounted for the humidity and the deep variations between seasonal temperatures. They had also not accounted for the number of mosquitos that hatched this season, drawn to and sucking away at the magic on the window, until they exploded prematurely from their own greed.

Ivan wipes away their husks from the side window, easily unlocking the brass bolts, and slipping past the torn web of incantation. Meeks's work is sticky and delicate, whereas his grandmother had created tapestries so complex, it often took years to dissolve them. Ivan plays with the web, disappointed with the shoddy craftsmanship. All it had in common with Arcana Meeks's work was the feel of sticky, lightweight silk disappearing underneath practiced hands.

"No respect for the craft," he says.

It does make this job easier. "Find one of the entryways to the core of Locke" the mission statement said. "You'll feel it when you find it." Which might not make sense to an amateur, but to a professional like Ivan, he knows it means he's after something old, that rattles the bones upon discovery. It's his favorite form of danger to test his luck against.

There's a distant sound of feet coming down the hall, but he'll be in before they round the corner. He has his technique timed to the second.

A burst of pain from his curse hits him, and it feels as though all the neurons in his brain are being burned alive.

Silent swears fall from his lips as he tumbles headfirst through the window, closing it a little too loudly behind him.

He draws the hood of his cloak over his head, clenching the bear's ears in a vain attempt to redirect the pain somewhere—*anywhere*—else. He hears someone walk by: their footfalls intermixed with a hard cane hitting the ground.

"I don't know if this will be enough, sir." It's a low, gravelly voice.

"I'm not paying you to fix it. I'm paying you to break it."

Ivan bites down on his cloak to muffle the pain, but a deep groan comes out of him, unbidden. The feet pause. There's shuffling as the passersby grow suspicious.

"It's nothing. We should go. We can't be caught here this late."

The footsteps get farther and farther away, and Ivan's tremors become sparser as well. His skin feels hot, even though it is cold and clammy. This mission has gone too wrong, too fast, and he's not one to take risks when his magic is on the fritz. Time to head back and try another day. His fingers, now shaky where they were once steadfast, open the window latch again. He pulls himself out back onto the grass, laying his overheated cheek against it before climbing to his feet.

The punch to his left side catches him off guard, knocking him back to the ground.

"This is no place for you, halfling."

Ivan rises, trying not to hold his injured side. He keeps his face tucked so far beneath his hood that no one can see his features. He whirls around the next hit.

He recognizes the voice from inside the building. A squat man, with black hair and a nose ring, holding a walking staff like a weapon. Ivan makes for a tactical escape. The little bull can't keep up with him, and Ivan's symptoms recede the further away he runs.

As his blood pumps with adrenaline, his gut is full of dread.

Years of running, and the family curse has finally caught up to him. As he escapes through the loud night, sirens wail and lights flash as he cuts back and forth between familiar alleys until he's sure he's safe. Only then does he stop to take a breath.

"I'm not a fan of bad luck," he says to the open air. He'll return to Delius as soon as he can and let him know he's quitting. There's not enough money in the world to make him take a job that might worsen his curse.

12

NEW FRIENDS

The school fair is filled with mages of all ages and creatures of varying species. The crowd is still, however, predominantly human. So human that it feels off. It makes her feel strange about the way her eyes are set, and the color of her hair. Behind her, an imp father of twelve struggles to wrangle all his kids, despite the fact that they're all tethered to him via child backpack leashes.

"Might as well come see it all," he grumbles, "if half my paycheck is going to 'public school.'"

Elaine thinks that's odd. Surely, a man with so many children would look forward to free education and lunches. Today, she's wearing a purple dress with brown leather flowers woven in. She opted to leave her blue cloak at home and wore her school-issued one. School spirit, and all. But as the year's worn on, she's noticed the city's peculiarities when it comes to its social structure. Unlike Alappan, the city's not a mix of species. It's humans that most often occupy the downtown residences. Those same neighborhoods also cater to human biology. Hospitals are 93% human doctors, and coffee shops have no gravel for claymen, or nectar for pixies. Flies are drowned instead of fed to frogs, and while frogs are not outright banned, there's not a shop within five miles that serves insects.

When she'd gone to the general hospital for a migraine, the nurse had been unable to fix it. After a while, she asked Elaine "are you sure this is the right hospital for you?"

She'd replied, "I didn't know there was a wrong one."

The nurse wrote down the address of a place on the other side of Garriver, so Elaine just walked to Neil and asked for his help instead. His potions left her nauseous for a few minutes, which is why she preferred the doctor's office. But the doctors here clearly didn't know how to do anything other than the human way, all stethoscopes and magic that only works on human cores. The doctors in Alappan worked on all sorts of people.

A group of students pass by, laughing and holding a Venus fly trap above their heads while singing the school anthem. She feels a pang of...something. She's not lonely. She has her uncle, and Ivan, too, if one were to squint their eyes, cross their fingers, and be incredibly generous. She wishes her uncle wasn't away on a work trip; it would be nice to have one familiar face here to support her. She doesn't have any faith that Ivan will really show up, though he said he would.

She makes her way into the auditorium, which has been expanded and converted into a gladiator-style stadium. It's as though she's stepped into a colosseum, if said colosseum had blue felt chairs with neon retro shapes drawn on them.

"Mind if I sit here?" someone asks.

She turns and sees a fairy with short purple hair and iridescent eyes, reminiscent of a dragonfly. When she sits, Elaine admires her strong profile.

"Are you presenting today?" she asks before losing courage.

The fairy shakes her head. "My affinity is for comet magic, but it's more mental than physical. I can feel when they grow closer, but I can't draw them in or push them away. My professor thought making me present a thesis in between elementals shooting fireballs out of their eyes would bore the audience."

Comet mages often hold honored and spiritual positions in society. Their magic is used in a wide range of ceremonies, festivals, political trips, and predictions for the coming year. One specific family, Calamity, is in charge of predicting the future of the entire city. When working with the general public, they predict minor events that won't send them into hysteria, like if it would be a hot or cool year. One region has opted out of the predictions and, instead, trusts a groundhog with their meteorological future.

Elaine curses. "I wish my professor thought that. I'm an accountant following someone's presentation on controlling an entire ant colony."

The fairy laughs.

"Elaine Aquae," she introduces herself.

"Haley Kuiper. What's your affinity, Elaine?"

Before Elaine can respond, the show starts.

"Excuse me, is this thing on? Welcome, all, to day two of the Locke University Symposium—Metaphysical Computations, Expulsions, and Other Hybrid Applications of the Magical Affinity. Today, we'll be showcasing a wide breadth of academic talent. First, our keynote presenter, Alec Cardoc, who has studied the link between fire affinities and the neuromuscular system."

Elaine is saved from answering the question, but now her looming presentation weighs heavy on her mind. What if she can't do it? She looks frantically through the crowd for any possible sign of Ivan, but she can't spot him in the dim lighting. She ends up listening to Alec drone on about what could have been a fascinating study of the brain and body's relationship with a user's affinity, but instead, was forty-five minutes of him sharing pictures and statistics of his progress at the gym, with no significant change in his heat output.

"Maybe if he used his brain," Haley muttered. "This is why so many taxpayers want to cut back on free federal education. Twenty more seconds of that, and I'd be right with them."

Elaine hadn't known people were upset about that. But she *had* noticed the increasing gas prices and grocery bags costing extra gold coins if you didn't bring your own from home.

"It's a bit ridiculous that humans get so much help," she admits. Her hands shake. "All other intelligent species understand magic implicitly. Humans? They need at least thirty years to grasp what others do in ten."

Haley looks Elaine up and down. "I'm here to see if I can spot one of the Calamitys too. There's been rumors they're desperate for new talent. The family's been spending their way through the city faster than they can make it. I know if I can just get an audience, they'll hire me."

She nods. It's all about connections. Secretly, she worries that the family would overlook someone like Haley—no ties, not human. But she supposes that's what Locke is supposed to be about: meeting someone who can give you a chance at something better.

Elaine claps with everyone else when Alec gets off the stage. A few more presenters go before her name is finally called. She's the last presenter of the day, and she feels the energy of the crowd dwindling. It's accentuated by the increase in murmurs and whispered conversation from the audience.

"Elaine Aquae, showing us some of the theory behind probability magic."

There are a few groans around her as she makes her way to the podium. The audiences' faces are all hidden in the darkness, as the fluorescent blue of the will-o'-the-wisps lighting the stage blinds her. She waits for the crowd to quiet but settles for a quiet murmur.

"Hello, thank you for having me." Her throat is dry. She reaches for a water bottle, but instead, knocks it off the stage and into the first row.

Someone smothers a laugh with a hard cough, and she speaks over their whispers and the pounding in her ears.

"While I love theory as much as the next student, I believe some practical showcasing would be better." She pulls a pair of dice from her pocket. "Now, do I have a volunteer?"

A hand from the front row raises politely. The murmurs hush when a lilac-haired man comes forward. He's wearing white robes with golden, minute details along the edge. Elaine thinks that color is highly impractical for a mage, and his entire demeanor comes off as stuffy.

"Alright, sir, I'll have you roll the dice."

He does so, a three and a four.

"Again."

He raises a brow but does so. Two threes.

"Now that the volunteer has shown that the dice aren't trick dice, I will throw snake eyes, every time."

Silence. She focuses on the feeling in her gut and wills it to spread to her fingers. She rolls snake eyes, and the volunteer's eyes flash with interest.

Emboldened, she does it again and again and again. While bile still rises in her throat, she now knows that's her magical core activating and not a symptom of stage fright. So many years of it living dormant made her magic feel like a separate entity from the rest of her. Much like a sedentary creature who starts running, her muscles have remembered the feeling, and recognize it not as a foreign body, but as an old friend.

"This might not look like much," she says to the crowd, "but think beyond something as simple as dice. What if I entered the lotto, over and over? Or decided to rob a bank?"

A few laughs from the crowd.

"I'm not quite that good. But when there's barely any documentation on your magic, even something small, like dice, feels like a miracle."

The audience claps politely, as does her volunteer. She smiles and motions for him to retake his seat.

There are a few questions on the classification of probability magic, and a few on how it might be used practically.

"And *legally*," they add in response to the laughter of the audience.

She answers them, before moving to a final raised hand.

"You call it probability, but is that really what it is?"

She squints against the stage light and is only able to locate her questioner by the bright pink heart glasses perched on his nose.

"Seems more like luck, even enhanced intuition," Ivan remarks.

She pauses, heart beating fast. How long had he been there? Did he sit through all those other presentations just to see her? "One of the few strengths of having an understudied affinity is that my mind isn't influenced by what's worked historically. Another mage with my affinity might call it luck. They also might move more impulsively, more instinctively. I am in the habit of crunching numbers, of needing to see the odds before I can even visualize overcoming them. For me, my magic is probability."

The moderator politely interrupts, saying that's all the time they have. Elaine thanks the audience before walking back down the steps and to her seat. She's still buzzing with excitement, and this isn't even the biggest project of the year. Her first-year practical exam, a tradition at Locke, is upcoming, and she's planned a research-based project that she's sure to pass with flying colors, if the expectations at this showcase were similar.

When the lights raise and the crowds leave the auditorium, she follows Ivan's cloak through the crowd, closing the door behind her. They've ended up in a lab with all sorts of beakers and tubes organized on the outer tables, waiting for the next class.

"Did you see me?" She smiles, bouncing on her toes.

Ivan picks her up with a laugh and spins her around. His hands are warm and firm against her waist. "Wonderful! You were wonderful. Dice trick and all."

"I don't think they really understand what they were seeing," she rambles. "But *some* will. And if I keep working, studying the relationship between magic and physical manipulation born from *desire*, not just affinity—" She breathes deeply. "Well. Let's just say it would make a mark."

"That's important to you, making a mark? Getting the accolades?" There's no judgment in his tone.

"The accolades are nice, but what matters more is knowing it could get me invited to all sorts of things. Trips to new places, exchanging stories with people at the forefront of their fields. It opens doors to once-in-a-lifetime experiences."

His hands move to hold hers up to his eye level for inspection. "You could get that by helping me with my missions."

"*Legal* experiences," she emphasizes. "So, I can make *money*. And money means doing things independent from other people's demands."

He picks her up, setting her on the end of a desk and making her heart pick up speed. She barely stops herself from pointing out the intimacy of it, not wanting to scare him off.

His hands move from her waist to her knees. "Everyone's beholden to something. You just have to make sure it's the right thing."

"I can't imagine you being beholden to anything but yourself."

Even now, as he rubs his thumb absentmindedly across her thigh, she expects him to disappear beyond her reach. The independence of his lifestyle is what she envies most. But she's missed something, clearly, if even he doesn't think he's free.

"And what are you beholden to?"

She doesn't mean to upset him, but his face washes clean of emotion. He pulls away from her, and there's a cold space at the front of her body where he once stood.

He gives her a strained smile. "A secret, Elaine." He looks at his bare wrist. "I've got to go. Running late." He moves towards the door but pauses just under the archway, still facing the exit. "Great job."

Then she's alone.

~

"How did your showcase go?"

Despite his uselessness, Elaine is still disappointed Professor Sap decided not to go to her presentation. This morning's lesson is a free period to work on her writing assignment, and they do so in relative silence.

"Without a hitch," she replies.

He nods. "You'll need to start prepping for your practical exam. Have you decided on if you'll work with anyone else?"

She shakes her head. "I'll be doing a paper-driven exam, alone."

The exam is oftentimes a display of a magical feat linked to an academic theory. For example, an animal mage would show the practical applications of a sheep-led grass clipping service. Her favorite practical exam she read about was one of a mage with an affinity for weaving. The student collaborated with an asteroid mage to weave a cloak made of meteorite. Scouters had attended that exam, and the student duo both sold the patent to interested parties, setting themselves up for a very cushy life.

Elaine doesn't have any groundbreaking ideas for her exam,

but already her mind tinkers around with the idea of a mock business to show off her financial savvy.

She stops working on her familial rune essay when there's a knock and the door opens. Elaine recognizes Haley from the showcase and waves to her in greeting.

Haley smiles before turning to the professor. "Excuse me, Professor. I wanted to come in to congratulate you and Ms. Aquae. You've been invited to the Constellation Ball." Haley turns to Elaine. "Due to the impressive nature of your presentation.

"Yes!" the professor shouts, making them both jump. "About time!" He turns to Elaine, smiling more genuinely than before. "Great work as always, Elaine. Perhaps you're ready for some of our more rigorous extracurriculars at the university."

A smile flashes across her face, and she nods firmly.

When the last bell rings and she's nearly out the door, Professor Sap hops out of his chair and stops her. "Due to your impressive showcase, Elaine, you're eligible to join the school's familiar ritual during the new moon."

A familiar ritual is an opportunity for a mage to become attuned to an animal that most aligns with the core of their magic. Made legal again in only the last twenty years, it allows for mages to connect with a creature that is willing to be attuned to their magic. The familiar chooses to come forward to the mage when they sit within a circle made up of wards and spells. While difficult to do on one's own, schools like Locke have a room dedicated to this giant step in one's journey as a magic user, with a permanent and powerful ward.

Elaine winces. "Thank you, sir, but animals and I don't really get along." She loves them, yes. But something about her sets off anything warm-blooded. Most people are too worried about themselves to notice anything off-putting, but babies and animals tend to have a great distrust of her.

"Oh, nonsense! Why, I once had a Mediterranean Olive

Dragon, till—" His eyes glaze over, but they clear up again when he shakes his head. "Familiars are very useful companions for those who earn their loyalty! An anonymous report, in fact, showed over eighty-two percent of mages prefer them over their marriage partners."

It would be nice to see Ivan jealous, at the very least. He's been regrettably good with boundaries since she poked him too hard.

"I'll think about it," she concedes.

He nods. "I want an essay on it, due before the waxing gibbous."

She nods, noting the moon rising in the afternoon sky. She had twelve days.

"Again."

Elaine flops back down on the patch of grass in front of her house. The magic doesn't come easy, no matter how hard she tries.

Ivan moves towards the haystack in front of them. He sticks his arm into it, immediately pulling a needle from it. "Listen to your intuition."

She scrunches her nose. Intuition has nothing to do with reality. Numbers, solutions, all backed by peer reviews. *That* was real. Not this "feel it in your heart and know it to be true" bullshit.

"Lainey."

She stays silent.

"Lainey," a bit more sternly.

She stays happily splayed along the grass.

"Elaine?"

"I can't do it."

"No, no. Not that. Why is there a rat staring at us?"

Her head whips up. Sure enough, the rat is back. This time, he's sitting atop a piece of scrap paper.

"He's been loitering for days now," she moans. "And I can't seem to get him to *leave me alone*." She aims her last words at the vermin sniffing a blade of grass with interest.

Ivan crosses the boundary and approaches the rat, who shifts to the left, allowing Ivan to retrieve the paper. "Well, maybe Roger can help us with our little crown problem."

"Roger?"

"Yeah. That's what the paper here says."

It's a torn-off piece of advertisement, the surrounding information all chewed away with only the name "Roger" left on it.

"Aw, he named himself!" Ivan bends down to pet Roger.

The rat snaps at Ivan's hand, and Ivan pulls back just before he can make contact.

He scowls at the rodent whose eyes have once again returned to Elaine. "So, you're just going to let him sit here? Menacingly?" It seems he's changed his opinion on how cute the rat is.

"What am I supposed to do?" She waves a dismissive hand before returning to the haystack. "He can't get past the wards, anyways. My uncle resets them every week."

"Hm." Ivan doesn't look away from Roger. "Are you sure his runes will be enough to hold him?"

She nods. "He used to be a warden."

Wardens are rune and spell experts for hire. To become a warden, a mage has to pass a series of security tests that only five percent of the population achieve. A small percentage of wardens each year are lost in fatal accidents.

Ivan only returns his attention to her once he's sure Roger won't be coming closer. "Try again. And remember—"

"Listen to my intuition. I know, I know."

She looks at the yellow haystack in front of her and wills it to reveal its secrets. Her head starts to hurt as she stares at the stack, thinking about how many straws there are. If she could count them, she could figure out the straw-to-needle ratio. One in two hundred thousand is a nice, round number. 0.000005%. Easier than winning the lottery, harder than getting struck by lightning.

The yard looks just as yellow as the hay to her as her vision changes, almost as if someone stuck a yellow film over her eyes, that familiar nausea in her gut, and a new foreign pang of pain, humming against her frontal lobe. The hum feels like it presses against her skull like a cat squeezing into a tiny box it has no business resting in.

The world's colors seep back into her sight, all the yellow shrinking into the bold "0.000005%" in front of her. She raises a hand to the number, and it changes to "0.00013%." Her hand slips past the ghost digits and touches the hay instead.

Testing it, she moves her hand to the left, the number getting smaller. She walks around the haystack, eyes narrowed and assessing. It could not be a perfectly round 1 in 200,000. Was she seeing the true odds, or just her subjective perception of it?

She looks over the stack again. It is approximately five feet tall, and the straws are about 3 mm in diameter. She calculates it, and her approximation comes out to 1 in 329,115. She's sure of it. Still, when she reaches out a hand to the same spot, the percentage stays the same. She moves it down, and the number gets larger.

She ignores the roar in her head as she circles the stack, testing and prodding at this visual magic. It looks as though no matter what her brain calculates, her magic shows the chances of getting what she wants based on her actions.

She blinks her eyes as the woozy feeling becomes too strong to ignore. She drops to the ground, her ears ringing. She places her head between her knees. Ivan touches her back, but she pushes him away. The contact is too much. She opens her eyes for a second but closes them when she sees the whole world is yellow again.

She hears what sounds like a voice, but it's muffled, like she's underwater. Her vision goes black before she can make sense of it.

WHEN SHE WAKES UP, she's in her bedroom, her vision is normal again, and Ivan sits by the window. By the time her bleary eyes focus on him he's already looking at her. His relief is palpable, and he moves to stand at the edge of the bed.

"What happened out there?" is what he settles on.

"It was my magic. I was thinking about what you said about instinct. And then I was thinking about how stupid that was."

He scoffs, indignant.

"And I estimated how many straws of hay there were in the haystack. These percentages started appearing, and wherever I moved, the numbers would go up or down. I think it was showing my odds."

"Odds of what?"

"Odds of finding the needle in the haystack."

She can see when he turns to inward contemplation. He paces the room, face blank, even as his eyes flit around the room, racing as fast as his thoughts probably are.

"It's believed that an affinity's skills manifest according to the user in some cultures."

"No, it's been proven and reviewed in several academic studies that your affinity is predetermined by genetics," she says.

"Well, yes. But what if a person's magic is unlike other people in their family? What if you aren't given textbooks and secrets passed down generation to generation about your technique?"

She stares, unable to see where his point is headed.

"I am the only luck mage in my family. For me, my magic is based on a gut feeling. I'm impulsive and rely on feeling more than planning. You love logic. Having problems written out with clear solutions."

She nods. "So, you're saying my magic is manifesting according to my personality? That's unheard of."

His eyes alight with excitement. "I know. But it's not impossible, is it? We have no teachers, no preconceived notions. I was taught growing up that I was special, and so I believed my magic would be too. You believed that you were useless, and it didn't manifest until you met me."

"You're claiming that magic's strength is reliant on the conscious self's belief in its own potential," she says.

He claps. "I'm saying that your magic is what you make of it. Your core is unchangeable, but your affinity is shaped around who we are, who we've learned to be."

Once again, he's stating an opinion as fact. Her disbelief must be clear in her eyes because he shakes his head. "Lainey. Whether or not I'm right, your magic is getting stronger. It's a good thing."

"It hurts," she mutters under her breath, though her head is hurting instead of her stomach this time.

"Who cares about hurting? There's practice to do."

"I'm done for now, Ivan." She shakes her head. She still doesn't feel right.

He snorts. "You just made a breakthrough, and now you want to stop?"

"I said I'm done," she snaps, pushing away from him.

Even as she pushes him toward the window, he says, "We'll stop here for today. We can practice another time."

"Great idea."

With a final push, he falls out the window, and she closes it behind him.

Uncle Neil is still away on his work trip, which means the entire house is available for her to have a good cry in. After Ivan leaves, Elaine fiddles with her shaking hands, thinking over and over about her fight with him. It wasn't a bad fight. It never is. But every time they disagree, it rattles her into remembering they are too different. He is a comet, shooting across the sky at an impossible pace. He makes her feel human: with steps too small and eyes so glued to the earth that even if she tries to see the forest for the trees, it will never compare to his view from the sky. She scowls, angry even, as she cries into her hands. She didn't think about it at all during the day, but as soon as the sun sets, their irreconcilable differences are all she can think about.

Why did she keep letting him in? He disappoints her, pushing her for his benefit without thinking about her own. This time, she promises herself, it will be the last. Every time he grows closer, he snaps away, angry and confused and taking it all out on her.

Scratches start scratching, scratching at her kitchen window, and her fury is projected onto the incessant rat at her doorstep. He must have gnawed and wormed through a weak ward somewhere. Neil is getting sloppy with all his sudden work trips and late-night office calls.

She flips open the window, "Not tonight, Roger. Nor the next night, or the one after that. It's never going to happen."

Her long speech about boundaries peters off when she sees the morose and faraway look in his beady, wet eyes.

Does he feel lonely? She wonders.

He's a creature of circumstance, completely reliant on those with opposable thumbs. Her heart clenches. He waits here every night, hoping that she'll change her mind, and her occasional crumbs of bread or shelter from the rain probably made him think he could wear her down with his loyalty. His consistency. It wasn't his fault he was born into serving an ill-tempered master.

Still trembling, Elaine stands from her window's ledge. She walks down the watchtower stairs, opens the front door, and stands at the stoop. Roger stares back, ears perked. Her stomach roils in fear, and her brain warns her that she's being a fool.

"Don't make me regret this," she calls out.

He stares back, patient.

Her fist unclenches. "Come in," she says the magic words.

He places a hesitant paw against the invisible barrier and easily passes through. He trots through the barrier and right up to Elaine. Her hands tremble.

Scurrying bodies, tiny paws, tiny maws.

Scratchscratchscratchscratch.

She tenses her hands to stop shaking, her nails leaving imprints in her palms. The rat stills once inside, hunching over, looking smaller. She takes a deep breath and exhales while he waits for her to calm down. She shakes out her hands in front of her. She shudders when he puts a tiny paw on her finger, and they're both frozen in place. A whole minute passes without them hurting each other.

"Would you like...?" She clears her throat. "Would you like to come inside? I'm sure it can't be comfortable waiting in the cold."

When she turns, she hears the pitter patter of feet following. They follow her through the living room, bound up the stairs, and all the way into her room. Her skin is crawling, but she's more lonely than afraid. It's not enough, having Neil. And with all her studying, she hasn't had the chance to make friends.

This is crazy, she thinks as she grabs a pillow from her bed for Roger.

"Here." She places her least favorite throw pillow on the floor. "This can be yours."

He sniffs the pillow and, sensing nothing wrong, settles into a little ball on top of it. Elaine gets into her own bed and lays back, arms straight next to her.

"This will be fine," she says to her ceiling. "I am going to be fine."

There's a rat lying in her room, and she'd let him in. A rat who serves a master that wants her dead. A rat that, under regular circumstances, would send her running and screaming and asking her uncle to get it out of her room. But animosity offers its own intimate form of connection, and it's the safest one she has. Roger can't break her trust because he's never had it. And if he bites her, he'll prove her right. If he betrays her, she can say she saw it coming.

This will be fine, she thinks once more, before slipping into an uneasy slumber.

13

FAMILIARITY

Four mornings later she pets Roger, the rat, cautiously, tapping at the top of his head, him blinking with each touch. In the first morning after letting him past the wards, she'd screamed when she saw him before remembering she let him in. Roger was a familiar, simple enemy, and if he wanted to be a part of her life, she was willing to give him the chance. She wants to be someone who believes people (and rodents) can change for the better. Her mind becomes occupied by thoughts of her upcoming familiar ritual.

"You're not the jealous type, are you?"

The rat sniffs the air. Her uncle being away on work left her with only the rat to talk to, and she's relieved she heard him return early this morning. She needs to talk to someone about Roger, but Uncle Neil would reprimand her for hours about safety and stranger danger. Unfortunately, she knows who she really wants to see: Ivan. She pauses, wrinkling the cookie sleeve in her hand. Maybe she could just force a barista to listen to her talk about her rat instead?

"Knock knock," Ivan says, opening and sliding through the watchtower window.

"How do you keep climbing up here? Stop doing that." Her smile betrays her attempt to scold him.

He heaves a great sigh, ignoring her question as he slips off his cloak and places it over her head. He pauses when he sees the rat she'd sworn to be her enemy sitting next to her.

"Is that one of Titon's rats? In your bed?" He backs up a few steps and looks around the room cautiously. He whips around and opens a closet door, but there's no rat king in there, only clothes.

"I decided to let him in," she says. "I think he's been abandoned by his pack."

He looks at the rat, cautiously. "How sure are you?"

She looks at Roger, and Roger stares back. While she's still terrified of him on a primal level, there is now an inexplicable draw to the creature that wasn't there before. Maybe it's because she got used to seeing him sit outside, day in and day out, with no idea if she'd let him in. But his eyes no longer felt piercing and instead, looked like smooth onyx stones. His fur is soft, even softer after the bath she gave him on their third day together. And his tail looks like a trustworthy length of rope meant to secure boats to docks and shoelaces together, no longer a slimy, squiggling worm in her mind. Perhaps most important of all, he smells different. He still smells of rat, but the magic that sticks to him isn't that of the rat king.

"Positive."

She turns her face into the cloak he draped over her and wrinkles her nose in distaste, even as she commits his scent to memory. "Where'd you even get this cloak anyways? The magic smells strange."

"It belonged to my dad. When he died, he gave me his cloak."

Elaine freezes. Ivan spooks as easy as a horse when it comes to intimacy, and so she forces her voice to stay neutral when she asks, "when did your father die?"

"My dad's cloak, not my father's," Ivan corrects. "I was still a kid. Fifteen, I think? It's been so long." He laughs under Elaine's horrified gaze.

"Your dad?'"

He settles down on the bed next to her. He places his hand just so, allowing their pinkies to touch. "I had a biological father, but when I ran away to Garriver, my dad found me. He taught me how to hide, how to steal, how to sneak around. And then, one day, he just didn't open his eyes again." He looks off, brows furrowing in contemplation. "It wasn't even my twentieth year. I was fifteen? Seventeen?"

She sniffles, and her vision becomes blurry.

He turns to her and smiles wanly, "How time flies." He does a double take when he sees the tears in her eyes. "It's not *that* bad. Why are you crying?"

"Oh, Ivan." She pulls him into a hug. Her heart aches at the thought of losing her dad at fifteen, before she was old enough to have her first heartbreak or join him for a drink at the bar. It hurts more when she can't remember the last drink she'd had with her dad. A dragon's breadth? A rose vow? "You must miss him."

His body melts into her touch, even as his arms hover around her back. He takes a deep breath before he puts his arms around her. A warmth blooms in her chest as he leans over further, fingers clutching tight. His head burrows further into her neck, breathing in deeply. She wonders what she smells like and hopes it's magic, glittering pebbles, harsh fires, and a little like him. He shudders, and Elaine holds him tighter. He shifts his arms, threading them under hers, palms clasped at her shoulders. Her back starts to ache as she stands there, slightly bowing back to accommodate his height, but she stays still, too afraid to move. Her breath hitches when she feels his heart beat against her chest now, fast and loud. She places a hesitant hand on his chest and pushes lightly.

"Sorry," he lies. He retracts only to kneel, melting into her lap.

Elaine watches, hands frozen in the air and unsure of where to land.

"Lainey, you must feel this." His tongue darts out to lick his lips, eyes scanning her.

"Your...cloak?" she asks, thumbing a tuft of bear fur.

He looks like he's about to beg her to do that to his ear, when he falls off her lap and onto the floor, stomach twisting and cramping as he curls himself into a ball. Pain seems to envelope his body.

"Nellie, come down here and reset these wards," Uncle Neil calls from downstairs. "You can't let someone new in, then not reset them."

"Coming," she yells back. She whirls towards Ivan, fretting over him. "He has horrible timing. Ivan, we need to get you to a hospital."

"No need."

"No need," she repeats, incredulous. "You look like you've been poked with a hot iron."

"Something to try under happier circumstances," he says. "But it looks as though our time has to be cut short."

"Nellie!" her uncle yells.

"One second! Ivan, please, stay." He was close, nearly begging for attention in one second, then gone the next. It's whiplash—why run from physical pain, when he'd been so ready to be vulnerable with the emotional?

He eyes her staircase. "I'll be safer in my own apartment." He reaches for his pocket, wincing when he unzips it. He uncorks a yellow shot before downing it. He stumbles to his feet and gives Elaine a delirious kiss on the forehead.

"Lainey. Roger." He's gone through the window, a moment later, leaving her flushed and bewildered on the ledge.

THE NEXT MORNING, she makes her way to the familiar ritual at Locke University. She's still not sure she really wants a familiar, and the thought of tying an animal that hates her to herself for the rest of her life leaves her jittery. As she makes her way towards the assigned classroom, she passes by a frustrated looking Haley. It's hard to tell because she doesn't have eyebrows, but frowns are a universal sign of distaste.

"Hailey, what's wrong?"

Her wings are vibrating, agitated. "They won't let me into the familiar class. Said they 'weren't prepared to meet a wide set of needs.'"

"I'm sorry." Elaine says, because there's not much else she can say. She can't help, and she certainly can't advise. She reads between the lines: they weren't prepared to offer the class to a fairy. Or any other non-human, likely.

"It's stupid. I study, I work hard, and they aren't prepared to teach every type of student. And I can't ask my family, who has lived in Garriver before it was even built, because fairies weren't allowed familiars for hundreds of years. No one was. And now there's apologies and regret, and there's money and power in familiars, and 'oh, why didn't we see this before', and they repackage it as new and modern and chic, but it doesn't change the fact that we were forced to forget."

"And it's not written down?"

"It was all burned," she gestures angrily. "Or buried. It was all destroyed to build this place, and they don't even have a record of how the old rituals were done."

The wind picks up around them, and Elaine tugs her cloak closer to herself. Haley screeches, sending a few birds flying out of a nearby tree, and drawing concerned glances from other students.

"I suppose you might have some luck. Tell me if you learn anything about slipping through their rigidly human rituals." Haley storms off, leaving Elaine torn between going after her and joining the class. Her stomach twists, yellow numbers appear, and she decides to make her way towards the ritual with the human mages.

SHE STANDS in a large classroom with a myriad of other undergrads, all the desks and chairs pushed to the walls. But now she's more nervous than before, and nervous about how the state of her blood might affect things. The room itself is an old classroom, with crown molding framing the walls and corners. The floor has a ring of runes engraved onto it, and someone has placed fresh, evenly spaced candles around its circumference.

"We stand above the circle of power of Garriver. The fairy ring enhances our wards, the strength of our architecture, and the strength of all your cores. Usually, you need to have an extraordinary well of magic to call for a familiar. With the ring, anyone can do it. " The irony of the fairy ring powering a ritual without a single fairy in sight, is not lost on Elaine. She shuffles her feet, uncertain. Not about tying an animal to her for the rest of her life, but instead, about her own place here. Righteously, she doesn't believe she deserves to be here more than Haley. She martyrs herself in her imagination, refusing to partake until everyone is allowed in, those in attendance applauding her and asking for forgiveness; but larger and louder, selfishness trumps her virtue with a single thought: *will they notice?*

"We begin with Alakazam, Melos."

Elaine hears the snickers around her. It is, she supposes, a terrible last name.

The man enters the circle and sits cross-legged. A lightning crack fills her ears, and the room goes white. When her eyes clear, Melos is sitting in front of a rabbit. Elaine thinks it's rather mundane, until the rabbit shakes, and a scorpion's tail sprouts from its stubby tail. Like children, the mages in the room gasp in awe, clapping for the ecstatic mage, who leaves the circle with his new familiar.

The ritual has less blood and screaming than she pictured it would. In the mountains, there were always whispers of cruelty when it came to city magic. "They're always shooting spells at each other. It's lucky any of them live beyond thirty," they'd say.

"As you all saw, the speed of the summoning matches the nature of the familiar. Don't worry if it takes a moment for your familiar to appear. A few years ago, we had a tortoise summoned that took three hours to appear."

Puffs of laughter come from the crowd, their shoulders loosening.

"Aquae, Elaine."

She steps forward, excited despite her hesitance to have an animal, and her apprehension of her place in this practice. She didn't even think her magic was usable before getting to Garriver, but since meeting Ivan, she's learned to dream bigger. If she could do magic, then she could certainly find a suitable familiar. And the companionship of someone that willingly attaches itself to her soul is enticing. Not *every* animal can detest her, surely. Maybe her soul would connect with a dragon? A snake? Or, she hopes, an air-breathing fish?

Just like the textbook instructs, she envisions herself alone in the place she feels most herself. It manifests as the mountain cliff she's fondest of in the Allapan. Instead of sitting, she's staring off the edge, excited, and thinking of the unknown of the jump.

Another voice urges her to sit back and do things the way she'd been instructed.

A gust, and the voice is gone. She's left with impulse, and it screams for her to take the leap. She steps one foot out, and instead of falling, she stands.

Her eyes shoot open as her body is forcefully ejected from the circle, wind flying around her. Her last conscious view is the circle, the flames, and solid ground.

SHE WAKES up in the nurse's office. She, perhaps naively, had not considered what effect her biological parenthood could have on her education. And that perhaps her problems with her magic weren't due to her natural weakness, but by learning through only one lens.

Ivan is the first person she's known to operate with magic beyond the "mind". The part of his mind he uses is intuition. He doesn't use his mind the way a telekinetic uses their mind, with thought. He uses it like one would an arm to throw, or their voice to speak—like an extension of both the body and self. He can't even write a full five sentences on how it works and would fail tremendously as an academic. That doesn't change the fact that he has an intimate understanding of how his magic works, in a way others spend years studying to learn. He can't quantify it, can't compare it to luck mages that came before him, though the lack of history isn't his fault. He simply is, and the magic comes from him. It's simple. She's come to admire the instinct, his assumption that a net will always be there to stop the fall. He doesn't need a plan because the plan is to succeed. She's not one to leap without knowing where she'll land.

The doctor, a redwood elf with large, spanning ears, fusses around her. "Oh, you're awake! I was worried we'd have to give your family a call." She checks Elaine's vitals, and after confirming Elaine is indeed all right, purses her lips in disapproval. "You shouldn't be so careless around other mages, dear."

Elaine sits up and winces, a hand to her stomach. "Using magic is just...new to me."

The doctor looks around, double-checking they're alone, and sits in a chair next to Elaine. "You don't have anyone to teach you your own magic?"

"I recently met another probability mage—"

The elf shakes her head. "I don't mean affinity. Do you have anyone available to teach you about your core?" Carefully, she says, "Human cores can handle different magic than that of... others."

Elaine's eyes widen. "I don't know what you're talking about."

The doctor places a hand on top of hers. It glistens almost silver. "People in the city may care less about your background. And you hardly show it. But there are eyes everywhere, especially in academia, so full of human magic. And despite recent steps forward, there are those that would want to make the school segregated again, at any cost."

"They wouldn't expel me," Elaine scoffs.

The doctor's eyes flash in annoyance. "Not for now. But do you really think they wouldn't be eager to get rid of an elf, much less a nymph?"

The word strikes her to the core. *Nymph.* Emotional, unpredictable, moody, manic. She has always been logical and reasonable before anything else, but something like that could change it.

She nods tersely at the nurse, closing the door harshly behind her in her rush to exit. Was it really that big of a deal, to not be fully human? She hadn't known for seventy-two years, and it hadn't affected a single aspect of her life.

When she leaves the infirmary, no one is waiting for her. Tears well in her eyes, even though she shouldn't have expected Uncle Neil to be there. She scrubs them away with frustration. While it's protocol for medical offices to send a message to an emergency contact, Neil was surely too busy to come help a fully grown woman who'd had a fainting spell. She begins the lone march home and pauses when she hears scratches against the cobblestone behind her.

"Roger," she whispers. The tears come back fatter, and she can't stop them when they roll down her face. "How did you know how to find me?"

He doesn't speak, but he does leap into the hand she cautiously holds out, and perches on her shoulder when she lifts him there. Together, they walk home.

14

BOUNTY ON A LUCK MAGE

Ivan strolls through one of the under layers of the city. He takes a deep breath, the underneath a strong but familiar blend of moss and curios and wares. Unlike the food market on the surface, here they sell skills, along with unregulated goods. The place is devoid of the sunlight, relying on bioluminescent crystals and flora for visibility, and a fog hangs permanently overhead, giving the illusion of a low cloudhang instead of a ceiling. The ground is mossy and covered in hard-shelled creatures that are hard to stomp under your boot; roly-polies with steel shells, and ants made of bullets.

He passes by a booth with an array of salves. They don't tend to work on his condition—he hardly ever gets scraped or bruised. When he first moved to Garriver, he tried all sorts of ointments and medications to ward off the lasting side effects of his family curse; but his aches run bone deep, pulsing and expanding, contracting and scratching, against him from the inside. It isn't something medicine can cure. Lainey could use it, though, the thought of drawing his feet back to the stall. She's always stumbling into a scrape, a bruise, an amputation. He picks up a circular dish with an ointment that smells like clementines. He places it down when he thinks better of buying her something scented, as she has a particularly sensitive nose.

"Lotion seller. What would you recommend for someone clumsy?"

The merchant moves him towards a shelf labeled "All-Encompassing Salve."

Ivan's mind drifts back to Elaine. He finds himself thinking of his protégé more and more these days. He supposes that's what happens when a teacher is gifted with a particularly wonderful student, even one so stuck on the idea of academic excellence. University is a bandage she puts over her life's profound lack of personal skill. When he shows her how powerful a tool luck magic is, then she'll see she doesn't need school credentials. Skill makes more money than a degree ever could.

He haggles down the price to something well below its value, following his instinct to compliment the seller's shiny table, before snidely commenting on the dandruff in his hair.

"How lucky," he says, rolling the half-price cream bottle between his palms. People like him and Elaine hardly have use for degrees. The world is a treasure trove, and they alone hold the skeleton keys.

He'd been thinking a lot more about his luck, nowadays. So many things had gone awry since he'd stolen the rat king's crown. He'd omitted that bit of information from everyone else, yes, but he didn't take it just for fun. He needed to study it for the Locke break-in job he'd quit. The crown magic's ability to distinguish between the rat and the human enough to suppress the magic that makes Titon transform goes way over Ivan's head. But he feels things, the way a mother feels her child forgot to take her cloak to school or when a sailor predicts the rain, all from instinctual magic. He knows he needs that crown to break in and take whatever is hidden beneath Locke and get past whatever's protecting it. The crown's familiarity with half-things is somehow the key.

He hadn't meant to drop it, on his way out. He hadn't meant for Ophelia to pick it up and keep it for herself. But that job was bad news, and it was no longer his problem. He'd get around to returning the crown eventually. Nature returns all to its rightful place at its own pace, it's the magic that complicates things.

His eye catches on a gold ring on the ground. It's garish jewels are shoved asymmetrically into a poorly melted hole. Looking at it activates the greedy bird part of his brain that appreciates an object with a bit of sparkle. He has to have it.

He crouches down and feels a slight breeze waft through the market.

Fwip.

He slides the ring onto his thumb, and what do you know, a perfect fit. Maybe he'll drop by Elaine's before his next contract job, and she'll give him a hug for the lotion. He grins as he thinks about how nice hugs are and almost misses that, just up ahead, an arrow has struck an orc, and his friend is trying to pull it out.

"Peculiar," Ivan says.

He looks behind him for an archer, but the crowd is too busy to pick a hunter out of it. The hairs on the back of his neck prickle, and when he has the sudden urge to lean to the left, he listens. Another arrow flies, whizzing past the area his innocent neck was just moments before, arcing through the air and landing a second time into the same orc, who roars in pain.

"Bounty hunter!"

"Grab the coins!"

"This is the third this week!"

The market buzzes as the public realizes there's an arrow-happy archer amongst them, and the crowded room devolves into jabbing elbows and scrabbling feet. Ivan pulls his hood down lower over his face and hunches over, surging into the crowd and changing his gait to be wide and hobbling, moving forward like he doesn't have full use of his hips. He pretends to struggle as he moves through them, allowing himself to be elbowed and stepped on.

Beneath his feet, a frog with a wizard's hat squeezes herself through a sewer pipe, escaping into one of the many exits. The fastest and most conniving, move through the crowd like smoke and are already long gone. Those left are the weak, the clumsy, and in Ivan's case, the hidden.

Behind him, he hears, "We lost him!"

"He might be at the head of the crowd. Move through and push them down if you have to. We bring back the luck mage, and this'll be our last job."

Ivan's heart beats faster when his pursuers move past him. He keeps his head low, continuing his tired, "injured" gait as he winds his way forward. Ahead, the leftovers are shoving themselves into different alleys and pathways. One even squeezes herself through an open window about one hundred feet ahead. The epicenter of this city layer lies past a long pathway leading to a steel room that makes this market perfect for merchants without permits—God's Loophole. Pipes, grates, steam, and darkness all coalesce in this room of infinite escape. To an amateur, it's an experience quite like learning to drive blind. Every pulley, lever, pedal, and switch could start or stop your escape. The holes and ladders go up, down, side to side, then backtrack into dead ends, or exactly the layer you're looking for. It's an architectural nightmare born from a lack of funding and knowledge, and every fifty years or so, the city hires someone new to "fix" it. The room is reclaimed by the swamp a few months after each project ends, twisting and opening pipes and filling them with local flora and fauna.

The city is constantly changing, but the land is just as persistent. The end result is God's Loophole, which frustrates the most talented thieves and determined cops alike. For Ivan, who's gifted with the magic of near-perfect intuition, it's a magical portal to wherever he wants to go.

He's just twenty feet away from the exit when he feels the ointment fall from his pocket. He's not sure why he panics when he drops Elaine's gift, but he whirls with speed to catch it, his hood falling off in the process.

The cloaked assassins turn to him, and he knows he's been spotted. It's a fairy, with large black eyes and gray, shiny skin. They have human-sized palms, too-long fingers wrapped around a wand, a learning aid for less talented mages who never learned to aim.

Abandoning his ruse, he leaps towards God's Loophole, the hunters right behind him. They take four steps for every one of his two, their legs long and spindly like tree branches, the bend of the joints resembling a deer. His body still aches from the recent flare of his curse and makes him run slower. He can see the eerie glow of the escape room and the exits he could lose them in. He will not be bested by a mage using a *training wand.*

A fairy steps out from a hiding spot at the wall in front of him, and another behind him. He scowls, turning his head side to side to keep his eyes on both of them.

"Are you here to kill me?"

They both step forward. He tilts his head, revealing his neck. "Make it quick. I've got tender sensibilities."

"You're lucky today. There's more money if we take you alive."

They walk forward and his hands are cuffed behind him.

"So, the Grays have finally decided to capture me?"

"We don't work for old money."

"No? The selkies, then?" He hopes not. He's not yet ready to part from the cloak around his shoulders.

They lead him towards a pipe with a downward slope, slipping into a shadow so dark he can't see the end.

There's a sweet cooing sound, and one of them holds out an

arm to a landing pigeon. They pull a tiny scroll from the bird's leg.

Elaine must hate pigeons, he thinks. *The rats of the sky.* The whole thing with Roger is an exception in his mind.

"It's your lucky day. Someone's put a time lock on the luck mage bounty for a few months."

A time lock is when someone pays to postpone a bounty's execution. This usually happens when the wanted man is still needed for a job. It's half the original amount, and it's added onto the bounty as incentive to let them live. In Garriver, time is as honored as money.

Something they say catches Ivan's attention: it's a bounty for a luck mage. Not Ivan Gray specifically. As of now, he's the only one the scum of the city know exists, but what if they caught wind of Elaine?

"There's a message for you on it too." the hunter clears its squeaky voice. "'Incentive to keep the mission as promised. We aren't done with you yet.'"

The fairies disperse into one of the exits, leaving Ivan alone in the now-empty market. He pulls his hood back over his head, thinking of home as he heads towards a ladder that splits off in four different directions.

Who would care enough to time lock the bounty? What's the point of keeping him temporarily safe?

"I don't like this at all," he mutters in the solitude of God's Loophole.

A time lock was security, but not a guarantee, and there's more than one luck mage in Garriver now. It's unlikely his mysterious employer is looking to put Elaine in danger just to get Ivan to finish a job, but the thought of someone going after her makes his stomach curl in a new and unpleasant way. He rubs his hand against his chest. All around him, people return to the market through pipes and grates and tunnels. It's a much smaller number than before, but the low mutterings break the complete silence, echoing around him in cautious murmurs. He climbs a ladder and enters a pipe he can feel leads somewhere safe.

He needs access to Locke, and to keep a closer eye on Elaine. As he passes, his eyes catch on a rotting poster of the great university, the words 'PRACTICAL EXAM SHOWCASE THIS THURSDAY' printed boldly, naming a date from twenty years ago. Still, he stops to examine the fine print:

First-year graduate students present their practical exam via scroll or skirmish. NOTE: Beheadings banned since XXX.

The school's so traditional, surely this is something his apprentice is taking part in soon. He grins, moving up the ladder with a new purpose. Two birds, one stone.

ELAINE GOES to class today with a spring in her step. She'd planned her practical exam out for weeks. Finally, she could get graded for her math. Math is her oldest friend—if you were a child with no useful affinity, being good at something no one else liked to do could change your life. Her siblings could transform into animals and save the rainforest, but she'd be the one with the solid nest egg for retirement. She's certain her brother thinks a ROTH is a congenital disease.

He doesn't have to know, she thinks bitterly. A fire mage as strong as him will be able to work until the day he dies.

She'd written up a report on a fake potions business with an apprentice owner and two wizard financial backers. She'd inserted several common issues a new business owner could come across—a wyrm infestation, a minimum wage blood oath broken and challenged by an unsavory employee, and surprise health inspections. It's all wrapped up in tax relief knowledge the city bylaws expect from someone in a much higher schooling year. She'll present it to Sap, and when he approves, she can edit a few things here and there, but otherwise have a stress-free exam season.

When she enters class for the day, Professor Sap is already awake in his pot and speaking to a cloaked figure. He turns to her, green eyes glittering with more excitement than she's ever seen. "Ms. Aquae. Due to your recent achievements at the school showcase, the school has hired a TA to help you with your practical exam presentation."

She knows why he's excited, now. It's because he can pass on the very little work he's already doing, onto someone else. She's surprised that the school has allowed her another opportunity, given how poorly the familiar ritual went. They'd offered her another chance to participate, but she'd politely declined, now knowing that much like Haley, it would be impossible to get a familiar with so much of the ritual for non-humans lost to time. Despite not having a familiar, Roger the rat has been accompanying her to school every so often and has yet to bite her. Their tepid acquaintance has grown warmer, and she now enjoys bringing him along with her to class. Today, he's at home, but she's thinking of popping into the grocery store for fresh cheddar before she gets back to the watchtower. He has a particular fondness for sharper flavors.

When the cloaked figure turns around, her smile drops.

Ivan puts out his hand for her to shake. "Ivan Gray. A pleasure to meet you."

She glares at him, squeezing his hand hard enough to make her wince. "Elaine Aquae."

"Well. I'll give you the rest of the day to get acquainted. Elaine, I'll expect a timetable of your work plan for the next few months."

She nods, excited at the prospect of making a schedule. As suspicious as she is of Ivan being here, she could finally show him parts of the city he hadn't yet seen. Locke University is hard to get into when you don't have a school-issued ID.

When Sap leaves the room, she turns her attention to Ivan. "What are you doing here?"

"I figured this is an easier way for us to continue to work together. You learn in academic time, I get paid. That's that."

"Suspiciously efficient," she says. "Come on. We can talk somewhere less stuffy."

She leads him towards the courtyard along the lake, where the water expands so far into the horizon that many people confuse it for an ocean. Today, the gnats are out and swarm around the heads of nearby picnickers, and though they swarm midair in random spots all along the shore, they leave the probability mages alone.

"I'm doing a non-mage exam." She brings out her binder, presenting her plan with pride. "I color coded with the CMYK color wheel."

She says it with a bright flush and whispers it like a dirty little secret.

"Well, throw it away, because I've come up with something even cooler."

"Yeah right," she laughs. When Ivan just smiles dumbly back, she stops laughing. Frowning, she points an accusing finger at him. "I'm doing this project for my exam, Ivan."

"Not anymore," he says. "Now you'll get to lead with your heart. Can I see your binder?" he asks, wide-eyed.

She hands him the binder, color coded by crisis. He pushes his giant rectangular sunglasses closer to his nose, hmm-ing and nodding.

"As if you know what any of that means," she hisses.

"I'll have you know A-11 C-E is my favorite penal code." He pats her knee, standing up and offering a hand to help her.

She ignores it to stand on her own and snatches the binder back. Ivan has once again crossed what would be a very distinct boundary to most people. This idea doubles her workload, her stress, and her anger. "You don't deserve to even see that penal code." It's one thing to question her magic, but to dismiss her intelligence bruises a previously unmarred portion of her self-worth, and it's not an assault she'll stand for.. If she leaves now, she might be able to catch Professor Sap and change his mind about the T.A.

She grabs her satchel instead of responding, marching back towards the quad. Maybe Professor Sap has already forgotten he pawned her off on someone else.

Ivan sighs. "I guess you don't want to see the surprise I have for you on training field seven."

Her curiosity is piqued, but she doesn't stop walking.

"It's only available to TA-assisted projects."

She falters.

"And it's too bad that I've already *planned* ahead for this project." He walks towards her, throwing an arm over her shoulders.

His lips are close to her ear, and she shivers when she feels his breath against her lobe.

"It required me to complete a *complex* and *term-heavy permit application.*"

His words go straight to her core, and she clenches her thighs together in an attempt to squeeze the pleasure away.

He thinks he knows everything. She'd show him. She wouldn't give in, not even for a well-planned-out schedule curated to her needs. Just for her. She bites her lip.

"So, what do you say, Lainey?"

Her leads her to school field seven for their first practice.

"As your TA, I hope that you understand it is of the utmost importance to listen to what I have to say."

Elaine rolls her eyes. "You don't have any credentials."

"Bup bup." He holds up a spindly finger in the air. "Any sass will be filed as a class disruption. Enough of those, and there'll be a disciplinary hearing."

She pictures his shoe hitting the rock in front of him, the

yellow number rising from 5% to 55% when she grabs his arm and forces him to veer left. He yelps, tripping over said rock and ending up on the ground. He sits up, searching her for signs of guilt.

"How did you get this job?" she says. Now that she's no longer girlishly thrilled at his increased presence in her day to day, suspicion takes over. As far as she knew, he was staunchly against his name being included in anything resembling official documentation.

"A few false papers here, actual recommendations there. A series of favors called in or blackmailed."

"Just to teach me?"

He smiles, arms in the air as if to say, "what can you do". While the thought did make her heart squeeze, Elaine doesn't believe his only motive is to be close to her. He's certainly a lonely, pathetic man, but long-term employment doesn't fit her understanding of him.

"Fine. Don't tell me, *Professor.*"

A blush spreads across his cheeks, his eyes widening. He pushes himself off the ground and saunters closer to her. He whips his cloak aside, hand coming out and taking hers.

"Do that again but say it more like you *really* need to pass this class."

She snatches her hands away. "You're an asshole."

"Ms. Aquae," he purrs, "I'd be cautious of the curse words you use around me."

"And why is that?"

"I'll fail you."

She pushes his arm in warning.

He laughs, unmoved by her shove. "We'll be collaborating with mages of different affinities. One of the most important tools in your kit in real life is flexibility. I reached out to some mages who could prove useful."

She doesn't bother to ask why. Ivan's in one of his "I want you to beg me to teach you" moods.

They make their way to the courtyard, and a young woman comes over to introduce herself. She's got a short black bob and plain features. She's tied up the top of her hair in a small ponytail that sticks straight up in the air.

"I'm Nero. TA for ceramics mages, mostly remote bomb detonation."

Elaine's eyes widen, and she whips her head toward Ivan. "Bombs?!"

"I'm Ivan."

"Hey," Nero eyes him appreciatively.

Elaine scoots in, shoving her hand in front of the woman. "Elaine, math apprentice with Professor Sap."

"So, Ivan," Nero takes a step closer, "when did you graduate?"

His eyes flick to Elaine before returning to Nero. "I'm a contract employee. I made my name in field work."

"Sword for hire?"

Elaine scoffs. Nero blinks her long lashes up at Ivan, who is acting the part of a professional teaching assistant.

"Unemployed loser, actually," he replies.

Nero laughs, batting his arm lightly with her hand.

Elaine steps between them again, her own fist clenched against her side. "Where's *your* student?"

Nero's eyes flick to her, smiling politely. "Clarke's on the bleachers. You should introduce yourself."

"I thought the department was sending over a few candidates." Ivan frowns. He crosses his arms, the perfect imitation of an upset instructor.

"Most of them probably chose their partners for the practical exam earlier," Elaine chimes in. "You know, since partner proposals were due *two weeks ago*." She has a later deadline for the solo project. Well, *had*.

Ivan laughs, avoiding eye contact. "Well, what's two weeks in the grand scheme of things?"

Elaine leaves them to greet the only man on the bleachers. He'd be hard to miss, large and imposing, with skin a pallid gray hue. It's clear that he must be part clay creature. As societies developed, several sects of creatures were born from several different elements. Golems and gargoyles are the most common types in Garriver, sharing similar ancestral lines that diverged over the millennia due to climate, evolution, and biome.

"I'm Elaine, the probability mage. You must be Clarke?"

Even his hands are huge, she marvels as he reaches out to shake her hand.

"Yes. Thank you for meeting with me. I had a family emergency back home and had to leave for a month, so I thought I was going to have to do a write-up exam instead. Can you imagine?" he says.

That sounds perfect. "Sounds dreadful."

He looks at her for a moment, clearly thinking before he snaps his fingers. "You're the probability mage from the school fair. It's the first time I've seen one of you."

"We're a bit of a rarity these days. My TA is the only other one I've met." She points a thumb back at Ivan, who watches the two of them raptly. When he's caught, his head snaps back to his conversation with Nero.

"It's a relief to get to work with another cross-species student. I never know how the others are going to react to my magical core."

She stiffens at the casual recognition of her past. No one else has noticed or didn't bring it up so far. She touches the ends of her locks. "Was it my hair?"

"No, no. I knew a half nymph that had the same looks as you in my youth." He bites his lip, looking a bit nervous. "I hope that's alright to say."

"No offense taken," she says. And she does mean it. He's the first one to notice, and he says it like it's a relief instead of a burden. "I actually haven't met a lot of...us."

Now it's his turn to look surprised. "Really? I know downtown Garriver is almost entirely human, but non-humans live all over."

"I grew up in the mountains with just my family and a town of a hundred. And in the past few months that I've been in Garriver, I haven't had much time to see the rest of the city."

He slaps a hand against his knee. "We have to fix that! Goblin Town welcomes everyone that isn't a gnome, and frat parties always draw out more of the student body that you wouldn't have even known existed."

Maybe this whole group project thing wouldn't be awful after all. At some point, they move back into the grass so Clarke can work on his clay and explain how he uses it.

"My aunt and uncle own the Golem Brothers' Demolitions, LLC," he explains. "In my free time, I prefer making things, but they're preparing me to take over the business once they retire. It's why I'm excited to work on this potions-focused project with you. Potions are sensitive, delicate things, and the formula matters down to the material."

So, Ivan's assigned her a potions project. It's not his worst idea.

"I've always loved the minutiae of things." Elaine says.

Clarke nods his head. "No need for questions when you know exactly how, when and what's happening."

A huge smile crosses her face. She looks over, gratefully, to Ivan. His scowl falls of his face and is replaced with surprise. It softens, and his face turns red.

Thank you, she mouths. This isn't what she expected from him: it's better.

They discuss their hobbies and interests, and when Elaine

mentions that she's always had a sensitive nose, Clarke has an explanation for it.

"You are magic-sensitive," he says. "It's very common in fairies and nymphs, satyrs mostly. In the country Nero and I come from, our savannah satyrs say Nero smells like nitroglycerin." He looks at her for a moment, assessing. "What does mine smell like?"

He kneads the clay in front of him. Elaine takes in a deep breath, concentrating on his magic. "I smell—olives, a wood oven. Something dry I can't quite put my finger on..."

"The nymphs back home say it's like hardened clay."

Elaine closes her eyes, sniffing again. "Pewter?"

He bobs his head side to side. "Never heard that one."

"Elaine!" Ivan calls.

She turns, shoulder to shoulder with Clarke, and wonders why Ivan's frowning. He marches over to them and plops down next to Elaine. Clarke leans over her to offer a hand to shake. Ivan ignores it, and Clarke puts his arm down, face neutral, even as his fists pull grass out of the dirt.

"So," Ivan begins, "Nero has a great work-study idea."

Nero nods. "Right. Clarke and I discussed potion making from scratch. He makes the materials, like the pestle and mortar, from scratch, using his expertise in matter and chemistry. Elaine will use her probability magic and background in potions,"

Elaine glares at Ivan. *Background in potions?*

"To create the recipe. Since this is an advanced project, we're going to wow with some big ones. Precipitation, Fermentation, and Decay."

"We can all meet three times a week and study the similarities between our in-the-moment magic fluctuations. The project should only require two mages, so she can act as the project partner instead of a TA. Of course, it won't be as exciting as I was hoping, but you love boring stuff like this." He finally acknowledges Clarke. "You won't have to participate, of course. Nero said you prefer working alone."

The golem man stiffens.

Desperate to keep her new friend, Elaine says, "Clarke is the best clay mage in his year. That would make him perfect for a potioneering exam. We'll have to work out the thesis, but it's a solid choice."

"Lainey, Clarke hasn't even accepted yet."

"And he hasn't said no, either."

Their eyes move from each other over to Clarke. He makes eye contact with Ivan over her head, who is glaring at him. His eyes narrow back.

"You know what, I'd love to work with you, Elaine."

She brightens. That means no Nero.

"Perfect!" She claps her hands. "You can meet us this weekend."

Ivan looks between them with narrowed eyes. He switches to a pout when Elaine's attention turns back to him.

"Weekend," Ivan whines. "Work isn't supposed to bleed into weekends!"

"Ignore him. Clarke, a fermentation potion should be the easiest to start with. Want to bring the clay and I'll bring the other ingredients?"

Despite his protests, Ivan's there with the rest of them on Saturday morning.

Elaine has pulled her hair back into a tight bun and is currently lining up her ingredients carefully on a table in the classroom they're working in. She'd talked to her uncle about the potion, and he assured her it's not much different than one made for fertilizer in the gardens back home.

"Cutleaf toothwort, dandelion root, bergamot syrup," she mutters as she double checks her supply.

Fermentation potions are used to help things grow; plants, people, and even objects can be made stronger and larger depending on the ingredients used. When making one with natural ingredients, it's important to use supplies native to the region in which it's being made. The fermentation potion ingredients in South America are entirely different from those being used in a city built atop a swamp like Garriver.

"I brought clay from the marsh bank a few miles south," Clarke says next to her. "It should blend well with the ingredients. I'll make the cauldron, then you can make the potion?"

"Sounds good to me."

And while she would've relied solely on her academic knowledge before, she had probability magic now, and percentages flash unreliably as she tries to perfect the potion recipe. On her first try, it's too dry. On the second, it smokes.

"I've got enough ingredients for one more try," she bites her lip. As she pushes three drops of bergamot syrup, she sighs in relief when it glows a subtle green hue.

"It worked," she smiles at Clarke.

Ivan pushes his way forward, eyeing the potion. "As if you know what that looks like," he says.

She pushes him back, but he just leans his shoulder further against her.

He pulls an empty vial from his cloak and ladles in a batch, sealing it with a cork and returning it to his pocket. "This is good, Lainey," he compliments. "I might need you to make me something stronger someday soon."

She rolls her eyes. She stands, pulling Ivan to follow her. He hisses in pain, and she turns around in alarm.

"Are you alright?" she frets over him. "Do you need anything?"

He sighs, rolling a shoulder back. "I should be fine. It's just my spine..."

She shakes her head, and the salmon on her cloak swim frantically around her shoulders. The last time he said that, his curse sent him careening out her window. "Let's get you on a cot at the nurse's office. No passing out in the field."

"I'd rather sleep in my own bed."

"That's too far!" she protests.

"Lainey," he pleads.

"We'll go to the watchtower." She turns to Clarke with an apologetic smile. "We'll meet up soon to work on this. Talk soon?"

He looks between Ivan and her, a somber expression on his face. He nods tightly. "Sure. Good luck trying to figure out what's wrong with him."

Elaine supports Ivan as he wraps himself around her, oblivious to Ivan switching which foot to stumble on as they walk out of the courtyard.

15

FRAT PARTY GHOSTS

The first day of training starts at seven a.m. So, of course, Ivan isn't there. Elaine is instead greeted by Clarke and Nero.

"Hello," she greets them both.

"Morning," they intone, neither looking up from the clay in front of them.

Nero's clay takes the shape of a dozen tiny soldiers, with details so precise that each soldier has its own face. Clarke focuses on one large piece of red clay, a wet blob he toys with. Unlike Nero, who works the clay with clinical precision, Clarke works it like there's no end goal. When it looks like he's about to form it into a pot, it's squeezed between his two large hands, and he starts the process over again. Nero is done with her tiny army and sits back to look at Elaine. Today, Elaine brought Roger with her, and the demolition expert scrunches her nose up at him.

"Is that your familiar?"

"Roger's a..." She pauses. *Pet* seems too diminutive for their history. Allies? Roommates? "He's my associate."

"So, he's just a regular rat?"

"Well, he used to be a part of an animal mage's informal militia."

Nero regards him more critically. "And what can you do?"

Elaine raises an eyebrow. "What do you mean?"

"You're a mage with an impractical affinity studying accounting. Now you're doing a practical exam dealing with advanced and volatile potion making?"

Nero crosses her arms and looks Elaine up and down.

Elaine had opted for an ankle-length, emerald-green gown today that is actually two billowing pant legs. She'd chosen the color as a farewell to fall as Garriver creeps into winter. Even the salmon on her cloak feel the change, moving in sluggish circles along the borders of the fabric.

"Ivan is training me to use probability magic to see the odds in any given situation."

Clarke looks up from the clay he's molding into a seagull. "There are safer ways to test that than putting you in an experimental potions exam."

"Just whose side are you on?" She puts her hands on her hips. "You don't believe in me?"

"I believe in you," Clarke says. "I just don't know if it's your best interest he's looking out for, or his."

Even though she's arguing, she agrees. Everything Ivan does seems to be an attempt to remind her of him: adrenaline pumping, blood curdling, life-threatening. Maybe it's unfair to compare the assignment to Ivan, as Garriver itself has proven to be a quick and vicious beast. She can now see she'd come to the city with a certain naivety, unaware of the imposing danger derived from systems created long before she'd arrived, and which will exist long after she's dead. To live here means to live with looming threats as varied as the city layers. Ivan avoids danger largely because of the affinity they share, an affinity that she had been told her whole life wouldn't be useful. And a secret part of her hopes that he feels that kinship as much as she does, and that he's funneling all of it into the work they'll do together on this project. She knows he's here because he cares. That thought makes her insides feel warm, but she ignores it in favor of answering Clarke's question.

"He believes in my skills. You can too."

"Ah, such high praise from my best student." Ivan approaches from an archway, strolling over to the trio of them.

She flushes when she realizes she's been caught defending him. "You're late."

"I was going to be on time, but then a black cat walked across my path, and I had to take the long way around." He sits down next to Elaine, putting an arm around her with a cheery grin. "We'll start with an ice breaker to get to know each other better. I'm Elaine's TA. I have luck magic. I like Neapolitan ice cream, swimming, and crowds. I hate bears, ghosts, and liars."

Elaine looks to the others. Nero nods so much she looks like a bobble head, that indifference from before wiped from her face. Clarke's face is carefully polite.

"How about you go next, Lainey?"

She nods. "I'm Elaine. I use probability magic."

"I thought you said you had the same affinity?" Nero interrupts.

"We have different ideas on how to define it."

No one else speaks. Clarke, obviously eager to dispel the awkward air, says, "Perhaps it would be helpful for you both to define it?"

Ivan takes his arm from her shoulders and holds his hands together in front of him, fiddling with his rings. "Well, I suppose it's like a gut feeling. I know how to act to get the result I want."

"But our options are predetermined," Elaine adds.

"Not necessarily. Nothing in life stays the same."

"Right. But you can't stack the odds higher in your favor."

"Maybe *you* can't, but I'll have you know, I've escaped more than one death-defying act."

She huffs. "That was because of the magic, not because you can *bend reality*."

"And what if I can?"

They stare at each other. He looks at her with determination; a playful air of competition surrounds him.

She's annoyed with his claims based on his "feelings." Feelings aren't empirical evidence.

"They don't sound alike at all," Nero says. "How do you know your affinities are actually related?"

Elaine sees Ivan's face grow red, and by the heat in her cheeks, she assumes her face is just as flush.

"The magic has made it clear," she says before Ivan can answer for them. She thinks of the prison cell and the dripping of water. "Like attracts like."

Here, Clarke and Nero eye each other suspiciously. He pulls his clay mound closer to him.

"Let's keep going," Ivan says. "Nero, you're up."

She sits upright at the attention. "I'm Nero. My last name is none of your business. I specialize in plastic explosives, learning, and learning about explosions. I dislike slow-moving students—" here, Clarke scowls, "—and spiders."

"I'm Clarke. I'm studying potions as a subset of claywork at the university. I like pottery, eating good food, and daisies. I dislike arrogance and the Locke grading system."

Ivan rolls his eyes. "All about school with you people. As we discussed before, we'll start with an example of our affinities. Elaine can go first."

She pulls her dice out of her pocket. Her stomach problems related to her magic are a thing of the past. Now, the odds of rolling snake eyes flash yellow in front of her. The percentage flips with each turn of her hands, the odds rapid and volatile. She throws them before she can think.

"Two fives," Ivan says.

She nods. She'd been aiming for snake eyes. She rolls again, the dice rolling into a five and a five.

She hisses and pushes a hand against her forehead when a sharp pain hits. "It still gives me migraines," she says with a warm face. Her head aches with the effort.

"Right. That's what school's for," Clarke says.

She smiles at him in gratitude.

Ivan's eyes flick between them suspiciously. She pretends not to notice the way his eyes linger on her as she gives Clarke a thumbs up.

ON IVAN'S second attempt to break into the Locke dungeon, he discovers he might have to break Elaine's heart. Just as he'd thought, it's easy to sneak by the "DO NOT ENTER" signs when you have a pass to be on campus. The window he crawled out of last time had been re-sealed but was still no match for him.

He creeps further into the guts of the university and keeps his eye out for signs of a secret door.

The greatest weakness in protecting a circle of power is that they require that hints be left behind so anyone can access them. Since his near kidnapping, he'd looked into Locke's history and deduced that must be what his employer's after. The strongest casters in the world can't avoid having to leave clues at the entrance, due to the nature of the magic being for everyone. So, Ivan searches for those clues within wobbly bricks or the loose slats of a metal locker.

He's in the men's locker room, checking the sinks for clues, when the door swings open. He curses, slipping into a nearby locker and shutting it gently behind him.

Step-step-thunk.

The odd footfalls he'd heard on his first break-in attempt are back.

"I know you're in here."

Ivan steadies his breath and his heart beats too loud in his eardrums. The voice is one he's heard before while in Lainey's bedroom. The uneven steps grow closer and closer. A locker door snaps open, and the disembodied voice curses.

"There are only so many lockers in this room, thief. Come out, and I won't hurt you."

Ivan stays where he is, biting his lip as, one by one, he hears the locker doors being opened. The figure is only a few paces away now, he can tell, and he prepares to leap from his hiding spot, when he hears the door open, and another person enters the room.

"We have to leave. Night rounds are coming this way."

"I'm sniffing out a rat."

"*We're* rats. Let's get out of here before they call the police. We'll find the dungeon another time."

The feet are visible right in front of Ivan's locker. Through the grates he can see a shadowed figure holding a cane, but it's too dark to make out his facial features.

"Time waits for no one, Neil."

The locker room door opens one last time, and bathed in the light, Ivan stares into the eyes of a mage between the grates of the locker. Ivan thinks he almost sees recognition in them. Elaine's Uncle Neil turns on his heel and makes his way to the door of the locker room.

When Ivan's sure the coast is clear, he jumps out of the locker, and runs to go find Elaine.

THE BASS BEATS loud against her heart. Clarke and Elaine end up at a fraternity house along Greek Row. Alpha kappa yadda

yadda yadda. Immediate regret hits Elaine as she smells stale beer and sweat, but she's determined to have a good time. In a moment of impulsive inspiration—or stupidity, only time will tell—she left her personal cloak at home in exchange for her school-issued one that reaches her hips and flares open at the front. She wore a short dress, all black, with built-in shorts underneath. It's the one she favored when the summers back home were particularly hot, and the trails were spectacularly perilous.

Clarke grabs her hand, using his larger body to push his way through the crowd and towards a series of overturned barrels with Scrabble red letters that, after careful inspection, are supposed to spell out "The Bar."

"Two shots of Algae-spark," Clarke says.

A pimply young man whose smile never leaves his face hands him a shot glass. Clarke clinks his glass against hers, and she downs it before she has time to think. It tastes a bit like pickle juice, she decides. The sour taste makes her nose scrunch, and it gets worse when she feels the leftovers pop in her mouth like fleas.

"It's like fireworks." Clarke smiles at her.

She smiles back and decides at this moment to never drink something that foul again.

The resolution is forgotten as one drink turns into two, then two into four, and she's lost in the whirl of the technicolored party. The frat house is a large spout of coral with a skylight in the middle, so whatever room you find yourself in, the night sky is overhead, a few bright stars twinkling in defiance of the city's polluted air. Elaine recognizes them, two points within the Big Dipper. She used them to guide herself the right way down the mountain when she stood at the cliff's edge too long, fantasizing about how it would feel to be the wind.

Astronauts say space isn't like that at all. There's no wind to push you, nothing to alter your course. Just the gravitational pull between planets in orbit around the sun, and a void of nothing. If you're lucky, the pull will keep you in rotation with the earth. But if you're pushed off towards nothing, you'll constantly move that way, slower and slower until you're left praying an anomaly will come and alter your path.

"More shots?" Clarke pushes a cup her way, glowing green algae juice spilling out and landing on her arm.

She takes it without complaint, smiling as she guzzles it down.

"This is my friend, Leon." Clarke gestures to the man that she only now notices standing beside him. He has brown hair, brown eyes, and his head is just a bit too narrow for his body. He also looks petrified, she thinks. Like a bunny. She giggles at her own comparison.

Clarke grins and nudges Leon. "Say hello, Leon."

"Hello, Leon. I'm Leon. Hi." He clears his throat.

Elaine likes nervous men. She holds out a hand for him to shake.

"Clarke says you're working on a practical exam demonstration together?"

With Ivan, her brain supplies. Stupid, unpredictable Ivan, who won't kiss her, and thinks it's funny to change her course curriculum.

"Mm-hm," she answers. Her eyes are back on the coral. How does it survive so far from the ocean?

"He also says you're a probability mage."

She nods. "Best in the biz." A lie. The best is at home, probably stealing her stuff as a punishment for having her attention on anything other than him.

"Well, I—" Whatever he was going to say is lost when a man with a dragon head walks by, shooting flames into a tray of—now fried—cheese.

Elaine rubs her stomach, eyes following the dish as it gets farther and farther away. "Clarke. Cheese." She points.

He nods and understands immediately. "Cheese."

They move towards it, his hand pushing against her back and forcing her into a slight jog as they follow the draconic dairy delivery man. Gods, she loves cheese. She scarfs down a pile, and Clarke does the same next to her.

"Another shot." He pulls her back towards the bar.

Why not? she thinks, *I'm alive.*

That night, she has an epiphany: she's never going to die and she's the most incredible mage alive.

She pulls Clarke onto the dance floor, feet sticking to the floor, and the bass thrumming all the way from her ears into her heart. Clarke grabs her by the hand and twirls her.

Delighted, she shouts "again!" and he does, twirling her to the world's best song at the world's best party. About seven twirls in, she feels lightheaded and pulls back from her project partner. She ignores her spinning head and continues to dance, but then the crowd starts to feel too hot and too close. The smell of sweat and stale beer becomes overwhelming, and she pushes her way outside for reprieve.

She gasps in a large breath of crisp winter air, and the wind pricks at her arms, sweeping away her nausea. Her hair scrunches up against the brick wall behind her, scraping against her scalp as she tilts her head to stare up at the moon.

"Pretty moon," she croons at it. She wishes she could kiss it, kiss anything. Unwittingly, her mind drifts to admiration beneath large hands and tired eyes. She imagines them holding her own hands, drawing her curled fingers up to his lips. She sees him in front of her, brown eyes soft and full of an affection so deep it makes her breath catch in her throat. "Pretty Ivan," she sings to the apparition in front of her. "You'll never kiss me."

"You're wasted," he whispers.

"And you're not here," she replies.

Before the ghost can disappoint her, she wraps her arms

around his neck and kisses the ghost. In her drink-addled state, she doesn't mind that Ivan doesn't kiss back. It's not real, after all. Then his arms wrap around her, and his lips move with hers, soft and plush like she remembers.

"I think about the cell sometimes when I'm alone," she confesses.

The ghost moans. Just how Elaine always thought a ghost would sound. The apparition pulls her closer, and she's eager to push her exposed cleavage up against his chest.

"I'd try so many things if I got you all alone again."

"Lainey," he breathes out, before cupping her head in its hands and pushing his mouth harder against hers. This time, he bites her lip, pushing his legs between her own before lifting her up to his face.

Her eyes land on familiar brown ones, brows creased as they search her own. He moves to her neck, kissing up along her collarbone until his lips are right against her ear.

"Why did you come here with Clarke?" he asks against her, breath fluttering hot and heavy on her skin.

"He's just a friend," she says. He sucks on her neck, and she lets out a pleased moan when he hits her pulse point.

"I don't like him," the ghost admits, something she already knew.

She grinds down on the leg between her thighs, body jolting in pleasure at the sensation of something pressing against her clit. He grunts and moves his thigh against her core to help her along.

"I don't want him," she confesses.

"What do you want?"

"You're warm for a ghost," she says.

"Lainey, baby." He takes a warning tone. "Tell me what you want."

She bites her lip, nervous to confess even to her own mind. To speak truth to her feelings could make it her reality, and reality means there could be consequences to her affection. Reactions from others, instead of the sweet and familiar self-intimacy of control. The ghost must notice her hesitation because he presses his thigh against her again. He presses more kisses and teeth to the expanse of her neck, making her forget that she's all alone, and this is just a beautiful illusion.

"You," she breathes. "I want you."

He lets out a pleased moan against her neck, sucking her skin so sweetly she sees stars.

The door to the party opens and sounds of the frat house filter outside.

"Elaine?" Clarke asks. "What are you doing out here, it's freezing! Come inside, someone's pulling quarters out of people's ears."

The alleyway is empty except for the two of them.

She gasps for breath, a chill breaking over her front that wasn't there before. She holds a hand to her chest, trying to steady her rapidly beating heart before rejoining the party.

"Yeah, I'm coming." She pushes herself off the wall. "I want at least three more shots of whatever they're serving tonight." She hadn't truly indulged in drinking since the River Speak.

That's the last thing she'll remember saying that night.

"I'M DYING," she moans.

She's unsure where she's woken up. It's quiet out, so it can't be her uncle's watchtower in the city center. The curtains are drawn over tiny windows that line the four walls around her. She opens one and is greeted by the sight of a bike and a mother pushing her child in a pram. She breathes in deeply, wondering how she's going to sneak out of whoever's home this is, when she realizes it smells like clay and Clarke, and her shoulders relax. There are low voices and muttering from behind the door. She opens it and bright light stings her eyes.

The home is painted in a limewash, with open archways and glassless windows. There must be a ward on them to keep the bugs out. The sweet smell of maple syrup and coffee is wafting towards her and making her forget she woke up with a headache.

When she finds the kitchen, Clarke and a brunette man are talking quietly, but they stop when they see Elaine standing in the doorway. She waves a hand, moving to sit at the bar in front of the kitchen setup.

Clarke slides a glass of orange juice towards her. "Feeling alright?"

She grumbles a thanks as she takes the orange juice from him. She chugs it all in one tilt of the glass before turning her eyes on the stranger, who eyes her expectantly. She squints, trying to place him.

"Leon," he says, before she can ask. "I'm studying to gain my warlock status."

"I remember," she lies. "We met somewhere between my first shot and this morning."

Both men laugh at that, and she relaxes further into her stool. She and Clarke discuss the project for a bit, working out whether they should change some variables.

"So, the title is The Effects of Materials on Potions of Natural Transformations," Clarke says.

"Tentatively."

"Right. Tentatively. And we'll demonstrate a potion on precipitation, fermentation, and decay. The city being built on a swamp will make those potions easier to make. I'll focus on clay type. One cauldron will be made from clay indigenous to Garriver, another from New York, which has similar build but an entirely different soil type. Finally, somewhere dry."

"Just dry," she raises an eyebrow.

Clarke shrugs, smiling. "A desert. Sahara, maybe? The school can help us source the material."

Elaine hums in thought. It would be interesting to get clay from another continent entirely, but using variables from the same land mass also shows off the vibrant diversity of the land. How a potioneer working in a dry, sandy climate has to think differently about their potion recipe than one in a humid environment. The clay is not the only material that changes in different locations. Even materials react differently when dealing with complicated, higher-level potions. It's what makes Uncle Neil's affinity for proportions so useful. It allows him to adjust for environmental factors like temperature, humidity, and weather conditions. Though, it's never advised to make a potion in the ocean air, but sometimes a potion maker doesn't have a choice. She's excited for the project now that she's started. That's how it usually goes. She is not a fan of change, but just like her decision to go to university, she bites down on a challenge and doesn't let go until it's seen through.

Leon nods where appropriate, though she's sure he has no clue what they're talking about.

"What's your affinity?" she asks to be polite.

A grin overtakes his face as he proudly states, "Dirt magic."

It sounds useless, and she's intrigued. "Tell me more."

Leon's eyes flit to Clarke, almost nervous, before returning to her. "Maybe over dinner?"

Warlocks are tricky creatures. They often have the academic training of wizards, but the debts and lack of life experience that makes them eager to pawn off their problems on others. They are the object of mischievous creatures' pranks and curses, which the cowards often pass onto naïve creatures —unsuspecting babies and the like. Leon is not to be fully trusted as far as she's concerned.

Her face still flushes hot at the offer, and she smiles. He's cute, with humble manners and seemingly honest intentions.

Maybe a date with someone new would take her mind off things. "Sounds like a plan to me."

She leaves her address and tells him to send a message, then heads home to the watchtower.

When she enters the kitchen, it's empty save for an open box of crackers on the kitchen counter. There's a small furry rump sticking out of it, and a long worm-like tail thumping lazily on the table.

"Roger!" She pulls him from the box. "What did I tell you about going through the pantry?"

Roger, clearly delighted that she's returned, avoids reprimand by climbing up and into the sleeve of her cloak, settling in for a mid-morning nap. Elaine pulls up a stool and works on her class assignment, abandoned last night on the counter. She scribbles a doodle on the draft of an essay when her uncle enters the kitchen.

"Afternoon," she greets him, eagerly putting the pen down to give her uncle her full attention in service of procrastination.

He smiles grimly, unwinding his scarf from his neck. He moves towards the tea kettle. With his back to her, he says, "Elaine, I have to go off on a work trip for a couple weeks."

She wiggles in her seat, disappointment filling her gut. "Oh. Again?" she replies quietly.

The teapot whistles, and he pours her a cup before serving himself. She curls her hands around the mug, steam swirling up into her face. He'd poured a dollop of honey in her water, one mint leaf soaking at the bottom.

"It's close by, but I'll need to be on site. The work is delicate."

The tower would be empty then. Roger's presence would be a welcome distraction from the silence. Once again, she wishes she had a few more classmates to hang out with. She thought once she left the mountains, that degree of separation from people would leave her too, but being in Garriver hasn't made her less lonely, it just makes her less alone.

"If anything happens, call me," he says.

"You're leaving now?"

He winces and pats her shoulder roughly. "I've reset the wards, just in case."

"A little warning would've been nice," she snaps. Her hands grip the mug tighter. Quieter, she says, "You promised you would go to the Constellation Ball with me."

It's the ball Haley invited her to after the school showcase. Her social life, networking and otherwise, is dismal, and Neil said he'd take her for an hour before coming up with an excuse for them both to leave early.

"I don't like leaving you here alone." A beat of silence. Then, "There have been rumors of a hit out on a luck mage."

"No," she breathes. Her uncle nods his head solemnly, most likely thinking she's scared for herself, but her mind goes to Ivan. "As in they want him—or her, dead?" The worry seeps into frustration. Of course, Ivan would get himself killed within months of them meeting.

He shakes his head. "Not dead, no. I know you're not listed as one, but probability is a close enough descriptor to luck for a hunter who wants that money badly enough. My brother asked me to keep you safe, and I'll do so."

Elaine scoffs, arms clenching tighter around herself. "Your *brother* hasn't talked to me in months." Anger at her dad comes back up. He hasn't cared enough to write to her, so why would a bounty on her head matter to him? "And according to him, you shouldn't even see me as family."

Neil's nostrils flare. "Don't be stupid. Albert is a fool with the nature of a clam. That's never been my burden, and your blood doesn't concern me."

The frown sticks to her face, though her heart feels warm at her uncle's declaration. She can read into the sentiment between his angry words.

He takes a deep breath, pinching his nose. "Nellie, this is serious. I'll be leaving some...extra precautions around. So don't be scared if your cereal isn't where you left it or if some silverware disappears."

As her anger dissipates, fear takes its place. It's likely for Ivan, not her, but there's no way for her uncle to know that. And there's no way for Elaine to be sure about it either.

"When did the hit go out?"

Neil frowns into his tea.

She's spoken of Ivan, in brief moments, but enough for him to get an idea that they're seeing each other regularly.

He sips it, before turning his dark eyes back on her. "Around two weeks after you got here, best I can tell."

"Oh." She slumps down.

"I think it's a coincidence. And I wouldn't leave you alone if this work wasn't of the utmost importance, Nellie. You're family and what my numbskull brother does or says doesn't change that."

She feels delicate. While Ivan may be the target, it might not be his skills they're after. If anyone with their affinity will do, then that means she's in danger every time she leaves the house. She moves her cup of tea to sip too fast, and she hisses out in pain as it spills hot against her collarbone. Perhaps the stress of this life, of school, Ivan, and her family, is getting to her more than she thought. "Do you promise I'll be safe here?"

"I promise."

He must feel like he's comforted her enough, or this project is more important than he let on, because he grabs a few things from the living room and then he's gone.

16

CAT CAPERS

She looks at her reflection in the mirror before entering the banquet hall where the Constellation Ball is being held. One last check to look for any mistakes. Each of her salmon pins holds one of six braids in place, and smaller, less important pins litter the back of her head to keep stray hairs taut against her nape. Her spider-woven dress, the same silver as her hair, gives her the air of a snowflake, delicate and priceless. The woman who looks back at her is identical to when she first arrived in Garriver, when all she had control over in her life was the plaited braids in her hair. She'd taken to wearing it down since her move, enjoying the way it could stay loose without getting stuck in brambles and branches and how it looked peeking out of the hood of her cloak or splayed out around her like a halo. Before her is a colder version of herself that she forgot existed, someone tucked away in the mountains, and a frown crosses her lips. She cocks her head and sighs. It's a pretty pout, at least.

A hand reaches over and plucks the front pin from her hair, freeing the frontmost strands of her hair from the tight crown.

"You bastard."

"That's Professor Bastard to you."

She reaches out to snatch the pin back, but Ivan holds it high above her head.

"Sweet Lainey, allow me this token of your favor."

"You snake."

"It's been so long since a lady has granted me her blessing."

He puts it in his own hair, one section now pinned down amongst his bushy brown tufts. He smiles down at her, victorious, then eyes widen for a moment when he looks at the dress she's wearing. "Wow," he breathes, the grin dropping to accommodate his now-gaping mouth. "You look like starlight."

"What are you doing here?" she hisses. "What about the bounty?"

She'd told him about it the next time she saw him, to which he scoffed and said, "That's the fifth this year, they all pass." He'd become more interested when he realized it was a way he could tease her about caring for him, to which she blushed and waved him off until the subject changed to something practical.

"I told you, it's not a problem," he says. He looks over the top of her head, eyes brightening when he catches sight of the ballroom. He leads her to the door, painted pale blue with snowflakes and thin branches empty of leaves. A bored, squat guard in a waistcoat and bow tie stands there, white gloved hands clasping a list.

"Name?" he asks.

"Elaine Aquae."

The guard allows her through, his frown deepening when Ivan steps up next, wearing his regular clothes, blatantly disregarding the dress code.

"Name."

"Ivan Gray."

The guard takes his time perusing the list before he shakes his head. "You're not on the list."

"Not on the—but I'm a Gray."

The guard looks him up and down. "I only see one Gray on the list. No Ivan."

Elaine smiles at his misfortune. Ivan would have some choice words for her blatant glee, if it weren't for the one-sided argument he was holding with the guard. The guard, though, is speaking to the next person in line as if there isn't a disheveled mage threatening his livelihood.

Ivan tries to walk past the doorman while he's talking to the next guests, only to be pulled roughly back with a surprising amount of strength from the man with the list. Ivan looks pathetic to Elaine, a sheepdog kept out in the rain by a more dominant chihuahua, guarding the pet door with a stern glare. Elaine enjoys the sight for a few moments more before Ivan's eyes land on hers. He pouts and gives her big weepy eyes she's sure are accompanied by a grunt of dismay she's too far away to hear. She can hear a loud crowd ahead, and can't see a familiar face as strangers weave in and out of the room.

"I'm going to regret this," she mutters. Taking a deep breath, she calls out "he's with me."

The doorman looks back at her with the sneer previously used on Ivan.

It's worth the trouble, she decides, when Ivan's frown becomes a beaming toothy grin. He limbos under the velvet rope before the doorman can unclip it for him, trotting up and wrapping an arm around her, which she shoves away with a wrinkled nose.

"Why do you smell like petrol?"

"I had a bit of an incident on a mission involving a dinosaur activist. Ooh, crostini!"

When he pulls away to chase the unsuspecting waiter passing by, she snags his arm. His eyes flit to her grip on him before going to her lips, then her eyes.

"You're lucky Uncle Neil was too busy to come and that I had a plus one spot available. Please don't make me regret it."

He puts a hand over his heart in mock offense. "Me?"

"I'm serious, Ivan," she warns. "I'm here to make some connections so I can get a job after I graduate, and I don't want them to remember me as the woman who came in with the guy who stole all the bread."

He grabs her other arm, guiding her further into the ballroom and against a back wall. From here, she gets a better view of the room, all dark wood with burgundy rugs, and chandeliers that glitter under the light of floating wax candles. The windows are stained glass, all depicting various winter scenes. They're next to the champagne glass pyramid, which she will be indulging in as soon as she can.

The winter solstice ballroom only opens for one day, and is a holiday celebrated across almost all cultures. Solstices are often regarded as moments of transition in the magical world, and are common times to reset wards, cast powerful spells, and due to the potentiality of great destruction, it's considered polite to engage in social activities to show you aren't casting any ill will magic on others. It's an old tradition from when towns were smaller and human settlements were few and far between. In Garriver, it means an influx of holiday parties and police patrolling the streets.

She turns her attention back from the room to the luck mage in front of her. This close, she can see the arch of his nose and the tiniest scar right above his upper lip. He's still holding both her arms, but his eyes are looking decidedly lower than usual.

She snaps her fingers. "Eyes up here."

She's expecting him to be sheepish now that he's been caught, but he frowns instead.

He reaches out to grab at the bottom of her school-issued cloak, rubbing the thin fabric between his fingers.

Her breath catches as she watches him gently rub at her

clothes. She clears her throat and worries he can feel the heat emanating off her skin.

"Where's your cloak? This one's practically useless."

She grabs at the school-issued fabric in his hands. "It's just for university events. They offer spells at an extra price, but they're not very strong."

He can't draw his eyes from the green and purple fabric. He bites his lip, clearly thinking something over in his head. "Do you want to wear my—"

"Elaine, how lovely of you to come to our event."

Startled, her head snaps to her left. "Oh! It's you," she says. It's the volunteer she'd called up on stage during her dice demonstration. Tonight, he has purple eyeshadow across his cheeks to match his hair. He wears that same white cape with barely any family magic on it. Instead, Elaine smells a strange jumble of magic, and runes litter the inside layer. None of them feel personal, save for a few inscriptions across the clasp at his neck.

Noticing she and Ivan are still standing entirely too close, she pulls away from his grasp and turns to give the newcomer her full attention.

Ivan doesn't say anything as he moves to stand right behind her, the ends of his own cloak nearly wrapping around her as he looms, his breath coming out in short puffs across the top of her head.

"I don't believe I caught your name the last time we met," she says to the man.

He bows his head. "Reginald Calamity, head of the space mage members of Garriver and holder of their council seat."

The Calamitys are the newest family to make predictions of the future for the upper echelon of Garriver. Fortune magic has made a recent comeback due to the recession that has swept the nation for the past few years. Their rise to power was indeed serendipitous, as several old families specializing in fortune-telling found themselves penniless and in incredible amounts of debt for their inability to predict the economic downfall, leaving a power vacuum for the Calamity mages to swoop in and take advantage of. Nowadays, their work is used by Wall Street, the queen, and occasionally the princess of Mississippi.

Reginald brings his eyes up to Ivan behind her. His face tightens for just a moment, so quick she believes she imagines it, before loosening again. "I don't believe we've met."

Ivan bows to him. "Ivan Gray."

"Of the old family?"

"The very same," Ivan says. His voice is static, switching to match the other man's tone so seamlessly that she wouldn't know he argued with the doorman moments ago if she hadn't been there herself.

Reginald eyes him with clear interest. "I'd heard rumors the most recent heir had run away from home."

"Old family gossip mills do get imaginative when they're bored." Ivan laughs, a charming laugh that sounds nothing like the snickers and cackles she's grown used to. "You'll get used to sorting out fact from fiction with time."

Reginald laughs, too, in that "I own a boat and you don't" pitch, and Elaine chuckles nervously to blend in.

"Thank you for this invite," she interjects. "I'm grateful to be able to meet so many new people."

His purple eyes turn back to her, and he nods. "Of course. We were quite impressed with your display at the showcase."

She feels a draft at her back and turns to see that Ivan has used this change in topic as an opportunity to escape. She continues to converse with Reginald, but her mind stays on the luck mage. He slipped into the role of a pompous asshole quite easily, and it seems like the Gray name carries some weight within powerful circles.

The conversation feels more daunting now that he's left her

alone, and she finds her eyes drifting from Reginald and around the ballroom, searching for his scrappy cloak. It's nerve wracking having him out of her sight, especially when he never told her why he was here.

She searches for him in the crowd, but all she sees are glittering gowns and suits, and defeated, she settles back into focusing on the conversation in front of her, hoping he doesn't do anything that will get her into any real trouble.

Ivan is about to do much worse than steal some bread. His plans lean more towards mischief than mayhem, but it's still not "lawful" in any sense of the word. Catching Lainey on her way in had eliminated his biggest obstacle—getting in. He'd had no luck so far breaking into the school dungeon, but a solstice offers a weakness in magical barriers that won't be available again until the spring.

He moves into the crowd, looking for any sort of carvings in the wall that would denote an entrance. There are rumors there are dozens hidden in Locke, and all led to the all-powerful fairy ring at its center. His feet move towards the other end of the room, instinct pulling him to where there's an electrical switch box. He opens it, and huffs in dismay when he doesn't see any sign of magic, that pull now tugging him back in the direction he came from. His instincts are on the fritz, and they're usually never this crossed. His eyes are naturally drawn to Lainey, who grimaces as she speaks to the blonde woman standing next to that space mage. He itches to go back to her and make sure she's okay.

Focus on the mission, he scolds himself. He's able to look away for a few seconds before he can't help but steal another glance at her pretty visage.

Since the bounty hunter incident, he'd been increasingly

worried about her safety. The whole mess is his fault, and now every time he leaves her alone, he can't help but think that the worst will happen to her. To quell his anxious heart, he decides to just be around, always. The TA work is a great way to search for the dungeon *and* keep an eye on his most protégée. Two birds, one stone.

The longer he stares at her, the more his nerves calm, shoulders loosening and fists unclenching, and his mind is able to focus on the reason he's here. Even if he doesn't tell her the whole truth, even if he doesn't stay out of trouble, if he can keep her trust, everything will be okay.

His gaze drifts back to the electrical box in front of him, concentrating on why his luck brought him here. There are no markings on it other than the name of an electrical company, and he's about to start cutting wires when his eyes trail up the wall, following the wires up and into the ceiling. There, the sconce has an odd, crest-like shape, shining light down oddly onto the chandelier.

"Bingo."

SHE'S FUMBLING THIS CONVERSATION.

It was all going fine, then a woman with silky blonde hair joined Reginald during the conversation, clutching his arm in a clear show of ownership. Which is fine by her. She does not want this man, but there's no way to make that clear in a way that would be appropriate in an academic setting. So, she politely endures the conversation as the woman, Ruby, falsely assumes Elaine wants Reginald carnally.

"What's your affinity?" Ruby asks, nails making indents in the white of Calamity's cloak.

"Probability magic."

Ruby's eyes lose most of their interest, going to inspect the red polish of her manicure.

Reginald smiles politely. "I was intrigued by your ability. Most of our history states that probability has incredibly low rates of practical use, and yet, here you are."

"Here I am," Elaine says.

She opens her mouth to say something else, perhaps something he'd like to hear from a future salaried employee but is instead interrupted by a couple who Reginald and Ruby are decidedly more excited to see.

There's a half minute of her staring wide-eyed and bobbing her head up and down like an idiot before they turn back to her. She wishes she'd left while they were distracted when there was a noticeable silence between the three of them.

"Do you know where Gray wandered off to?" Reginald asks.

"No."

"Mm."

Abort, she thinks.

The woman's eyes flash to her cloak, a smile lighting her face. "My, what a unique cloak."

"It's school issued."

The woman pets her own cape, elbow-length and studded with diamonds. "I find the newest capes available at seamstresses to be more suited to my tastes."

Elaine wishes Ivan was here, someone interesting and able to hold a conversation about something that isn't completely banal.

Something behind Ruby catches her eye. It's the problem consuming her thoughts, sliding down the pole of a chandelier in the middle of the crowded ballroom, everyone dancing below blissfully ignorant of his presence. She gasps before she can stop herself, hands coming up to her mouth.

The couple in front of her looks confused and begins to turn to see what's shocked her.

"The magic in your cloak is weak," Elaine blurts, trying to distract them. "Were anyone to come at you with ill intent, you'd be a goner. I've barely lived in this city for four months, and it's already tried to eat me alive."

Ruby's eyes narrow into a glare, clutching Reginald's arm tighter. "Are you threatening me?"

"Hah!" Elaine laughs but chokes when she realizes that Ruby *isn't* laughing.

Behind them, Ivan unscrews a lightbulb and tucks it into his cloak.

"No. It's a fact. You—"

"Thank you, Elaine, but I'm afraid we must head off." Reginald cuts in and wraps an arm more firmly around his date's waist. They look at her with caution, and she wants to scream that it's his precious Ivan Gray hanging like a bat, not her. But that would cause chaos. Reginald is only one of the many people who could help her get a job, and Ivan dangling from the ceiling is so much worse for her reputation than a few stolen trays of crostini.

She excuses herself and walks away from the couple, eyeing Ivan hanging precariously above the ballroom.

Ivan catches her eye and blows her a kiss.

"You bastard," she mouths to him, which only prompts more silent displays of affection.

Frustrated, she turns to the champagne tower, sees a flash of yellow numbers, grabs a glass, and keeps walking.

There's silence behind her, one thick with the intent to gossip about her as soon as she's out of earshot. She's not interested in hearing whatever half-baked comments they have about her clothes or her off-putting nature.

"Elaine!" Reginald calls out.

She turns. He's not quite running, but he's not taking his time.

"I apologize. Ruby can be protective of my attention." He

smiles, like they're sharing an inside joke. "And it'd be a shame to burn a bridge with a woman who can pull a glass from the middle of a tower without it coming crashing down."

"What?" She looks behind him to see that she had taken a champagne glass from a corner, but the structure still stood. Her eyes flick back to Ivan, who is now climbing back up the chandelier and to the side of the ballroom. "Oh, yes. Water under the bridge."

"Well, she'd love to apologize to you. If you'd let her."

She notices Calamity puts all the blame on his date and feels a sudden, undeserved protectiveness over Ruby. She wants to call him a coward and ask him why he didn't say anything before, but Ivan's started swinging back and forth, making the crystals of the chandelier ring like windchimes.

"Thank you, Mr. Calamity. But it's been a long night." Her feet stop and turn when she thinks better of going home without a single career prospect. "I'd enjoy talking to you another time. Send word to the watchtower along the river, and I'll tell you why you should hire a probability mage."

She takes off before he can say another word. Ivan is now scaling down a large pillar, a few dozen feet from the floor. People notice, and one woman cries out "He's going to jump!"

Ivan looks up and has the nerve to look surprised. "Oh, don't mind me. Can't believe how hard it is to be an electrician in a place where half the rooms are closed until cosmic intervention."

Elaine corners Ivan just as his feet touch the floor and yanks him by the cloak, causing his pockets to clank quite conspicuously.

"What a bust. It was just a sconce after all," he whispers to her. His dull eyes sparkle anew when he sees her glass of champagne.

She glares when she sees where his attention has been

drawn. “This glass is the only thing standing between you and my fist.”

He makes a grab for it, but she pulls it back. She can feel the eyes of the entire room on the two of them as she keeps the champagne out of his grasp, but she refuses to let him take it from her, even as it orchestrates an antagonistic dance show for every Constellation guest.

“You’re no fun.”

“You need to leave.”

They both turn when the guard from the front door speaks, having come over during their spat. He stands in front of them with his arms crossed.

The walk home is mostly silent. She rubs her chilly shoulders, walking at a breakneck pace.

Ivan is forced to speed up from his usual meandering, nervously chittering to drown out her fuming silence. “I think I found some clues for something I’m working on. Isn’t that great?”

She walks a little faster, ignoring his attempt at conversation. He holds out a hand, her silver pin resting in his palm. She snatches it back and continues to ignore him.

“C’mon, Lainey. I’m sorry I ruined your night, I really am.”

“This wasn’t just a training session, Ivan. This is my future.”

He can gallivant around, getting kicked out of events all he wants, but she still has people she needs to impress, and she isn’t strong enough on her own to have the reputation that Ivan does that lands him his jobs. So, yes, she’s mad at him.

“It’s more than the ceiling, Ive. I’m not strong like you. I don’t come from an old family, and I don’t have a backup plan. If I fail at this, I have to go back home to the mountains.”

He shakes his head. “We’re different, Elaine. We don’t need accolades or achievements. We have luck on our side.”

“*You* have luck on your side.” She points an accusing finger at him. “I am a late bloomer, trying desperately to catch up.

Reginald probably thinks I'm insane because I was trying to keep them from turning around and seeing you hanging from the chandelier. He might have offered me a job."

He looks guilty, then frustrated, then guilty once more, sighing with his whole chest. "I'll talk to that Calamity guy. The new players in the game always want to get a hold of the old families. Maybe get you…a meeting. I'unno."

She looks at him for the first time since they left campus. Almost shyly, she says, "really?"

His eyes soften. His hand cups her cheeks, rubbing his thumb fondly across her skin. His eyes linger on her lips, then they look back up at her. His pupils dilate, presumably because of the dim lantern-light on the street, and he appears to be in deep thought.

"Anything to make you happy." He stands up straighter, seeming to come to terms with whatever he was thinking about, and grabs her hand in his, holding it the rest of the way home. "Tell me what you want, and you'll have it, Lainey baby."

She tightens her hold on his hand.

"Lainey baby." He takes a warning tone. "Tell me what you want."

He looks back at her when she stops walking, one eyebrow raised in inquiry.

She shakes her head. "It's nothing," she says. "You just reminded me of a ghost." She picks up the pace again, and he follows her all the way home.

SHE HASN'T BEEN LEAVING the house for the past week unless necessary, as the guilt of leaving Roger now that he's fallen ill is too much to bear. Today she braided her hair up into a loose, romantic crown, and wears a long lavender gown that cinches just below her bust before flowing the rest of the way down.

She put the salmon pins along her braid, head to tail, to give the illusion of them swimming in a constant loop.

Her original plan had been to go to the market to pick up ingredients for a pumpkin soup. It was definitely winter, so she put long johns underneath the thin sheath of her dress to protect her from the bone-chilling winds, already anticipating curling up in the living room with a book and a cup of tea after her soup begins to simmer. Then, Roger, who has noticeably lost some weight, sighed heavily from the throw pillow, and she immediately changed plans.

She brushes cracker dust off her dress, munching on a last-minute meal of salami and saltines with fig jam. Her rat is curled up along the nape of her neck, taking his fourth nap of the day. He sighs deeply, his warm furry body melting into her shoulders as she sits on a stool at the kitchen table.

She writes to her mom by candlelight. It's been too long, and she knows prolonging it will only make it harder.

Dear Mom,

I hope you're doing well. School has been off to an interesting start. The city is strange, but I haven't decided if that's a good or bad thing yet. My professor is lazy, but harmless.

SHE WONDERS if she should tell her about the discoveries she's made about her own magic. She bites her lip and decides to keep it close to her chest. She hasn't kept a secret from her parents since her siblings moved out and on to the next steps of their lives.

I'VE BEEN WORKING with a really talented TA. I haven't been able to find as much time for math as I'm used to. Uncle Neil has been great. He took me to see a giant monarch migration, and the international conservancy brought along one of their teams. I'd never seen such powerful lightning magic in my life!

I do miss home. It's never quiet here, and it feels like my mind will never get the chance to be, either. I miss the river, the simple days, and the deep black nights. But overall, I know this was the right decision. It's like looking at the world for the first time all over again. I am grateful, but it feels as though I left some of myself with you.

Tell Dad I say hi, if he's around.

With Love,

Elaine

She moves to the windowsill. Roger puffs air against the nape of her neck. Garriver's evenings are kept bright by the lights of apartments and skyscrapers rather than stars, creating a multicolored light show from their windows and lampposts. Unlike the sky, the variation in existence and distance between these light sources changes the view as people leave their offices and return home. She opens the window just a crack, letting the crisp sounds and air come through clearly. She takes a deep breath in, basking in the breeze. Roger is not a fan and skitters off to her bed when the breeze grows too cold for him.

Her favorite window lights up around 5:30 p.m. on Saturday nights with a kaleidoscope of explosions from what she can only assume is a potioneer. It's the wildest window in her view, and she can see it best from her bedroom in the watchtower. The mage stops working around 6:15 every night, and a fluorescent overhead light comes on until 6:30 when the lights go out, and she has to wait for the next show.

She considers writing to her father, but that thought is quickly brushed aside. A lack of response from him would do something nasty to her heart.

"You'd write to me, wouldn't you, Roger?"

He huffs. She returns to the bed and lays beside him.

Uncle Neil's work trip is taking far longer than she expected. She tries to reset his customized pest control spell on her own with very little success, evident because there are spiders in the kitchen again. Roger hunted them before he fell ill, and now they're weaving homes in the back cupboards she can't reach.

She sits up and scoots to the foot of her bed, pulling on a pair of socks before slipping into her house shoes. She heads down to the empty first floor, her steps echoing loudly as she checks the latches on all the windows and doors. She locks the door to her bedroom, then unlocks and locks it again, just in case.

ELAINE SAVORS A SIP of her tea as she reads the morning paper. Again, she sits at the kitchen table, a soft morning glow casting an irritating glare over her eyes. Roger lays in a basket of towels next to her, having been carefully wrapped like a burrito in a plaid red and white towel, still enjoying dreamland.

LOCAL SOCIALITES SUCKED DRY IN THEIR OWN HOMES

Garriver police are investigating a string of murders affecting the Abraham Parks District. Rumors state the victims are found in near-mummified states, sucked dry of all bodily fluids, a state most commonly found after vampire attacks. The police chief did not respond to requests for comment.

SHE SHAKES HER HEAD. Vampire attacks are nasty business. Still, they usually keep out of the USA, and favor the more sparsely populated Transylvania. Most tend to leave a symbol on the homes of their victims to signify to other vampires that the hunting ground is already claimed, which makes it all the more strange that this one didn't. It's possible the police are hiding it from reporters, she supposes.

Her eyes go to the dwarven runes carved into the doorway. She'd realized Neil was part dwarf after she'd accidentally stumbled upon a book collection in his room. She'd thumbed through *Dwarf Magic* and learned that, along with being a mostly reclusive species, their magic also only works if one has dwarven blood. When she realized that was the reason he never taught her how to carve them herself, it softened the blow. Her paternal grandmother had been a serious woman. Her father and uncle told stories of early bedtimes and a suspicion of anyone new in town. That's what had made her affair with a dwarf, nomadic and secretive, such a shock.

Her mind goes back to her father, who fell in love with a woman who, later, unbeknownst to him, had an illegitimate child of her own. Was he drawn to them, women with secrets? He could hardly blame Elaine if that was the case. He could also bother to write, but that was neither here nor there.

She twirls in the barstool, bored. It's too cold to go outside, and the street is covered with a thick sheet of ice instead of deep snow. She ends up spending the day cleaning everything once, then reading a book, then cleaning it all again. She takes Roger's temperature, which has been steadily declining for the last two weeks. Then she gets in bed only an hour after the sun sets, having done an intense skincare routine.

When Ivan climbs through her window again, it's with the same newspaper she'd been reading in hand.

"Midnight training session. Put on your—" He stops, eyes trained on her short, semi-translucent nightgown.

She throws a blanket at his face. "Turn away, pervert."

He grumbles and settles on the edge of the windowsill, blanket untouched.

"Alright, you can look."

When he turns, she's wearing a black gown with lace at the bottom edges, long sleeves, and a high neck.

"What do you see in that photo?"

She scans the article for some clue, but all she sees is one of the women attacked and her large, empty house. "A tragedy."

Ivan tuts. "And opportunity. The woman who died was a great collector, and a lot of people are looking to nab some stuff from her cold, shriveled hands. I happen to be the greatest sticky fingers this side of the river. One tragic MILF's trash is our treasure."

She frowns at the newspaper. Learning how to use magic is what she's here for, and jobs are where Ivan's luck is at its peak. But to steal from the dead?

"I don't know, Ivan."

"Oh, come on. If we don't do it, someone else will. At least we won't destroy her house."

"Seems like a waste of time," her eyes drift back to the paper. She scowls when his hand pushes the paper down to look her in the eyes.

"We had fun at Shark Tank, didn't we? This is like that, but with more adventure."

Her eyes drift to the op-ed in the corner about the ethics of necromancy.

"I'll give you a cut of the reward," he bargains.

Elaine puts down the paper. She looks him up and down. "How much?"

"Fifteen percent."

"Thirty-five."

"Twenty."

"Deal."

She shakes his hand, before getting up to grab her cloak. She clasps it around her neck all while moving to the window, peering at the steep drop below. At this time of night, there's only darkness below. "How do you get up here every time anyways?"

"Faith, trust, and a little pixie dust laced into my aglets. Now come *on*, or they're going to clear the scene before we get there."

"Fine, but I'm bringing Roger. He needs some fresh air."

The rat grunts but doesn't fight her as he's stowed into the inner pocket of her cloak.

THEY TRAVEL by a boat docked along the river next to the watchtower, Ivan rowing. He ropes the boat just under a bridge. Ivan tosses a solid gold coin at the troll, bright orange, beard dragging along behind him.

"Come back before midnight, or my price doubles," the troll warns.

Elaine and Ivan climb up the unpaved hill.

"The police put wards up around the house," Ivan says. He pulls out another gold coin. "We'll have fifteen minutes. Keep your eyes out for an emerald-green cat statue."

The brick house in front of them is decrepit. There is ivy permeating and crumbling the brick, and there's a weathered "44" across the front, rusted over.

"A socialite lived here?" Elaine scoffs. It sits in stark contrast with the rest of the block: all clean bricks and well-lit entryways.

Ivan doesn't respond. He's frowning and looking over the eroded foundation, eyes calculating. He takes a step closer, hand touching hers. "Stay close to me. I don't like this."

"A trap?"

Fear flashes through his eyes, but he stands straighter, stepping back to stand next to Elaine, rather than in front of her. He takes his umbrella-shaped sunglasses off, slipping them into the breast pocket of his shirt. "If it is, we can get out of it. Now come on, we've got twelve minutes."

With the police's overconfidence in their wards, they'd left the front door unlocked.

The place is a lot larger than they originally thought, most certainly due to a room expansion ward. The first floor extends forward almost 100 feet more than the outside. It's as grand as it is disgusting. The wood is termite-filled, and the smell of mold seeps in the air, making Elaine's head spin. The woman who died here must have been living like this for years, as it's impossible for this level of rot to form over such a short time. She walks forward into a cobweb and bats it away with frantic hands, screwing her mouth shut to make sure none of it gets in her mouth. She's overcome with the desire to steam and press her cloak until it's free of wrinkles, free of anything that could ever lead to a home like this.

"Stay inside the cloak Roger. The floor's rotted, and I don't want you falling through."

The rodent inside her cloak shuffles around in her pocket before becoming still again.

"Stars, this place looks like...change of plan." His eyes flit, calculating. "Take the first floor. The damage will be lighter. I'll take the top." He doesn't give her time to disagree, and his footsteps are barely heard over the groaning of the stairs.

The magic in the air grips her senses. "A cat," she has to remind herself what she's looking for. "An emerald cat statue."

She tests the floor before stepping on it. Overhead, she can hear Ivan moving quickly across the floorboards. She huffs and —pridefully—steps faster, channeling that feeling of nausea into probability.

"Cat," she chants. "Cat. I'm going to find a cat."

"No!" There's a quick snap of wood as Ivan's foot shoots down through the floorboards above Elaine's head. At the same moment she hears rhythmic clanging, like porcelain teacups rattling across the floor away from her head, and towards the staircase. Her head whips towards the sound. She breathes in at the same time, and gags at the smell that overtakes her senses. That moldy magic sits in the air, polluting her lungs and touching a memory in her brain she can't quite recall. She breathes in again, and as terrible as it hurts, this time it feels as though she's about to remember where it comes from.

"Meow."

She turns to see a green cat running down the stairs, and she moves forward to intercept it. The feline is smooth, its muscled edges look sculpted out of marble, and as it runs, she realizes it's the source of the sounds of glass bouncing. Elaine stands at the bottom of the staircase, fifteen feet between the cat statue bolting down the stairs and the probability mage blocking the front door.

"Close the door!" Ivan yells.

She whips her head back to the entrance, which is a mistake. The cat's feet land heavy on her head. She tumbles backwards, and the cat's momentous push off her skull and towards its freedom forces her backwards. Her back meets the floorboards with a sickening squelch, and wood collapses wetly around her body, sucking her slightly into the foundation of the house.

Ivan tumbles down the stairs, halting when he sees her stuck to the ground. "Are you alright?" When she groans, he takes that as confirmation and jumps over her prone form. "Five minutes!"

She pushes herself upwards, squeezing her eyes shut when she feels something crush under her hands. A sticky brown liquid covers her palms. She shudders and pulls herself the rest of the way upwards, wiping her hand along the walls. She doesn't close the front door behind her, instead using it to wipe the rest of the residue off her palms.

Ivan's past the barrier, and Elaine picks up the coin Ivan

dropped before as she crosses it. Hopefully, the police won't be able to detect their work. She sees him running after the tiny green blur down the wide, well-lit road.

With a wild dive, he reaches out and grabs for the cat. There's a moment of struggle, and Elaine's heart is in her throat. What if he broke it? His arms shoot up in triumph, a hissing cat in hand. She whoops in glee, jogging the rest of the way towards him.

"Client could've mentioned it was charmed," he pants. "But we got him."

The cat tries to whack Ivan with his paw, but he holds it further out from his body.

He leans to the side to smile at Elaine. "Next stop, the morgue!"

"The morgue?"

He doesn't answer, gleefully carrying the cat to their next destination.

They get back to the boat, and the troll grunts. He eyes the moon and snarls. "Back already?"

Ivan waves him away, motioning with the cat still in hand for Elaine to get in the boat first. He holds out the cat. "Take this. I'll get us to the client before sunrise."

She holds out her hands, and the cat shrinks away, ears flat.

Ivan grins wider. "Perfect. He's afraid of you. Now let's get—"

The cat shatters as soon as it touches her hands. It breaks again when the remains hit the floor of the boat, and it echoes over and over against the troll bridge ceiling overhead. Ivan's eyes flit around, looking for someone else, something else to blame.

"I don't understand. Did I...?" His eyes turn to her. His eyes widen in the effort to keep emotion off his face. "Did you grab the coin?"

She cringes, flashing him a nervous smile. “Yes?”

He tugs his hands through his hair. “Lainey.”

Oh.

“Elaine.”

Oh, he’s *angry*.

17

DOCTORS ARE THIEVES AND LIARS, TOO

The only thing audible is the wet *plap* of the paddles on the surface of the water. Her eyes avoid the shards of the broken cat and Ivan by trying to find the night's hidden horizon line. If she looks hard enough, it will appear, surely.

"This job was *really* important. You shouldn't have touched the coin."

"You never told me," she says.

"Do you not remember what happened the last time?"

"Oh, you mean when you got my toe amputated?" she snaps. "I remember."

He cringes. "Alright. I didn't think someone who was thinking would forget! It destabilized the runes of the house, Lainey! Why—"

"The police! I thought the police would find it suspicious."

Silence. He turns and rows the boat towards their next destination. His rhythm is aggressive and choppy, water splashing onto her legs each time the paddle slaps the surface. The landscape shifts from lines of brick townhomes to empty parking lots, with bursts of wild grass interspersed between them. Ivan is rowing them away from the residential buildings and towards the business sector.

The boat inclines, the river dipping not into another layer, but rather land on the precipice of one. There are a few places like this in Garriver, so close to major entrances to the undercity that the land is near-impossible to sell or rent, save for a few businesses already associated with the unsavory. Businesses that open up here are those that need low rent, easy access to the river, or frequent trips to multiple layers of the city.

Many of these businesses must be able to survive a reputation of being on "cursed land." Between our two earths, there are many similarities in culture and language. One phrase that's come to be common in both is "the only things guaranteed in life are death, and taxes." The usual suspects are businesses of death, terminal illness, and elder care on these parcels of land.

In front of her, she can read the signs lit up by streetlamps. House of Hope Assisted Living, Custom Tombs and Custard Emporium, and Nygard's Mortuary and Accounting. In smaller script, a sun-dried tagline reads "Fifty percent off for upper and lower torsos, respectively."

The building Ivan docks in front of is tiled in dark-green ceramic bricks. It's low to the ground, circular, and the size of a small house. Quietly, Ivan starts to gather the remains of the cat in his hands.

Filled with the overwhelming need to do something, to fix *anything*, Elaine bends down and picks up some pieces.

"I'll do it," he says.

She places them in his hands. He does not thank her.

When they enter, they find themselves within the fluorescent hallway of an office space reminiscent of Uncle Neil's but dated and with a staleness to the air. The ceilings seem shorter than they should be, and the walls closer together. An uncanny feeling settles in Elaine's gut, but she's not sure what's setting her off in a building she's never entered before. She takes a step closer to a stone-faced Ivan.

"Ivan," she says. "What is this place?"

"The office of the dead woman's daughters. Sit here while I go check in. Don't get caught up in anything while I'm gone."

The miserable put in her stomach grows larger. "Right."

She's hurt he doesn't bring her. It's hard enough making a mistake, but surely this office building is somewhere she's more useful than he is. Less mortal danger, more social cues.

Ivan goes up to the front desk. The receptionist is a nervous looking fellow who sighs in relief when he finds his name is indeed on his list before guiding him towards the elevators.

The feeling of being discarded leaves a sour, fuzzy taste on her tongue. Her father abandoned her for a mistake that wasn't even her own. Would Ivan do the same? It would accurately reflect the path her life is going down, at least. She squirms in the hardback oak chair. Yes, she can see it now! Ivan's cold face as he makes sure she gets home, sweeps off into the night, decision made that he's better off without her. It feels highly probable.

Abandonment—?

She shoots out from her chair, overtaken with adrenaline. The chair rocks back into the blank waiting room wall, startling her fellow abandon-ees. But she's not a waiter anymore. She's a probability mage whose every action can be bent in her favor (hypothetically).

She struts to the desk with a faux confidence, the fish on her cloak giving away her true nerves with their frantic swimming. The secretary eyes her from his hunched over seat, sweaty fingers clicking rapidly over the keyboard. Up close, she can see how the stress wears on every physical facet of his form. His brown eyes sag, his ears are stretched from tugging, and his suit is two sizes too small—but to be fair, so is his body.

"I need to join my colleague upstairs," she says.

His fingers twitch, tugging at a piece of hair. "Do you have an appointment?" He flinches away from her before she even answers.

"Yes," she says it slowly, as if she hasn't decided on the answer.

His shoulder sag in relief. "Name?"

She'll give him a fake one. "Aquae." Oh. Alright, no problem. She'll pivot and give him a fake first name.

"Elaine?"

Her heartbeat quickens. How did he know her name? Her head swivels across the lobby for a threat, but it's still just quiet businessmen, one who has fully fallen asleep in that uncomfortable chair, which is a feat in and of itself.

"Yes."

His shoulders sag further in relief, and now she's sure she hasn't met him before. In Garriver, the only things she's been associated with are theft and her ornery uncle. Nothing relaxing about that.

"You're slotted as our summer intern."

That's why Nygard is such a familiar name: *Dr., Doc and Nygard PhD's Accounting LLC*. It didn't match the signage outside, but this was certainly the accounting firm she'd accepted an internship with. She'd applied to work with them months ago; what business could they have with a shady character like Ivan? She straightens her posture, knocking the tips of her shoes against the floor to get rid of dust still clinging to the tops of them.

"Yes, that's me. I wanted to see if I could tour the office before I begin?"

Now he looks at her strangely. "I thought you wanted to meet up with your colleague."

"Well—yes. But I was hoping to get the tour first, of course. Two birds, one stone."

The secretary looks harried again, shushing her. "No jokes about animal harm around here. You'll get me put on a PIP." Whatever good fortune he had towards her is replaced by derision, slow brown eyes sweeping up and down her. "And aren't you too old to be an intern?"

Elaine stands up straighter, taking full advantage of her willowy form to stand high above this secretary. "I am exactly on time for my own life," she sneers. "Are you going to let me up, or not?"

The secretary leans over to push the P.A. button. Questions loom on his face, but he responds to derision like Arap, Biakal, Bek, Nord, Norka, Rex, Druzhok, Jack, Sokol, Sultan, Rosa, Lis, Toy, Zmei, and Max Pavlov slobber at the ring of a bell. "Dr. Nygard, there's a summer intern requesting a tour today. Yes. Yes, alright. I'll send her down." There's a strange screeching through the speaker, and the secretary sits up straighter. "Thank you for pointing out my posture, Dr. I'll work on it further."

He leaves her at the elevators, which only have a button pointing down.

"There's no upper floors?"

"All the elevators fritz when we tried to install them to go up. The upper floors require you to take the stairway. But you won't need to go there." The steel silver doors open, and she steps inside. He leans over and presses a button reading "2B", before stepping out. The elevator doors ding shut, leaving her alone in a box with faded blue carpet and fuzzy speakers playing the same saxophone solo, over, and over.

Now, in the long trip down this elevator, she plays the events of the night over and over in her head. Logically, she did nothing wrong. The whiplash of his emotions is irrational. He came into *her* home, brought her to a crime scene, and made her steal from a dead woman that definitely would not have appreciated their presence. If he wants to be difficult, that's fine. She can be difficult too.

Her eyes feel heavy and blurry to the point where she can't see her fingers in front of her. She presses a hand against her cheek, and the tears fall unbidden from her eyes. She laughs, but it doesn't stop the tears from streaming, and no matter what expression she pulls, she can't stop their flow down her cheekbones, each new tear easily following the path the previous tears forged down her cheeks.

Let them fall, she thinks, picturing the headlines. *"Elaine Aquae, Conveniently Dehydrated to Death Inside an Elevator."*

The ding of an elevator pulls her out of her stupor.

"Are you alright?" a voice calls out. A woman appears in front of Elaine, wearing a pastel pink coat and a spiky silver crown around her forehead. Elaine pretends to scratch her nose as she wipes her tears away from her eyes.

"Yes. I'm looking for a Dr. Nygard?"

"That's me." She nods. "I do hope you weren't waiting too long. Nygard has a habit of hiding from new guests."

A bit odd, referring to herself in the third person. The woman's voice is in a register too low, vocal fry clear in every word she pronounces. "I was hoping to get a tour before my internship starts next summer."

"Right. Come along, then. We usually request notice ahead of time, but the company's in mourning right now."

"I heard someone passed, recently."

"Yes, my mother," she sighs. "It's a terrible shame, but we've stored her in the mortuary wing for now. Fresh as a daisy."

"Is that normal?" The Aquae burn bodies as quickly as possible, and then celebrate their lives with a week-long feast.

"The Nygard family has a penchant for preservation of dead things. But that's all a bit too serious for your first tour," Dr. Nygard chirps. She spins on her heel, waving Elaine to follow.

"You'll see the main floor where our accountants work soon, but first I want to show you the water room."

Dr. swings open the door to her left, to reveal a stark white room, paler underneath the fluorescent lights above. There's a slight buzzing through the room that could be coming from any of the old devices littering the world. Everything looks a little too old to be useful—a cooler with a leaky faucet, a toaster that smells burnt even from across the room, and a table that, as she approaches it, is wobbling on just two legs. The other two look torn and bitten by something very angry.

"This is where our hardworking Nynauts—that's what we call our employees—get the job done."

"'Because we go where no firm has gone before,'" Elaine quotes.

Dr. raises her eyebrows. "So, you've studied up. I knew you were sharp from your application, Elaine."

Elaine smiles. "I like to know everything I can about a company before joining it."

Dr. Nygard shows her other equally dull rooms in the 2B office floor. Most notable is the breastfeeding closet. Not because it was updated and top of the line, but because a woman shrieks when the door swings open to her boss and the almost-intern coming in.

"Oops," Dr. laughs. She shuts the door and moves on, and Elaine quickly follows, red in the face.

"Does that happen often?"

"Yes, the lock is a bit finicky. I'm sure you noticed how everything here is antique."

Dated and on its last leg more like, Elaine thinks.

"The Nygard family's love for preservation is hereditary. When my mother's mother died, she cursed this place by making it so no equipment can be no younger than thirty years old. The dust adds to the air of seriousness required in an accounting firm, don't you think?"

She knows she should be concerned with finding Ivan and getting out of here in one piece, but all Elaine can think about is how desperately she doesn't want to work here. Every other desk is empty, there's a new mother that already despises her, most likely, and she will never hear the end of it from Ivan about how right he is about corporate.

"It's certainly blown my expectations out of the water."

Dr. Nygard claps. "Oh, wonderful. I'll have to introduce you to my sister, Doc. A true woman of the shadows, but she should be around here somewhere."

"While we're looking, I saw my T.A. when I came in. I wanted to go over some homework I have coming up before I leave. Any chance you'd know where Ivan Gray is?"

Dr.'s shoulders tighten up, and it puts Elaine on high alert again.

"He's meeting with HR. Better to wrap up the tour here and see him during your next class."

She begins to usher Elaine out of the office and towards the elevators.

In a panic, she shouts out, "what about the paperwork?"

"What paperwork?" Dr. crosses her arms.

The doors are getting closer.

"For the internship. I need to fill out the liability wavers. It's why I came." A lie. But a good one.

Dr's face relaxes. "Right. I'll bring you back to the front desk."

"I'd love to tour the office again. Get a feel for it."

Dr's finger taps against her elbow. "You're not allowed down here alone. It's very easy to get stuck here."

"I'll be quick," Elaine says.

There's a beep from Dr.'s pager. She lifts it up and rolls her eyes. "It'll certainly be a *long* time before you see your T.A. again. Go ahead and take a look around, I have to take care of something."

Her heels clack as she walks off, leaving Elaine alone. She peeks her head back into the break room, where three pallid accountants stand clustered around the lukewarm water jug.

"Do any of you know how to get to HR?"

Only one turns her head to look at Elaine. She's wearing a gray pin stripe suit, and her eyes seem on the verge of never opening again every time she takes a languorous blink.

"It's like her eyes are on the verge of death," Elaine mutters to Roger.

"Hm?"

"I asked if you knew where HR is?"

The string-haired woman looks through Elaine as she speaks. "Oh, you don't want to go there. People disappear for weeks at a time in the HR Department."

"There's some paperwork there for me." Elaine tries to keep speaking, but the woman's already turned back to stare at the water cooler with the rest of her coworkers. They all chuckle when a few air bubbles float up from the bottom of the jug.

At the same moment there's a rustling from the inside of her cloak. She pulls back to see Roger's nose peeking out from her breast pocket.

"Any chance you know how to get there, Roger? You've got a good nose, don't you?"

Roger squeaks in her cloak but doesn't offer any solutions. Elaine returns to the main office, but everyone she tries to talk to is entirely unhelpful. She has learned one thing: she should not be trying to find her way into HR. Yet here she goes, all for a very difficult man who told her to stay put. She circles the final corner of the office and sees what she was looking for: a door labeled 'HR'. She strides towards it, yanks on the door, and it doesn't budge. She wiggles, turns, and twists it every way, but the door stays firmly shut. Her eyes catch on a smaller ledger beneath the original sign that states 'locked for employee safety. See Nygard or Administrative Assistant for entry."

"He better be grateful for this," she mutters, heading back down to the lobby. "'Trust your instincts', he says. You know where that's gotten him, Roger? Into imminent danger, all alone."

The elevator doors open with a ding and she's back in the lobby. She strolls up to the secretary, whose clicking pen echoes loudly in the deathly quiet office space.

"You have to let me into HR."

He startles and shoots up out of his chair. When he sees it's just Elaine, he huffs. Sitting back down and returning to the papers in front of him, he says, "I don't have to do anything."

"I have paperwork to fill out."

"The Nygards didn't approve any paperwork to be filed. HR is off-limits to guests and employees under a certain title. A not-yet intern doesn't meet that standard."

Her magic flares up uncomfortably in her gut. Something terrible is going to happen in HR, she can feel it. Ivan will have to face it all alone.

She raises her voice, startling the other in the waiting room. "You will let me into HR, and you will let me in now."

His eyes flash in annoyance. "You want to go to HR so bad? Fine. I'm starting to think you deserve this."

He gets up and walks through the hallway behind his desk. Elaine follows, heart hammering in her chest. Roger still lays hidden in the inner pocket of her cloak, but she can feel him rigid and alert against her arm. The secretary comes to a halt at a dead end in the hallway. He moves to the side and pulls a key from his lanyard. He points to the ground.

"Stand here."

His key, old and ornate, sinks into a hidden compartment in the wall, and sticks with a solid *thunk*. She turns to the blank wall in front of her, ready to face the HR department ahead. Her stomach falls into her throat when she plummets downwards, and she clutches Roger tight against her within her cloak.

"See ya never, intern," the secretary hoots, his laughter echoing as she falls further and further downwards, into the HR Department.

Elaine gets a migraine, and then an explosion of letters and numbers swarm her vision. The odds are passing by too quick for her to read as the cracks and rivets of the cavern walls move by in a blur. Opportunities like *grab here* or *kick off here* pass through her hands like smoke.

But the ground is always going to be there, she thinks.

She looks downwards at the fast-approaching cavern floor.

Land Safely—2%

I need a miracle.

Something new comes into vision. A shadow appears, standing right where she's about to land. She wants to shout at them to get out of the way, but all that comes out is a guttural cry of anguish. Instead of immense pain, she feels the air around her change—and for a moment, she's light as a feather. She swears her hair isn't whipping through the wind but floating with it.

She lands with a solid thump into a pair of strong, familiar arms.

"I told you to wait, Lainey."

She gasps for air, nearly smiling at the luck of Ivan being the one to catch her when she falls. But she remembers that he's mad at her, and she's a bit mad at him too, and decides to argue instead.

"You—I had—knew you were in—danger."

He smiles for a moment, but it quickly turns back to a frown. "I told you to leave me to finish this alone."

"My magic was freaking out. You said it wouldn't take long, and it's nearly been an hour."

"Well, my magic was acting up too!"

"What was wrong?"

He clamps his mouth shut. His eyes shift around the cave, looking everywhere but her.

"It doesn't matter what was wrong. It seems to be fixed now."

She huffs. "Fine. Then can you at least put me down?"

He does so wordlessly. When she takes a step forward, his hand reaches out to grab hers.

"Just for safety. It's dark down here."

She looks at their joined hands. She squeezes his palm with her thumb. "Just for safety."

After a few more minutes of walking, she asks, "What are we walking into, here? And why are my future bosses involved?"

"The house we robbed was their mother's," Ivan explains. "There used to be seven daughters in the Nygard family. They took over the business after our father ran off with some sphynx tamer in Tanzania, and in a mysterious accident, four of them died. Their mother never was the same, and kept buying older and older artifacts, looking for something that can bring her girls back to life. Now it's just the three Nygard sisters left."

"So, who's the third sister?"

Ivan purses his lips. "The third was originally the fifth. And she's the mysterious accident that killed the other four."

"Killed?" She'd never considered killing family, no matter how many times she threatened it. "Why?"

"That's what makes it a mystery. No one knows."

Hand in hand they walk deeper into the caverns of HR. The walls are flush with gradients of blue-gray stone. It's mostly cracked and uneven, but the worn and smooth paths they're walking down are clearly well-traversed. Elaine's mind wanders to the silence between them even as she continues to hold his hand in hers. It's been so long since she's been so removed from constant noise and stimulation, and HR reminds her of home more than anything else has in months.

"My dad and I learned I wasn't his. That's why I applied to school here."

He holds her hand tighter.

"Do you still talk to him?" In true Ivan fashion, he takes the information in stride. He doesn't make a big deal out of it, and it emboldens her.

"I don't. I wrote one letter, and he didn't respond. Haven't tried since then."

His eyes are focused on looking for any danger around them, but his thumb brushes across the back of her hand, and he hums in confirmation to let her know he's listening. "He's missing out but count yourself lucky. I'd do anything to not be related to my father."

She does her best not to reveal how excited she is that he's revealing something new about himself. Everyone comes from somewhere, even Ivan Gray. "Do you keep in contact with your family?"

"Family's for fools and dogs, Lainey." He looks around them. "This cave is echoing too much; we'll have to stop talking. Help me keep a lookout for monsters instead." It's sharp and blunt, and it surprises Elaine to hear him be so curt.

"How convenient," she mutters. But she does keep quiet, and they make their way through the cavern in silence.

Ivan was right: whatever was blocking his magic before is no longer an issue, as he guides them both confidently through the caves even as it gets darker and darker. Elaine can't see much farther than her hand clutched in his. They come across a sign with "HR" printed across the front. In tinier font just below, it is written *Dr. Nygard, PhD*.

"I'll go first. Stay here." He says.

"No way." She grabs his hand tighter. "We're in this together."

"Elaine." He squeezes her hand before loosening his grip, but she reaches out and grabs him by his cloak.

"It's dark, Ivan."

She's never been afraid of the dark, but she knows her complaint works when she hears him shift. Then, slowly, the door creaks open, he pulls her next to him, and they step through together. The room is well lit, and she's able to see that while it is a cave, it's been decorated with dark wooden furniture, sconces, and an antique red rug. Stuffed animal heads line the wall with their mouths wide open in a silent roar.

"Ivan Gray?" A voice comes out from the other side of the room. There stands a slender brunette woman with large rectangular glasses framing brown, owlish eyes. Her hair cuts sharply across her tight jaw. The shape of her face is an indicator that this must be Doctoral Nygard, PhD, her similarity to her sister uncanny beneath her plain appearance. Those raptor eyes snap to Elaine. "I don't believe that's the statue we asked for."

"I have it here." He pats his cloak gently.

The woman inclines her head. He takes the cue and moves closer to her, but Elaine is stuck to the ground. Her heart hammers against her ribs, and the hair on her arms rises in alarm. This woman looks human: two arms, two legs, two eyes. But there is something about her that's hungry, and Elaine's body screams at her to turn around and run back out that door. In defiance of every instinct other than the magical, Ivan strides towards her and takes a seat, sipping a cup of something on a chaise. He's unharmed and landing a punchline, if the laughter from the Nygard in the room is anything to go by.

She sets her tea down with a small *clink,* uncrosses her legs, and turns to Elaine. "Come closer. You're the intern that came to visit, no?"

Elaine nods. Her tongue feels fat in her mouth, and she doesn't take a seat like Ivan does. She's frozen in place, and she clenches her robe closer. Roger growls against her neck, covered from sight by the loose waves of her hair.

Doctoral Nygard glides closer, coming up just in front of Elaine. She grabs Elaine's chin and lifts her head, so she's forced to look her in the eyes. "You won't come sit with us?"

Doctoral's a little too tired, too cranky, and too lean for Elaine's comfort. Her gaze reminds Elaine of an animal who's gone too long without a kill.

"You're very rude for someone who wasn't even invited."

Her magic flares in alarm, but she doesn't need to read the yellow words flashing in front of her to know that she's about to be eaten alive. She pedals backwards, but Doctoral's tight grip on her chin keeps her in place. She pushes Elaine back into a bookshelf, wood shuttering against her spine.

"Elaine!" Ivan moves to rise from her chair, but the ornamental claws at the end of the arms of the chair turn and grasp his hands in their own, keeping him stuck in the furniture.

Elaine lashes her feet out, but Doctoral presses herself closer, trapping Elaine against the wall with no room to move. The HR employee laughs as she's not at all injured by her attempts to escape.

"It's been a while since an employee acted out of line, especially one so rare."

Elaine feels her mouth against her neck and squeezes her eyes shut tight.

"And I'm ravenous."

Doctoral is about to eat her alive.

A high-pitched snarl comes from Elaine's neck, and Doctoral screeches in rage and pain, rearing back and grabbing her now-bleeding face, giving Elaine enough space to slip past her and run towards Ivan. Roger has latched onto Doctoral's face with a determination Elaine knows all too well and refuses to let go. Ivan struggles against his chair, but the claws have a firm grip on him. Elaine runs over and tugs on the arms, but the gilded chains don't break free under her grip. She feels around the sides and the bottom of the chair.

"There has to be an emergency brake."

"Get me out, Elaine!" Ivan shouts.

"I'm trying," she snaps. She circles the chair, frantically searching for some sort of switch. Sharp pain hits her shoulder as a clawed hand reaches out and pulls her away from him. Doctoral's face is inches from her own, and her eyes are no longer a muted brown, but a vibrant yellow with pupils slitted like a snake's. In her other hand is Roger, whose long maw is snapping and reaching for the HR employee's hand, just out of his reach.

"I am going to boil you and your rat in a stew and feed it to my employees during the company potluck."

Elaine snarls back. "Hurt Roger and die."

Doctoral throws her head back and laughs, high pitched and sinister. "I am going to enjoy this bite." She leans in toward Elaine's neck again, the tips of her white teeth pressing against her soft, exposed skin.

"Stop," shouts Dr. and who Elaine presumes is Doc.

Doctoral's head snaps to her sisters. "I see you've decided to join us," she says.

Dr. and Doc grasp at each other's hands. Doc is a carbon copy of her sister and dressed entirely in black.

"Doctoral Nygard. We think it's time for our guests to leave," Doctor stutters.

Doctoral cocks her head. "What for? There's no rush. It's been so long since a body came in warm."

Ivan wrestles in his binds against his chair. "This has to go against at least a dozen company guidelines. Let my Lainey go!"

"Your Lainey," Doctoral mock with a deeper voice. "Your Lainey is company property, luck mage. You're free to go once you give us the statue, but she's ours to do with as we see fit."

Elaine flinches as spittle lands on her neck.

"Doctoral," her sister snaps. "That is our summer intern, and she has *not* signed her release forms yet."

Elaine feels the teeth pull further away from her neck.

"*Summer* intern. Why is the summer intern here when it's barely winter?"

"For a tour. You can't eat her, Doctoral. All we have right now is the contract stating that she will work here for three summers. No signatures, no onboarding, nothing."

The predatorial tension in the air seeps away. Doctoral places Roger back on Elaine's shoulder and takes several steps back from her. Her angry face loosens, brows unfurrowing, and a sickly-sweet smile replaces the hungry gaping maw that was against Elaine's throat just moments before.

Doc and Dr. step forwards into the space their sister left in front of Elaine, faces painted in polite smiles as they look her over.

"Minor bruises, no piercings in her neck," Doc mutters. She tries to touch Elaine's throat, but Roger reaches out and snaps at her fingers before she gets the chance.

Elaine gives him an appreciative scratch under the chin. His illness makes his bites too slow to land, but it's the thought that counts.

"No visible broken bones or sprains," Dr. confirms.

All three sisters make eye contact before nodding in confirmation. "No viable lawsuits."

"Apologies for the hands-on introduction to our HR Department, Ms. Aquae. But as you can see, this was a demonstration, with no documentation, so there's no proof of distress to present to the worker's union. If you'd be so kind," Dr. starts ushering her towards the door, "we will conclude our business with Mr. Gray, which is separate from your contract with Nygard, Nygard and Nygard.

Elaine moves Roger from her shoulder to her chest as she's pushed forward to keep him from trying to bite anyone else.

Ivan struggles against his chair behind her, and his cries startle her out of her complacency. She moves out of Doctor's hold and turns back around, pointing an accusing finger at her future employers.

"You horrid wretches," Elaine snaps at them.

"Ms. Aquae—"

"No." She holds out a hand in protest. "I have had the worst week of my life. I disappointed Ivan, I failed my familiar exam, my rat is sick, and I'm pretty sure my hands are covered in spider egg residue. My professor thinks my name is Elmer," she growls, "and—"

"Professor?" the scary one, Doctoral, asks.

"Professor Sap."

Doc and Dr. stop breathing. Ivan freezes in his struggle to shoot her a panicked look. Doctoral Nygard's eyes fall on Elaine, where she stands glaring at the mortician for interrupting her speech.

"Don't you mean—" Doctoral leans towards Elaine, "—Dr. Sap?"

Even the mounted taxidermied animals seem to be holding their breath.

"He doesn't ask to be called that."

"He doesn't need to ask. Doctorates are where the term 'doctor' originally comes from. Those in the medical field *co-opted* it."

The goth one shuffles in her platforms.

Doctoral brushes her mousy brown hair out of her eyes, her glance scathing when she looks to her sisters. "Some take the name on even when they only have a technician's certificate—"

"Oh, grow up," Dr. snaps. "Some people just have a doctor vibe."

Doctoral's brown hair flares in anger, magic spewing into the air. It smells like cinnamon, old books, and something spoiling, like the magic itself is molding. It's distant, but it brings forth a memory Elaine can't quite remember, like passing by a stranger wearing the perfume of an old teacher, or the taste of a pizza you swear you've had before.

"Well, it sounds to me like your sisters don't really respect your title," Ivan pipes up from his chair.

Doc and Dr. peer around Elaine to look at him incredulously.

"Especially since you graduated sumo tumo wumo."

"*Suma cum laude,*" the women in the room correct him.

"That's what I said."

Elaine catches on to Ivan's plan.

"At least Doc and Dr. are keeping up with the family business," Elaine argues, "what do you do, use big words?"

"Well, she keeps up with the records, even if she's a bit squeamish with bodies—"

"Squeamish? She killed your other four sisters!"

"I did not!" Doctoral's nostrils flare. "It wouldn't have happened if you two hadn't drugged my coffee!" She turns to her sisters, hands outstretched in claws.

Doc and Dr. scream in what seems like fright at first, but transforms into a predatory shriek as their own hands slip into talons, stepping away from Elaine and towards their irate sister.

"Animal magic," Elaine breathes.

She's never seen a transformation like this in real time. Animal magic often goes one of two ways—inward or outward. These honed talons are a sign of animal magic changing the mages themselves. The rat king's ability to control and communicate with rats is an example of external manifestation, and his rat head an example of internal. Families with animal affinities hold their secrets close to their chests, but it's widely believed that as they grow older, the animal magic takes root in their core like a symbiotic parasite. Whether or not the mages get to choose the animal is still highly debated.

"This isn't fair," the twins cry, even as their feathered, sharpened hands raise in offense.

Elaine moves towards Ivan, fussing again with the knobs and pedals on the side of the chair.

"Hurry up," he hisses.

"Trying."

When she twists one of the chair's knobs counterclockwise, the hands detach from Ivan's wrists. He rises and pulls the cat statue from his cloak, fully intact. Elaine's eyes grow wide at the sight. Last time she saw it, it was scattered into pieces. Ivan moves forward and places it gently on a side table, turning his head and signaling for Elaine to follow behind him as the sisters argue in between thrown furniture and vicious swipes of their claws. The Nygard's eyes flit to it before returning to each other, and the fight they're all in. The cat statue is the last thing on their minds as they argue about a topic they've clearly covered before.

"Fair this, fair that." Doctoral's serpentine pupils widen, eclipsing all the light in her eyes. "What about anything in my life has ever been fair?"

She swipes a hand out at her sister who ducks, causing the room to shudder. Doc takes the opportunity to strike at her sister from below, sinking her claws into her ribs and pushing her backwards, forcing Ivan and Elaine to leap out of the way. As they do, something shatters. The women grow still.

Ivan wraps his arm around Elaine's. "Bad luck, ladies." He gestures with his free arm to the shattered cat at their feet.

Elaine gasps. So do the Nygards.

"You," the three snarl at each other. There are no sides after that, and the sisters circle each other with equal loathing.

"That's our cue," Ivan says, tugging her towards the door. "I don't think we want to be around when there's only one."

The sisters lunge at each other, forcing Ivan and Elaine to

use their magic to dodge the flying vases, books, and one unfortunate houseplant.

Ivan guides her through most of it, but Elaine sees a flashing yellow of *Hit in the head—88%.*

"Duck!" she shouts, and Ivan obeys, both of them narrowly avoiding the flying giraffe head.

The cacophony of sound grows further and further away as they run back the way they came. They finally burst through a set of doors Elaine sees an *Exit, 100%* glowing over, and end up exactly where they first entered. An entire night of running has gotten to them, their steps clumsy and heavy as they trod over grass, onto the dock, and into their boat, tripping over each other as they fall into the dingy, which rocks precariously. She ends up on top of him, his hands catching her waist to keep her steady as the boat levels out. One hand glides up her spine, gently pressing her chest against his to hide them.

They're silent, panting as he presses them closer together, wet clumps of dirt sticking to their cheeks. The faint sound of arguing grows louder as the sisters' voices grow closer to the dock.

"You idiots let them get away," Doctoral hisses from somewhere nearby. "Dorian said he needed them!"

"Well, *you* went crazy when we broke the damn cat!"

"That was Mom's—" A sharp inhale. "You know what? I'm not helping search."

"Of course," Doctor drolls on. Their voices start to fade away. "Run when Mom's brought up."

The duo's breaths are loud in the night. Even as escape is within reach, Elaine can't shake the feeling of dread that sits in her stomach. It's hard to tell the difference between her magic and her fears sometimes. Even now, yellow percentages flash by before she can read them, her breath coming harshly and her thoughts scattered, unable to focus on what odds will help her most right now.

Doctoral had said "Dorian" needed them. Did she mean someone was after them? It has to be the same person who put out that ransom for a luck mage. But who was he?

As much as she wished it could be, she knows that it's no coincidence a warrant went out for a luck mage the same year she moved to the city. It's too convenient. Ivan might be fine believing in luck, but Elaine is not so starry-eyed. Coincidence is the warning with which life prepares you for a blow to the gut.

Elaine sits up—with her hands pressed against his heavily beating heart—when her breath catches. He's smiling, his lips parted, revealing his even bigger smile, chest rumbling in silent laughter. She joins him, though she's still angry at him for trying to face HR alone. She's not sure if she wants to kill him or kiss him.

As a compromise she punches him in the chest, a gust of air spewing from his chest with an "oof." Then, she leans down and presses a kiss to his cheek, soft against the rough stubble. "You're incredible," she whispers.

He orchestrated their escape and saved their lives. He kept her from a deadly end at the hands of HR. She wanted to laugh, wanted to praise him, she wanted to—

She derails her own train of thought before it can go any further, slowly lifting herself from his lap. "Who do you think is after us?"

He frowns, placing his hands on her waist and halting her escape. "Whoever really gave me the job in the first place. We can figure it out later. I'm tired." He draws out the last word, eyes sliding closed.

Feeling daring, she reaches down and slides a hand through his thick hair. He groans in approval. The stress of the job bleeds out of him, leaving a smug creature nestling far too comfortably into her touch.

"Soft hands," he states.

"Astute."

They lay there in silence, but Ivan begins to twitch. She can see he's wrestling with a thought in the way his eyebrows scrunch, reminiscent of the look he gives her when he's struggling to write down his 'class objectives' as the teacher's assistant.

"I'm cursed."

She's afraid to say too much, in case he brings his walls back up. "Cursed?"

"The Gray curse is older than Garriver and the House families. All the ailments and destitution of the family are transferred onto the first son of the patriarch. Bad luck, disease, aging. On the outside, the entirety of the family prospers. While they travel the world, the bearer is meant to be stuck in the main household his whole life. They make investments that will secure their future for centuries, and I can't seem to save even a penny."

"And what about the aging?" she prompts. She looks at his tired eyes, thinking of the way his body creaks and cracks like an old forgotten house.

"The extended family ages like normal, save for the Lord and Lady of the House of Gray. In exchange, the eldest ages quadruple speed. At least on the inside."

"But then you should be dead," she gasps. The stories Ivan tells of his time in Garriver take place over a twenty-year span at least.

"Nice math. Maybe you should be an accountant—ow," he hisses when she tugs his hair in warning. "I'm the first in a long line of bearers to have luck magic. The luck got me out of the house of Gray, and it brought me here. According to history, I've outlasted all my predecessors by a full sixty years."

He says predecessors, but she knows what that really means: siblings. A long line of children born just to fuel the family's prosperity. Her family always expected her to stay and take care of the Aquae River like her mother, but they still let Elaine go to Garriver and make her own choices. To take away the life and freedom of your own sons for generations, and every ten to fifteen years from the sounds of it, is a hell she can't imagine is worth it.

I think I'm going to be sick, she thinks, holding her stomach.

"It is quite grim, now that I've said it aloud." He laughs. "It's just a fact about my family now to me, but I won't judge. I really did throw up the first time I heard it."

He laughs hollowly.

"I've found myself wondering more and more these days about who I would be if I wasn't cursed. Would I be stronger? Would I no longer be tired all the time? Would I save my money to spend it on something that lasts, instead of on expensive ingredients for a potion keeping me alive?"

The questions sit in the air, stale, used and easily answered: yes.

But the sure answers are not what interest Elaine. Selfishly —and she knows it's selfish—she wants to ask the question that's been on her mind since he first used the phrase 'family curse'.

The words, "Do you know when you'll die" come out of her mouth, stinging like a scorpion atop a hungry shrew.

"No."

A weight is lifted from her. "So, it could be never."

"No one lives forever. Anyone chasing immortality dies the day they choose it."

They stay there for a while, this new vulnerability settling over them like a blanket. This is the first time since leaving home she's floated in the body of a river. She'd forgotten about the lullaby hidden within the waves that rocks bodies back and forth within it. Ivan clearly feels it, too, his soft snores filling her ears, head caressed by her long fingers moving intricate, senseless patterns against the skull of his head. He sleeps so long that Elaine is able to put three tiny braids in his hair before he snorts awake.

His body jerks, eyes bulging as he tries to see in the dark of night.

"C'mon." She gets off him. "Drop me off back home."

They pull the rope off the dock, and Ivan pushes the boat further into the water using the paddle in his hand. "My back hurts," Ivan complains.

"Let me paddle."

"No."

Another ten minutes of his complaining, and she wrestles the oar from him. He doesn't put up much of a fight, swinging himself so he's lying down, head in her lap.

"If you're going to steal from me, the least you could do is provide a place of rest for a weary traveler."

She can't even pretend to be annoyed. "Of course, Lord Gray." She bites her lip, contemplative. This is as good a time as any to discuss what Doc brought up. A family secret connected to his curse, and someone named Dorian. Who is Dorian? What's his connection to the Nygards? And why does he need two luck mages?

"I can hear you thinking up there." He doesn't even open his eyes. "Either stop or share with the class."

"It's nothing," she says. They can discuss it in her home when they aren't stuck in a boat together.

She keeps paddling until they reach the watchtower. They tie the boat back to the dock, deboard, and walk towards her tower. Ivan's eyes travel up the long expanse of stone, rubbing at his back as he contemplates the sheer size of it.

"Has this wall always been this tall?"

"You can go through the front. My uncle's out until

tomorrow morning, and you're the one who decided you never want to knock."

He side-eyes her at that. "And enter like any other guest? Guests go through the door. Family takes the window."

She laughs, pulling out her key and stuffing it into the lock. Her hands feel heavy after the night she's had, and it takes a concerted effort to unlock her door this time. He goes in first, leaving her to find the light switch.

Ivan heads into the kitchen. She turns on the light, and he turns to shout, "Want to order whole turkey legs and saltwater taffy?"

With his back turned, he runs into a lump slumped against the kitchen table. His fingers are just trailing along the object curiously when it leaps up to shove him.

He yelps as the lump reaches out a gnarled hand to yank on his hair.

"Who the fuck are you?" Uncle Neil snarls.

"Lainey," Ivan howls, "there's a troll in your kitchen."

"Uncle!" Elaine says. "He's my TA." She holds her hands up, as if placating a startled horse.

This wasn't how Neil and Ivan met in her five-month plan. The first month would be her sprinkling in positive stories of Ivan, perhaps a few repeats of "he's very responsible now". Months two and three would show a slight decrease in bringing him up so as to not arouse suspicion of romance. Month four would have physical proof of his worth, vis-à-vis his help culminating in her acing the practical exam. And if Uncle Neil didn't show intense dislike, then she'd bring them both to a neutral third-party location to have their first twenty-minute interaction; twenty-three if they catch Neil in a good mood.

Neil yanks on his scalp harder.

"Let. Him. Go," Elaine demands.

He lets go of Ivan's hair, if only to point a finger at her. "I let

Roger come and go as he pleases, but I draw the line at vermin."

Roger, while mostly sticking with Elaine, still occasionally slips through the holes and cracks of the city for his alone time. She respects his boundaries; all good friendships do. He needs his own personal rat time, and if he was working with Titon, surely something would've happened by now.

"He's a probability mage!" She stomps her foot. "You always do this. I'm not twelve anymore. I can decide who I put my trust in on my own."

"Trust breeds deceit," he scolds, wagging a finger at her. "And I was right about that Girl Scout. She wanted to take your spot in front of the dispensary!"

"How many times are you going to bring that up?"

Ivan moves behind Elaine, rubbing at his sore head. His eyes move with interest over the room, and she realizes this is the first time he's seen anything other than her bedroom.

As she and her uncle continue to argue, the luck mage beside her shifts uncomfortably, eyes flitting around the room's windows and doors.

"I should go," he finally says when their voices grow louder, thumb pointing at the door.

"Yes," Uncle Neil says.

"No," Elaine disagrees.

They glare at each other. In the end, Ivan takes his cue from Uncle Neil, who is now turning an interesting shade of red, and he exits their home with a quiet 'bye' and a squeeze of her shoulder.

"Uncle Neil!" Elaine scolds. While she hadn't been expecting him to roll out the red carpet, it's strange of him to be so protective. They'd always been kindred spirits in their independence, and he'd always trusted her to make her own mistakes.

"That mage is bad news, Nellie," he warns.

"What's so bad about him?"

He purses his lips and holds his hands up in surrender. "Just be careful who you let past the wards. Has he told you of the curse?"

The hair on the back of her neck stands up. "He has," she says. "How do you know about that?" It raises a red flag in her head. How did her uncle know anything about Ivan Gray? She'd only just learned about his magical malediction.

"The Gray's have been in power longer than most because they're crueler than cruel. The family tree is filled with nasty hearts and personalities to match," he says.

She crosses her arms over her chest. "He's kind. He's in pain, but he's not a bad man."

"The curse doesn't just erode the body, Elaine. It erodes the soul, and I promise you that man is rotting from the inside out."

Elaine touches her stomach, and an awful feeling fills it. Ivan may not be perfect, but he's *fun*. He's an adventurer. "The curse isn't his fault. He's helping me."

"He's a dead man walking with nothing to lose. Whatever he's doing, he's acting upon his own self-interest. You're grown, but you're far from streetwise, Nellie. You'd do well to listen to me." His eyes shift guiltily, then he straightens up and looks her straight in the eyes as he asks, "Does he know you're part nymph?"

It's clear he regrets it when she freezes.

"Nellie, I didn't mean—"

"Don't 'Nellie' me. Is everyone in this family going to hold that against me forever?"

He reaches towards her, but she pulls away, arms tightening across her chest.

"You know it's not a problem for me."

She runs a hand through her hair, "Then why do you treat it like a dirty secret?"

Internally, she knows why: it's because she hasn't accepted

it, and her uncle sees her discomfort and stays quiet; but she's too angry to remember he's not trying to ruin her life. Her mom had an affair with a wind nymph and said she could hardly remember enough about it to tell her anything. Mom had always been more drawn to wild magic than most human mages, but that was as much explanation as Elaine would ever get.

"Can't you listen to me, this one time?"

"How about this: when you give me a good reason to listen, and you look beyond your personal vendetta against people who need a second chance, I'll be happy to." She goes upstairs to her room, plants her face into her pillow, and screams.

Her mind replays the evening, except this time Ivan enters through the window like he usually does, and she asks him who Dorian is. At first, he refuses, but as the night wears on, he tells her everything. In exchange she tells him about her father—and when he tells her he likes her, nymph or not, the confession stops itching at her throat like a bad cold. Sleep doesn't come, and her paternity runs circles in her mind to the point where she turns over to her nightstand, rustling through her drawer until her fingers touch the textured leather surface of a book she's been avoiding since she bought it. She sits up and opens it to the cover page:

Mages, Magic, and the Creatures That Live It.

It's an incredibly offensive title, but one of the only books she could find on nymphs.

While a marvel, nymphs are prone to outbursts. Though often compared to fae folk, they are capable of lies if they have developed the ability to speak. Their feelings are often as changeable as the element they represent. Most common are water, air, fire, and earth nymphs. Air and earth are on opposite sides of the spectrum—short vs. long lives, changeable vs. determined. Fire and water are opposites in that they avoid collision. But earth and air find they need each other, despite not understanding the way each other lives. It is well reported that they have the most amicable relationships of any of these forms, but unlike water and fire nymphs, the air and earth do not move in packs. Earth, because their lives are so long and settled. Air, because their lives are quick-changing, and sometimes as short as a day.

18

THE RATS ARE UNIONIZING

A full day has passed, and she's back to lounging in her bed. She'd scoured all her books for more information on nymphs, but the literature all melts down into calling them forces of nature. It could be true, that all earth nymphs are stoic and slow to change, and that the fire nymphs are passionate and raging. But the literature repeats itself over and over, and it never comes from a primary source. The only nymph she's met is Ophelia, and her life in the city is a far cry from what the books say a nymph should be drawn to. Instead of shying away from polluted waters, she has made her own domain in mage-made sewers. The front door thumps closed downstairs, which means Neil is leaving again for a late-night work assignment. It's gotten to the point where sometimes they catch each other sneaking back home in the early morning, say nothing to each other, and just...let it go. They used to ask each other snide questions, half disapproval and half a familial habit of nosiness.

Neil would ask, "Where have you been? I made soup."

"Oh, the same place you were last Tuesday at 2 a.m."

The mint soup was delicious. Ivan has been taking her on

increasingly difficult jobs, and most of them leave her exhausted for the next day of classes, especially if she has training with Nero and Clarke. It leaves her short tempered, and Neil bears the brunt of it.

Today she gets home before midnight, covered in magical residue from class, but it's mostly from the anarchist pixies Ivan was paid to take down. Each faction lived in its own plant, and these had been stuck in a willow tree, which carried its own magic. The combination had been combustible, and she leaves a soot fingerprint on the door as she pushes it closed behind her.

Uncle Neil lays on the couch, looking similarly worse for wear. He wakes up with a jolt when she drops her boots on the floor. They stare at each other. He thumps his head back down without another word, and she doesn't waste the opportunity to escape scrutiny, grabbing a packet of crackers before heading up to her room.

Now she sits on her bed, reaching out to console her current biggest problem: her sick rat. Elaine pets Roger along the ridges of his spine, his eyes opening briefly to greet her before sliding shut again. He'd been getting plumper along his sides, even as his spine sits raised and ridged across his back. One more week of this, and she's sure the vertebrae will be clearly defined. The vet didn't know what was wrong, and when she'd mentioned seeing Titon for a remedy, Roger worked himself into such a tizzy that she promised not to ever take him back to the sewers.

He gives a deep sigh.

"We'll figure it out, buddy."

She'd even written home to see if her parents knew of any remedies. Dad had once looked for a cure for half a decade when her sister developed furunculosis.

A swath of brown cloak rattles her windows, rings clanking against the glass. She pushes off her bed and unlocks the latch to let Ivan in. He arches his spine and stretches his arms upward, his chest bumping into hers before he brings his arms down to wrap them around her shoulders. He only moves out of her personal space to check on Roger, who's bundled in blankets atop a throw pillow.

"How's the little guy?"

Elaine's heart drops back down at the mention of her tiniest friend. "He's eating enough, but I'm worried, Ive. He's in pain."

At that, Roger heaves another great sigh. She rushes back over, picking him up and holding him close to her chest. Ivan eyes the way Roger sits nuzzled against her.

"Alright, he's not a baby."

She gasps and kisses the rat on the head. She lifts him higher to talk to him directly. "He's just jealous because I like you more." She puts Roger back on the bed and turns to give Ivan her full attention, catching the end of the scowl he shoots her rat before focusing back on her.

"What're you doing here so late?"

"I need some help with a job I'm doing. It's...logistical." He scrunches up his face like he's talking about kissing a dead fish.

"Already?" But inside, her chest feels lighter. *He thinks I'm smart,* her heart sings.

He rambles on about logistics. It's hard to focus on his words when he's so clearly frazzled, hands fidgeting with one another. He paces around the room, refusing to look at her, then swooping towards her and fidgeting with her, mumbling about a misplaced hair or wrinkle in her robe.

Ivan finally stops and stares at her. Then, gently, he places a hand on her shoulder. His gaze is soft, caressing her as gently as his arm. Something intense passes through his eyes, and it electrifies Elaine. He looks like he wants to love her. He looks like he wants to eat her alive.

His eyes sharpen back into the moment, but that intense gaze never averts from her own. "Look, Lainey. I know I said we should just be friends. But I can't help but feel as though—" He's cut off by his own shout of pain.

"Ivan," she gasps.

He's hunched over, and for the first time in a very long time, she thinks he's small in her arms. Another shiver wracks his body.

"Ivan," she whispers.

His eyes clench shut in pain, and he gasps out. Elaine, unable to communicate, starts to wish. She runs her hand under his shirt. Takes the top of his spine, muscles flexing, and runs her hand down it. She thinks of soothed joints, of relaxed muscles. She breathes in and channels the thoughts out. For a moment, his breath evens.

Then Ivan's back spasms, arching as if struck by lightning.

Sharing magic doesn't work. She's not strong enough. Not good enough. Not anything. Something to lose in the wind.

"I..." He winces. "I have to go."

"You can't move." She gapes at him, pulling the tufted cloak back over his shoulders.

"I'll be back," is all she hears before he jumps out the window.

She sits on the edge of her bed, petting Roger and watching the window for his return. After a half hour passes, she settles into the bed to wait for him, turned towards the city view, eyes glued to the open latch of the glass pane. Roger grunts as he stands, walking a whole three steps before collapsing against her arms. She only looks away from the window to look down at Roger, whose wispy breaths worry her as much as Ivan's curse. She can't rest knowing two of her closest friends are so sick.

She's almost asleep when she hears it—a skitter. She pats her hand around the bed and feels Roger huffing in distaste at being disturbed so late. The distant blare of a horn brings her fully back to the land of the living. She lifts herself off the bed.

The source of her disturbance is clear—she'd forgotten to lock the window and it had been blown open by the wind.

She bemoans the loss of her warm bed, feet thumping across the wind-chilled floorboards, fingers clutching and turning the cool iron lock shut.

She's got one knee back on the bed when she hears it again —the skitter.

Roger picks up his head this time, nose twitching as he sniffs the air. Elaine looks to the back of her door for her cloak, a reflex from the mountains, but it's downstairs hanging on the coat rack as always. She looks down, noting her sheer cream nightgown, and ties her robe closed around it.

When she nears the door, Roger squeaks louder than he has in weeks, stumbling off his pillow towards her. His feet scratch against the floor as he chases her. She bends over and scoops him up, body warm against her cheek.

Feet scratch along the wooden floors.

She stumbles back with a gasp, and her hand lands on her heart, beating fast against the cage of her chest.

There's something else in the watchtower.

"ELAINE," Ivan coos, swinging through her window with a pair of scissors in hand. "Lainey darling, your favorite TA needs a haircut."

The watchtower is empty. He makes his way down the stairs, peering into the kitchen. Her uncle's gone; he knows that. His boots crunch as they step into the kitchen, the ground covered in broken ceramic shards and spilled ingredients. The couch is upturned, and the only light still on comes from outside on the stoop of the open back door.

His heart beats faster as his eyes scour over the evidence of struggle, noticing the tiny scratch marks where feathers and foam bleed from the upholstery, dirtying the wooden floorboards.

"Titon," he hisses. He slams a closed fist against the stone wall. "Always getting into trouble, Lainey."

Ivan feels a righteous fury so overwhelming he begins to laugh. The rat king is so *silly* to think he could take from Ivan so blatantly. He'll smash his face into the ground so hard that even his dear Ophelia won't be able to recognize him.

He cackles with glee, magic sparking off him dangerously, his hand twiddling with the handle of a dagger. He takes a deep breath to calm himself. Infuriating your target to make them sloppy is one of the oldest tricks in the book. When they're startled, angry—or whatever it takes to set them off balance—they become easy to kill. So, he'll be calm.

His steps become quiet, his cackles no longer filling the ruined living room. He's not a scared boy, skittering across the undercity, trapped, and trying not to die at the hands of his pseudo-father. Predator's instincts run in his blood, and he stands up straighter, flipping up the hood of his dad's cloak. He closes the back door gently behind him and smiles broadly up at the moon. It's been so long since he'd had a good chase.

He'll have to be careful, as he drank the last of his potion in order to return so soon. He planned on surprising Lainey and taking her to the night market to see the oyster booth that only appeared under the full moon instead of a job, but her sudden abduction puts a stop to that. He pulls back a manhole cover and climbs down. If anyone is going to distract her from her work, it's going to be him.

He stands in the sewer, close to the water treatment plant, the smell less pungent than it would be close to the rat king's throne. Before him are several tunnels and giant pipes. Some are well-lit and clean, with the water treatment plant logo emblazoned on the entries. The rest are in varying degrees of disrepair, though that's what makes them so perfect for sneaking.

"Eeny, meeny, miney—that way."

He takes a step through the third option and starts walking just until he's totally shrouded in darkness. His hands reach for his satchel, fumbling for a flashlight, or a glow worm if he hasn't left his at home.

The water splashes in an odd rhythm from the path he just came from. He presses himself against the side of the pipe, listening to the slap-slap-*thunk* of uneven movement across the paved path.

Peeking around the corner, Ivan sees Neil grumbling to himself as he moves further into another pipe.

"What's an upstanding potioneer doing in the underneath?" He narrows his eyes. And more so, where was he when Lainey was taken?

He moves to follow Neil, but his magic flares in alarm.

Lainey, Lainey, Lainey, it blares, even as he tries to give chase to her uncle.

First, the girl. Second, a thank you kiss—

He shakes his head.

Second, get Lainey home safe. Third, find the increasingly suspicious uncle.

He straightens out his shoulders. He can do this. He's got his priorities straight. And Lainey will see there's a reason she's under his mentorship. Ivan's sure this would've never happened if she'd mastered their magic.

Elaine is quite cross with Roger.

"Traitor," she hisses at him.

He nuzzles his weak body against her trapped one, standing atop her horizontal chest as the rats carry them down the sewer gates, uncaring of his mutiny. Their magic is less seductive this time around, and that urge to be a part of the hoard is a mere passing thought. She feels separate from them and feels fondness only for Roger.

Instead of being in Titon's throne room, she's been brought into some sort of abandoned mine hidden within the layers of the under city. The crystals that light the cave push out from the mining walls, raw and untouched. They strike a contrast against the hole below, the crystals getting smaller and dimmer, leaving a pitch-black dot in the middle.

It's clear now to Elaine that Roger was playing the long game. It was always his goal to get her back in this underneath and subject her to the whims of Titon, his master. She'd even allowed him to lay in her bed, worried over him when he became ill. The rats must have been circling the house for a while, poking holes and using Roger's familiar scent to find ways to gnaw themselves in. Rats are good at that, infesting and swarming in places they aren't welcome. And with an analytic mind at the helm, it must have been so much easier to sneak in and steal her away in the night.

The rats shuffle her down a path, away from the throne room, pulling off a rusty grate that leads to a single antechamber. Inside sits a chair, stacked with bits and bobbles—a shiny button, clumps of hair. Rusty old keys decorate it: all different shapes and sizes.

As she's deposited onto the throne, she realizes the cushion is made up entirely of left socks. The rats disperse once she settles on her throne of trash, hissing and clicking their teeth at each other. Roger sits in her lap and watches them warily, hissing whenever one wanders too close to her. Each hiss tires him until all he's doing is huffing out in breathless warning.

"Roger," she whispers. "What in hells is going on?"

The rats grow silent. Then they chitter, which turns to chatter, then a synchronized screech of a chant.

"One of us," they say. "Rat king, rat king."

She looks around for Titon.

"Rat king!" they insist. "Rat king!"

They circle her, and Roger's hackles raise. He wheezes at them, eyes flitting rapidly as they grow closer and closer to Elaine.

"Rat king." They move closer. "New king."

She'd grown used to Roger's presence, but being surrounded by so many rodents brings back bad memories. She breathes rapidly, feeling ghosting teeth and nails and tails clamoring over her.

They're looking for a limb to bite, her magic screams. *They want to bite and rip at you until the chair sits bloody.*

"What," comes a snarl, "is going on here?"

Titon, ugly rat face and all, makes his way through the room.

"Thank the stars," she cries. "Control your rats, Titon. They've kidnapped me."

A smile curls over his snout. He leans against the wall, eyeing her throne with a sneer. "They've been in a tizzy since Roger left. Perhaps they saw a need for a bit of retribution." He glares at Roger. "He's been going on and on about the pillows and the blankets and the Gruyère cheese." He makes a noise. He tries to approach the throne, but the rats don't move. He snarls, retracting his foot back into his original stance. "Beatrice! Mary! Move aside."

She scowls. So that's where Roger had been when he left her side. She's been feeding what she thought was a stray all this time, but he'd been sneaking off home once he'd gotten what he needed from her. Like a cat loyal to the warmest bed available.

Two large rats tremble, but they don't move at his command.

"Someone take these traitors to the dungeon." He snaps his fingers.

The horde shuffles, but no rat moves forward to obey him.

"N-no Gruyère!"

"No pillows!"

"No blankets!"

"New king, new king!"

He looks to Elaine, a look of realization washing over him. He laughs in disbelief. "This waif of a woman? She wouldn't know a thing about leading you. And we don't *need* those things."

A few more unusually large rodents flank Beatrice and Mary.

One brave little soul utters out a stuttered, vulnerable, "No hugs."

Titon's eyes widen. "Hugs? You don't need hugs. I'm not your father."

They hiss.

"Alright, clearly we all need to have another talk about expectations—"

The rats let out a collective screech, and the rat king is pushed out of the room.

Elaine grips Roger tighter in her arms. She can feel his bones trembling beneath her grasp. She combs through his fur again, and realizes he is not trembling. Instead, something inside him squirms, like a centipede just under his skin.

She screams, startling Roger into standing on his hind legs. When she reaches out again, her fingers touch still, solid bone. But she could've sworn...

The other rats eye her curiously. In front of her, the word *Escape* flashes at a dismal 17%. Elaine tries her luck and stands up to leave. She puts one foot forward and is quickly snapped at, stumbling back onto her makeshift throne.

"Stay," they hiss. "Stay!"

"Alright, alright, I'll stay."

Their teeth retreat from her feet.

There's a sound of something at the entrance of the antechamber, and their heads snap.

"Thief." They move, a plague. "Thief! Thief!"

There's another sound, this one further away, and they filter through the door.

Ivan appears, able to pass by them with ease.

Elaine eyes him, relieved. "What are you doing here?" she whispers.

"I'm here to rescue you."

Escape, 5%.

"Help!" she yells. "Thief!"

He turns back to her, eyes blazing. "What the hell are you—"

"Help. Me," she mutters. Louder, she hollers, "Take him to the dungeon!"

The rats scramble back into the room and hasten to obey. In their rush, they knock Ivan's struggling body unconscious, and she watches the door until he's removed her sight. They leave her with just a small security detail this time, rats roaming, occasionally looking at her with admiration.

One rat, it seems, is not happy she's there.

"Traitors," it murmurs. "Traitors." Its voice echoes throughout the empty chamber.

Roger peeks open one eye, trained on the limping, geriatric rat.

"You know, Roger," she says loudly, "I bet if a faction decided to stand up against the other rats, Titon could get the title of rat king back. I'm sure he'd be incredibly grateful."

It eyes her, limping off with a mutter, "Traitors, mutineers, betrayers."

~

IVAN WAKES from an unusually pleasant dream when breath is puffed onto his face. "Mm, Lainey." He grins. "Again?"

"Wake up," a nasally voice snaps.

Ivan yelps, flailing back from the rat king. He tries to push him back but fails when his two arms jut forward, cuffed together at the wrist. Titon's hands are free and smack Ivan's away from his chest.

"Titon! Give a guy some space, would you?"

"We need to get out of here."

Ivan rolls his eyes. "Obviously. But I'm not leaving without Lainey. Trying to add kidnapping to your rap sheet?"

"Abduction. Despite your behavior, you're not a child."

A rat guard paces by their cell, eyeing them warily before waddling on. The cell is an old boiler room with the front doors replaced by irons bars. Ivan runs a hand over it, unable to feel any magic in them. It's definitely iron, he can tell that much.

"Trying to catch a nymph?" He shakes his head, turning his judging eyes on Titon. Ophelia would not be a fan of this.

Titon turns pink. "This grand adventure was not my idea. After your last failure, I didn't want to see the pair of you again until you had my crown."

"You expect me to believe the rats kidnapped Elaine on their own?"

"She took Roger! Made him soft. Now the others have been muttering about 'unions' and 'class inequality.' They are—" Titon pauses, looking like he's tasting the sour words in his mouth, "—trying to...dethrone me."

Ivan laughs. "Treason against the crown." He eyes Titon's bald head. "Well, metaphorically."

He hisses. "Laugh all you want, lucky boy. I'll be back on my throne, and your little lover will be dead. The rats plan to absorb her into the swarm, then decorate my neck with the bones left over."

Ivan's nerves alight at the thought of her being consumed. His heart rages against his chest, and his fists curl in distaste.

"Absorb? How would they absorb Lainey?" He asks in a terse tone.

"They'd eat her, Gray. Obviously."

His laugh this time is mean. "If they do that, I'll suck the marrow from their bones with a curly straw."

Titon shrugs at the threat to his legion. "You can try. It won't make her any less dead."

Ivan stands up, rattling the bars of their cell. "Let us out!" he yells.

The rat guard snickers, leaving the cellar behind.

Ivan runs a hand through his hair, pacing the cell floor.

There's a moment of silence, then: "So, you're sleeping with her?"

"No."

"I don't believe you," Titon responds breezily.

"I'm her teacher."

"Ah, your 'student.' How unethical."

"Unethical? We wouldn't be in this mess if you were better with women."

Titon scoffs, "Me? You're the one holed up with *a student* twenty-four seven. Roger is baffled by your cowardice."

That rat.

"I'm protecting her," he hisses.

"From what? Having a normal relationship? You don't want her badly enough to ask her out, but you'll bat your eyes and moonlight as her TA? Pathetic."

"I don't see Ophelia running in here to save you."

"That's different."

"Is it? 'Get my crown, Ivan. Ophelia's mad at me, Ivan.' Why don't you apologize to your wife like a normal person?" His cuffs clank against his wrists.

Titon sniffs, turning his snout to the air. "Marriage is

complicated. Not that you'd ever understand. It'll be three more years of pining before you get tired of Elaine going on dates."

"She doesn't date," he snaps. "She's dedicated to accounting." It's the least sexy job Ivan can imagine, and he's incredibly grateful for it. He pulls a silver pin out from an inside pocket of his robe, and starts to pick at the lock, wrist awkwardly swiveling around the tight grip of the cuffs.

Titon grins. "That's not what I heard."

Ivan scrunches up his face. Titon's just trying to rile him up. She's delightfully introverted, and he knows everyone she speaks to. Clarke is a non-issue. He's too boring, too dedicated to his work, and his Lainey would eat the man alive. Elaine is off in the same way Ivan is—unpredictable, primal, angry. But they also make one another gentle, more understanding. Their magic makes each other more powerful.

Ivan grinds his teeth. Lainey is kind to others, yes, but he's sure he's the only one who sees her sweet. Though her insistence that he be taken to the dungeons does make him question her. Just a little.

The conversation ends when the lock holding his wrists clicks open. He places the silver pin in the cloak pocket over his chest.

He rubs at them. "Despite you being a nuisance, I do need your help to find Lainey and get out of here."

Titon eyes the pin he's holding with surprise. "Where did you get that?"

"I helped her unbraid her hair and...forgot to give it back."

"I thought you couldn't pick locks."

He shrugs. "Lucky, I guess."

"You're intolerable." Titon eyes the pin like it's obscene.

"It's not like I'm her boss."

"Oh, not that. I believe you haven't touched her. You wouldn't be so...wound up otherwise. I'm just wondering when you'll tell her about your curse."

"She knows. It's not a problem."

"Oh, but it is. Don't you think it hurts her when you leave with no explanation? Even I've noticed you getting worse, Ivan." Titon raises his nose in the air. "The smell is clear as day."

"The curse is unpredictable. You know *nothing*."

"I know enough to recognize when a man is dying."

Ivan grinds his teeth. "I've always been dying. As are you. As are all of us."

"Oh, but not like this. Not this fast."

Their conversation ends when a wheeze echoes through the hallway, followed by the thumps of tired paws. It's the old rat from the throne room.

The rat king sits up. "Mr. Notters. I knew you wouldn't stand for mutiny."

Mr. Notters perks up at the sound of his king's voice. "Traitors."

"Traitors." Titon nods. He reaches a long, clawed hand through the iron bars, and Mr. Notters leans heavily into his touch. The rodent stands upright, a prison key placed carefully between his teeth.

The lock clicks open with a twist of Mr. Notters' head, and the men step free.

ELAINE EYES the pot in front of her dubiously. The rats had forced her onto a pedestal with a large cauldron below. Roger hisses whenever any of them come too close, but he's unable to stand up again. The rats shuffle in with all sorts of goods—carrots, celery, paprika, cayenne. She hopes Ivan comes up from the dungeons soon. Not even luck magic could keep him safe from a constantly changing swarm of rats; and although her magic had seen their escape as nearly impossible, Ivan can escape any trap, and they might have a chance with the element of surprise.

"Hold the walnuts," she calls out. "They give me hives."

Her eyes flit around the cave. She's running out of time, and Ivan's still not here. If there's no one to help, she'll have to help herself.

"More spices," she commands. "And more vegetables. It's not enough!" Stalling can only work for so long before she'll have to break out, but how? She leans a bit to the side to look over the edge, and the chair she's in creaks with the movement. It's a sharp drop, one without a visible bottom. She leans back quickly, swallowing nervously. Jumping is not an option. Elaine is not one to shy away from a cliff's edge, but with both the ground and the sky missing, it's more symbolic of an unknown cage than the freedom of the sky and solid ground.

The rats have decided it's time and approach the creaky pseudo-throne, a poor copy of the one Titon usually sits upon.

Sweats beads on her forehead. "You know, if you really want a new king, I'm sure a democratic election amongst yourselves would fare much better."

There's a resounding crash and muttered panic amongst the rats. Two large figures run by, one a blur of brown, the other with an extraordinarily long snout. Her heart leaps in anticipation as the rats look back to her for guidance.

"Well, go on, stop them!"

Their feet stumble over the gravel as they take off with a war cry. Elaine fiddles with her restraints. They'd begun to nibble and fray her ropes, but they used multiple tiny knots to keep her here, and she has no way to get them off.

Roger perks up and moves to gnaw at her ropes.

"Roger," she breathes. Perhaps he hadn't betrayed her, but rather followed her to the gallows, and like a good sneak, too weak on his own, waited for the right moment to save her. "I do love you, Roger."

There's a hissing at a lower register than Roger's. One of the sentry rats has stayed behind and discovered his treachery. Roger turns to face the enemy and they war in the low, complicated hisses of their language, circling one another. Roger jumps from Elaine to spar in front of her throne. They snap and scratch and claw as they fight over her freedom along the pit's edge. Roger bites the edge of the other rat's ear. The larger rat screeches and thrashes around, trying to throw Roger off, but he clings on. She wrestles against her ropes, a few snapping and breaking off from her body.

The larger rat succeeds in throwing off Roger, and he skids across the floor, body stopping just before the maw of the pit. Her left hand snaps free as the other rat approaches Roger. She fiddles with her other hand.

"Stop!"

It sniffs Roger's form. Breathing deep, Roger looks into the eyes of his brother.

Her left leg snaps free.

Roger closes his eyes in acceptance.

A yelp is the last thing she hears before she watches as Roger's weak body plummets into the cavern below.

"He was sick!" she cries. "You had no right! He was sick." She repeats it over and over, tears streaming from her eyes. Her hands strain harder against the last of the ropes to no avail, even as she stands alone on the edge of her death.

"HOW DID THEY HEAR US?" Ivan yells.

"They're rats! They're incredibly intelligent and don't deserve the reputation they have."

One flings itself at Ivan, clawing his cheek before being flung away.

"Yes. Smart and docile, how did I not see it before? Have

you considered loaning them to children's hospitals as therapy animals?"

Titon dodges a thrown brick. "Maybe I will."

They take a left, and alarm bells ring in Ivan's brain. "Where are you taking us?"

"Out."

"We have to go back for Lainey."

Lainey, Lainey, Lainey, his magic thrums. *Lainey, Lainey, Lainey.*

Titon jumps over a blockade of traffic cones. "*Elaine* can handle herself. The rats aren't able to use magic; their strength is in numbers."

Titon lets out a cheer when he sees light coming from a tunnel up ahead. "Do what you want, I'm leaving."

Ivan tackles him to the ground.

"You idiot," Titon hisses. "You'll get us both—"

The rats corner them.

"—captured."

The rats move them into the room Lainey is in and tie the three around the same pole.

"You are rather unlucky." Titon sneers to her. "Are you sure you're a luck mage?"

"Probability isn't luck," Elaine says.

"You look beautiful in the crystal light," Ivan offers.

"Shut up!" she snaps. "Both of you. I'm in no mood. Roger is… He fell."

"Fell," Titon says.

"One of your servants pushed him!" Her voice cracks.

His face doesn't change. "As I recall, they're your servants now. I've been impeached."

"Guys?"

"You—"

"Guys."

"I—"

"Your Majesties!"

"What!" Titon and Elaine snap.

"That cauldron looks about ready for cooking."

It's true. The rats stand gleefully around it, as two of the larger ones approach to untie Elaine. They tip her body over, shuffling her towards the pot. She squirms in their hold, and the tears that come to her eyes now are those of frustration.

"Put. Me. Down." She yells at the rats.

Ivan turns to the rat king. "This is ridiculous, Titon."

"What do you want me to do about it?"

"Negotiate!"

"No!" His eyes flit to his legion, who coo and flutter over their sacrifice.

"If she dies, I'll make sure you never see that crown again. I'll bury it so deep, with so many ridiculously expensive and cursed wards, that not even a starving dragon will be able to sniff out the gold."

Titon's narrowed eyes shift between Elaine, his rats, and finally back to Ivan, the mage who still owes him a crown. "Fine." He clears his throat. "Alright, everyone. It's become clear you plan on following through with this ridiculous ploy for attention. I'm willing to discuss terms."

The rats pause and turn to face him, shuffling Elaine around with them. She's a mess, red-eyed and crying.

"Compensation!" they screech.

"Fine."

"Brie?"

"Farm-raised white cheddar."

More muttering.

"Hugs?"

Seeming embarrassed, Titon's eyes flit to Ivan, but Ivan doesn't take his gaze off Elaine's teary face. "My—yes, fine! Fine. But there's too many of you. One hug per year!"

More utterances.

"King Titon! King Titon!"

Some rats untie Titon, and he makes his way down into their ranks. Elaine is moved next to Ivan by another pack and dropped without care. She winces when her bottom hits the hard rocky floor. Titon is once again the rat's king, and Ivan and her can find a way to the bottom of this cave.

"Roger can't be left there, all alone in the dark." She murmurs to Ivan.

He looks at her with pity. He opens his mouth to speak, but she cuts him off before he can.

"He would never leave me down there," she hisses. "He'd do it for me."

She wishes she hadn't been afraid of him for as long as she had. She regrets those nights she let him wait out in the rain, and how long it had taken her to believe him. How she had lost trust in him so quickly when things went south. Perhaps she's more like her father than she thought. So quick to let trust slide away from her, just for a mistake. For something that Roger had no control of her and tried his best to fix. He shouldn't be held accountable for the crimes of his family.

Titon straightens his cuffs out, that smug smile back on his face. He looks over the luck and probability mages, eyes flickering with something soft and hateful. A frown takes over his face. "Now, throw the mages in the cauldron."

Elaine and Ivan shout in dissent, but their protests fall on deaf ears.

"You think you're so irreplaceable that you can threaten me? My crown? You're arrogant, Gray, and I don't *need* you. No one needs you. There will always be new mages for hire, ones younger and eager and cheaper."

They are pushed to the edge of the boiling pot, arms tied behind them, but legs free. The rats nip at their heels to keep them moving forward, edging closer and closer to the pot. The heat is hitting her face now, and the scent of all the spices she demanded wash over her, embracing her as if a grim reaper of her own creation.

"We could push the cauldron over, but then we'd fall into the pit," Ivan mutters to Elaine. "Not enough time, not enough room." He shakes his head at his words implying impossibility. "There *is* enough room," he reprimands himself.

By miracle, or luck, a bat flies and knocks the cauldron over, sending bubbling broth towards the rats and Titon. They scatter, crying in pain as they disperse, leaving the mages tied up and on their own.

Something small and dark flies to Ivan and gnaws on the ropes. Ivan struggles against the ties, shouting in triumph when they come loose. Ivan moves around to her back to untie Elaine, and as soon as the ties come loose, she spins and embraces him, face tucked into the crook of his neck. She takes a shuddering breath in and pulls back, only for him to pull her close again. One of his hands slides between them to press over her chest, desperately searching for her pulse. Her heart beats fast against his palm, eyes wide.

"Ivan," she breathes. The red rims around her eyes are fading, resigned relief taking the place of her grief. "Sorry about before. I knew you were outnumbered, and I thought if you had the element of surprise, you'd have a better chance."

The cauldron's bubbling waters have cooled in front of the exit. From the corner of his eye, he sees a familiar figure.

"Roger?" He says.

Elaine opens her mouth to yell at him, but Ivan squishes her lips between his fingers, turning her head toward the approaching animal. A bat swoops towards them, but there's something wrong with it. The creature has four legs, a long, worm-like tail and familiar snout. The flying "rat" soars closer, newly sprouted bat wings coming from his back.

~

"ROGER!" Elaine cries out. She pushes away from Ivan to grab hold of him. She knows it's him, as the black veiny wings blend into his fur where that ridge once sat along his spine. "I knew you'd be okay." Her voice is choked and wet, but she's smiling, touching the marvel of his wings. "Falling to his doom? Not my Roger. He's much more than they all think."

He'd sustained a nasty blow to his left eye, which was scabbing over, but that's the worst of it. Uncle Neil can fix that with a healing potion. She huffs out in relief.

"This is incredible. Elaine, he must have reacted to your magic, somehow. But wings? You can't fly, as far as I know. And you can't turn into a bat either."

Ivan prattles on, and Elaine watches him fondly, a soft smile stretched across her face. The affection for the man who entered her life just a few months ago is making a warmth spread across her chest, and she can't help it when her smiles grows larger as he gently grabs Roger and inspects him, now talking to her rat like an old friend. Roger blinks and lets himself be manhandled, wings stretching out to appease the scarecrow of a man looking over them. She's not quite sure why her heart feels lighter. Roger surviving is reason for joy, but it's more than that, and whatever it is has to do with the way Ivan held her, and the way that he came back for her. She'd betrayed him, knowing he'd know she didn't mean it and come back for her. She hurt him and knew that he'd come back anyways.

I trust him, she realizes, clenching her fist against her heart. The realization inspires the rapid beating of her heart, and her feet itch with the impulse to run away.

Ivan stands up and offers the hand not holding Roger out to her. "C'mon, Lainey. Let's go get something to celebrate." He looks at Roger again, brow furrowed in deep contemplation. "Maybe some kites?"

"Get them!"

Titon and the other rats are returning. Elaine's body

clenches in fear. Titon enters the room first, eyes alight with murderous intent. The rats file in after him, curling around their king. There's no way they can take on Titon's entire horde. But then something strange happens as the rats turn on Titon instead, climbing over him as his eyes grow wide.

"No! No hugs now. You can't all redeem them *at once.*"

The rats ignore him, clamoring over him and entirely disinterested in the other mages in the room. Elaine looks to the exit, and using her magic, thinks of how likely it is for them to be able to get away.

Escape, 95 %.

Keeping hold of Ivan's hand, she leads her boys out of the cavern, and follows her magic along the most probable path to home.

WHEN SHE GETS HOME, Ivan drops her at the door.

"I need to get some medicine stat." He kisses the top of her head, startling them both. But when her cheeks warm his face softens, his eyes shining with unfiltered fondness. "Get some rest and have your uncle make you a healing potion. I'll check on you as soon as I can."

"Promise?" she asks coyly, looking at him from under her eyelids.

He grins down at her, kisses the top of her head again for good measure, then turns to leave, a spring in his step as he disappears into the night.

She knocks on the front door, Neil answering with a slight raise of his eyebrow before letting her through.

"And where were you? And why did you throw a party without asking me?"

Elaine leans down to hug her uncle, breathing in his magic. He reaches around and pats her back. When she pulls back, his face screws up as he examines her dirtied clothes, and the look of exhaustion on her face.

"Why do you look like you've just run to the mountains and back?" He says.

"Rats got past the wards."

A look much more frightening than his scorn crosses his face. It's one Elaine has never seen before on her uncle, in all their trips through unpredictable terrains—uncertainty.

His eyes flit around the house, landing on everything but her. "I reset the wards twice. I know I did."

Even so, she can see the dark shadows under his eyes, the twitch of his lids from dehydration. Uncle Neil's been off, the stress of his work weighing more heavily on him. It's manifested into a sloppy version of the proportion mage she's never seen.

19

SELKIES IN THE SEWERS

IVAN

Many years ago...

"You wanna work for food?"

Ivan looks up at the man talking down at him from where he rests in the grim dirt of a Garriver alley. He entered the city a month ago, and his health has only worsened. He sold his gray cloak for a pouch of coins but quickly found himself missing its warmth and protection. Here there are creatures much larger than him, and ones much more cunning.

The man's face is hidden. "I know a man who takes in orphans. You have to work, but you'll be clothed and fed."

Ivan stands, unsteady. The man's hand is steady on his back, leading him further into the alley, until they come across a manhole.

"Go ahead," the man says.

Ivan takes the ladder down until his shoes touch the cement below.

"All yours, Liam."

The manhole closes with a screech, and Ivan is bathed in darkness.

"Hey!" He crawls back up the ladder, banging on the steel exit. "Let me out of here!"

"Sorry, kid," he says.

Ivan bangs his shoulder against the manhole to no avail. He pauses when he feels the hairs on the back of his neck stand on end. Something moved in the water. He slides down the ladder, wincing as the friction turns his hands red. He runs deeper into the sewer, following the primal part of his brain that screams he's being chased.

Something reaches out with a splash, and he leaps in the air, feeling clawed hands brush against his nape. With a crash, someone barrels into him. They sniff at his hair.

"This one smells all wrong."

Ivan scowls. "*You* smell wrong."

The kids surrounding him snarl, moving around him in small circles. There's an uncanny air to their eyes, which are a bit too close together. Their nails are a little too long. "You're lunchmeat, human. You're in the domain of selkies."

There's a rumble, and the kids move back to reveal a man, large and gruff. "What's this? I ask for a mage, and I get a child?" A large man sighs, as if it's a burden. "Well, a deal's a deal. Since you're so young, I'll give you a head start."

The kids at his feet whine.

He turns to address Ivan. "Run and see if you can make it until morning light without getting eaten."

Ivan scrambles to his feet as childish giggles intermixed with growls follow closely behind.

This shouldn't be too hard, he thinks. *Seals can't run on land.*

But what hunts him are not seals, but three bears. It is true that, traditionally, selkies are seals that can turn human by shedding their sealskin. But challenges to survival create new, powerful strains of evolution, and these selkies are a product of that.

Ivan dives into the water, swimming with the current. The

water is fresh, and magic is surely keeping it from spoiling and polluting with what comes out of the drains. Ivan can feel it all around him, and he knows he's the most rotten thing in here.

A paw reaches out and grabs him by the ankle, dragging him under. He turns his wide-eyed stare to the bear behind him, paddling along the river. It grasps him in its jowls and carries him to shore. He coughs out the water in his lungs, but otherwise stays still, all too aware of the ivory teeth clenching his middle.

"'Aught 'im," the bear says. It drops him in front of the other two within a cavernous antechamber, littered with bones and furs.

Ivan rights himself, trembling beneath their giant, hungry teeth.

The bears are taunting and laughing, unconcerned with him. Playing with their food. It is that arrogance that allows Ivan to slip beneath one's giant belly and disappear further into the cave. As he runs further, the walls turn from concrete to slabs of rock, jagged and dry, and most importantly, warm.

Ivan is bare in a way he's unused to. Without a cloak, drenched in water, hungry, and alone, he is drawn to that wave of heat like a moth to a flame. A roar of outrage echoes behind him, and he moves faster. Before him, he can see a warmly lit living room. It's still a cave, but there are couches and beds and a stove with hot soup. His mouth waters, but his magic is thumping faster than even his own heartbeat, warning him away from the comfort of a home.

He stops in his tracks. Behind him, he hears the fast-moving clicks of large claws against the rocky floor. He leans a hand against a wall, looks up, and sees a hole. His heartbeat slows when he looks at it, and he scrambles upward, sliding into the slim escape from the bears. He wiggles along, heart and magic both slowing down despite the darkness of the hole, and how it grows tighter and tighter against his shoulders, until he emerges finally into a hovel. It's filled with silver light, bioluminescent crystals jutting out of the wall like candles. Exhausted, he curls up in some moss and rests.

He's woken the next morning by a sheen of light from above him. Blinking his eyes open, he squints up at the sun. When he remembers where he is, he scrambles up, climbing one, two, three crystals before his head hits the ceiling with a dull thud. He pushes one hand up on the clear ceiling. It's cold and rough to the touch.

"Ice," he curses. At least four inches thick.

Three days pass in that hovel, and he knows if he doesn't leave, he'll starve to death. He looks back at the entrance and climbs back through. He stops just before the opening, and hearing nothing, drops down.

"Don't assume you're the quietest thing in the cave."

Ivan whirls around to see the large man with his bearskin slung across his back like a cloak. He motions for Ivan to follow him into that cozy living room from before. "My kids will get you eventually. Until then, you're a guest until nightfall."

A bowl of porridge, fresh and hot, is dropped into Ivan's lap, the first fresh meal he's had since leaving home. He eats quickly, before the monster changes his mind.

Ivan's days pass like that for a few months, days spent fed, warm and sleeping, nights being hunted by enemies that learn from their mistakes and come at you with some new way to eat you the next time. He learns the man is named Liam, and his family lives in this tiny piece of Garriver.

In the fourth month, Liam's eldest, Mort, gives up.

"You gave us Ivan just to keep us here," he accuses his father.

Ivan keeps his eyes on the squash soup in front of him. It's his favorite, and Liam bought it as a memento to his success, and to shame his children for their failure.

"It is tradition to hunt and defeat a mage before you leave," Liam says. He is calm in the face of his son's accusation. He rubs a hand through his beard. "He is young and cursed. And none of you can catch him? That's a reflection on my parenting maybe, but not a scheme to keep you home."

Mort snarls and leaves the cave. Liam watches, never taking his eye off his son.

That night, Ivan dares to steal Liam's cloak. Liam roars with anger, so much less frightening when he can't turn into a brown bear. Ivan tucks it into his hovel for safekeeping. The next morning, when the remaining two selkies cannot catch him, Ivan taunts them all.

"You talk about how much stronger you are, but I stole right from under your nose."

Lucinda and Junior snarl, stepping forward, but they're stopped by their father's hand.

Liam steps toward Ivan, who cranes his neck up to meet his glare. With his cloak gone, Liam cannot leave home for long, and he's unable to bring back his eldest.

Liam laughs, loud and wheezy, an acquiesce. "I will find my skin. Selkies always do."

Lucinda is the second to leave. She is the youngest, and her departure does surprise Liam. Ivan sees the shock in the way Liam reaches to pull the second bed mat out the next dawn, hesitates, then puts it back again. He turns to look at Ivan.

"Junior will get you," Liam promises.

"Junior can try."

Junior does his best. He is the middle child and has always been Liam's favorite, due to the shiny sheen of his coat and the cinnamon coloring of his fur. Junior is loyal to his father because he can feel the affection, can feel his father's belief in his excellence. It starts to fade when Liam leaves one of the extra bedrolls out for Ivan.

"The hardest prey is healthy prey," he explains.

But then he buys Ivan new clothes, new boots. He shows him how to wield a knife, how to sew a shirt. The final straw comes when, one morning, instead of leaving Ivan in the living room, he lets him come into the den.

"You treat him like he's one of us," Junior says, in a calm manner, so like Liam. "You treat him like he's a selkie." He paces the living room just after dawn, when Ivan's scampered off to escape his deadly blow. "Do you even want him to be caught?"

His father looks away, ashamed.

Junior wraps his bearskin around him, growing and morphing into his true form. He strolls past the place he can smell Ivan hiding, dips into the river, and swims beyond Liam's wards.

Being childless changes Liam. No longer does he warn Ivan when the sun is about to go down. Instead, they spend their nights training, that deadly edge gone from Ivan's nightly trial. For five years, Ivan learns how to breathe right, how to silence his steps, how to swim, how to fight. While he sleeps, he can hear the slow steps of the selkie, searching for the skin he's tucked away in a hole he's too big to squeeze through. Five years pass like this.

Liam is nearing eleven years old, which is quite old for a jupiter bear. Ivan cares for him now, going to the surface to get goods and medicines, keeping the fire stoked and the blankets in piles where Liam can reach. It's when he's wheezing, so weak he cannot feed himself, that Ivan returns with his cloak.

"I'm way stronger than you now." A twenty-one-year-old Ivan juts out his chin. "So don't even try to fight me." He places the skin on Liam's chest. His heart does something strange in his chest when he sees his pseudo-father place a fond hand along the ears of the hood.

"Keep the cloak, Ivan." He coughs. "Give it to my kids when they come of age, won't you? They'll come back to kill you. I know they will."

He pulls the cloak back. "Of course."

When Liam passes, the magic keeping this haven of the sewer leaves with him. All sorts of creatures come to lay claim to the new real estate, and Ivan isn't skilled enough with wards to stop them. He takes what he can and moves into the rafters of an abandoned warehouse in the golem district, notoriously soft-hearted to wayward souls despite their stoic nature.

The survival training with the selkies lends itself well to all sorts of dangerous work. No punch hurts more than Lucinda's claw. No target has better hearing than Junior. And no one is as true to their word as Liam, making Ivan realize that no one can be trusted when his magic flutters with every lie that comes across their lips. So, he fights and stumbles and fails until he moves upwards, and he's left with a new appreciation for the family that tried to kill him.

This is what fathers do—train you to take on the world, he thinks. And this must be what love is, because Liam taught Ivan the same lesson he taught his other children. But he made Ivan his enemy, which made him stronger, and perhaps it means Liam always loved Ivan more. He loved him like piers love oysters, how bears love the sea.

HE'S REMINDED of this because today is weapons training with Elaine, and she's managed to get a good swipe across his cheek with a pair of brass knuckles.

"I told you I have great aim," she scolds, dabbing at the blooming bruise with the hem of her dress.

Oh, Ivan thinks. *This is what it's like to be cared for.*

"You're an idiot," Elaine says. Her hands are gentle across his face, wiping delicately across stinging, shallow cuts. Ivan can't help but compare it to Liam's rough hands slapping ointment across a newly healed knee. They only had so many wipes, so many bandages, and so much patience for Ivan Gray.

His heart clenches as he watches her peel back an old bandage cover on his elbow, revealing the star pattern underneath. He stops breathing when she places both hands on him, but he forces an inhale.

I was wrong, he thinks. *That wasn't love before.*

"A guy could get used to this," he says, voice wobbly.

She smiles, thumb smoothing over the now-stuck bandage. "I'll be meaner next time."

"I don't know if my heart could take it." He presses a hand against his chest.

His heart has been one of the most reliable organs over the years, only suffering from the curse with an arrhythmia here, a clogged artery there. Once it had even threatened to stop beating at all. He's never been so grateful to feel it skip a beat.

20

UNWELCOME GUESTS

The winter melting into spring makes Ivan go a bit mad, Elaine decides. He's been more attentive as of late, walking her to class on his days off, bringing her breakfast. Today, though, it's clear something in his brain has snapped.

"Show me all your favorite corners."

She frowns. "Corners?" She puts down the paper she's reading, with the headline *ANOTHER HOUSE BURGLED, WOMAN FOUND MUMMIFIED*.

"Everyone wants to be in the highest tower, the newest labs. I want you to show me the best corner walls Locke has to offer."

When she doesn't move, he adds, "When you've seen as much as I have, you tend to look for new curiosities wherever you can."

So, after their project meeting, she shows him to the corners she thinks are best.

"Is that pewter and marble?" he gasps, crouching to touch the point where the walls meet reverently.

She rolls her eyes, but that doesn't keep the smile from her face. "You look mad. Or like you're looking for weak spots."

He grins at her. "Oh? I thought you didn't like defense magic."

"I don't," she sniffs. "But my uncle is an expert. He once took me to a bar for what I thought would be my first drink, only to have me inspect wall crevices for moss."

"Hm." His attention is still on the corner molding.

"My uncle's working on a project with the dean, too."

Ivan sticks his tongue out in distaste. "What kind?"

"Something to do with security? All the break-ins on powerful houses have the city leaders up in arms."

There were at least two new robberies a month since the Nygard break in, and the police were no closer to catching who's responsible.

Ivan's grin is tense. "I didn't know the city consulted potion masters."

"Well. He's a retired spell caster. And he knows the university better than most." Enjoying his attention, she adds in a family secret. "He worked for the university for years until they fired him. Something has them worried enough to hire him again, and now they have to pay double for his consulting fee."

Ivan stands from a crouch, pocketing something inside his cloak. The sun is bright despite the clouds painting the sky gray. Under it, she can see the deepening of the dark circles under his eyes and his thousand-yard stare.

He bends down when he notices her attention, stuffing his face into the side of her neck. Her hand comes up to pat his curved back.

"I don't like your uncle," comes out muffled against her collarbone.

She pulls back, and he lifts his head from the empty air to pout at her.

"He doesn't like you either," she bristles.

It's unfortunate they don't get along. Uncle Neil was there for her when the rest of her family couldn't understand her need for isolation, how her flighty behavior wasn't rooted in something as changeable as fear, but as essential as breathing.

Neil's own need for isolation is much more predictable than hers. Every six years, he goes to the eternal mountains of Alacra. Alacra is a range eclipsed by the Allapan Mountain Range, and it's easy to mistake them as simple hills if one doesn't know their history. It's believed they originate from the world's first fault line shift; before plants, before anything we would define as life, when the earth was just simple cells that accidentally collided.

Neil spends months on end beneath that sacred range. So, when Elaine's dad engaged her in another fight about how dangerous leaving without a word could be, Neil had interrupted. "It's bad luck to keep a mage from wandering when they need to, Albert. What if Mom had never trusted me enough to leave and come back?"

Elaine's penchant for disappearing is why her mother had insisted she stay in the mountains.

"You wander like the wind." Her mother sighed the same thing every time Elaine reappeared. "If you're not careful, it will blow you farther than I can reach."

Neil showed her parents that wandering was natural, instinctual, in the family. For them, sticking to one home stoked their magic. For Neil and Elaine, staying meant snuffing it out. She will always defend him, especially to Ivan.

"I wouldn't even be here without him, you know."

"Yes, you'd be naked in a forest brushing your hair while the salmon sang sweet nothings in your ear. I know."

She blushes and, angry, leaves him behind. "We're going to be late to training."

"Don't be sad, I would have found you and brought you to me!"

~

They all turn up at eight a.m. on a cold Tuesday at the training field. Today, Ivan has decided to do something a little more dangerous with all the smoking potions they've made. These ones do more than just cloud your vision.

Today, they work on the precipitation potion. It's a mix of rain from Garriver, rain from the Amazon, and a tear shed by both Clarke and Elaine. The clay Clarke brought in is from the Tongass rainforest, and ancient place known for its muskegs, temperate weather, and lack of snakes. Snakes were outcast millions of years ago, though there's only whispers left as to why. Some say it was a powerful vengeance spell, and others say it was during a great war between birds and lizards. The snakes are the descendants of disgraced reptiles who lost the land for all their kind. The Tongass sits over its own fairy ring, making a clay that can naturally withstand rain that has magical properties.

A precipitation potion is as easy to make as scrambled eggs, but it's the potioneer that makes it powerful. Using the right ingredients is what makes your rainfall change from a mere drizzle to a downpour. The tears are the heavy cream and spice of this recipe, and they'd both collected enough to make at least seven. One tear for each batch. Clarke is tired looking today, skin dry and cracked.

"Are you all right," Elaine asks.

"Not used to crying. I get dehydrated pretty easily."

She frowns. "Let's wait a bit before beginning.

"No," he shakes his head, beginning to stand, "I can power through."

She pushes him back to the ground. "No. Drink some water, then we can start. I have accounting homework to get through, anyways."

He nods, settling back down and taking a large gulp from his bottle. They sit there in silence, and when Clarke feels better, he peers curiously at her work.

"Accounting?"

"I'm aiming to be an accountant when we graduate," she says, without stopping her pen from moving. "I'm good with numbers."

"It's certainly less volatile than potions."

"And whatever else Ivan's got planned." To Elaine, numbers aren't just a way to make money. Because they are certainly that. But it's the way that there's only one right answer; and you're either good, or bad at it. You either follow the letter of the law, or you get fired. Numbers are the most consistent thing in her life, these days, and accounting at its core stays the same.

"General ledger," Clarke reads over her shoulder. "That's where a business does all their bookkeeping, right?"

"Very good," she nods.

"That's basic knowledge," Ivan chimes in, turning away from his conversation with Nero. "Lainey, test me."

"No."

He groans. "Come on. I know lots of stuff about math. And if I don't, luck takes care of it."

"Probability magic doesn't teach you words," she takes a breath. "All right. Fine. What does 'Yield' mean?"

"Slow down or stop."

"Wrong. 'Yield refers to the return on investment (ROI) or the rate of return earned. It is typically expressed as a percentage and represents the income an investment generates relative to its cost. Yield is an important metric for investors in assessing the profitability and attractiveness of different investment opportunities'."

He blinks blankly at her.

"Alright. I think I'm ready to give the precipitation potion a go. Elaine?"

Clarke and Elaine go to work at their table, Nero and Ivan watching closely. They have to be careful with this one, as the wrong proportions can end in a twenty-minute nap at best, and a coma at worst.

"We'll get right to it. Clarke, you'll pull back once you finish making the cauldron. Lainey, the temperamental nature of the potion is a great chance to test your ability to see the odds."

"Don't you think she should be wearing some PPE to make this safer?"

Ivan shrugs. "She doesn't need safe. She needs practice."

Clarke crosses his arm. "I don't know if I'm comfortable jumping into putting her into a possible coma," he says.

Elaine can see the word *wuss* on the tip of Ivan's tongue and decides to intervene. "I'll be fine, Clarke. I have to jump in headfirst, either today or another time."

"It might be fine for *him* to injure a student, but it could cost me my scholarship."

Ivan groans in dismay. "Fine. We'll find a mask for her to wear. Happy?"

Clarke looks to Elaine, and she nods in confirmation.

"And we'll get goggles for you as well."

"Academics," Ivan says, shaking his head. He turns to Elaine. "On the field, you wouldn't have any of this. It'd just be you tracking the odds to make sure you succeed."

"I'll use them when I'm portioning out the potion."

"Boring," he groans. "Nero, could you go find a mask and goggles? The last time I tried to enter somewhere my T.A. pass didn't grant access to, a cabinet bit me."

When Elaine is properly suited, she stands in front of the table once more. She sets the instructions she had her uncle check over before she left the house. There were textbook recipes, but she trusted her uncle more than a textbook. Neil wrote:

Heat local rain to 180 degrees Fahrenheit

Pour half out into a separate vial. Add Amazonian rain to pot at exactly 104 degrees

Stir clockwise twice

Stir counterclockwise once, then again when temperature reaches 200 degrees

When potion turns carmine red, add in potioneer and cauldron maker's tears. NOT when it's magenta, and it's TOO LATE IF IT TURNS BURGUNDY

Potion will be a shimmery cornflower color when complete

The spell is simple, but not easy. It will require her full concentration, and even with the instructions she'll need to double-check the temperatures between every ingredient. She's muttering the steps aloud to herself when Ivan reaches out and crumples up the instructions.

"Ivan," three voices shout out.

"This is about using your affinity, not your brain," he tells her.

"That's not mutually exclusive for most people," she hisses, reaching out for the crumpled paper in a panic. She knows that even without the instructions, Ivan still expects her to brew this potion.

"You can do it. I have a good feeling about this."

She did not have this. Her failure happens over and over again, until she's trying with the seventh and final batch. Her magic doesn't show her percentages, and instead washes the world in a yellow pallor, so she's left to rely on a gut feeling she hasn't mastered yet. For the first time in weeks, she has that queasy feeling in her stomach while trying to use her affinity.

"Seventh time's the charm!"

She closes her eyes to shut out the yellow (and the yelling), but that only makes her nausea worse. Instead, she re-opens her eyes and looks down to see a carmine red potion. She smiles to herself beneath her mask and grabs the vials of her and Clarke's tears. Adding them, her shoulders relax when the potion turns a shimmering light blue. As soon as she's done, she turns away to puke away from the potion.

Someone hisses in sympathy. Elaine is covered in sweat, bent over her knees.

"Elaine."

She winces at the tone. "Do not come near me." she says.

"You did it, though. I knew you could."

She throws her arms up in the air.

"I would've been done ages ago if you'd let me keep the instructions. Throwing them away was a waste of time.

"It wasn't a waste of time; I need you to *focus* on your magic. You've seen me use our affinity a thousand times. I've seen you do it before, and you proved me right again today."

He trains her how he lives—pushing adrenaline for results. But Elaine isn't Ivan. She is cyclical. She is a train always on time, and he thinks she'll improve if he takes her off the rails. Her magic pours out under stress, overexerting while only using a fraction she can scoop out, mercury in frantic hands.

"This can't just be a game, not if you want to make a living off our affinity."

"It's not a game. This is my life. If I can't find a job with magic..." She stands up, shouting in frustration, "You're a terrible teacher." She storms off the field, toward the locker rooms.

"Well, I'm all you've got." He strides after her.

She can feel Clarke and Nero watch them with rapt fascination.

"Honestly, Ivan, would it kill you to be kind?" Elaine says.

"No, but it might kill you."

She slips into the women's locker room before Ivan can stop her. She hears Ivan's shout of alarm behind her but doesn't turn around to help.

"Sorry," Clarke's muffled voice comes through the door. "Magic slipped."

Elaine scrubs her skin raw in the showers, flecks of dried potion clogging the drain, the colors sticking easily to her pale hair. She changes into a fresh coral-pink gown beneath her blue cloak and makes her way home uninterrupted.

When she enters her bedroom, she screams. Glowing eyes blink at her from the corner of her ceiling, observing her curiously.

"You need to find another corner to sleep in, Roger," she scolds.

Roger flies about the room with an exuberance that would've been impossible before his transformation. His once brown fur is now the same inky black color as his bat wings, which he has slowly but surely learned to navigate with. He's taken to hanging upside down like a bat, which is admittedly very cute when she remembers he's not a random creature in her room.

He lands on her head, wings blowing hair into her face as he settles on the crown of her head.

"Keep me company while I study these wards."

He makes a pleased noise when she scratches a finger on the underside of his chin.

The rest of her evening is spent studying protective wards for Uncle Neil. His constant exhaustion has culminated in a few ruined potions and warrants her adding a complex alarm spell to his cloak. The one she chooses will make the whole fabric vibrate when within fifteen feet of malicious magic. The constant vibration is sure to anger him, but she doesn't trust him to keep himself awake in the face of danger these days, much less detect it.

His perceptive and cautious nature has spoiled into something paranoid and vicious since her kidnapping, and he's acting like a badger does when backed into its den, the only exit blocked by a reaching hand. She writes out the ward before she begins to practice it verbally. It would be easy enough to recite the book word for word, but the shields that truly stick have a personal touch, a truth that makes the caster's magic stick better to the surface.

Her blinks grow longer and longer, and she stretches, spine popping in release from her hunched studying position. She changes into her nightgown and heads down the stairs to grab a cup of water for bed.

A shiver passes through the house, and then her own body, the change in air chilling her exposed toes. She clutches at her elbows to fight off a full-body shudder. The reason for the sudden danger in the air becomes clear when she looks out the window—someone new has moved past the wards.

She rushes into the kitchen where Neil scrubs at a spotless pot. It's a testament to his fried nerves that she felt it before him.

He looks up, takes in her horrified gaze, and drops the pot with a clang into the sink. He sniffs the air, unmistakable fury taking over his gaze as he spots the same shadowed figure through the window she did moving towards their front door. He growls, moving forward and wrapping her tightly in his cloak. She wheezes when he draws the string too tightly around her neck.

As she rearranges it, he swears and prowls the kitchen, muttering until the runes etched into every available surface of the watchtower begin to cover the whole room in a raging glow. Their home no longer quivers in the cold but shakes with his magic so strongly she collapses forward onto the kitchen counter, grasping at it for stability.

Magic is connected to someone's core. The affinity is its personality, the way it most easily manifests. But much like people, magic's power is rooted in its existence. It is used like legs help you climb, and eyes help you see. Magic, like all other ligaments, boils down to the three base instincts: fight, flight, or call for help.

She's never felt so clearly smothered by her uncle's magic—

it's in her lungs, it's wrapping around her to the point that she begins to sweat, like a hug one would expect from a dragon guarding gold. She falls back onto a kitchen stool when her knees shake from its force.

"I told him not to come here anymore," he snarls, grabbing his staff, which shakes with the same rage as its master.

The watchtower glows so warm it must be like what lies beneath the eternal mountains—smothering, intense, bright. The door swings open and she recognizes the intruder instantly. It's clear he's put up illusions and charms around himself, as that sickly ominous aura isn't emanating like it did when she visited Neil's office.

"Aren't you going to invite me in?" says the Someone.

Neil grips his staff tighter. He repositions his body in an attempt to hide Elaine, but all it does is draw attention to her and the stark height difference between them. The mass of shadows below the hood turns from Neil to her, but there are no eyes for her to stare into.

"We can talk outside." Neil's eyes now flit between the intruder and Elaine, a hint of fear in them.

"No. I'll let myself in."

When he penetrates the threshold, it ignites another ward, blowing the shadows and gray hood off his face. This, too, must be an illusion, as the face revealed is the most beautiful she's ever seen.

He's boyishly good-looking, with blond hair and bright-blue eyes with a startled deer in the headlights glare to them, and a natural downturn to pink, pouty lips. Those lips hiss and soft-looking hands bring the cloak back over his head, shielded once more. But the house has cleared whatever illusion protected his identity, so he must rely fully on the hood to hide himself. She notices he's leaning on a cane gilded in silver, and the hand holding it is adorned in gaudy rings covered in a rainbow of gemstones.

He steps outside their home's threshold, and his illusion shadows his face once more. "Ever deceptive, Neil Leatherforth."

Neil steps forward and a bright, blaring yellow percentage takes over Elaine's field of vision, accompanied by only one word:

DANGER - 72%

It's vague, but she knows what her brain is implying. On shaky legs, she joins the two men and takes Neil's cloak off, handing it back to him. He pushes her back, but not before taking the cloak, and shuts the door in her face with a scowl.

The watchtower gives her space to breathe when Neil and the beautiful creature step beyond its boundaries. Safe, she drops to her knees, gasping for air.

Who is this shadowed stranger? And what business could he possibly have with Uncle Neil?

~

SHE SHOWS up to morning training at Locke rattled, Clarke and Nero already waiting.

"Y'alright?" Nero grunts from a pushup.

"Fine."

"I only ask because you're looking as tired as Gray."

When she doesn't respond, Nero replies between push-ups, "Don't worry. Pushing through is what makes us stronger."

The camaraderie surprises her. Nero has been kinder lately. Perhaps she can get through practice with less tension.

Ivan appears and says, "Wow, you look like shit, Lainey. Morning," Ivan greets the rest of them with a closed-eye smile. "We'll start with the final potion: decay."

Decay potions are not very common in academic settings, due to their inherently sinister nature. Quickening something's death, or making it rot faster, hardly has practical uses beyond grim and malicious reasons. There are three types of decay potions: radioactive, temporal, and true. Radioactive decay potions use radiation to further the death of the object it's poured onto. Temporal decay is a bit trickier, as it speeds up the deterioration rate of whatever it touches. A potioneer has to make sure the item they use the potion on has a faster decay rate than the container they put it in. True decay potions are categorized as an Impossible Potion. Not because it's truly impossible, though there are only a handful of potioneers alive that can brew it correctly, but because it always kills the potioneer that makes it. Making one is like signing your own death warrant.

They'll be working on making a Temporal potion, today. Time is the easiest form of decay to reverse in Garriver, the city of timeliness, and Elaine called the nurse's office a week ago to make sure they have anti-aging potions ready in case anything goes wrong. They've scheduled time in one of the hazard labs just in case something goes wrong.

"I brought clay from the first grave of a cemetery," Clarke says. "Take this one as slow as you need. Temporal decay is the most reversible, but it's still not fun if you get splashed."

Ivan steps forward. "Lainey, a moment."

Nero and Clarke scatter, happy to leave Elaine to her fate.

"What?" She eyes him warily.

"I believe in you." He nods, looking her in the eyes. He clasps his hands on her shoulders.

Her heart rate increases. Gods, his hands. Maybe this was his apology. She opens her mouth, filled with words of forgiveness.

"And I'm a little sorry for this." He shoves her.

She flails, falling backwards into the lab, alone with the cauldron and the ingredients. Ivan air locks the door behind her.

"I took the instructions. You should be terrified."

"Ivan," Nero warns. Even she's nervous in the face of Ivan's risk. "What are you doing? This goes against school protocol!"

"She'll be fine. She works best under pressure." He looks into her eyes. "You can do this."

Elaine takes a deep breath. He's right. She can do this. She feels the magic even now, flowing through her like it has so many times before. She lets out a deep breath, and sees a percentage appear in front of her:

Pouring half of the manticore tail powder—85%

"See? She's fine, Nero."

There's a loud bang and then all goes black.

ELAINE GROANS, vision blurry as she comes to. There are white ceiling tiles above her and a large blob to her right.

"Ive?" she mutters, confused.

"Oh, you're awake," a voice breathes. It's off, a little too low, too calm.

"Clarke?" she tries again.

"You had a bit of an incident and ended up in the nurse's office. The nurse said your nymph blood made you less susceptible to decay, since as a species you're made for transmutation, not rotting. You're lucky you didn't end up a vegetable."

Clarke is taut with anger, and she reaches out to place a reassuring hand on his.

"I'll get him back. Put a venereal disease in his coffee."

He scrubs a hand over his face, looking a bit tired and mostly horrified. "Elaine, that's illegal."

"I'm joking," she lies.

"I'm not sure exactly what's going on with you two, but I did hear a bit of your argument. If I may...there are many with an explosive affinity. But we all connect to our cores differently. Nero uses her mind. I use my hands. Ivan seems to fly in with reckless abandon. But you like math, statistics, thinking things through before jumping in. To connect with your magic, don't think like Ivan, think like you."

She nods as Clarke excuses himself to get a cup of coffee.

A knock at the door breaks her out of her thoughts. Ivan clears his throat, approaching her bed. He stares down at a crack in the tile, looking abashed at the floor. He looks worse than she feels, sweaty, like his mind is parsing through a thousand thoughts at once. "I...did not expect this outcome. If you'd trusted me, we could've done it."

"We made a mistake. You can't finish a potion right when it's already been ruined."

"That might be true, but we could've made something new."

"That wasn't the assignment."

He shakes his head. "Success in the real world isn't about getting it all right, it's about getting it done."

She raises a brow. "If you're not here to apologize—"

"I'm sorry," he interrupts. "So, so sorry. I can't imagine life without you. And that's the problem. Being around me is deadly. I worry that if you can't handle the work study—" he swallows, like his throat is dry, "—then how could you take being around me?" Then, quieter, "Around my curse."

Elaine reaches out a hand to pat him. "Ivan. You're not going to kill me. And I'm not going to kill you. We're *lucky*, right?"

He breathes out. "Right. Lucky, I..." His face turns ashen, and he coughs blood up onto the white sheets.

The smell of mold and copper fills her nose, and she covers it. She wishes she wasn't wearing this stupid, backless hospital gown, or he isn't sitting out of arm's reach. Ivan's face is sweaty, and he's staring down at his bloodied hands. Elaine's eyes shoot to the door. The mold smell is fading away, too quickly.

"I've smelled that before," she mutters. "If I could only remember where I smelled it before."

"What?" Ivan says, eyes far away.

"Nothing. You alright?"

Whatever wall crumbled is back up, that cold politeness back in his eyes.

"I'm sorry," he says. Then he swoops back out the door.

She flops down, groaning. So much for talking it through.

MUCH LIKE THE WEATHER, his mood has oscillated between hot and cold since her trip to the hospital. Today, they're crammed into her windowsill, backs on either side and feet tangled together. Cold slips in through poor caulking, but she stays warm wherever they're touching.

Ivan stares at Roger, who hangs upside down from the open cabinet. "Aren't you curious about why he got wings?"

Elaine shrugs. "Nature adapts and changes. When my sister decided she was a fish, she became one. Change is a part of living."

"Do you think we'd be a good couple?" he asks.

"No."

He lets out a sharp breath of laughter. "Alright. Friends with a multitude of benefits?"

"No. Try again."

Ivan ruffles his hair, the bits at the end sticking back up.

It's unfairly sexy, Elaine thinks. It makes her think of his skilled hands elsewhere. In silver hair, arms slowly curling up and in—

"Besides, you're supposed to be abstaining. You're my TA. It's a conflict of interest."

"You are...annoying." He presses his foot harder against hers.

"Oh, that's nice. Now you're definitely not going to be my boyfriend."

He scoots closer. "It's true! What, you only want my praise? Because that's going to take hours."

"Backtracking, are we?"

"No, it's just easier to name your one fatal flaw."

"Annoying?"

"Annoying."

Elaine pushes him away, only for Ivan to move back into her arms. He smiles up at her from her lap. His hand entwines with hers, calloused and scarred. It's silent for a long moment, and she almost relaxes enough to enjoy it, but he opens his mouth again.

"It's clear how badly you want to kiss me."

She grabs each side of his head, forcing it to jolt side to side. *It can't be pleasant*, she thinks.

But he sighs and goes limp at her violent touch. He lets her slip the yellow triangular glasses from his eyes and place them on top of her head.

"You have magic hands, Lainey."

"We all have magic hands."

Ivan's brow furrows, as he takes her hands back in his. His fingers brush over her knuckles, her nails, the pads of her fingers. He hums in affirmation. "Not like these. I'd be able to tell these were your hands in a room full of thousands. Even if you had no magic at all."

Her cheeks grow warm at his statement. It can't possibly be true. Still, the way he looks at them makes her want to believe him.

"You're an idiot."

He ignores her, closing his eyes and fluttering his lashes against her palm.

~

She's writing an essay in the courtyard when she sees Ivan speed walking by. His eyes flit to each corner of the yard, occasionally looking behind him. Taking pity on his search, she stands and waves a hand to get his attention. The panic leaves his face, and he strides over in long, quick steps.

"There's my girl!" he says, eyes roving over her lying atop her blue robe in the grass. He unclasps his brown pelt and lays it on the ground. He drops down and wordlessly gestures for her to join him on top of it.

Rolling her eyes doesn't stop the grin from coming over her face. "There's barely enough room for you."

He grasps at her arms, pulling her forward until she's half across his cloak, her feet still laying on the tips of her own.

"My cloak is better suited for makeshift spontaneous blanketeering. Yours is for protection!"

She wants to point out that she's only been using the cloak for much more hazardous situations thanks to him. The girlish voice in her head whispers, *What if he lets you pull away?* So, she scoots the rest of the way forward, knees knocking his as they sit together on just his pelt.

He bumps his shoulders against hers. "Isn't this much better? And your pretty cloak *must* be shown off." He lifts it, but instead of placing it on her shoulders, he places it along his own. "Mm. I can feel the self-righteousness flowing through me." He raises his voice to a mock-girlish tone. "School is very important. I can't come out, Ivan, I have a report due on where all the professors store their sticks when they're not shoved up their—"

She scowls and reaches out to grab the cloak. "That's enough. If you're going to be mean, I'll take it back."

He leans away from her, and she follows, moving into his lap to reach for the clasp. He pulls the hood up, then uses both hands to grab her wrists. She laughs and wrestles to free herself from his grip. It's no use, as he's got a tight hold on her and won't let go.

In his high voice, he says, "I'd never lay a finger on my dear Ivan. He's so big and strong, even if I won't admit it. I do so hope he'll teach me *much more* than magic."

A frown twists her face, and she pulls back.

He realizes he's gone too far and lets go of her wrists immediately. "I didn't mean—"

"It's fine," she cuts him off. Without thinking, and led by the petty thoughts in her mind, she blurts out, "I have a date tonight, so we won't be able to hang out."

His mouth drops open in shock. He clamps it shut again, muscles twinging along his jawline. It's Ivan's turn to scowl, his back straightening from his slouch. "A date? With whom?"

"You wouldn't know him," she replies, keeping her face carefully neutral. She tries to climb out of his lap, but his hands move from her wrists to her hips. She grabs his green, frog-shaped glasses and puts them on to try and lighten the mood, but the subject matter has fully sobered Ivan from his previously playful mood.

"And your uncle's allowing it?"

She scoffs at the implication. "I'm not an infant, Ivan. My uncle couldn't care less who I get dinner with. And he's out of town." While she's still worried about the subsequent exhaustion that follows Neil after working strange hours, now that she has a date, she's grateful.

His playful smile drops, and his eyes narrow, seemingly trying to find someone in the crowd.

Her hands move to her scalp, fiddling with the braided crown she'd put her hair in today. "I have class. Cloak, please?"

He keeps his eyes on everything but her.

"Ivan," she hisses.

"Fine," he replies. The fabric clenches in his grip for a moment. Taking a deep breath, he loosens his hold and leans forward to place it onto her shoulders. His hands brush against her bare shoulders for only a moment, but she feels her breath catch at the motion. Their magic tingles between them, kindred sparks. He must feel it too because his eyes soften.

The words are on the tip of her tongue: *Do you wish it was you?*

But as her own face softens, his grows sharp and cold. He fixes the clasp, and she pulls off his lap, both standing and redressing in tense silence. For a moment, they stand there. He opens his mouth, closes it. He raises a finger and opens his mouth as if he's going to make a point. She waits, expectant. Instead, he turns around and storms off.

Elaine feels tired all of a sudden. Anger, confusion, and bafflement all sit on her chest like an anchor. She wants to follow after him, demanding he kiss her if he's so upset that someone else cares enough to take her on a date. She takes a step forward but stops once she realizes she doesn't know what for. To demand an explanation? Maybe he'd grovel, and if he did a good enough job, she'd tell him he can take her instead.

The bell chimes, signaling there's only five minutes to get to the lecture hall. She can't be late again because of Ivan Gray. She heads to class to give a report to her narcoleptic tenure professor who still occasionally calls her "Elmer."

Class is spent reading up on the practical uses of human saliva in potion brewing, and Professor Sap only snorts awake when the final bell rings.

"Read chapters ten and fourteen! And bring in an essay on the hierarchy of runes."

She'd written that three times already, each garnering a better grade than the last.

"Thank you, Professor." She waves goodbye.

21

THIRD FAILURE'S THE CHARM

IVAN

Ivan waits outside the classroom for her. He slants against an arched doorway, a mockery of aloofness. He had quite a stressful dream about Elaine the night before. She'd been laughing with an aardvark in a very fancy looking cloak, and he'd been stuck behind glass, and when he looked down, he was a goldfish! And every time he tried to scream no sound came out, instead it all turned into bubbles floating to the top of the tank. He wears an intense frown, and he agitates and twists magic between his fingers. He stops and stands up straight when she exits, clearing the space between them with a few long strides.

"What makes him better than me?" he demands.

Elaine rolls her eyes. "Ivan, he's not better than you."

"Then why are you going out with him?"

She eyes Ivan up and down, eyes never softening, even under his best pout. "You're the one who didn't want to date. You think it's more important for us to be partners. So, if someone else takes notice of me, I have every right to go with him on a date." In her final blow, she remarks coyly, "This isn't very 'just friends' of you, Ivan."

He eyes the wall behind them.

He could press her against it, flick up her skirt—Is it new? It's pretty—and make her come against his hand before her next lesson. Make her forget the other man's name.

"Who's touching you," he'd ask. "Who makes you come quicker than anyone else ever could?"

"You," she'd breathe. "God, Ivan, you."

"Ivan," snaps the real Elaine, "you're not listening. We can reschedule to next Thursday. Don't be weird about this."

Ivan flicks a finger against the skirt she's wearing. "Is this new? It's pretty."

Elaine bites her lip, but he still sees her smiles before she can hide it. "I will see you *later*, Ivan."

He shifts his pant leg. When did he start to get hard again? It's so difficult to remember when he's around her.

"Right." He nods. "Later."

He waits to watch her walk away, salmon swimming across the bottom hem of her cloak. He runs his fingers through his hair, shoulders squared, and chest puffed in case Elaine looks back at him. She doesn't, and her hair shimmers like silver scales as she leaves him behind. When she turns the corner, he slumps over, thumping his head onto the wall in front of him.

"I'm in trouble," he breathes.

He has a check-in with the apothecary about his Locke mission, and he still hasn't even found the entrance to the fairy ring. Ivan kicks open the apothecary door with an excuse on his lips.

"You know I'm good for it, Delius."

The imp looks up from the document in front of him, tail swishing with agitation. He plucks the cigar from his lips, puffs a few rings of smoke, and watches them disperse when they hit the low ceiling. Green slitted eyes turn on Ivan before they close again, and he puffs on his cigar once more.

"I've been on that campus, day in and day out, with no new clues. There's too much ground to cover and it'll be years before—"

Delius picks up a pouch of gold with two long nails and throws it at Ivan's feet. "Mission's been pulled, full payment delivered."

Ivan grabs the coins, opening to confirm it is, in fact, gold.

When he doesn't leave, Delius rolls his eyes and pulls his cigar from his mouth. "It's all there, you're free to double-check in the back room."

"No one pays full price for an unfinished job."

Delius hums. "The luck mage bounty's been changed too. Only paying for a live one."

By all considerations, Ivan failed. He still has about a month to completely botch it, technically, but he is no closer to finding the entrance to Locke's dungeon. Something here stinks. Considering the time lock on the luck mage bounty ends just before the solstice, and his mission's been pulled a month before that, something's amiss. Those two things should be good news, lucky news, but he's no fool. The two events are definitely connected, even if he hasn't figured out the why or the how. He's certain the answer to both questions lies within the *who*.

He strolls right up to the imp's counter, who still hasn't looked up from his book. "Did the client drop the money recently?"

Delius closes the book and rolls his eyes up to the ceiling, sighing so long and loud that Ivan worries he'll pass out from exertion before he answers his questions.

He flops his head to the side, looking down on Ivan. "Paid in full. No name left."

Ivan runs a hand tightly through his hair. The lights are

suddenly too loud, and he pulls his hood over his head, muffling the outside stimulation. The wards are getting old, and beneath the pelt, it no longer smells faintly of the selkies who taught him to survive.

The mission being cancelled, and Ivan not getting paid? That would be cause for an argument. An attempt to ruin the reputation of whoever requested his help. But to have it happen just a few months before the bounty is active again, with a change in requirement to "alive", is alarming.

His affinity tells him this reeks of connection. Whoever wants him to break into Locke has cancelled the mission before the solstice, when Locke is holding a ball. If the bounty and mission were set by the same person, that means the bounty was a threat to complete the mission. But why is he getting paid in full for a job he technically doesn't need to do anymore? And why, suddenly, do they absolutely need a luck mage alive?

"It's not just for me." He paces back and forth in front of Delius. "It's for the woman I came here with. She's like me. But she's clean, no history with the undercity, no experience with being hunted down. She's good, Delius. And if they realize what she is—what if something happens to her? I need to find them, not for me, for her." If Ivan doesn't complete this mission, his gut tells him Elaine will have to. And worse: they might have already decided to use her instead.

He must strike an intimidating figure, wrapped in his cloak like a pouting child being made to leave the pool, because Delius speaks again.

"Someone's coming in after you to officially clear it. If you stay, you can see if you recognize them."

His shoulders slump in relief. "Thank you, Delius."

Then, with horrible timing, his magic urges him to leave.

"No," he curses under his breath. "Why? What else could possibly matter?"

Lainey, it whispers. *Lainey, Lainey.*

He's out the door with a curse, the chilling breeze of winter greeting him on his way out. The city is beautiful, even when there are no stars in the sky. His shoulders bump into those of passersby as his feet lead him forward. Thinking of Elaine, Lainey, Elaine Aquae of the watchtower. He wonders then if the world can truly hold the both of them kindly. Before she came into his life, good luck was guaranteed. Now it's like another force is working against his. It can only be her, and he worries every so often that as her magic grows, her power over the outcomes replaces his.

The first time he theorized that she made his magic weaker, he'd decided he'd gladly suffer endless unlucky days. If to be in her presence is to be hurt, for his curse to worsen, his luck to run out, his life picked apart by the silver-haired mage who descended from the mountains just to gift him his own misery, so be it. It's with a heavy heart that he watches her in the warm glow of a small Italian restaurant. Their affinity for luck leads him to her date.

Selfish, he thinks. *Selfish and foolish and spellbound.*

It must be a spell. He clenches his chest out in the blue, blue rain. She sits safe and warm in a short dress he's never seen, smiling shyly (and when has she ever been shy?) at the stranger, the back of his head obscuring where their hands lay on the table. She isn't in danger, but a desire he's too scared to name is.

Ivan walks around the side of the building, stuffing himself behind a tray of empty crates. He slips in when a staff member comes out for a smoke, trading his cloak for a server's coat and bow tie. On his way to her table, he grabs a bottle of champagne.

Lainey's smiling, and his own gaze darkens when he sees her date reach out to touch her fingers with his own.

Bite him, whispers someone left over from his days of

surviving the selkies, someone smaller and dirtier and more feral.

"Champagne for the table?" Ivan asks. His sunglasses are shaped like flamingos wearing their own, tinier sunglasses.

The man she's with, blandly dressed and offensively unoffensive, doesn't notice the angry look on her face; but Ivan, as he always does, watches her from the corner of her eye.

"No, thank you." Her date waves him away. "I'm going to the bathroom. I'll be right back, Elaine."

He goes off to the bathroom, and Ivan settles into his seat. He pops the champagne cork and pours her a glass, then pours one for himself. He spreads his legs out, pressing one against her bare thigh like it belongs there.

"Stop," she hisses.

His grin widens and he slides his foot higher. Her cheeks grow pinker, but she counters, placing a well-heeled shoe against his groin. His arrogance wavers, eyes growing wide before he drops his foot back to her ankle.

She presses lightly against his inner thigh in a warning she clearly delights in. "Why are you here?"

I'm selfish.

"You still have my frog glasses."

"They're in my room. Go get them yourself."

He grabs her ankle, running a thumb across the bone even as she scowls at him for it. "Can't a teacher come to see his best pupil?"

She rolls her eyes, but a smile creeps onto her face even as she does. His hand is traveling further up her leg, and she jerks it back from his hold.

"I'm also here to make sure you're not wasting your time."

"If that were the case, I wouldn't be hanging around you," she says.

He puts a hand to his heart in mock hurt. "You wound me, Lainey baby."

"Excuse me?" her date questions, as he appears back at the table.

A real date would *say* it. *Excuse me.* There. Done.

If it was Ivan coming back from the bathroom, he would have sat on her lap, reached over the table, introduced himself, and asked what business he has with the two of them. Because it's not just him anymore, it's "us." They're a coin, a working clock, a light with a match.

Ivan looks her date up and down, then leaves without another word. Selfish. Even his magic is selfish, taking him away from finding out who his mysterious employer is just to spoil Lainey's night, but he walks back into the apothecary to see if he can outdo himself.

Arms spread wide, he asks, "Where did they go, Delius?"

Delius doesn't look up from the book he's scribbling in. The message is clear—you had your chance and lost it.

Ivan clenches the doorframe and pushes off back into the night, following his gut wherever it leads.

It lands him in front of the same bar it does every night he's worked this case; a place called The Broken Record where he habitually fails to find any clues. He squints as he crosses the threshold, hot air blowing the cold winter night off his shoulders. Who knows, maybe tonight's the one where he gets lucky.

Ivan swirls his finger around the rim of his negroni, and sighs.

"Lady troubles?" The bartender asks.

Elaine's shy smile flashes through his mind. Ivan takes a swig of his drink, a hot flush blooming on the high ridge of his nose.

"Like you wouldn't believe."

The open-air djinn joint sits on top of a three-story brick building, serving cheap alcohol for cheap prices. At night, a misspelling in the ward allows for observation into Locke, excellent for reconnaissance. It's perfect.

"Women are nothing but trouble," the bartender says.

Well, almost perfect.

The bartender wears a tank top with the threads fraying and has a bit of shaving cream drying on the edge of his ear no one's bothered to tell him about.

"Couldn't agree more," Ivan says. He wonders if Lainey is watching a movie to de-stress after her boring, last first date. He scowls at the courtyard. *He* should be watching a movie with her before bed. Then she could compare them back-to-back and remember how much fun she has with him. "They do smell nice," he tags on. He likes when she lets him use her shower and he can go a few days with the scent of her shampoo in his hair.

The bartender grunts, wiping the counter with the same towel that wiped up spilled ketchup half an hour ago. Ivan watches as it makes the wood before him stickier.

"My last girlfriend is the one that rubbed my gas lamp. She rubbed it real *nice* and *slow*. She knew what she was doing." He slaps the dirty towel over his shoulder. "Next thing I know, she's wishing for an open-concept craft cocktail bar with bite-sized eats, and for me to run front of house. That bitch took off with the last wish, and I'm stuck here running a small business."

"Make a lot of money?"

The djinn smiles, revealing sharp teeth. "We're deep in the red."

Ivan spots someone new in the courtyard. The fool's not wearing a mask or a hood, and moving in the most suspicious way possible, head swiveling constantly for anyone that could catch them.

"Amateur," he mumbles, taking another sip.

"Well, not all of us spend our free time smiling at pretty girls then getting sucked off."

Ivan blinks in surprise. He'd forgotten about the bartender.

"I'm sticking to one pretty girl as of late, and she's much

more likely to bite than suck." Ivan stands up, neck craning to get a better look at the figure through the dark. "Damn," he mutters. "I know that cloak." He throws a few gold coins down and hurries outside, slipping through the crowd and towards the empty university courtyards.

Elaine's Uncle Neil is, indeed, trying to break into the college. He's far less skilled about it than Ivan is. The short man taps his staff against several stone blocks. A door opens wide, and Neil steps through.

Ivan has never liked the way his curse acts up around Elaine's paranoid uncle. If he's lucky, the man isn't involved in darker magics, but only a powerful wizard could infiltrate Locke's defenses. And lately, Ivan hasn't been feeling so lucky.

He must be the one who both posted and canceled the mission. His instincts set off alarm bells when he saw him in the sewers, and he realizes, seeing him in the darkened halls of Locke, he must be the man that attacked him when Ivan broke in all those months ago. Neil must have found the entrance, but what is it he's hoping to find inside?

The answer is simple: money. The cold, defeated glaze Ivan saw in his eyes the night after Nygard's office can be found in millions of faces all across the city—people who hate their boss, who hate their job, their life, their friends, and think only money can help them escape.

Elaine's own words flash through his mind: "Money means experience independent from other people's demands." It must run in the family. And what better way to cruise into retirement than with a treasure from the depths of Locke University, the institution that had so cruelly fired him years before? Neil had set up a red herring, then when Locke had gotten scared, they hired the very half-dwarven man who wished to steal from them, giving him the perfect alibi for his crime.

That doesn't matter, Ivan thinks, when he pictures what Elaine's reaction will be to this betrayal, another family member out to hurt her, and willing to put her in the sights of bounty hunters on the off chance they could, what, hurt Ivan? The only mage alive with her affinity, and the only one that could free her from society's shortsighted visions of a perfect future?

He'll hurt Neil before he lets him hurt Lainey. All families fail their children, but Ivan can be her new family. And after doing her this one last, terrible favor, he won't betray her ever again.

22

MY LIFE IS YOURS

Elaine throws her pack to the side and collapses headfirst into the bed. Ivan was a pill at training again. Since he learned Clarke had introduced her and Leon, he's been testing his limits and seeing if he can push him into losing his temper.

He seemed far off in thought the entire morning. It had to be about her date. His reaction had been childish at best, though a smile curls on her lips at the memory of his hand on her ankle, and the dangerous glare he gave Leon when he took his seat. He covets her attention and time the way silverhoppers covet silver, but just because he's decided she's strictly "look, don't touch" doesn't mean the rest of Garriver thinks so. And Clarke introducing her to Leon is no reason to be so cruel to the potter. A nice man that she had an okay time with, and probably won't see again. She can't be preserved like something in a museum. Pinned butterflies look pretty, but they smell of chemicals and can't be touched.

She pinches the ends of her cloak between two fingers, splaying them like wings. The salmon swim along iridescent currents, winding and whirling around the runes and protections of her family.

"I'd make a pretty butterfly," she informs Roger.

Roger lifts his head to check for treats and, seeing none, goes back to his nap.

Anger licks at her heart the more she thinks about Ivan. Still, the way his face pinches when she pays attention to another man...it stirs a prideful satisfaction in her. She cackles until Roger squeaks in protest at being woken up again.

After class, she changed into something more daring than usual. Her dress is gray with blue undertones, marbled in a pattern you'd expect from a statue. It's off the shoulder, and a thorn of raspberries, blueberries, and blackberries run along the sides of her corseted waist. She only put her hair up for practice, but it's now hanging loose around her, an expression of her current high self-esteem. She has her probability, the potions Uncle Neil makes, and a rat willing to bite and claw his way through anyone who dares to hurt her. In pushing herself out of her comfort zone, she's found things out about herself beyond her heritage. She's learned she's brave, that she's quick on her feet and even quicker with her mind, and has created a new home in a city she would've never considered moving to on her own. She's found love and a new, independent future for herself. She admires herself in the mirror, sliding a hand over the sides of her body, but her vanity is interrupted by a gray blur fluttering into her apartment. A messenger pigeon sits on the top of her mirror, holding a very tiny scroll.

Meet me at my place in 10. Bring your A-game. No bad attitudes.

Ivan's place is barren of domestic goods, but the floor is littered with random objects he has to dance around. When he greets her it's with a smile at the door, spilling with such unbridled joy that it does strange things to the butterflies in her stomach. He spills a haphazard armful of vials out of his bag onto the table in front of him. They all vary in color, shape, and size. Many of them have dried crust around the rims, illegible labels, and—most horrifyingly—several of them aren't sealed properly. One rolls towards her before he scoops it back onto his side and lays out a cocktail shaker and several shot glasses in front of them.

"All right," he says. "Pick one and tell me how much to drink."

"Are you serious?"

"As a heart attack. Which I might have if you don't concentrate. This is the collection of potions that currently keep my fragile, nubile heart beating and my body from collapsing into that of a particularly handsome vegetable. Because my medical routine is illegal and entirely self-funded, I have been relying on my intuition to measure out my doses. Now, you'll use your affinity to do it for me."

It feels as though the butterflies are gnawing their way out of her intestines. "I will not put your life in my hands."

"It's not so different from the caves under Nygard, Nygard and Nygard."

"Yes, but that was life or death."

He raises an eyebrow. She looks at the potions in front of her dubiously. Instead of immediately following orders, she takes her time reorganizing the potions on the table so none of them are tipped over and their corks are all tightly closed. Focusing on the pooling magic in her stomach, she allows her core to guide her eyes. The numbers appear in front of her in cardinal yellow, percentages and fractions—and, after a week of practicing her visualization, a pie graph. Her eyes flit first to a red vial, a 2% flashing above it. Next, a long opaque green flask: 52%. She goes through the pile methodically, pleased with how tiny the variances in percentage are. With the potions organized, she can easily mentally categorize them, to resulting in a yellow pie chart.

Her eyes finally home in on a golden potion, shallow with a tiny, spherical case. "That one." She points at it.

Ivan picks it up and shakes it in her direction. "Pour me a glass?"

Elaine skims her hand over the tacky bikini shot glass to grab a normal one and, with shaky fingers, pours a mere two drops in. The numbers shift above her, startling her. Had she made a mistake? The red potion now sits at 95%, and the purple at 15%, where it had been 0% before.

"It's changed," she says. She looks to him, a silent plea for guidance.

He gives no sign of a willingness to help. Finally, he rolls his eyes. "Think, Lainey. We have here in front of us a bunch of illegal vials for curing medical maladies. Why would it change?"

She stares at him then looks back down at the pile. The order is critical for this potion, but order-sensitive medicine has been banned from household use for a century. Which means...

She gasps. "Are these unstable?"

He grins. "We have a winner, ladies and gentlemen. Feast your eyes upon my collection of highly volatile ingredients, frowned upon outside of government-controlled laboratories." He picks one up and shakes it in front of her face. "This one would have me serving three life sentences."

Her nerves are replaced with anger. "This is awful, Ivan. Go to a doctor."

"With what insurance? Pick the next potion."

"No."

He's silent for too long, and when she looks, he is picking up the unfinished shot. She reaches out to slap his hand away, but quicker than she can grab it back, he downs it in one gulp. Their eyes widen in horror.

"Oops."

"You idiot."

"Pick, Lainey!"

"You *idiot.*"

"Pick!"

Her hands scrabble over the available potions. The pie chart disappears, and she must move her eyes frantically over the bottles in order to collect her data.

32%, yellow.

5%, purple.

93%, blue. She drops half of the blue bottle in a glass.

40% yellow.

83%, purple. A drop of purple. Its odds of helping decreases to *7%*.

From the corner of her eyes, she sees Ivan turn a pallid blue. She knows something's missing, and her eyes scan frantically over the spread. She digs through the pile, avoiding anything with a starting number lower than seven. She's running out of time, and it's still not ready to drink. There's a flash of yellow out of the corner of her eye. She turns and sees *72%* slipped under a low dresser. She dives, skinning her knees as her hands scrabble along the dusty surface, sweeping through dust and grime until she grasps a cool bottle.

When she pulls it out, she wastes no time dumping it into her cocktail of poisons. When the shot glass reads *93.5%*, she decides it will have to be good enough. She rushes to a collapsed Ivan's side. His face has deepened to a navy blue. She forces it into his mouth. She cups the back of his neck and tilts the glass with care. His eyes are wide, surprised by his near death. He gulps in breaths of air, no longer choking on his own stupidity.

Finally, he finishes drinking and turns back into his normal hue. He sits back, supported by his palms. She knows he's fine when he laughs, breathy and short.

"Asshole," she snarls, whacking him upside the head. Her heart beats fast in the adrenaline rush. "I could've killed you. Do you have any idea—"

Ivan pushes off the floor and kisses her. She gasps and his tongue sneaks between her waiting lips, tasting sour and sweet and of cough syrup. Despite that, she only pulls away when it starts to taste like soap. She pants, looking up at his wild eyes.

"You saved me," he breathes.

"From yourself," she says. She's not quite as angry as before. "You shouldn't trust me so blindly. Especially with something so important!"

He opens his mouth, then closes it. His expression flits between what she believes is confusion, anger, and then something darker. Something wild.

He pushes back up against her. "I'm incredibly hard right now," he says. As if it's an explanation.

She can feel it, she wants to say. But her tongue is dry. He grinds against her leg, cautious. Hers spread open, and a grin spreads across his mouth even as that dark shadow remains.

"Saved me from myself," he mutters, kissing her, sinking lower and lower and lower.

"You're awful," she says.

He hums against her thigh, either in agreement or contemplation, before continuing up under her skirt , making her shiver as she feels his hands pass her knees. He looks at her through his lashes, and her breath is taken by the softness of them.

"Push me away," he says, even as he grips her thigh tighter.

She feels his magic in his thumbs, begging to stay right where they are. She puts a hand in his thick hair, and he nuzzles against her touch.

She's still stunned at his change, from near dead to reverent and aroused. Part of her wants to keep him on his knees, finally at her disposal instead of the other way around. But something curls uncomfortably in her gut when she sees him down there.

"Come kiss me," she requests, softly.

He rises and closes the gap between them, lips pressing together. She grasps at the back of his neck, tugging at his nape and pulling him closer. Their lips touch gently. Soft, slow. His large hands skate up her sides, grasping at the nape of her neck and the small of her back, firm in their caress of her skin.

The kiss stays sweet, like something might break if they move any harder, any faster. *Trust me*, his lips say. *Trust me blindly*.

Even as she grows wet with want and his erection presses against her thigh, they keep the kisses soft. He is the first to shift the energy as he moves to her neck, and a zap of warmth hits her when he sucks, pressure against the slope of her neck. His hand moves from the small of her back to the front, undoing the lace of her corset. His other hand tightens against the back of her neck, and she lets out a moan. He squeezes it again, but when it doesn't elicit the same reaction, he slips a hand against her breast, finger caressing her nipple. He rubs in circles, watching darkly as it grows erect under his touch. Elaine shivers against his open palm, slightly arching against his touch.

"So sensitive," he says against her neck as he continues to lavish her neck with kisses.

She squirms, desperately looking for stimulation where she needs it most. He alternates between her lips, her neck, her breasts, never reaching lower, and she's reminded of her drunken fantasy outside the frat house, when he refused to move south.

Perhaps, she thinks, *it wasn't such a crazy dream.*

Elaine grinds, ready, against him and sighs in relief when she feels his erection against her own arousal. He pulls away and smiles at her, but instead of reaching down to where she so clearly wants him, he cups her face in his hands. He kisses her once more, readjusts himself in his pants, then sits back and puts on his cloak. He settles behind her to lace her dress up.

She watches, mouth slightly agape, as he searches for hers. With a flourish, he settles it around her, clasping the silver together. Her eyes flicker to his erection, but it's hidden behind his cloak.

"We're going for a walk, Lainey."

"Now?" she says.

"Now," he confirms, kissing her forehead before taking her hand.

She sits there for a moment, bemused. "Now?!" She follows him out the door.

He walks her to the edge of the watchtower, just behind the ward that separates her home and the river. Ivan splays out a thick, woolen blanket along the snow, which covers the entire city in white. Tomorrow it will be slush and slick the streets with black ice and mudholes, but tonight, the city is crisp and biting, and the lampposts replace the stars they cannot see.

He sits down and wraps his arm around her when she sits next to him. The heat draws her in, and she shuffles further into him, melting into his chest.

"I was destined to be cursed and live out all my days trapped in the house of Gray. It's a tradition set by my father, Dorian, and his curse."

Elaine doesn't stop rubbing a hand across his broad chest, even as her mind itches at the name Dorian. Where had she heard it before?

Taking a deep breath, he continues. "I thought if I was away from the casters, it would dispel the curse."

It's basic knowledge that the only things that can stop a curse are the death of the caster, true love's kiss, or the blessing of a power ring. The blessings can only be obtained through seemingly mundane rituals. The odds of receiving a blessing are as high as the odds of you winning the lottery—negligible... and possibly rigged by higher powers.

"I was fifteen," he says. "I ran to the closest city. I was completely unprepared for the real world. It's loud, and no one there cares if you're in trouble when you're as tall and old-looking as I was as a teen. The symptoms didn't get better, but for the first time, I was in control of my own fate." He chews his lip, eyes staring off into the city. "One of the cruelest parts is that I can't ever live outside cities. I need immediate access to a constantly changing recipe just to walk around without being in constant pain, which means I can't see the world."

She can't keep her breath from catching this time. Relief fills her when she knows he's not dying and there's potions in Garriver that can help him, followed by grief for the life he might have lived had he not been dealt a foul hand at birth. Offering condolences doesn't feel right, but crying feels even worse, like she's reorienting herself as the star of his tragedy.

Quietly, she says, "What can I do to help?"

The arm wrapped around her shoulder tightens. "This helps."

The city's blare is muted by the watchtower's protection spells, but the slap of the river's water is clear along the shoreline.

"It hasn't gotten worse, has it?"

"Hm?"

"The curse. You said you don't know when you'll die. Since meeting me. Have you...lost any time?"

She fears that two mages of the same affinity subtract from one another's strength, that the magic can't handle both of them so close at once.

Something like panic flashes through his eyes, but it disappears before she can understand it. "Nothing's changed."

She pushes herself further into his lap, until his cloak is

wrapped entirely around her. She looks up at him through her lashes.

"Don't look at me like that."

She cups his cheek in her hand. "Like what?"

But when he opens his mouth to tell her, fear floods her like a tidal wave and she kisses him, and he wraps his arms eagerly around her. The tension is different than it was before. Before, it was carnal, vibrant, a powder keg finally set off. Now, she kisses him with her eyes closed, not because it's right, but because she's afraid if she looks at him, he'll run again. Imagining life without him now is impossible, and she's already decided she'll stay, even if the length of his life is uncertain. He's brought her a kinship that no other living being could, a friendship built upon humor and adventure and a magic that no one else alive shares, save for each other.

When he walks her back to her room, through the window and beneath her sheets, her heart pounds alone and filled with deeper affection for the man cursed by those that were supposed to protect him.

His own cloak, given to him by a selkie moments before passage, stands the test of time. The mages of today are frivolous, buying mass-produced cloaks with petty, shallow spells. The cloaks fray within the decade. No. A cloak given by a loved one carries so much more. Elaine knows that, the clever mage. She carries more power than most in the city, coated in protection that can only come from a strong home.

He thumbs the side of his hood. His cloak could use a new incantation or two. Perhaps she'd be willing to help him with it. Later tonight, when her uncle sleeps and she worries on and on about things that don't matter.

Elaine doesn't turn around when his feet sweep over the

ledge of her window the very next day. She doesn't turn around when his boots thud as they come off or when he moves to stand behind her, head bowed down next to hers to look over her work.

Feeling a twitch of annoyance, she says, "I have a door."

"You have a roommate," he counters.

She pushes his face back by covering his mouth with her hand, and he grunts. She feels his lips move up into a smile before her hand is licked and covered with saliva.

"Gross, Ivan!" She smears it back onto his cheek.

Desperate for her willing touch, he relishes in her palm wiping drool across his stubbled cheek. "I came here because I want to test our bond," he says.

He twirls a strand of her hair. "I want to see if you can put an incantation on my cloak." He leans in as if to kiss her.

Her breath catches. His eyes flit across her face, and then he snaps his body towards her workbench, meticulously ordered like a series of Tetris blocks.

A hand comes up to her fluttering heart, then drops when he turns his gaze back on her.

"You know," he remarks, "it wouldn't kill you to have at least one pen out of place."

"Magic like ours requires precision."

He looks up from where he's fiddling with her pens, raising an eyebrow.

Instead of conceding, she asks, "What incantation do you want?"

His smile broadens. "Strongest you've got for me. Positive, of course. Don't need a curse on a family heirloom."

She scrunches her face. "Isn't it too new to be an heirloom?"

"It won't be by the time we have some Ivan Juniors running around."

She splays the cloak across the workbench. She puts a careful palm across the bordered edge. It's been years since someone else put a spell on this. There's something inhuman in it too. Up close, she can see the subtle tufting along the edges. Her hands move further up the hide, noting the softness of the fur inside the hood. She knows the spell she's going to cast. It's family magic, the spell her mother learned from the river, which she taught to her kids. Each caster has to tweak it, but it's only possible when they feel a deep bond and desire to protect the cloak's owner. Ivan's cloak will be tricky. Now that she's able to get a closer look, she can see there's no other spells at all. She can tell the selkie it belonged to held little affection for him. Other than that, it's empty. Completely devoid of any love, any warmth, not even an incantation made for a comrade in arms.

She can feel Ivan watching her hands intently, rubbing the lobes of his ears absentmindedly.

"Nervous?" She teases.

"Just don't accidentally spell it to make me blue."

Elaine closes her eyes, focusing on the microscopic in-between of the fabric. It rumbles, a beast emerging from a pewter cave. Snowy, and yet green grass puffs up through the melted snow. It's easy for her to home in on good intentions.

I want him safe because he is my closest equal. The only other probability mage. Please keep him warm and let him slide past unpleasant probabilities like a fish past the wrong current.

There's no glow, no proof that it worked. She frowns down at it. She's always casted spells that gave off no signs they worked, but she'd hoped her increased strength would mean her wards would be flashier.

She turns her attention back to Ivan to assure him the incantation worked, and he's frozen, red, and open-mouthed. "What?" she asks.

"Nothing," he snaps. He scoops the cloak up in a flurry of arms and disappears back through the open window like a bat in the night.

She shakes her head, staring into the empty starry night. "What a freak," she mumbles.

Elaine drops back into her chair, not turning when she hears movement at her window again. Her professor requested a four-page explanation of the nature of a bonsai, and it had no relevance to—

Ivan is kissing her. Her eyes are wide open, his own furrowed and closed as he smashes his mouth sloppily against hers. His cloak is across his shoulders, shinier, and she can feel no gaps of air escaping through the hide anymore.

His large hands cradle her cheeks as his mouth continues to move over her. To her nose, her forehead, her mouth, over and over again. This time is slower, more harmonious than their frantic kisses from the other night. Her mind focuses on moving her tongue lightly over his lips, tingling as he takes his time, even as his breath quickens. He moves his right hand down to cup her waist, left hand lifting her chin down so he's granted easier access to her neck. She lets out a breathy moan as he sucks and licks at her throat. He reaches the edge of her collarbone, and she moans louder.

Ivan's eyes open slowly, lidded, and hazy. He smiles, still panting, pupils blown so wide his eyes are more black than brown. "Feel good, baby? You like that?"

Elaine's legs splay apart, and Ivan is quick to move between them. He places his knee in between her thighs, mouth returning to hers, now open and pliant. He presses against her core, and Elaine feels a rush of warmth in her lower stomach that's almost painful.

"Ivan." She breathes.

"You prepped my cloak so well, Lainey baby. I can feel your magic like a second pulse. What did you put in here?" he groans.

As if desperate for contact, he straddles her lap, his erection now pressing against her rapidly growing arousal.

And with him so cloying, so desperate and hard and ready, how can she turn him away? Why would she? She rolls her hips upwards, and he groans low, hips jolting after hers when she moves away. She cups his cheek in her hand, and he looks down at her, wanting and ready.

"Bed," she commands.

He scoops her into his hold, hands on her thighs as he kisses her once more, tongue slipping against her bottom lip, nibbling and prodding. His hands press her back and forth against his groin. She's dropped onto the bed and he's on her immediately, pulling the top of her dress down to expose her breasts. He palms one and lowers his head to lick at her other nipple.

"You always do this to me," he says. "You—*mm*—just love to see me in distress, don't you?"

She pushes his head back onto her breast. He closes his eyes, mouthing over the entire areola before suckling gently against it. His other hand rolls her pert nipple between his fingers, and a well-placed tug has her hips rising to meet his.

"Ah." His hips grind down to meet her own.

She whines when his hands move away from her to slide her dress the rest of the way off. He stands up off the edge of the bed, unbuckling himself and pulling his cock free. Her tongue rolls across her lips, eyeing the slow motion of his hand rubbing up and down his length. It throbs under his hand, red and beading with precum. He slows at the head, squeezing it ever so harshly, and his eyes roll back, hips bucking into the hand still stroking himself.

When he looks at her again, he's back to his cocky self, eyes lidded, and mouth stretched into that impossible grin. "Like what you see?" He picks up the pace, hand slick with his own arousal. "Bet you can't wait to have me inside you. I know you like the way I touch myself."

"Shut up and come here." She tries to sound mean, she really does, but it's lost in the hazy truth of her arousal.

His hands grasp her ankles, tugging her towards the edge of the bed. He drops to his knees, hitting the rug with a dull thud, eyes and nose now the only thing visible over her mound. Not breaking eye contact, he kisses softly against her clit. Her body jolts, and then he's pushing his tongue slowly across the outside of her folds, licking and sucking and laving up the arousal that spills out of her achingly empty hole. It's infuriating...he's too low to incite real pleasure, and not deep enough inside her either. He's doing it on purpose, she can see it in the taunt glittering in his eyes, even as his mouth glistens with her slick.

"Please," she pants, despite herself.

"You wanna come, baby," he mumbles against her. His lips are shiny, coated in her arousal. "I'll make you come." He speaks to himself more than her. "And then I'll make you come again and again. And then I'll put you on my cock, and you'll be begging for me to do this every night." He moans and leans forward to flick his tongue rapidly against her clit. "You want me to come here every night? I can eat you out until you're exhausted, put you to bed every night with my tongue. I'll be so good for you," he vows, sucking gently at her clit again.

"Ivan, I need you to inside me," she says.

He pulls back, chin shining below his toothy grin. "Not yet. I want you to come in my mouth."

He presses into her entrance, finally tongue-fucking her. Her walls clench around the appendage, and Ivan moans in approval, moving his thumb to her clit, rubbing slow circles against it.

"Faster," she whines.

"Hmmm?"

She glares down at him. Ivan closes his eyes as he whines

and tries to push his tongue further inside her. His head bobs slightly, and it's clear he's too lost to listen.

"I said *faster.*"

She grabs his thumb and sets a rough, rapid pace that sets her body on fire. His eyes open when her moans grow louder. With a new vigor, he keeps his eyes trained on her, thumb moving rapidly against her clit as her cries of "yes" and "more" and "good, so good" spill freely from her mouth.

"Tell me I'm good," he begs.

"Don't stop."

"Come for me, please, Lainey, god, I need you to come while I'm watching, please come, baby, I need you, I need to see it come, come, come." The words spill out of him, two fingers replacing his tongue, moving inside her.

His fingers press against her softest part, and she comes undone.

"Ivan," she cries.

He watches with rapt fascination as she comes against his hand, because of his hand. The way her body writhes, her eyes closed, her mouth moving wordlessly across the open air. The experience is only heightened by the context: she's achieving physical release because it's Ivan who cares enough to give it to her, and she's comfortable enough with him to receive it. She's lucky enough to, for the first time in a long time, have feelings for the person so desperate to hold her.

"*Ivan.*" She breathes his name over and over.

He pulls his fingers out and puts them inside of her mouth. "Suck," he demands, and she complies readily, tasting herself on his fingers, moving her tongue in between them and imagining it's his cock. Said cock weeps, precum dribbling and cooling against her stomach as he pumps his fingers in and out of her cloying mouth.

She props herself up, eyeing the painfully erect dick in front of her. She grabs it, Ivan falling forward, his arms resting on either side of her head.

"You like that," she breathes, playful and a little mean. "You like when I touch your cock?"

"Careful," His eyes flash in defiance.

She puts more pressure on the head of his cock, just like he did before, and he keens.

"Sorry." She pouts, feigning remorse. She's not sorry, and he knows she's not sorry. She leans in for a kiss and he eagerly follows, mouths meeting and melding and sliding across each other.

He pulls back, moving her legs over each of his shoulders, and with ease, he slides the first few inches inside of her.

She gasps, locking her ankles around his hips, attempting to pull him closer, to make him enter her completely.

He places a warning hand on her throat. His teeth glint in the candlelight, tongue flashing briefly across his open lips. "My turn."

He moves slowly, too slowly. Ivan's eyes focus on the way his dick slides in and out of her pussy, so eager to swallow him to the hilt.

"You must want to go faster," she pleads. "You have to want it harder."

He revels in her pleas, her desperate moans. She looks so perfect beneath him, wanting and ready. He's the luckiest man alive, and he has to savor it, in case he never gets another chance.

But then she mutters a low, keening, "Ivan," and he swears there's never been a sweeter sound. His hands move to grasp at her thighs pressed against his chest and pushes the rest of the way in, hands sliding up to her ankles and wrapping them around his neck. It's enough to set off Elaine's second orgasm, and it tightens and pulls his cock further inside.

"Fuck! Fuck, fuck, fuck," he moans, setting a rapid pace as

her walls clench around his cock. "I'm not going to last if you keep...fuck—" he shudders, "—clenching around me. Oh *fuck*, baby."

He never shuts up; Elaine thinks in her post-orgasmic haze. She places a hand against his cheek fondly, watching his wild gaze scrunch up as his thrusts grow erratic and frenzied. The bed is creaking frantically under his ministrations. She's floating in her own body, relishing in the power of watching Ivan come undone.

"Oh, baby, I'm gonna come, you gonna let me come inside, huh? Yeah. you are, you want it. You want me to—" He comes loudly, hips stilling right against hers as he spills inside of her.

She's filled with the sensation of his release, and the gentle pulse of his own orgasm beating like a heart. He doesn't pull out, their breaths in sync and their bodies meshed.

This is intimacy, she thinks.

This must be what all the fuss is about because she's sure she's never felt so close to anyone before. His eyes soften as he looks down at her, and she's positive no one has ever loved her so tenderly.

He slides out of her, lying down next to her on the bed. It's quiet, save for the sound of their heavy breathing. Then, a harsh smack as he slaps one of his hands onto her breast. She makes a noise of discontent, immediately undermining herself when she places her hand on top of his. He squeezes her gently in his palm, and she makes a satisfied noise.

"Ivan," she breaks the silence. It's a pity—it's the longest stretch he's remained silent while awake, the steady hand rubbing her back confirming that he hasn't fallen asleep. "There's a spring equinox ball in a couple months."

"Yes," he replies before she can ask.

She kisses the nearest patch of skin, before nuzzling closer. "Alright. It's a date."

He squeezes her even closer. Her paper can wait until the morning.

23

THIEF, MURDERER, SNITCH, LOVER

When Elaine wakes, only Roger's in her bed. She rolls over to the still-warm part of the sheets, smiling. Last night had been far better than she could have hoped. Sex had felt transactional so many times in her life. An itch to scratch. And the few times it had meant more, it had been with the fumbling earnestness of youth. With Ivan, it was not just kind, it was intentional. He remembered how she'd lean into his palm if he cups her cheek, and asks for her to look at him, to see him. She'd always thought it came one way or another: it was either kind, or good. But he'd once again proved that there is more to life than expectation, and there's more to a man than being merely kind or good.

A paper crinkles under her head. She scrunches her eyes open and sees Ivan's scrappy handwriting.

Be back soon. Told Roger he's in charge.

Roger huffs out a breath of air, burrowing further into the pillowcases. Elaine reaches out a hand and runs a finger over the bridge of his nose. He's another creature that's proven to be more than her assumption. Garriver has proven to be full of surprises, but the largest one has certainly been that trusting those who don't seem to deserve it reaps a bounty far greater than coins could ever buy. All those stories about wolves dressed as sheep and dragons stealing little girls had proven to be half-truths. The wolves here dress as sheep to steal from other wolves, and the dragons do not hide the girls, but instead show them the world atop their scaly wings. They can bite and maim and hurt you beyond recognition, but they choose not to, over and over again.

There's a knock on her bedroom door.

"Nellie," Neil's voice comes through. "Breakfast meeting. Get decent and get downstairs."

"Be right there," she replies. The bed creaks as she swings her feet and places them on the ground. She hums as she dresses, opting for a gown made of the colors of river stones: grays, reds, whites, and tan swirl together and warp the way they do under a bed of water.

Roger finally wakes, stretching as a morning yawn squeaks out of his tiny snout. His wings flap lazily, swooping down and into Elaine's open palms. She descends, still smiling as she rounds the corner into the kitchen.

"Morning Uncle Neil," Elaine sings, taking the cup of tea he offers her before sitting across from him.

He snaps the morning paper closed, another story about the vampiric serial killer roaming Garriver. This time, the victim was only forty-five. "You're in a good mood." Neil eyes her.

"Things are going well at University."

He doesn't hear her, eyes roaming her face. She winds Roger's wings around her neck. Just in case.

"There's been a development in the Locke break-ins."

Shop talk is normal at the watchtower. But what's not normal is the fact that Neil's put too much sugar in her tea, or that he's squirming like he's wearing pants two sizes too small.

"Why are you nervous?"

"There's something I have to tell you. And I don't want you to think any less of me for it."

Her smile lowers. "What do you mean?"

There's a knock on the front door, and they both ignore it.

"You know I've been working with the city to secure Locke, but I haven't told you the trouble that's been following me home."

Another knock.

He walks around the table and sits next to Elaine, reaching out a hand to almost touch hers, before sliding it back. "Ignore that. I know you've not taken my advice on avoiding Ivan Gray. Because you're a grown woman, I've respected it. You've lost a lot and instead of stumbling, you've adapted. And adapting's something I've struggled with my entire life. I admire you for that." He clears his throat, eyes darting away. "The adapting. Not the loss."

"Right, I didn't think you meant the loss."

"I'm very proud of you," he raises his voice, the way he only does when he's not sure about what he's going to say next. "I'm proud of you is what I'm trying to say. But I knew something wasn't right with that man."

"Uncle Neil," she warns.

He holds up his hand. "Now listen. I—oh, for ring's sake."

The knocking has become an incessant pounding, muffled yelling coming through the door. Neil wrenches open the door and barks out, "what."

Well over his head, Elaine can see the uniforms of the Garriver police, rigid and stern in front of her home's front door. A smirk raises on her face when one reaches out to grab Neil, knowing they can't get past the wards and take him. He never steps beyond the entryway when answering. Then, the strangest thing happens. They grab him by the scruff of his cloak and drag him forward. In his exhaustion, and nerves from having to step into the role of an older male figure trying to teach Elaine a lesson, he stepped past the entryway ward.

"Neil Leatherforth, you're under arrest for participation in the purchase of an illegal bounty for a luck mage, and collusion to steal from Locke University of Garriver."

The handcuffs clink closed behind his back. Her hands raise to her mouth in horror. She's so focused on the scene in front of her, she doesn't hear the feet rapidly approaching her from behind.

"What's going on?" Ivan stands behind her, a worried look on his face.

Her eyes are locked on Neil being pulled further from the safety of the watchtower.

She should've known it couldn't last. She yells at the policemen as they take her struggling uncle away.

"What are the charges?" she screams, tugging against Ivan's hold on her arms. "You can't take him without a warrant and a charge." She knows they've told her, but she's already forgotten. What was he going to tell her? What was he warning her about? It's cycling through her brain in partial phrases and the brain fog of life changing so quickly, her left foot's still set back in the tower, in the peace she had moments before.

A police officer, in the city's sky-blue uniform, keeps a hand on his holster as he addresses her. "Aiding and abetting in plans to rob Locke."

"He *works* for Locke." She doesn't listen to their response. Instead, she pushes herself further back against Ivan, as if looking for comfort. He loosens his hold at the beginning of what she's sure is his attempt to spin and hold her in his arms, and she slips free and rushes after her raging uncle, who kicks his legs out at the surrounding police.

"I didn't lie down when you bastards tried to ruin the Union Strike of The Long Summer! And I won't go quietly into your overvalued clown car." His eyes flick to Elaine, and he grows panicked. "Trust no one, Nellie! And when you feel like it's safe, close your heart again. Don't believe them. Go home. No, no stay in the wards. Don't go anywhere without Roger. They can't hold me forever."

"Uncle!" she cries.

"You're in danger. They're looking for you, Nellie. For *you*."

Ivan tightens his grip around her, lips drawn into a frown.

She loses sight of Uncle Neil when he's shoved headfirst into the car and the door slams close. The cops whirl around to her, curious neighbors standing on the other side of the lawn. She feels Ivan at her back, standing so close it's like he's trying to absorb her into his chest.

"He's gone."

"It'll be okay, Lainey. I'm here."

She really does turn into his arms this time, taking comfort in the warmth of his palms.

A polite cough draws her out of her misery. "The captain wanted me to give you this." The officer holds out a yellow slip of paper to them both.

Ivan tenses his hold on her. "I'll take it for her."

"It's for *you*, actually."

It's her turn to tense in his arms. His hold tightens, but she's still able to twist herself around to face the officer. He lets her go when she reaches for the paper and snags it before he can. It's a check.

"For the tip," the police officer supplies.

"Thank you," Ivan grits out.

"Happy to help."

When Elaine was five, she'd brought home a plant pot full of snails. Her mom had told her they were invaders, that the green ones were killing local plants. She'd spent the afternoon far out in the wilds and away from her younger siblings, as they were practicing magic without her.

The snails hid away in the sticky bushes near the foothills

—they were tropical invaders, and the rocky paths were too hard for their mushy bodies to pass. She'd worked all afternoon to collect them, barbs from the shrubs pricking at the sides of deft fingers. Her hands were long and thin, unlike the stout and stubby ones of her siblings. She'd brought the snails back with a sense of relief, knowing the exterminators were coming in just a few days' time to destroy them. She'd spent all night watching them, whispering plans for an aquarium with tropical plants and water and fruit.

"It's my allowance for a whole month," she'd told them. "But you'll have a nice home."

The next morning, her open curtains woke her much earlier than usual, confusing her as she knew she'd closed them the night before. A sharp crunch, followed by the swish of a trash bag rhythmically sounded near her desk.

She'd screamed bloody murder when she saw her little brother squashing the snails. Her father walked into Elaine hitting her brother over and over with a textbook, screaming about snails, wind from the open window swirling her hair around in what was probably a vision of righteous fury.

"Elaine." Her father pulled her off Alan with practiced ease. She'd gotten so much better at controlling her anger, but that morning was one of vengeance, trying to crush her brother under her wooden sled, stealing the breath from his lungs.

"He killed them," she wailed. "He snuck in and killed them."

It was her first time getting angry about something that mattered, as tantrums were near constant in her youth, as dependable as August storms.

"You'd be calm, then spitting vitriol in the next moment. Your father and I could hardly figure out what to do with you." Her mother loved to recount the story like it was a fun family memory instead of a beast she'd had to bottle.

She never expected her brother to kill them, to squash something that had no reason to be dead.

"They're invasive," he cried. "Mom said it was okay."

Just as she has almost every moment after the snails, she doesn't share her anger now. She didn't when she learned of her illegitimacy, and in recent memory, she's only ever lost her good judgement when Ivan's been involved. A grown woman doesn't throw tantrums, she swallows them.

I hope he burns, she thinks. *I hope he makes all the money in the world, and it's not enough to make him healthy again.*

Rationalization doesn't keep her from her dark thoughts, condemning herself for the way her life has turned out. In cruel daydreams, she's crying and pleading to a Neil that won't forgive her. The men in her family love to blame her even when she's innocent, and this time she's responsible for ruining his life. She doesn't afford Ivan the comfort of a fight and, instead, steps out of his arms. Talking to him might make him think he can fix things.

The spectacle is over—the police leave, and neighbors rush back into their homes as a gust of bitter wind whirls, barren trees creaking and moaning under its force. The watchtower still stands, but to Elaine, she stands in the ruins of her lover's making, all part of a home that's destroyed in spirit without Neil in it. The wards hold, but they've allowed in Ivan, who doesn't deserve the comfort that's been curated and protected through her Uncle's loving hands. Not the care put into the lawn, covered in prairie flowers, or the kitchen and its perfectly worn utensils. Not her uncle, her care, or her trust; which she'd so neatly packaged away before he convinced her he deserved it. And through the thoughts of revenge and rage, she can't figure out the motive behind all this. He'd cased her life like it was a job, found the knots in her sails and pulled at them until the structure collapsed, fishing out the shipwreck to steal and shovel into his own boat in a bottle. Her anger devolves into fear as she realizes, horrified, that she doesn't know what Ivan's motive is. In the past she'd been worried he'd leave, or get her in trouble with the law, or expelled. It never occurred to her that having him in her life could hurt someone else entirely.

He opens and closes his mouth noiselessly.

"Now you have no words," she says.

"He was going to hurt you," he lands on. "He was the one who put out a bounty for us. He was going to use you to get to Locke's treasure!"

She shakes her head. Her voice is shaky, but it isn't sadness that makes it weak. "It's finally happened. You've successfully ruined my life."

"I saved you." He raises his voice. "Families use the leftover children like cannon fodder. Your parents *wanted* you gone, Elaine, and Neil decided to take you in because he needed luck."

"I'm the one who wanted to come here. My parents didn't— I'm staying in his house, why would he need the bounty?"

But Ivan shakes his head, clearly thinking of her as past rationality. "It has to be him. You're blinded by loyalty. He's the one tampering with the school defenses. He was the traitor all along. He was going to use you to get into the school's dungeon! He wants the circle of power!"

"What would he do with the circle of power? Neil doesn't need power to get what he wants!"

It stings that he looks at her with pity while he spouts conspiracy theories. She's not sure at what point he'd convinced himself her uncle wanted her dead, nor when he'd decided her choice to come to Locke wasn't her own. Somewhere along the way, Ivan had made theories about her life he's thought about over and over, and along that paranoid and irrational train of thought, without ever speaking to her about it, he'd decided it was the truth. The probabilities whirl over his head as she considers how best to hurt him.

Punch—22.12%
Groin Kick—33.6%
Scream—79.9%
Stab—15.24%

"He was going to use you, Lainey," he pleads.

The wind dies down around her.

Silence—88%

She turns to her house and slams the door behind her.

A WEEK LATER, Elaine wakes up to a low voice murmuring in her room. A figure stands in the dark corner where Roger hangs, his eyes now open, wings still drawn close around his body to keep warm. He leans his head out to receive fond scratches from the figure.

Not moving, she says, "I don't want you here."

The figure tenses. He turns from Roger to face her, expression neutral. "I wanted to check on you."

"Come here, Roger."

The loyal rat-bat swoops towards her, stumbling on his landing before nestling into the crook of her neck. They lean into each other. She knows what she probably looks like—hair askew, eyes red and lifeless. In the week since Neil's arrest, her laundry hamper has overflowed, clean clothes buried under the dirty ones.

Ivan doesn't move from his spot in the corner, and she wonders what reason he'll conjure up.

"I think you'll feel better if you yell at me."

She blinks her bleary eyes. That is not what she was expecting.

Before she can answer, he fumbles on. "You haven't yelled. You started to during the...when they took him away." He scrubs his hands against his hood. "I think you'll feel better if you yell at me."

She lays back in bed and turns to Roger, who has begun fiddling with some of her hair.

"Say something. You're freaking me out, Lainey."

"I don't want to yell."

"That's what I'm worried about. That if you never yell, you'll be gone."

An emotion breaks through the hazy fog she's been wrapped in—satisfaction. She smiles before she can stop it, and his body freezes when he catches it.

"I did it for you." His tone sharpens. "You're better off without him."

She counts the cracks in the ceiling.

A crash rings out when Ivan kicks over her chair. "Yell at me!"

Her shoulders tense, and he murmurs a soft apology. The soft scrape of him picking up her chair and putting it back where it belongs fills the silence. In a moment of weakness, she thinks about holding him. He's the only person she has left in Garriver.

Hug—99%

She closes her eyes after the room grows colder in his absence. She never wants to see him again.

THE DETECTIVES who'd come back to ask her more questions about Uncle Neil referred her to a Locke appointed counselor. The office itself is like any other corporate setting: fluorescent lights, large, unkillable plants and a glass table with expired magazines scattered across it. Elaine sits in a squeaky pleather chair and thumbs through a two-year-old edition of MAGES. She's halfway through an article titled "Not all Wizards: How

This Centaur Rose Up in a Human-Dominated Field" when the counselor comes out.

"Elaine Aquae?" Pam the counselor says.

Elaine fights off a grimace; the tone is too gentle, too pitiful. She doesn't want to be treated gently. She walks the short distance into the office with the tall, willowy woman.

Pam is starkly pale, very tall, and wears a serene look on her sallow face. When those sad, wet eyes home in on Elaine, she frowns. "I understand you were recommended for counseling through Locke."

"That's right."

Pam hums, looking through her file as Elaine fidgets in the seat across from her.

"Have you done therapy before, Elaine?"

She shakes her head no.

"I'll ask you general questions first. But because this was recommended by your school due to extenuating legal circumstances, I'll be asking questions about that to make sure we can get to what will help you the most. If you don't like them, we can move on."

Elaine nods.

"How long have you been in Garriver?"

"About nine months, give or take."

"Do you like it?"

Memories of danger, aquatic diners and moments on the floorboards of a too-small boat all flash through her mind. "It's different."

"Different good, or bad?"

"To be determined."

The questions go on like that, her studies, her friends, and she really only freezes up on one.

"What exactly happened with your uncle?"

Elaine's shoulders stiffen. "Didn't they tell you?"

"Yes, but I'd like to hear it from you."

She looks away. “They said he was trying to steal something from Locke.”

“Yes, but you mentioned someone else was involved with him getting arrested. Where is,” Pam shuffles through her notes, “Ivan?”

Elaine draws her cloak closer around her. The fish hide on the inside of the blue material. “He did something unforgivable, and we’re not talking.”

“Unforgiveable. From how you described him, he did a lot of things most people would describe as unforgivable. What was so bad this time?”

“I’d like to move on, please.”

Pam leans closer in her chair. “I understand this is uncomfortable. Let’s talk about Ivan being in your life before this ‘unforgiveable’ act. Why is it that this man, who you’ve described as impulsive and dangerous, is someone you kept seeing? You don’t seem like an adrenaline junkie to me, Elaine.”

Elaine’s fingers curl around the edge of her cloak. She knows why. It’s because he’s the only mage alive that shares her affinity. It’s because he’s taught her how to access her power, believed in her, and brought her along into danger—not because he thought she was expendable, but because he knew she could handle it. He makes her feel less alone. Even now, as angry as she is, she wishes she could see him. Her frustration veers from hatred into desire, when she’s alone in the watchtower. Part of her believes that if she had him one more time, she wouldn’t dream of him so often.

“He made me feel l-cared for,” she says. “But now I don’t even know if I’ll stay at Locke. Stay in Garriver at all.”

There’s a long pause, Pam waiting to see if Elaine will say anything more.

“Do you have any family who can come visit you?” Pam asks.

Her parents flash through her mind. "No," she said. "No one."

It's like he can tell when she's thinking of him. She comes back from therapy, insurance slip in hand because only the first court-suggested session is paid for to find him sitting on the chair in her room. She steps towards him and he freezes before relaxing again.

"Get out." She says it deep, low.

"I wanted to see if there's anything I can do for you." He looks up, eyes wet and wide.

When she doesn't react his eyes flutter back down to his lap. She takes notice of his broad shoulders, and the way he fiddles with his cloak between his fingers.

THIS IS THE LAST TIME, she thinks.

He licks a long stripe up her underwear. The dulled sensation feels like all too much, and she blames it on her therapy appointment leaving her wired.

"Gray—"

"Ivan," he says. "It's Ivan."

She replies with silence, his voice bringing up images of her uncle being arrested, of her life falling apart at his skilled touch.

His tongue halts, and he grins up at her. "Where can I touch you?"

To her dismay, he pulls back, wiping his mouth against her thigh before pulling away. She kicks at him, and he grabs her legs, kissing her heel before placing it on his shoulder.

His eyes are soft when they note her furrowed brow. "Come on, Lainey. Tell me where."

She nudges her knee against his cheek and delights in the

way his eyes shutter closed. He shakes his head, dispelling his bliss and turning his eyes on her, dark and serious.

He tightens his hand in warning. "I'll leave."

"Don't lie to me anymore, Ivan."

Still, she leans forward, unlacing her corset with practiced ease before settling back down against the pillows behind her, topless and stubbornly silent. He moves to push her ankles from his shoulders, and she squeezes her feet together, eyes panicked.

"Anywhere. Touch me, lick me. Make me forget."

He puts practiced hands on each side of her hips, tugging her underwear down and off her body. He shoves them into his back pocket. "Whatever you want."

He moves back in towards her clit, tonguing around and over it, just as she likes. No one knows her body this well. No one else could feel the ebb and flow of their shared affinity, guiding him with expertise.

He moves too far left, but when she grows quiet, he immediately returns to what worked without her having to say anything.

You're perfect, she thinks.

"You're nothing," she lies. "Inside, now."

He lets out a groan, shimmying up her body, eyes flitting over her face. He squeezes her cheeks with one hand.

"Tongue out," he demands, and she lolls it out obediently. He takes it all in his own mouth, and sucks on the appendage.

She moans, body tingling even warmer.

Weirdo, she thinks, even as her hips grind upward into his and he sucks a little harder.

"Taste yourself," he pants. "You're so sweet, Lainey. So sweet."

She moans, hips thrusting, desperately hoping he'll take a hint. Ivan's pupils are blown wide as he stares down at her, finally releasing her tongue.

"Ivan, inside," she begs.

He grabs his cock, stroking it a few times before finally sinking inside. Just the head, and they both hiss. Frustrated, she pushes her hips up further.

"Yes," he hisses when he slips all the way in.

They sit there for a moment, silent except for their panting. Ivan rolls his hips, and she feels herself clench and release under him. His eyes roll to the back of his head, fists closed on either side of her head, sheets crinkling under his grip.

24

MEAT TORTILLAS WITH MUSTARD

When TA training ends, she doesn't look Ivan in the eye. Professor Sap is joined by Nero, who tells them they'll have two days until the practical exam.

"It will be overseen by us as your mentors. No public viewings this time," Nero says.

"It's a terrible thing." Professor Sap shakes his head. "Trying to get a passing grade with an unfinished project."

She'd asked to be allowed to complete the exam early due to extenuating family circumstances. Begrudgingly, Sap agreed a relative being arrested for crimes against the university did indeed fall under the student advocate council's guidelines for an adjusted exam. Clarke and Elaine would complete the practical exam in its simplest stage, during the day, and with no additional obstacles as originally planned.

She looks at Clarke, who shares her amusement. Her smile falters when she makes accidental eye contact with Ivan, who looks especially disheveled today. Her head snaps forward, but she can feel his eyes boring holes into the side of her head. She makes for the door as soon as they are dismissed.

"Lainey," Ivan calls out.

She ignores him and walks a little faster.

"Ms. Aquae, a moment please," Sap says.

She turns around with a grimace. She approaches Sap and, consequently, Ivan, who looks far too hopeful for a man who got her uncle arrested.

"You're dismissed, Mr. Gray."

His devastated look deepens at his words. "Professor, I—"

"Go on, you can wait for her outside."

Ivan looks as though he's about to argue again. With a brief glance at Elaine, he heads out of the classroom.

Forget everything I've ever thought about you, Professor Sap, she thinks. *You're my hero.*

Professor Sap turns to her. "What's this I hear about you getting a familiar after all?"

She'd forgotten Roger didn't always have wings, and she'd failed the initial familiar ritual Sap signed her up for. And in the chaos of her life, she hadn't considered that in a roundabout way, before the ritual and far after she failed it, her familiar had made his way to her on his own. "How did you hear about that?"

"Mr. Gray was quite glowing in his review of your work. In fact, he even recommended you be allowed more university privileges on account of your magic getting stronger during your training."

Here, the professor looks at her with focus, that milky faraway look gone in a moment of clarity. "Is it true? Can you really do what he says? See the odds?"

What could Ivan steal from her this time, she wonders. Even now, he tries to rule her life. She's sure this is his last-ditch attempt at getting her to use her magic instead of her mind and, consequently, keep him in hers. Accounting is safe. It will feed her, clothe her, and retire her, and it will keep her from needing him ever again.

"Well—he might be exaggerating. But I am still committed to the path of an accountant."

Sap's eyes are still too sharp, and she shifts when he doesn't reply. Then, finally, he responds. "Of course, Ms. Aquae. You are dismissed."

She nods and turns to leave. As her hand reaches the door, he calls out, "I look forward to your practical exam, Ms. Aquae."

She smiles, brittle. "Thank you, Professor."

When Ivan tries to talk to her in the hall, she whirls past, diving into the crowd before he has time to get a word in edgewise.

Elaine walks into her empty home, flicking on the lights. It's been almost a month since Neil's been gone. Her steps echo across the floorboards as she makes her way into the kitchen. Her feet are loud in the quiet, so she changes her gait, scuffing and dragging herself along. The cauldron so often bubbling with experimental potions sits empty, dust evenly spaced around the rim from disuse. They'd let her see him once, but they wouldn't let them speak to each other. He'd looked safe, but that didn't truly comfort her. Neil belongs in custody as much as a fish belongs in a tree.

She opens the fridge and pulls out a pickle jar and salami. She can't find the mustard, but when she turns to put the other ingredients down, it's already sitting on the counter. She must have forgotten to put it away. She jiggles mustard out of the jar in uneven splotches onto her salami slices.

Plop

"He's the one tampering with the school defenses."

Plop plop

"He was the traitor all along."

Plop

"He was going to use you, Lainey."

There's a flash of yellow pain, probabilities exploding against her vision in a flash bang, and she drops the jar.

"Shoot," she says. The last salami slice had one-third of the jar of mustard piled on it. It was drowning in it, golden and tart, and now the whole meal is ruined.

Her magic has been erratic since Neil's arrest. She'll be taking a walk, and a series of sudden and bright numbers will flash overhead for questions she didn't even remember thinking, exhausting her physically and further weakening her addled mind. She opened the floodgates of her affinity, and she hasn't yet learned to close that connection, resulting in her magic overflowing and overwhelming her daily. Her intense jaundiced-colored migraines only go away once the pain gets so bad that she loses her train of thought.

Taking her finger across the salami, she slides the excess mustard back into the jar. Disgusting maybe, but she's the only one eating it.

She turns to Roger, pointing to her jar of lukewarm mustard. "You don't want any, do you?"

He does not respond. He never does. He does pointedly turn his nose up at the offer.

"The only rat in the whole city who can't speak English," she grumbles.

She pulls a few pickles out with the same hand, placing them carefully on the cold cuts. She wraps her meat tortillas, the name she gave her culinary abomination, and folds the ends in to make sure the pickle and mustard can't escape. She prepares it all on top of a paper towel, because plates require cleaning, and once you start a pile in the sink, it never ends. It's much better to never cook at all.

She goes through her nightly routine in silence, washing her face, braiding her hair, and putting on a silk nightgown. The latch of her window clicks open, and her head is once again filled with the disastrous visions of *him*. She is traitorously glad to be rid of the quiet, even if it means talking to Ivan again.

She examines Ivan within the frame of the window now. "Ivan," she says. He looks smaller, all hunched over like that. "Stand up straight," she commands.

He shoots up, wincing as his head bangs on the window frame he hadn't yet cleared.

"I came to see how you're doing," he says, raising his hands in surrender once he's in the room.

"Well, I've been a bit lonely, seeing as you *threw my uncle in jail.*"

Ivan rubs at his wrinkled brow. For a moment, she thinks he'll say something snarky back. She lifts a single brow, and he closes his lips into a tight fine line. She feels a vindictive satisfaction when all the ways she can hurt him scrawl across her vision like a yellow deli menu. Her brow furrows in pain, a tight, precise one, right behind her eyes.

"The magic is hurting your eyes," he guesses.

She ignores him, tumbling into bed and pressing herself face-first into a pillow. He approaches, pulling her vanity chair along with him. She turns to look at him, miserable gaze glaring at miserable gaze. He sits backwards in the chair, his hand resting against his cheek, big puppy eyes trained on her. She must look a sight if she's able to invoke a piteous glance from the worst man she's ever known.

His hand twitches, and she imagines he might want to pull a strand from her neat braid or wrap his large hands over the small of her back, the nape of her neck. His tongue darts over his uncharacteristically silent mouth. He pulls out a pair of sunglasses Elaine hasn't seen before. The frames are connected by a silver chain that she can wear like a necklace. She takes them when he hands them to her, their fingers brushing.

"Soft," he whispers.

"Hm?"

"Soft glasses," he corrects. "It's what I'm calling them. They should block out the visual component of your magic while you wear them."

Elaine twists and sits up fully, pulling the glasses onto her face. The world is all yellow for a few moments, but her eyes adjust until her vision's tinted in an almost unnoticeable golden hue. For the first time in weeks, her eyes have a break from the endless possibilities surrounding her. She lifts them off the bridge of her nose, wrinkling it at the cartoonish fish shape of each lens.

"These are incredibly tacky," she says.

Ivan's eyes narrow at her. "You love fish."

"Yes, but that doesn't mean I want them to be the lens through which I view the world." She purses her lips. "Yeah, real classy. I'm sure to get a real job wearing these to interviews."

"They're ironic chic," Ivan says.

He's currently wearing his blue half-moon glasses. She purses her lips.

His face turns red, and he snarls, hand reaching out to take them from her. "Well, if you don't want them, I'll take them back."

"No!" She holds them out of his reach. "I want them." Then before she can think better of it, "thank you" spills softly from her mouth.

Ivan's body relaxes, and on his next breath he leans towards her. His eyes are wide, as if he's afraid. Maybe that's why she lets him place his finger over the back of her hand, guiding the glasses back over her face. He stays close, eyes searching for something in quick passes across her face.

"Don't look at me like that."

He licks his lips. "Like what?"

She can hear her heart in her ears. "Like you want to devour me."

He swallows, drawing her attention to his Adam's apple. When her eyes flick back up, his look grows more hungry. "You told me not to lie anymore, Lainey."

She remembers her uncle's pleas, and that righteous anger snaps her spine straight and away from him. "Because you threw my uncle in jail." She moves away and towards the basket Roger's sleeping in. She picks him up, and he grunts in mild discomfort before he recognizes her scent and falls asleep in her arms.

His jaw grinds, following close behind. "He was going to use you, Lainey. I saved you."

He moves away from her electric energy, hand scrubbing against his jaw in annoyance. He paces her room, muttering angrily to himself. She watches, unwilling to kick him out when she doesn't know when she'll see him again.

He throws his hands in the air. "Do you really think your uncle didn't place the bounty?"

Elaine nods her head, unsure where this is going.

He points a finger at her. "Then I'll figure it out, Lainey." He says it like a threat, before climbing out of her window. He curses and mutters all the way down the tower vines, leaving Elaine alone with a rapidly beating heart.

A MONTH INTO HER GRIEF, she has given up on scrubbing the age-old stain from Uncle Neil's pot.

"It's useless!" she shouts to no one. "I'll never get this stain out."

Roger ignores her, winding his body up to jump on a spider he's trapped in the corner. She throws the pot down and collapses onto the couch. The more complicated wards are getting weaker and weaker, and she doesn't have the skill to bring them up to their full strength. She's lucky Neil chose to use familial runes, or the watchtower would be overrun with pixies and forest gnomes looking for shiny things to steal. Just the other night, she swore something rattled in her pantry, but when she checked, swinging the door open with one hand and a rolling pin in another, it was empty. Her brain is replacing her loneliness with fantasies of danger, as if pain is better than boredom.

She sits up and grabs her cloak. "Roger. We're going to the undercity."

He flies over, landing on her shoulder just before she pulls the hood up over her head.

"We're getting my uncle back."

She retraces the night Ivan had the imp work on her toe, through back-alley doors that lead to unlit staircases and boat rides. The layers of the city become more swamp than cement the further she descends. With no open sky, every leaky faucet echoes like thunder, and a hidden frog's croak roars like it's from the maw of a much larger beast.

She exits the boat and gives the boatman a jar of cricket song as payment. The market here is not selling food as much as it is curses and contractors. She veers towards the mages for hire. Her eyes skim over the job descriptions: *sellsword, butcher, bounty hunter, kidnapper*. They are all too vague, and they all look at her with suspicion. Perhaps if she'd spent more time with her classmates instead of with Ivan, she'd be looking for a lawyer, not an escape artist. In her panic, another headache comes on, and the probabilities of how likely those around her are to kill her fills up her line of vision. A fishman—*drowning—45%*. A statue—*petrification—82.6%*.

She reaches for her sunglasses, but they're not there. The odds whir across her sight so suddenly she has no chance to stop it, all horrible insinuations of her death.

She stumbles into an alley, head clutched in her hands to try to get the visions to stop. But it's all too much, too many, and every time she opens her eyes, she's presented with a new danger. She squeezes her eyes shut; skin drawn tight, unaware of how long she's been crouching there. She feels a shuffle at her feet and opens her eyes to her familiar.

Roger—*gnawed to death—.01%*

Her eyes fill with tears. "Sorry, buddy."

"Is this what you made all that fuss for?" Titon says.

Rat king—*decapitation—25%.*

She moans. "If you're going to kill me, can you at least take me home first?"

THE BAR the rat king guides her to is humid. When he took her, she thought it'd be somewhere awful in a dangerous way, but it's merely uncomfortable in the way a scab is itchy or a sock is wet. The bar is ceiling-to-floor brick, lit by green crystals and a glowing moss she's careful not to touch.

Titon eyes her carefully as she crosses the threshold. She feels a shudder overrun her body, and she continues forward.

"Why did you bring me here, Titon?"

He doesn't look at her, eyes drawn to Roger's wings. "Those are new."

Roger flares his wings, showing them off to his old master.

Titon takes another sip. "Let me guess, you're looking to hire someone to help break your uncle out. I'd be willing to help you. For a price."

She rolls her eyes. "It's always for a price with you city mages, all instant gratification and short-lived victory."

"My price is simple, and you'll be able to fulfill it now. I just want two things," he says.

"Go on."

"I want you to get my crown, and I want to tell you a story."

When she's silent, he takes that as the go-ahead. "When I first met Ophelia, I was drowning. A job went wrong, partners betrayed, and I ran into the thickest rim of the old forest, where the trees are thicker than trolls and taller than buildings. I was injured and starving, both things I'd dealt with before and could live through, but my dehydration was sure to kill me.

"It was then I came across a river, filled with predators waiting to snap up unsuspecting travelers. I couldn't hear the alarm bells going off in my head over the pull of the water. Beneath the waves was a pod of nymphs, hungry and ready to kill me. It was when I reached down for that first sip that they grabbed me. Thrashing, and lungs filling with water, my magic searched desperately for some animal to come and help. But they all knew to stay away from that riverbed, and every call for help was worthless.

"It was then that Ophelia felt my magic, fending off her podmates and pulling me back out of the river. She was a half nymph, visiting her father, and it was fate that she met me there, she says, because she'd never met someone with such compatible magic, and she hasn't since. I stayed another four months there before I convinced her to move back into Garriver with me."

Titon pauses, smiling fondly as his eyes look off into the distance.

"Back then, a half nymph and a civil adventurer together was scandalous. Humans had just desegregated their public institutions by race, but most weren't ready to do the same with other species. But Ophelia looked human back then, the kind of beauty men drowned for, and she had an intelligence many tried to dismiss on account of her otherness. She used that attraction to her advantage and gained enough allies to earn a place within powerful covens and companies. Unfortunately, she's also the most ambitious woman I've ever met, and didn't have the vanity to care about appearance over power.

"She believed she could cure the city of its polluted water, the jealous humans, and push Garriver into an industrial revolution. As her powers grew, her humanity diminished, and she lost her human beauty, thus the favor of her allies. To me, though, she was gorgeous. Only fools choose to hang onto something as artificial as a physical form."

Elaine takes a sip in lieu of mentioning the crown.

"Ophelia was a dangerous half nymph in the eyes of the magistrate, manic and willing to do whatever it took to change the city as she saw fit. They turned when they realized they couldn't control her and tried to throw her in jail. It started small, as subtle phrasing that kept her on the fringes of magical research groups. 'She's very changeable', they said. It always starts with little critiques, ones humans have linked to nymphs for years. Then it became 'she's unpredictable'. When the police finally came for her, it was 'She's too dangerous.'"

"What did she do?"

"She...attempted to flood the entire city using the circle of power. I convinced her not to, as I can't survive underwater. But I knew they'd kill her, and my name was mud for bringing her here. So, we staged a drowning and disappeared."

The rat king licks his chops, fingers clicking against the whiskey glass. "You must be careful, Elaine. Mages like you can't afford to be seen as rash, emotional. It invites speculation."

She's careful with her next words. "The world's changed since then. I won't be killed for what may or may not be true." For a moment, she feels like she's sitting at her old oak table, eating soup under the heavy watch of the mountains. "I belong at university as much as anybody else."

He slams the glass back down. "Forget about university and forget about 'what you deserve.' Elaine, you are in *danger*. You are *alone*. All you have are the agreements you make, and doors will close if they can confirm what you are." He takes a breath, and his expression cools. "So, what do you say about getting my crown in exchange for your uncle?"

She shakes her head. Titon made it clear before that he thinks she's useless and weak. "Why me? Why not Ivan?"

"You've grown," he says. "You've strengthened your magic, and if I can smell it on you, so will she. She hates Ivan, but maybe her heart will be softer to you. You're delightfully miserable." His laugh is a snorting, hissing noise.

She holds out her hand to shake, and her heart beats fast against her ribcage. "Fine. A crown for my uncle."

Titon takes her hand and pulls her in closer. This close, she can see every strand of hair beneath his eyes. Roger hisses in warning from beneath the safety of her cloak.

"A crown for your uncle. And if you fail, I will not just be taking a toe."

25

IVAN TRIES TO KILL ELAINE

Killers come for her the night her uncle's strongest wards give out. Fairies with long, twigged arms break into her home. Roger swoops and claws at the tallest one, but he can't keep them from pulling her from the watchtower, and her brain hammers with a magic-induced migraine as her vision fills up with a hundred different probabilities. She swings out with her free left hand, but it's grabbed, and she's struggles to break free as they pull her out of the warmth and into the cold fresh air of Garriver. The thieves snarl, looking down with greedy, bug-eyed satisfaction.

"He was right. She's much easier to capture."

Elaine lands a well-aimed kick at one of their middles, fumbling for the sunglasses around her neckline as her magic floods her vision, painfully calculating everything and making it impossible to see. While her fish glasses make it so she can't study the odds, she can at least now she can see her kidnappers in front of her.

"Who sent you?" she pants.

"Gray sends his regards." Not wasting time, the tallest of them reaches back and grabs the handle of their axe. Raising it high above their head, it swings down and arcs towards her neck. She scrunches her eyes closed, but the blow never lands as it's intercepted by a blur of brown.

The blur is tall, and for a moment, she imagines it's Ivan. But whatever it is can't be human, as the trench coat bends and lurches with movements that would break human bones, and there are flashes of green beneath the fedora they wear. A muffled sentence is yelled out by her savior, and with a flash, it blankets new wards over the watchtower, pushing the enemies out.

"Impossible," she breathes.

Neil is the only one who can grant permission to others to cast wards on the property. Her brain tries to figure out how this stranger could bypass Neil's permissions, but her adrenaline wears off too fast, and her last conscious act is letting go of her secret, naive hope that things could get better.

After all, Ivan Gray wants her dead.

ELAINE DESCENDS into the sewers of her own volition, ignoring the slight burn of the scrapes and bruises left by her would-be abductors. Stepping down the ladder feels like stepping back through time. The last trip to Ophelia's domain was filled with arguments and curiosity, but now only fear joins her into the sewer, the rest of the space inside her filled by anger and a confidence in her magic that wasn't there before. Those pearly gates gleam the same way—just as shiny, just as clean. Her heart beats just as fast, but the magic doesn't consume her as it did before. In spite of nothing else changing, she has.

She reaches Ophelia's pearly gates and is surrounded by that same humid magic. This time she is prepared. She can feel the magical pressure around her, but her own core has strengthened to the point that she cannot be overpowered, and the feeling is a nuisance instead of a death sentence.

It's quieter too now that Ophelia's magic isn't flooding her veins. The room is silent, and just like before, Ophelia lies on her chaise, asleep.

Numbers flash in front of Elaine's vision as she looks for dead spots in the water.

92%

17%

4.3%

She places her feet according to her greatest chances of sneaking by, hedging her bets and shifting closer with the help of her affinity until she's finally in front of Ophelia. Coiled up like a snake, breathing deep and slow, she looks smaller asleep. Sweet. Elaine reaches forward, slips her hand beneath the pillow, and pulls out what started this all: the crown. Why she'd keep something so close to her from a man she hates, Elaine doesn't know. Her lips pull back into a sneer. Titon and Ophelia are two creatures of habit, of a cycle built on mutual dependence and familiarity, addicted to the cycle of leaving each other, then coming back together again. Addicted to the adrenaline rush of leaving someone, only to inevitably fall back into one another's arms. Disgusting.

A hand reaches out and snaps around Elaine's wrist. Ophelia's eyes are open and now mere inches from hers. Elaine can feel her hot breath inches from her own and winces as her hand grips her wrist too hard, forcing the crown to drop.

Ophelia reclines against her chaise, forcing Elaine to lean forward into her. "Ms. Aquae, back so soon?"

"I'm here for the crown," she says.

Ophelia ignores her.

She tries to shake her hand free, and Ophelia allows it. Elaine takes several steps back but doesn't run. "Give me the crown, Ophelia."

Ophelia lifts one eyebrow, regarding her with some interest, then turns her attention back to her nails. "I heard he offered to help you break out that furball of an uncle of yours if you got it back. You should've told him you'd get him the pot of gold at the end of the rainbow. That would've been easier."

Elaine takes a step forward but is intercepted by a wall of water. She prods it with a finger, and the water sucks her whole arm in. She lets out a cry and tries to pull herself out of it, but the liquid holds steadfast up to her shoulder. Ophelia laughs loudly, and Elaine snaps.

"Of course you won't help," she snarls. "Getting that crown means getting a sliver of my once peaceful life back. But you don't have the capacity to care for what's best for someone else. I don't know what I expected from a reprobate like you."

Ophelia's form splashes as she whips her head around, nostrils flared. "I am this city's strongest water mage, capable of powers beyond your tiny brain's understanding. Be careful how you speak to me, mayfly."

In her anger, Elaine's magic acts up, her hair flaring wildly around her. It feels as though all the aimless anger inside of her stewing in the dark finally has found a target. "I was raised at the side of my mountain's oldest river and born to its chosen keeper. You're just like her. Selfish, moody, forgetful. I've known women like you my whole life."

"But we aren't standing in that river anymore." Ophelia rises from her chaise, drifting towards Elaine, eyes cruel and her magic roiling about like she's the eye of the cyclone. She circles Elaine, and the water rises past their knees. "No. We're in my river, and you're not a true child of water. You're of the wind. Vapid, hard to reach, lifespan of a change in temperature. It's no wonder you're so contradictory."

"I am not contradictory."

"No? Then why do you kiss Ivan one moment, then push him away the next? Are you going to promise me you'll stay forever, then wish for me to die?" She steps close enough that their feet almost meet and their chests touch with each harsh inhale. Ophelia's breath smells like minerals and is reminiscent of Elaine's home. For a moment, Ophelia's eyes look just like her mother's. "Water may be tempestuous, but it always returns. You, Elaine Aquae, are of fair weather."

Elaine steps back and crosses her arms across her chest. She'd let the conversation stray from her true objective. Still, she can't help herself from digging her teeth in further. "You stole Titon's crown! How are you not changeable?"

Ophelia's teeth sharpen, and her soggy mouth elongates into a mockery of a snout. She looks nowhere near human like this: all teeth and shadowy water and monstrousness. "It is mine to take and give as I please."

She leans forward as if to take a bite out of Elaine, who squeezes her eyes shut, trapped by the water. Instead, she feels Ophelia take a deep breath a quarter inch away from her face, and empty air fills the space between them as her jaw moves away. Elaine opens her eyes to see Ophelia's face shrink back to normal. The nymph looks tired, and she sinks back into her chaise. The look on her face is one Elaine's had pointed her way her whole life: pity. It digs under her skin like a worm, and she grits her teeth to hold back her tears of frustration,

"You have a new job. Forget the crown and go tell Titon to send a mage worth killing. I can't stand to drown someone so worthless."

But Elaine isn't done with her. She can't leave without the crown, without a way to get her uncle home, and her desperation tangles itself up in her fear and anger.

She stomps a foot and says, "advice from a coward—you may be above humanity, but Titon is as petty and forgetful as the rest of us."

A probability flashes across her field of vision:

92%--taking the crown.

"It's lonely when he's gone, I bet."

Ophelia scoffs.

"Are you afraid he'll forget you if you give him that crown? If you don't cause him pain?" Her logic is weakened by her anger, but she can't help herself from continuing. "Fighting is when you feel closest to him. Knowing all his attention is on you and connected to that which he cares most about."

Water builds up to her ankles, then her calves.

"It's intimate when you don't know when you'll speak again. You're in complete control of his absence when you know he's coming back for that crown."

The water rises to her waist. Elaine wonders if it will taste like the river back home.

"It feels like your heart's beating out of your chest. But then when you look around, there's no one to share it with. No one to share the anger with." She wades a step forward and holds out her hand. "The only way you won't be alone is if I tell him I stole it back. That's how the game usually ends, isn't it? He gets someone to steal it, and then you get to see him again. He doesn't have to know you gave it up because you miss him."

Ophelia looks at her open hand, and Elaine isn't sure if she's going to put the crown in it, or bite it. Ophelia strokes the diadem, eyes softening as her finger pinches the tip of one of the ridges. She places the crown carefully across the palm of Elaine's hand, and Elaine curls her hand around it, but the water doesn't recede, and she holds back a shiver as its chill seeps into her bones.

"You're different," Ophelia acknowledges. "You're crueler now."

"I'm efficient."

Those are the words she leaves the water nymph with as she walks out of that too-clean chamber, back into the grimy and familiar halls of the city's sewer system.

All it took was enough loneliness, she thinks.

She repeats those words over and over in her head, even as she smiles wide and her and Roger make their way back to the rat king's lair with the crown in her hand. It's near-stereotypical in quality, all gold and rubies and big pointy ridges. When she enters, the rats aren't scurrying or biting or trying to turn her into stew; instead, they're all asleep, a few scurrying or watching her lazily from the edges of the room. The rat king himself sits bored atop his throne. His large ear twitches when she enters, letting her know he hears her even as he ignores her.

"One crown."

He turns, eyes now focused on the crown. Like a wraith, he swoops down upon a sea of rats, all climbing up and around each other to create steps downward as he scrambles from his perch. Roger watches on, not shaking, but his wings unfurl and flap with the approach of his old king.

Titon grabs the crown in seconds, smelling it deliriously, eyes rolling back. He closes his eyes in bliss as he places it upon his head. His head changes shape, the teeth rolling back into his mouth, furry hands becoming smooth and pale. His hair stays that mousy grey, but now she can see pitch black eyes, and a beak of a nose. He's human again, and she finds herself underwhelmed by his appearance. He looks like every other shifty eyed man skulking alone through the alleys of Garriver. He turns back to his throne and steps much more patiently to his seat. She hopes he doesn't think she'll forget his unflattering scurry to his favorite hat. He lays back against the throne with a blissful sigh, head propped up by the palm of his cheek.

"What now?" She asks.

He doesn't bother to open his eyes to her again. "Your uncle will be returned to you. By the end of the month, give or take."

Her jaw tightens. "Give or take."

"I'll bring you your uncle when it's safe. Don't think you can speak disrespectfully just because you've finished one job," he warns.

The cold tone is accompanied by thousands of tiny eyes glowing in the dark.

"End of the month."

He nods, half-listening as he smiles at his human hands. "End of the month."

Before she can turn away, he clears his throat to grab her attention. She raises an eyebrow.

"Ophelia," he finally spits out. "Did she say anything about me?"

"Wouldn't you rather know if she's safe?"

"Of course, she's safe. But did she seem," the word struggles to come off his tongue, "lonely?"

She shrugs. "She seemed the same to me."

A half hour of limping through the sewer later, Elaine collapses into her bed, Roger swooping onto the perch above her head. She's bruised, battered, but she'd done it. All on her own, she'd returned the crown to Titon. She'd secured her uncle's freedom herself. If she's lucky, she won't see Ophelia or Titon ever again, and she'll be sure to keep away from his haunts. The sewers, the bar, all of it are in the past. And as the sweat cools on her chest, her heart returns to a steady beat, and the room dulls from yellow to a pallid hue; the echo of her hot breath no longer fills the room around her, but instead extinguishes into something small.

Yes, she'd done it. They'll all leave her alone from now on.

ELAINE STORMS BACK to the bar where she last saw Titon, and to her luck, there he sits, scowling down at his drink. His eyes drift behind her, and he sighs.

She sinks into the stool next to him, the fight seeping out of her. "Ivan sent someone to kill me," she confesses.

"I didn't ask," he mumbles.

Her shoulders slump, and she rubs her hands against her eyes until she sees stars. Ivan has put her in danger as constantly as he's chased after his own victory, passing tedious tasks onto her, and getting mad when he doesn't get his way. "I have to kill him before he kills me."

"And after?"

He's changed her life as much as he's destroyed it. She sniffs, grabbing the glass in front of Titon and taking a swig. "Miss him until I die."

"You're pitiful."

"Between the two of us, which one of us will Ophelia drown on sight?" she snaps.

He snatches at the hand holding his drink hostage, but she pulls it away from him before he can get it.

"That's what I thought."

He orders another one, and they sit there in silence. Titon leaves after finishing his drink, but she decides to stay for a few more. Elaine is three drinks deep when she sees someone familiar.

"Calamitous," she slurs. It's the stuffy man with the pretty lady. But there's no pretty lady. "Where's the pretty one?"

Calamity slides into the seat next to her, waving a hand at the bartender. "Ruby and I are on different paths these days." He turns to address the bartender. "A minotaur spliff in a Manhattan."

He turns to Elaine, face slack of its usual charisma. "Isn't this a bit out of your way, Aquae? University students aren't usually welcome here."

She rolls her eyes. "I b'long here more than you do."

"How do you figure?"

I'm not human, she thinks. *Would you work with me if you knew?*

Her eyes slide to the other patrons. "They haven't stopped looking over here since you walked in. Owe some gold?"

Calamity casts a blank gaze over the bar, confirming what she said as true. Every eye in the place is on him.

When he turns back to her, he hunches further into his seat. "I'm here to propose a deal, Aquae. I've heard we have a mutual enemy."

"I have no enemies."

He hums in amusement. "Not even Ivan Gray?"

She snarls, hand gripping the glass more firmly. "Ivan Gray," she mumbles, "stupid, self-centered Ivan Gray." She moans, head hitting the bar in front of her with a *thunk*. Saying his name makes her heart flutter. Anger sits funny in her chest when it's about him.

"I am not well-versed with the underlayers, but I am well-funded. I thought you would be in a position to hire someone."

"Hire?"

"A contract-for-hire?" He gives her a look.

"Like a stripper?" She crinkles her nose.

"No, you idiot. I... An assassin." His voice drops into a whisper. "A trained killer."

"I don't want to kill anyone."

"Not even Ivan?"

"Don't say his name." She slaps her hands against the bar.

The bartender eyes Calamity. "Everything alright here?"

"'S fine," she says. "He just wants me to kill someone."

Calamity rubs his eyebrows. "Can I get two shots of resting laurel?"

"Can you pay?"

Calamity flushes a deep red, slamming two gold coins onto the bar table. "Keep the change." The bartender serves them the drink, and as soon as she takes a sip, she feels lighter, and her situation seems more funny than tragic. A goofy smile slides onto her face without her noticing, her shoulders loosening with an easy feeling she hasn't felt in weeks. A fire alights in his eyes, but it is not a kind one. "Here's the deal. I leave the money, you find a contractor, and we'll never speak to each other again. Deal?" He holds out a hand to shake.

"Why d'you want him gone?"

"He's delaying the delivery of something I'm owed."

She grabs his hand and giggles. It's soft and hairy like a baby's head. He keeps a hold and wraps a thin cord around their joined hands, and she doesn't like how hot it feels. He mutters under his breath. She winces. His breath feels cold.

"Speak up," she says, shaking her hand free.

Her vision blacks in and out, and when she can see again, she's in a back alley with some goblins. They're common goblins—short, green, and with disproportionate features, everything normal except feet that are too big or a mouth that's much too small.

"All of it to kill Ivan Gray." The words that come out of her mouth don't feel like her own. She throws her sack of gold (where did she get gold?) at their feet.

They shoot nervous glances at each other, but one steps forward, clears his throat, and says, "You got it, boss."

They take the money and skitter off without another word. She slumps down onto the cold cement, holding her pounding head in her hands. What had happened? She'd been at the bar, then it was all a blur.

"No more drinks tonight," she says, rubbing the back of her head before she follows her magic home.

A bright "home" glows in front of her, flashing over different routes in the underlayer. She stumbles towards an exit, picking the highest odds all the way back to the tower.

26

ELAINE TRIES TO KILL IVAN

Ivan is confused by the goblins who have been following him for a few blocks. Not by their intentions, no. The daggers and comically large hammer make it clear they're here to do some damage. But the lock on his bounty is on for at least another month, and any working hunter in Locke wouldn't risk being blacklisted for a measly score. He takes a sharp right into an alleyway, and smiles when he hears the squawked panic of his would-be killers, scrambling to follow him. He scales the wall with ease, perching atop the roof as the green group runs into the alleyway.

"Where'd he go?"

"Down the alleyway."

"Mm-hm! I saw it."

"We all *saw* it. But where did he go?"

He drops down behind them as they continue to bicker. "You would all be much better at this if you had someone watching your six."

"Ah!" they all yelp, turning towards him with their weapons.

"Sneaking behind us isn't a very fair thing to do," one pipes up, even as his fingers tremble around the handle of what looks like a very large meat mallet.

"Trying to murder someone isn't very nice, either."

The goblins, to their credit, do not reveal their employer, despite the imposing figure Ivan cuts beneath his hooded cloak.

"We were just fulfilling the boss's oath." A goblin with an eye patch blurts out.

The others squawk again in dismay at this betrayal.

"What? You wanna die for some stupid promise?"

"We owe him a debt. We said we'd watch out for her while he's away."

"I don't owe nothin'," the one with the eyepatch remarks.

"Slow down. Who's your ward?" Ivan interjects.

"He told us not to trust you," one moans. "The man in the bear cloak. He said you were no good for her."

"For...do you mean Lainey?"

"It's Nellie!" one blurts out, slapping a hand over his mouth once he realizes his mistake.

"Now you've done it."

"It was a secret."

"The oath, the oath." A goblin tugs at her ears in distress.

Ivan is putting together the pieces of the puzzle now. He crouches down, and the goblins' kitchen tools clank as they brandish them at his body. "So, Neil asked you to watch over Lainey. That doesn't explain the attempted homicide."

"She paid 'em," Eyepatch says.

The others whack him with the blunt ends of their tools.

"Why would she hire you? No offense." A part of Ivan feels smug, as Elaine is not dumb enough to hire this group as true killers. In her own petty way, she's hoping he'll seek her out again.

"She 'ired 'em after stumbling out of a bar they followed 'er to. Then the 'ired knives 'ired me," Eyepatch huffs.

"We thought he looked tough. The eye patch and all."

He *is* the scariest looking of the bunch. Like a beloved doll that's been stitched up too many times by a well-meaning amateur.

"We keep an eye out for the watchtower and Nellie. She doesn't know we're there but she's safe with us. We followed her out of the bar, and when she looked possessed! Mumbling about finding a killer. We couldn't let her give all that gold to someone who wouldn't keep their word. We owe Mr. Neil a life debt."

"He even lets us sleep in the kitchen closet since the home we slept in got destroyed by that vampire," another goblin chimes in.

"The one killing the socialites? You lived with one of the victims?"

They nod vigorously. "We kept the gnomes out of her garden."

"Damn gnomes." They all spit on the concrete in disgust.

"Usually, this would end with you all dead."

Eyepatch sprints out of the alleyway.

"But since you're protecting Lainey, I'll play nice. I need you all to give her something for me."

The remaining goblins huddle together, whispering harshly.

"We can't be bought," one states. A life debt is no small thing to break.

Ivan taps his chin, as if in thought. "I see. What if I offered you a place to stay? My apartment is a pretty nice temperature this time of year. And it'll even help Nellie, if you're worried about what Neil will think."

They lean in as their enemy-turned-ally lists out the details of their new mission.

~

Little green goblins are massaging her rat-bat. Roger purrs from the window, where the low cooing of goblins awakes her from her slumber. She's gone mad, then. She slumps back into bed.

"Rise and shine!" a nasally voice yells.

Elaine groans. "What?"

"No time! Get in the tub."

"What tub?" Her room only has a shower.

"No tub? We're worse off than I thought. Boys, dry rub."

"Dry rub!"

"Dry rub!"

Elaine is swept into the kitchen by the goblins. One takes a towel and runs it under the sink before scrubbing at her, moving her around until he nods in satisfaction.

"Not that I don't appreciate this, but who are you, and why are you bathing me and kneading my rat?"

"Neil sent us. You must go to the ball."

Another nods his head vigorously. "Lots of webworking to do."

"It's networking."

"No, that's *fish*."

"Alright. To the dressing room!"

They dress her in a pink, scaly gown that shines with a pearly sheen if caught under a certain light. It's a testament to how bad she's been longing for care, because she lets them. Even if your uncle is framed and your lover tries to kill you, a 401k waits for no one. They're right, she needs to network, especially if she wants to be able to afford living in the watchtower. Then she's pushed out the door and walks to Locke University's Spring Equinox Ball.

~

She's smiling through a conversation on opportunities abroad when she sees him. It's the first time she's seen him out of his cloak. He's dressed for the occasion in a long black tuxedo robe, with the black garland crown in his hair. She looks away, heart pounding fast as she looks for someone, anyone to talk to.

She places her hand on her belt, feeling for the potions she stored there. A smokescreen, a minimizer, a detonator. The celebration isn't worth it anymore. She'll need to leave before he finds her.

Picking up the ends of her ballgown, Elaine moves towards the front door. She winces as her eyes flash probabilities in her panic, mind whirring with questions.

Escape—67% flashes over the exit.

Inebriation has dropped from a promising *72%* to an *11%*.

Conversation—5%

Conversation—81%

An orc wiggles his eyebrows.

Make out—95%.

She shudders. Most of the crowd has parted, but the yellow visuals make it harder to see where she's going. There are too many variables, too many possibilities that change with every new conversation and passing fancy.

As she passes him, Ivan's hand slips her yellow glasses from her hip onto her nose. The headache disappears only to be replaced by a taller one.

"Care to dance?" he asks, whisking her away from *Escape—2%* and onto the dance floor.

Ivan doesn't look at her as he scans the room for something. There are a hundred possibilities in a room full of people and food and magic, enough to make her head spin.

"I put out a hit on you," she whispers.

He holds her hand tighter. "I know."

They sway through the couples, all laughing, whispering sweet nothings.

She grips his arm. "I'm sorry."

"I know, Lainey. It's okay. I took care of it."

She nods, eyes screwing up as her vision grows blurry. "I miss you, even though you tried to kill me." His face pinches in agony, but her chest feels lighter after telling the truth. They dance with everyone else, swaying as the rest complete complicated dance moves she's never learned. "Titon's going to get Neil back for me."

His nose scrunches. "The rat king?"

She nods. "I got the crown back from Ophelia. He's getting Uncle Neil for me any day now." His frown doesn't disappear, and she notices. "What?"

"Ophelia's taken Titon prisoner. The underneath's been buzzing with the news. Rats chewing on cables, stealing food, the works. They don't know how long she'll keep him captive this time."

The world around her sounds underwater, now. "Captured? No. No, I need him to get my uncle. She can't just take him." That means she's back to square one with no way to get Neil back. Her breath speeds up, and Ivan's hold on her tightens.

He's going to kill you, her mind warns, even as their magic commingles, his pleasure at her proximity purring in her body like a cat.

Her anger comes back swiftly, and she narrows her eyes at him, gripping his hands tighter again.

"I'll get Neil," he says.

An awful feeling sits in her stomach, stewing up the acid pain of his betrayal again. He gnaws like an unruly dog at her ribcage, trying to make a hole big enough to squeeze through. He wants to come back with his ears pinned and head low, expecting sweet eyes to be enough to let him back onto the foot of her bed. Her tight fist wrinkles her dress. Will he wait to bite her until her eyes are closed, or will he wrap his jaws around her throat as soon as he passes through the front gate?

"I promise, love."

Her heart skips a beat, and his teeth make it past the first rib. "You've never called me that before."

"I'm going to teach you to hire better contractors," he says. "They were awful. How much did you pay them?"

"A year's rent."

He whistles. "I could've taken the job at that price, Lainey. 'Death by asphyxiation.'" He looks suggestively towards her thighs, but she scowls.

"Say you're sorry," she says.

"I'm sorry."

She gulps, even though the next words are the least vulnerable. She folds the crease of his suit jacket, staring hard at the crushed black velvet. "Say you'll call off the assassins." The words hurt to say, and her voice breaks at the end.

"I'll—wait, what assassins?"

She pushes him away. "Incredible. Even now, after you've abandoned your vendetta, after the hell you'll put me through, you can't admit your mistakes."

"I didn't send killers."

"'Gray sends his regards' they said. Who else, *Gray*." She spins and heads for the nearest exit, cloak fluttering behind her in an angry wave. She hopes he slips when he inevitably comes after her.

"Lainey...shit! Sorry..." Ivan's voice fades away as he stumbles into another dancer, and it allows her to escape from the hall, pink-scaled dress twinkling as bright as her tears.

27

LOCKE'S TREASURE

She's stopped by Professor Sap on her way to the bathroom. He looks as unkempt as she feels. His eyes are wild and alight, so unlike his usual foggy glances. His short green arms are outstretched toward her stomach, blocking her exit.

"Ms. Aquae! It's too early to be going home. Head back in." He shoos her backwards.

"But, Professor," she says, "I really have to go."

"It's almost time," he insists.

"I've seen seventy-two spring equinoxes, Professor. What's another?"

A burst of laughter fills the hallway as a group of students exits, paying no mind to them. As they pass, the smell of mold fills her nose.

"That smell..."

Sap stops pushing at her knees as she walks around him. She's smelled it before— at the hospital, in the dead socialite's home. The answer lies just beyond her reach, an itch her brain can't scratch.

Elaine follows her nose, maddened by the mold. "It's getting closer." She focuses on her core. Following the scent is easier with magic. "C'mon," she mutters. "Where are you?"

A sharp pain shoots between her eyes, and her vision is flooded with too much yellow. She touches the glasses hanging around her neck. Taking a deep breath, she focuses on wanting to find the mold. Her headache lessens. The yellow numbers appear like apparitions, and the smells grow stronger as they show the way.

The hallways twist and turn in unfamiliar directions as she follows her percentages, but getting lost is not a worry as the hallways light up with her odds of success. *Find the mold* floats above each path, and the sound of the ball fades into the background until all she can hear is her own steps.

She rounds a corner and sees 95%. She fumbles her glasses on now that she found her target, and in her excitement, swings the bronze double doors wide open.

"Aha!"

Calamity, the man behind her invitations to the balls, whirls to face her.

"You," she says.

"Elaine." he replies.

A figure steps out of the shadows. His gray hood is pushed back, the elegant features of his face so familiar it makes her heart ache. Beneath blond hair and blue eyes stretches a wide familiar smile, a little too young to be the right one. The teeth are too straight and the shadows under his eyes are nonexistent.

"You?"

"Me." Her uncle's coworker smiles ear to ear. The one that had stopped everyone in their tracks when he glided through the office, and the one who had come uninvited to the watchtower. He takes a step forward, and she notices he leans more heavily against his silver cane than the last time she'd seen him. "The guest of honor has finally arrived."

Calamity grabs her by the arm before she can run. She struggles against him, but it's no use, his grip is too strong.

Before them lies a copper spiral staircase within a room so dark that the only light illuminating it is the door she entered from. The room itself is cold and devoid of warming wards. In fact—Elaine sniffs the air—it's devoid of any spells and runes as well, as far as she can smell. It looks as though no one has stepped foot inside here for centuries. She shivers, the uncanny feeling of the liminal space making her feel as though the room is watching. It reminds her of after hours at an office.

They lead Elaine down copper stairs that rust green under each of the gray stranger's steps.

"You're so much easier to get to when that uncle of yours isn't around. Bounty or no, I don't think we could've gotten you with him still guarding the watchtower," Calamity says.

His words make a horrible pit settle in her stomach. "You're the reason Uncle Neil is in jail," she accuses. "You're the one who wants to steal from Locke, and you set the bounty to get a luck mage for the school's dungeon after you realized my uncle couldn't get through it on his own." She thinks back to Ivan's crazed rant about the circle of power as they took Neil away. "You're the one after the fairy ring."

The pretty stranger doesn't reply, but Calamity can't help himself.

He slows to walk beside her, nose stuck up in the air. "It was so easy. You were so desperate to prove yourself you didn't even notice Ivan's growing suspicion of your dear uncle. And that suspicion made him blind to the fact that I was the one who created the bounty. The Calamity family has put all it has into the funding of the city, and we hardly get paid, while the top brass get all of the profits. Those traditionalists of the Delphi family hardly make relevant predictions these days. They're so inbred, their eyes are too crossed to be able to tell you if you should turn left or right. If we take the oracle seat within the old families, we can shape the future for generations."

Elaine thinks back to all her interactions with Calamity: the constant purchasing of new cloaks, the bar full of people he owes a debt to. "You're broke, and you're doing all this just for money?"

He sneers, eyes fogging over with his rising superiority complex. "Money means security, and security means freedom."

She twists her face but pauses. Had she not said the same thing, over and over to Ivan?

"Money can do many good things," she reminds both Calamity and herself. "When that money is earned legally. Not through blood and theft."

"You've been doing a lot of thieving yourself these days, I hear."

"That's different! No one dies at the end."

"Well as long as no one dies," he mocks her.

She scowls. Her lack of strong moral boundaries is less deplorable than her abduction. "If your plan was to take me during the ball, what was the point of the bounty?"

"Insurance," the stranger steps forward. "It was an incentive for Ivan to stay under my thumb. If he ignored the mission, we'd get a luck mage by force. Your arrival to Garriver makes stealing a luck mage much easier. We didn't know you even existed before you met Ivan." He fiddles with his hands in a way that's familiar to Elaine, but she can't quite place it.

"You picked the wrong one. My affinity isn't trained enough to help you find an entrance."

"Oh, we found it," he replies. "Your uncle discovered those copper doors, along with five other entries, only open during an equinox. Of course, when he realized what it was leading us to, he tried to end the contract. But he'd already made me the potion I need to complete my plan, and Ivan jailing him was merely a well-timed opportunity to remove an obstacle before reaching our destination."

She struggles against his hold, but he just grips tighter. "And where are we going?"

"The ultimate source of power: Garriver's fairy ring."

Garriver's fairy ring, like all rings of power, is a natural, cyclical source of power.

"Then why do you need me?"

"We need a bit of luck."

"Probability," she corrects. "My point still stands: why me?"

Calamity looks at the gray cloaked man over her head. "Don't feel like sharing, Gray?"

The gray stranger looks back at them, eyes heavily lidded. "Watch yourself."

"Gray," she says. "Like Ivan Gray."

Her mind whirs with theories. If he's related to Ivan, he must be planning on taking him back as a prisoner to keep their family alive. But if Ivan's the only thing keeping their family from money and power, why are they still heading into the dungeons of Locke?

Gray shoves her forward, face red.

"You're related, aren't you," she says. "A nephew, a cousin?"

Elaine's first thought is that this relative looks nothing like Ivan. He's fairer in every sense of the word. His clothes are pristine, and his hair is combed back, carefully framing the face he'd previously kept hidden. But as she looks closer, she sees Ivan in the shape of his eyes, and the hard cut of his jaw.

"If I hadn't shown up you would've had to put the person keeping your family in power into mortal danger. Why would you ever risk dealing with the unknown consequences of killing off the family curse-bearer?"

Gray's hand tenses around his cane.

"We can always make more sons," he replies.

They reach the bottom of the stairs and stand in front of a steel-doored elevator, lit by a single green lightbulb above it.

"Calamity," Gray barks before pulling himself and Elaine back from the elevator doors.

Calamity pushes his sleeves up and steps towards the elevator. He rolls his neck side to side and stretches out his arms. He then cracks each individual finger before repeating the action for each of his knuckles.

"Any day now."

He shoots a glare at Gray. "Magic isn't all brutality. Some affinities require patience."

"I'm not paying for patience. I'm paying for results," he says. Even as he speaks of impatience, his body is relaxed against his cane.

Calamity ignores this. He raises his arms over his head, and Elaine feels the magic tingle in the air. He lets out a deep sigh and bends over to touch his toes. Gray's grip tightens on her arm, and she hisses in pain.

Calamity laughs at her discomfort. "Don't hurt your prized cattle, Gray." He pushes the elevator's down button.

The whirring sound of elevator pulleys fills the air around them, and after a few moments of waiting, the elevator opens with a ding. At the same moment, the area around them heats up, and Gray hurries to put himself and Elaine next to the comet mage. The floor below them flicks with bright orange tongues of new flames, and she can feel the sharp burn of them snapping against the bottom of her shoes.

"Fire is not my area of expertise, but all matter loses to the vacuum of space."

The fire at their feet flares momentarily before being sucked out of the room in front of Calamity. But the flames are not her biggest worry. Her vision goes black as matterless space, spreads across the floor and rises the wall, until all that remains is nothing and the sound of faraway static in her ears.

The fire flares for a moment before it flickers and dies within his vacuum of space. Onward, onward, and onward extends this expanse of nothingness, hungry to suck her in and make her nothing too, and just as she thinks this might be here forever, the room snaps back into view, and everything is as it was before. She wiggles her toes; the floor is cool beneath her feet.

Calamity waves a hand at Elaine to enter the elevator.

Gray clicks his tongue. "You'll be going through first. Not her."

Calamity's head snaps to him, eyes wide in outrage. "But—"

"You think I wouldn't find out you tried to get her to hire someone to kill Ivan?" Gray laughs sharply.

Elaine listens to this new information with interest. So, this relative doesn't want Ivan dead, and his partner tried to kill him. If there are cracks in their partnership, that means there's room to topple it.

"Sloppy work, and a lazy attempt to destabilize the Gray family's power." Gray waves a hand at the elevator, mocking Calamity's earlier motion. "I'll forgive you and will continue to consider letting your family take the Delphi family's seat if we get through this in one piece."

Calamity places one foot in first, and when nothing happens, he enters it fully. He turns around with a smug smile.

Gray and Elaine follow him in, and the steel doors shut behind them with a loud thunk. The trip down is long, and minutes pass in silence.

Unable to stop thinking about the darkness, Elaine asks, "What's your affinity? I thought you could see the future. But I couldn't see a single star."

"I come from a long line of comet mages, specifically working with fortune telling through the stars. They love to focus on what's there. But I focused my studies on something much more plentiful: the absence.

"How empty," she says.

"How all-consuming."

On instinct, she goes to clutch her cloak tighter around herself, but her fingers grasp at papery satin. She'd left it at home and worn her school cloak, per dress code, void of any protections.

The elevator doors slide open, and she's shoved out of it.

She wishes she could remove her glasses and use her magic, but her mind is so scattered that she knows the numbers of her probability magic will only incapacitate her.

There's a blast of heat at her back, and she's pushed the rest of the way forward, a cloak wrapping around her to protect her from the heat.

Calamity screams in pain still halfway inside the elevator, pawing at the flames eating his cloak. The shiny cloak he wears curls into charred and warped rubber, the plastic smell wafting through the air.

"New money cloaks." Gray sneers. He takes the side of his own cloak, infused with priceless years' worth of family wards and storied spells, and pats the flames licking at his dress shoes. "The trap must have a fail safe."

The air now smells of a noxious mix of burning plastic and barbeque, and Elaine's eyes water, at the smell or the sight she's not sure. Gray wipes at his own eyes with a handkerchief, watching as Calamity lays there, crying in pain, half naked and burned.

Gray moves towards the next elevator, leaving Elaine to stare horrified at the injured man now whimpering on the copper floor, pawing his way out of the extinguished elevator.

Gray taps his foot impatiently, and when she doesn't move, he taps his cane so hard it echoes across the room. "He should have been better. Faster." He looks her up and down. "Lucky."

He gestures for her to follow with a point of his cane. She turns and approaches Calamity, takes off her own school-issued cloak, and places it next to him. She pulls a painkiller potion from her hip, and places it against his lips. He gasps as she touches the raw nape of his neck.

"Drink," she insists.

He gurgles and spits as she forces the concoction down his throat.

"Keep drinking. Especially when it starts to hurt."

He leans his head away, but she forces him to face her again and presses the lip of the bottle to his burnt mouth. She started keeping pain relievers on her when Roger fell ill and doubled it after learning of Ivan's chronic curse. Just in case.

She lays his head back and puts her cloak under it once the bottle is empty. Gray's silver cane whistles through the air and whacks the back of her head, and a firm hand grabs her and hoists her back to standing. She glances at Calamity, a proud man reduced to a shivering slump along the floor.

"Don't dwell on the fate of vermin."

Visions of Roger run through her mind. She pulls her arm out of his hold and snarls into his face, "Do you have no heart?"

He laughs prettily. "I believe we share the same one."

He drags her to the other end of the room where there's a door instead of an elevator, and she's struck by a sickly-sweet smell of honey in the air as they approach it. The doorknob is covered in a thick amber slathering.

"Ladies first."

She's forced to grab the slimy handle, and she pulls the door open with a wince, trying to shake the goop off her hand and failing. There is a slab of honey in front of her, unmoving, and it's so thick that it distorts the view of whatever's on the other side. She looks back fearfully, but he just pushes her forward another step. Holding her breath, she takes a step forward, as her body is covered in the substance, muffling her ears, and soaking through her clothes. She pushes forward and takes a deep gulp of air when she feels wind on her face, coughing out the honey that gets into her mouth. She hears low mumbling and turns back to see Gray saying something. He rolls his eyes and says something else, gesticulating. His eyes widen, and he pulls her towards him before turning to face forward. This room isn't really a room, but complex walls of hexagonal honeycomb built over what used to be the freight elevator.

Low buzzing fills her ears. She takes a cautious step backward on the honeycomb. From the dark two red, hexagonal eyes emerge. Then a blue-and-yellow striped thorax, with three legs on each side, follows the head. A vibration thrums through her whole body as the insect chatters two large mandibles, but she's still unable to hear. Large iridescent wings beat furiously above the body of what can only be the queen bee to a royal hive.

Elaine's heard of the royal hives before. They were hunted to near extinction because of the rarity of their color and the hallucinogenic properties of their honey and were thought to be extinct until their rediscovery ten years ago. They are classified as nonintelligent due to their lack of complex dialect and the inability for a majority of their population to survive through cold weather. However, this verdict is highly debated because of their advanced telepathy, a technique that makes them the smartest predators in their domain.

A glob of honey drips from the ceiling and oozes onto her face, the smallest amount making it past her lips. This time, she swallows, and her ears pop.

"You idiot—"

She's at home, and her mother is making honey jam to go with her biscuits. She's humming a nursery rhyme from her childhood, sweet and rich and familiar.

"Oh, good. Your father and Ivan are about to come back with some more berries for our lunch."

She's alarmed for a moment at the prospect of seeing her father again, but that feeling is quickly washed away by excitement. By the stars, it had been months! Why wouldn't she be excited to see her dad?

The front door swings open, and the aforementioned men walk through the door.

"Dad." She smiles, opening her arms wide.

"There's my little girl." He grabs her in his arms and spins her around. He smells like home.

"Is the royal jelly ready? I'm starving." Ivan wraps an arm around her free shoulder, kissing the side of her head. Leaning against him feels like sliding into a hot Alappan spring on a cold winter's day.

She notices his cloak is different. "Where's your pelt?" She thumbs his new amber cloak, silky and covered in yellow four-leaf clovers.

"Honey, you know how I feel about bears." He tugs her hand and pulls her further into the kitchen.

She frowns. She thought he liked them.

"Come on, your dad was about to tell us about the time you two fell from that tower."

Her nails scratch over her skin, which feels dry and itchy. That gooey warmth she'd been surrounded by seeps away, leaving her cold and dry and—

She gasps in a deep breath, hands tugging away from the sticky substance keeping her immobile. She can't find purchase, and her feet start to kick out as well, further twisting the royal honey around her limbs.

"Stop moving," Gray says. He's ahead of her, across from the royal queen.

"I was at home." She coughs out a spittle of sweet nectar. "Put me back! I want to go back!"

"The honey convinces the weak-willed they want nothing more than to sit up against it and leave. Eventually, your body becomes emulsified in it, too, creating that blue royal jelly."

Gray steps forward, cane left behind him. "Lucky for you, I don't dream. I exist."

He reaches out a hand and touches the head of the queen. She shrieks, tugging away, but he has her in a firm hold against his palm. Her limbs thrash weakly until they stop moving, save for the occasional twitch. Her thorax, full of royal jelly, begins to collapse in on itself as Gray stands straighter. The honey around Elaine dissipates and she's able to break free as the honey dries up, along with the queen. Her mucous form husks over until she's a collapsed shell of nothing.

It reminds Elaine of grotesque photos from Garriver papers and police reports, and of the cat statue they stole after the article came out about the unsolved murders in Abraham Park. "You're the one who fed off the housewives," she accuses.

Gray stands straighter after using his magic, and his stride back to his cane lacks the limp he had before. "It's funny, how strong lonely people think they are, until they have the chance at affection again."

When he uses his magic, she finally sees Ivan in him—the wicked smile, the same playful twitch of his fingers after a powerful casting, the energy sparking over his digits in anticipation of the next blow. But this kind of magic, both his and Calamity's, is used to take and take and take. He gestures down the elevator shaft. They'll have to use the honeycomb to descend.

"Ladies first."

She jumps down onto the first step, and when it stands firm beneath her, she turns back to scowl. "You're vampiric. Both of you."

Gray shakes his head. "Calamity? No, he displaces. Space just shuffles matter around. But me?" He hoists his cane up and over his shoulder. "I'm something much worse."

"That's vile."

"That's power. And I only take what I need." He blinks his doleful eyes. "I'm not the selfish one in the family."

Gray steps behind her and she moves forward before he can push her again. They enter the next elevator, and he presses the down button.

"What awaits us now? Deadly mosquitos? Our worst fears realized?"

He sighs, forlorn. "I wish. Those are all things that could be conquered through bravery and valor, easily found in contract swords. No, the next task requires a bit of—"

"Don't say luck," she warns. "I'm not lucky."

She believes it now as much as she did before she met Ivan. Luck is for dreamers and the rich, not her. Never, despite her hopes rising in the past year, for Elaine.

He smooths out his collar. "No, not luck. We need you for a task that requires a fine-tuned touch."

The elevator doors open, revealing a simple stone room with a cauldron at its center. She steps out and checks the corners, the floor, the ceiling for traps.

"I believe we'll have to get closer to the cauldron to do anything."

She moves closer and takes a deep breath in when the room remains normal. The cauldron itself is normal, too. It's on a square wooden table, and potion instructions are sitting neatly next to it. It reads: *True Decay. Class: Impossible Potion. Odds of correct brewing: 0%.*

"You must be joking."

Gray taps the cauldron with his cane, peering inside. "It's a catch-22, even if you do solve it, the potion kills you instantly, but the final door is opened. If you fail to brew it, this entry point closes off forever."

"You think a probability mage has the ability to change the outcome."

He nods his head.

"You're asking me to change reality. A lethal potion is still a lethal potion." It's true that she can't bend reality. Once she thought she'd made a banana peel appear in front of Ivan to trip him, but it turned out a monkey had dropped it on his way to the financial district. "At best, I could try to change the odds of us surviving it. Maybe." She shakes her head. "You're asking me for a stroke of luck."

"Ivan could do it."

"Well then you should've taken him instead."

He narrows his eyes at her. He gestures back to the cauldron in front of them. "If you share an affinity, you share a skill. Calamity said success was written in the stars with the help of a luck mage. If Ivan's lucky enough to change the odds of us surviving the potion, that means you can too. You've learned potion making from a wizard rank potioneer, a skill I'm sure Ivan doesn't have the patience for, so," he waves his hand again, "alter."

She narrows her eyes. To give this man access to the fairy ring that Neil was so desperate to keep him away from, sends chills running up her spine. "I'd rather die."

"Oh, suddenly we're noble? Might I remind you, you will *actually* die."

She raises her chin.

"If not for you, then do it to cure Ivan," he says.

Her heart skips a beat, but she shakes her head. If there was a cure, Ivan would've found it.

"You can't do that. No one can do that."

"I know the family curse inside and out. You see, most old families stay in power because they have some trick. Our curse has kept us wealthy, well fed, and well bred. One of us just needs to take on all of the bad—the hunger, the malaise, the death."

"You think I'm going to fall for a story?" Elaine sneers.

"There's no cure. Your family will always need a victim to stay in power."

"If I get to the fairy ring, the Grays won't need the family curse."

The implication sits heavy in her chest. "You're lying."

"What reason do I have to lie? The tool I'm looking for will make Ivan's role in our family irrelevant. And it lies just beyond this potion."

"Liar."

"Liar?" Gray sneers. "The circle of power after this final trial has restorative magic strong enough to replace an eternity of first borns for the curse. The family will never curse a child again."

If he's telling the truth, Ivan could live a full life. But on the other hand, the ring is much more than a source of magic for mages. It isn't just the wine, but the water. Ivan may be free of pain, but the city will be drained of its magic. Though she doesn't understand it, she knows the metropolis covered in cement, and its air and water filled with toxins, still holds life. By the gods, life passes so vibrantly and volatilely, that it makes her feel like she lives amongst the stars—vivid explosions that die, and in their wake, create smaller microcosms of something entirely new. Over and over again, cycles on cycles, like rain to a river. To turn against Garriver would mean turning against the laws of nature. It's why so many rings are hidden in the first place. Terrible things happen to mages who mess with the natural order, and those disasters echoes for miles around the impact zone. This could take millions of lives and destroy entire ecosystems.

She breathes in and looks down harder at the instructions. They're written poorly in a script she's only used to seeing from Uncle Neil—it's in the common dialect, then the margins have runes with arrows pointed in between words.

1. Pour in the manticore hair.
2. Crush up a sprig of basil.
3. Bring the cauldron to a boil. Then add cracked porcelain, dearly loved
4. Wait until the potion turns green, then add in a whole page of the Gutenberg Bible

The instructions droll on, listing rare ingredients, some thought long lost to history. Her eyes catch on a mention of lightning mushrooms, and she thinks of Uncle Neil.

Gray drops a pouch next to her on the table. He pulls out the ingredients and closes it when it's empty. Her fingers twitch and she begins to organize the ingredients in order of use. She switches to color, then largest to smallest, common to rare.

"Any day now."

She looks over the organization. She picks up the tube of manticore hair, then puts it back. She'll do it in chronological order. Carefully, she rearranges them once more.

"You're stalling," he snaps.

"Do you want it done fast or right?"

The ball to celebrate spring is surely still going on. They had plenty of time, a priceless resource. Ivan's smile fills her mind.

Elaine uncaps the manticore tube, prays for forgiveness, and attempts the impossible.

When you're born unable to rely on magic, you create it yourself with practice. Cooking is a basic skill that can be enhanced by tasting, adjusting, and adding what you think will make it better. The best chefs are those that make cooking look like magic, ones that don't use measuring tools at all, or seamlessly integrate something new into a dish without testing it first. They know that saffron mixes well with poultry but is a waste in something sweet.

With baking, the exactness of each ingredient is key. It's the difference between a fluffy cake and one that won't rise. The amount of sugar used is the difference between a sweet cookie and a savory one.

Potions masters understand that their work is a bit of both —exactness and instinctual. They not only train in precision, but they study the chemical reactions and how they change with the humidity, temperature and, depending on the ingredient, measure out portions based on the time of year, month, and day.

Elaine may not have the instinct that comes with learning magic when you're young, but life granted her a different gift—because of magic's absence in her life, practice became the closest act she had to a miracle.

She takes off her sunglasses and the odds appear in front of her. She doesn't look away from the cauldron, knowing her mind will stray if she thinks too hard about the stakes. She tucks her sunglasses into the top of her dress, noting that the odds of success are low.

Brewing Correctly- 0.001%

Still, she goes through the steps, hesitating as the numbers decrease the more she proceeds.

"This is like nothing I've ever seen," she breathes. It doesn't matter how she thinks to approach the problem, the probability of succeeding won't go any higher.

"I've heard you can change the odds with dice. Do that."

Her hands tremble over the cauldron. "That was for one in thirty-six odds. You can't expect me to change the odds of a potion this complex, Mr. Gray."

"Yes, you *can*."

She panics and squeezes her eyes shut when the probabilities flare up like a flashbang. She presses the heels of her hand into her eyes, scrubbing at the acute pain just behind them.

Gray growls nearby, tapping his cane. "Don't you understand if you fail to change the odds, you die?"

"And don't you understand you're asking me to do the undoable?"

"Looks like you took the wrong mage, Mr. Gray," someone says from behind them.

Elaine's heart beats faster at the sound of that wonderfully familiar voice.

"Ivan," they both say, turning to find him standing nearby.

She opens her eyes and sees he's regained his brown cloak, though he's still wearing formal clothes underneath. His eyes run over Elaine.

"You alright?" he asks. He looks calm, but she's known him long enough to see the tell-tale sign of panic when he fiddles with his cloak.

Elaine nods.

After deeming her relatively unharmed despite the scattered scorch marks and honey, Ivan turns his gaze to his relative. He notices the Gray family crest on his cane and laughs.

"So, Daddy Dearest sent a pawn. Couldn't get his creaky millennia-old bones past the garden gate?"

"No, no, no. You—" Gray cuts himself off. Gone is the apathetic impatience in his blue eyes, now replaced by a cold fury. He points a shaking, accusing finger at Ivan. "It was all going to plan. All you had to do was stay away. Run off, like you always do. Now we'll all die if this fails."

Ivan grins, relishing in the man's anger. "Introduce me to your new friend, Lainey."

Relief fills her, even if personal experience has taught her Ivan's confidence in his success isn't a guarantee of it. "He claims to be a family member of yours."

"A Gray?" Ivan smiles meanly. "You all hate work. Me leaving really did do something to the curse, then."

Ivan collapses as the smell of mold fills the air again. When she turns to identify the source, her nose lands on the blonde, who points in the duo's direction..

It's him, *this* Gray, who makes the air smell wet and wrong. She remembers the smell from her uncle's office and those times in between; when Ivan collapsed around her uncle, it had to be that this blonde parasite skulked nearby, infecting the air with the effects of this terrible magic.

Gray regards Ivan like a particularly fascinating specimen as he lays on the ground. When he moves his eyes back to Ivan's face, a strange expression crosses his face—intrigue, confusion, familiarity? "You've always been so tired."

Ivan, Elaine bristles, *looks perfect.*

There he lays, his bear-tufted cloak now lined with her own magic. His eyes soften when he turns to her again, and she revels in his gap-toothed smile. He turns over, palms pressing his shaky arms upwards until he's standing and steps towards her, but Gray stops him with his cane. Ivan snags the aid and uses it to take his next few steps, and as his joints creak with every step towards her, she realizes he probably needs it.

He kisses the top of her head when he reaches her, and she clutches the front of his dress shirt to her, drawing him closer. His eyes flit to the title of the potion.

"Impossible," he scoffs. "You know nothing's impossible for us."

Her heart leaps in her chest.

"What do you need, Lainey?"

"I've followed the instructions down to the letter. But the odds don't change, and I can't figure out what I'm doing wrong." She licks her lips. "I also don't know if we should complete it. Getting down here is sort of a one-way ticket until you complete the challenges."

"Sounds like we'll have to figure it out, good idea or no," he mutters. He circles the table, eyeing the cauldron.

She smacks his hand away when he goes to lift the cauldron and check the bottom. Any movement could change its composition. A clock chimes, and her heart jumps.

"We have to do this before the spring equinox ends," Gray hisses, "or we'll die here."

"Right. No pressure, then." Ivan runs his hands through his hair, fingers catching on the back of his neck.

"It's not fair."

"It's not fair..." he repeats. He gasps, eyes lighting up, "Oh! It's brilliant. The perfect test for a school full of silly, law-abiding academics, who can't imagine not following things to the letter."

"What are you talking about?" Gray says.

Ivan turns a derisive grin towards his relative. "It's easy—come on, tell me you see it."

He turns his glittering eyes on Elaine. He grabs her hands and presses his forehead against hers. "You know it, Lainey."

"Ivan, we don't have—"

"Think."

She scrunches her brows. Potions are like baking, an exact science. But an impossible one?

Her eyes widen. "Of course. Luck is cheating."

Ivan nods, proud. He stands next to her and takes her hand. "They've never considered probability magic a threat to defend against. If you'll be my head, I'll be your heart."

She eyes the bottles in front of her. "We have to time this right. When I finish brewing, right when I finish brewing, you need to change the odds. When I see it reach 100, I'll grab it."

"100?" he blinks. "I didn't know that was possible."

She also has never seen the yellow odds before her go up to 100%. But with Ivan, she believes it's possible. She is a creature of science, and Ivan is a creature of true magic. She knows he can make even the most impossible, possible. He's the stroke of luck she needs to beat the odds.

"I've never cheated on a test before. But this is it," she says. "This is all or nothing."

"If anyone can do this it's you."

She works with Ivan at her back blocking all distraction. She follows the instructions to a T, finding a familiar rhythm as she works and not letting herself dwell on the possibility that she's brewing them all to their deaths.

"Alright. Put your hand over mine."

Ivan does so, intertwining their fingers.

"You didn't have to—"

"Are you ready?"

He gives her another squeeze.

"Now."

His magic thrums through her, like so many times before. The numbers rocket up, *80*, *85*, *87...83*. She panics at the decrease, and as if he senses it, he pushes more into her, warming her veins. Instead of following the instructions, she begins to add ingredients according to the odds as they turn in their favor.

"I love cheating," she breathes. The resulting potion will be different from the one on the ingredient list, but she trusts the yellow *Success—54%* gleaming in front of her.

Before the last step, Ivan pulls away. "We don't have to help him."

She shakes her head, grasping her free hand around his wrist. "Stopping now means we die."

Gray speaks up. "I'm facing these traps for you. Your mother won't stop going on and on about you. 'Where's Ivan? I want to see my boy.' It's driving me up a wall." He sighs. "You know what they say: happy wife, happy life."

Ivan's hand stiffens in her grip. "You?" Ivan says. "You're Dorian."

Her eyes flick between the two. They're opposites, Ivan wild and Dorian a controlled, clean creature, but there's a similar shape in their eyes and their noses.

"You're my father."

The father who cursed him, and who stole his life to make his own easier.

Dorian Gray looks down his nose at his most disappointing son. "In the flesh. I'm surprised she didn't know me, and that you didn't get suspicious when all those housewives started having the life sucked out of them. Surely some of the symptoms on the bodies sounded familiar." He frowns, but his eyes are mirthful. "But I know you like your secrets. You haven't even told Elaine the whole truth of your curse." He turns his elated gaze on her. "Has he?"

"I know all about it," she snarls. "And I bet killing you would solve it."

Dorian laughs. "You know my life is sustained by his, as with all my children. The first son carries the curse so the rest of the family can thrive. You know eventually, and sooner than most, the first son dies."

She scoffs at his lie "Ivan escaped that when he ran away."

But then Ivan looks at her with guilt, and her heart drops to the floor. "No." She shakes her head. "No, you said it was aches and pains. Not—" She cuts herself off. She turns away from him, a sudden mist coming over her eyes. Quietly, she asks, "When were you going to tell me you're going to die?"

He moves his hand to her waist. She searches his face for any sign that Dorian's lying, but Ivan's angry scowl is the same he wore when he had to pay for her toe, when she broke the cat statue, and when he got a check for her uncle's arrest.

He turns his head to the side, frowning. "I didn't want you to pity me."

"You can't know that I would've."

When he turns his gaze back to her, his eyes are pained. "You're too sweet not to, Lainey."

She clutches a hand at her heart, beating rapidly beneath her chest. "If I had known, I would've..." her voice trails off.

"You would've what," he laughs cruelly. His tone sharpens when he speaks, mouth in a wide grin. "Would you have loved me knowing I would die?"

Her breath hitches.

His words have a bite to them, his eyes fiery, like a former street dog ripped from its soft sheets.

"Don't, Ivan."

"You're saying you would." His tone is bitter, disillusioned, even as his teeth shine bright. "What, a pity fuck? Something to make yourself feel less like the weakest mage in the city?"

She pulls back from the hands on her waist. "You don't mean it." Her hands hug her bare arms, eyes pointed down at the ground so he can't see the tears in them. There are more important things at play here than the pair of them.

She eyes the unfinished potion—the last step is the easiest.

Scorpion's tail—86%

But his goal isn't to finish it anymore, it's to argue with her, and no matter how much it hurts, she needs to put a bandaid on this issue so he can focus on potion making, fast.

"We can talk about this after we murder your dad," she murmurs to Ivan. "We need to at least try to complete the potion and live."

His eyes are cold and distant, and it feels as though he's looking through her. "Why bother."

She looks away again, shameful tears falling from her eyes. They should bother because she's scared to be lonely, because she's scared that this really might be the end of her life, and—if Dorian's to be believed—Ivan's. "Because I don't want you to die."

Dorian sees them commiserating, and panic flickers on his

face. "Wait," he says. "If I can get to the power ring, I'll lift the curse."

She'd forgotten his promise from before, something she'd brushed aside as a lie to get her to comply.

Ivan turns to his father, Elaine positioned behind him. His hands ball into tight fists, a sneer across his face. "A likely story."

"With the power of the ring, I won't need the curse to sustain my eternal youth. I'll be able to use it until the end of time."

"Your promises are coming about sixty years too late."

Dorian moves forward, grabbing at Ivan. He tries to pry him off, but Dorian keeps a clawed grip on his forearm.

Dorian's visibly sweating and his doe eyes are wide and filled with tears, his once pursed lips now quivering like a newborn. "If you can create this potion without killing us, you can be free to travel where you wish. You can see your mom again."

Ivan pries Dorian's arm off his own, and the madman clasps at his own elbow, blond hair askew, tears staining the pink blush of his cheeks. His eyes move to Elaine, and the pitiful look disappears, as his Cupid's bow lips slip into a sinister smile.

"You can be with Elaine, for the rest of your natural lives," he says.

It's Ivan's turn to look surprised.

Elaine has to stop him. "Ivan, no. We have to complete the potion, yes, but we can't let him tamper with Garriver's ring. It's too unpredictable!"

"Quiet," Dorian says, and with a wave of his hand, she finds herself magicked into silence. He caresses the side of his son's face, looking at him imploringly. "Imagine, having all the time in the world with her. The way you are now you have, what, two years at most? That's certainly not enough time for her to forgive you for ruining her life, getting her uncle thrown in prison, and derailing her career. But a half century? More? The heart forgives when it's lonely."

Ivan bites his lip, eyes darting between a desperate-looking Elaine, and his horrible, scheming father. Unable to make the choice, he closes his eyes and seems to focus on his magic instead. It had carried him out of his horrible home, through dangerous situations, and into the arms of the only woman who has loved him, regardless of his sins.

He takes a deep breath, eyes widening, mouth moving into a grin, then fluttering back into a grimace. His face fidgets and twists between glee and horror and he squeezes his eyes harshly, breath pumping harsh and fast from his chest.

"I can do it." He opens his eyes and looks at Elaine. Even as his brows screw up in pain, his shoulders brace, and his hands flex and raise with a determination that scares her. "I'm sorry."

Blue eyes flash victoriously behind him. He completes the potion without her, and the floor opens below them.

28

GARRIVER'S FAIRY RING

I *failed,* Elaine thinks as they plummet down.

The metal walls are overtaken by a blur of natural colors as they descend deeper and deeper into the layers of the city. Her dress whips violently against her calves, and everything moves too quickly to see.

Moss beneath her cushions her fall. All around her crystals glow silver, sticking out of cave walls. Crickets, frogs, and a plethora of other fauna chirp. The air is humid, sticking to her skin like a second cloak. She sits up, blurry eyes focusing on the clearing in front of her. Something about this place has her hair standing up on its end, making her feel incredible despite the fall. Before her sits a small circle of garlic, pulsing and glowing much like the crystals all around them. She tries to groan, but Dorian's spell keeps her silent. The Grays don't land quite as softly, both moaning as they roll around on the ground.

She stalks over to Dorian and stands above him. She takes his cane in her hands, raising it above her, but two hands grab it before she can strike.

"Elaine!"

She twists, tears in her eyes, and tugs at the cane Ivan is holding back from her.

Dorian pulls a coil of rope from beneath his robe. "The ring's chosen Elaine as it's champion. It makes the selected mage go crazy, become irrational. You'll have to tie her up, for her own safety."

Her face is thunderous as Ivan twists her around to tie the proffered ropes around her ankles and wrists. She shakes her head, mouth open, but even her pants of breath are silent.

He rubs a fond thumb across her cheek. "When this is through, we'll travel the world together. Promise."

Dorian taps his cane on the floor. "Bring her here. I've found it."

He scowls at his father but takes Elaine in his arms and carries her to the center of the room. There, no larger than two feet in circumference, sits a ring of garlic. The garlic is silver instead of ivory, glittering in the dirt like crystal. Dorian smiles with unadulterated glee, and Elaine and Ivan share a moment of commiseration, trading looks of distaste at his joy. Elaine wiggles in his arms.

"I don't want to drop you," Ivan says.

"Bring her to the edge. I'll drag her the rest of the way in."

Ivan hesitates.

Dorian rolls his eyes, checking his watch for the time. "The rules of a fairy ring are simple. Circles of power can only exist because there's a trade off: they can be challenged for control over the land's magic. Magic likes to ebb and flow, but these circles take a large amount of magic and trap it in a circuit, building momentum and creating eternal, renewable magic sources. It's only natural that other forces of nature would challenge it for that resource. The ring chooses a champion, usually a mage connected closely to nature. When Elaine challenges me to a fight inside the circle of power, I will accept."

"The ring chooses a champion, and when Elaine challenges me at the right place, at the right time, I will accept."

"You won't touch her."

Dorian relaxes his face, giving the smile she's used to receiving from disgruntled clerks and adults she'd corrected as a child. She rolls her eyes, but Ivan's focus is split between her and the fairy ring, rather than his father.

"I don't need to touch her. The champion and challenger enter the ring, and whoever is pushed out first loses. There's a theory that since the founders cut the ring off from the city, the circle's been calling out to all sorts of...changeable creatures to be its challenger whenever someone approaches it with the intent to take the city's magic. When she's pushed out of the fairy ring, I will become the victor, and I will be granted access to all of Garriver's magic. You can both leave, unharmed."

She bares her teeth at the use of the word "creature."

Dorian breaks the silencing spell with a flick of his wrist.

Elaine hisses, "Shut up, just shut up."

He cocks his head, eyes wide. "What, he doesn't know?"

"He doesn't *need* to. It doesn't *matter*."

"Then why are you crying?"

"There's nothing wrong with me! Don't call us creatures. You don't understand why I— it's not *shame*, I'm—"

"You are the *bastard child* of a *wind nymph*. That makes you one of them."

The tears run hot down her face. Ivan's face screws up in anger, about to say something, when from the depths of the marsh, the water begins to move.

Out of it comes the unlikely deity Ophelia, moss and bugs falling off her pristine figure and sticking onto the human-shaped clump held by his collar in her hands like an unruly cat. She rises above all of them, striking an imposing figure among the crystals and moss of the circle of power. The sopping figure hacks and curses in her grasp, and she shakes it while making eye contact with Elaine.

"The river said we owe you a wish, Elaine Aquae."

Uncle Neil tumbles out of Ophelia's grasp, hacking water out of his lungs from all fours on the muddy ground. His staff shoots out of the water with a low whistling sound, clacking harmlessly next to him. He uses it to rise and points a shaky finger at Dorian.

"Step away from my niece, you twat."

29

AN UNCLE'S LAMENT

Neil Leatherforth was seven when his father decided he didn't love him anymore. The secret of his paternity began to unravel when he was birthed like flames from his mother. The doctor said it was the brightest birth the hospital had ever seen, and he was sure to have a powerful affinity.

It was a bit of luck, he decided later in life, to be born in a humans-only hospital. If the hospital had allowed other species to use it, perhaps they would have seen the early signs of his differences as a dwarf, and he would have spent his entire life without knowing a father's love. And, despite their cruelties, he loved his family to a frightening degree. He used to get in trouble for grabbing his older brother's hand and pulling both of them into their parents' room. His father took them both by the hand, Albert rubbing a fist against his eyes as he was awoken for the second time that night. Once Albert is returned to his room, Mr. Leatherforth tucked Neil back in bed. The half-dwarf's eyes were filled with tears, and he pouted even as he allowed himself to be swaddled in.

"You need to stop waking you brother up and bringing him

to our room." His dad rubbed a large thumb across Neil's wet cheek. "Is it nightmares?"

Neil shifted, fists shoved in his dinosaur pajamas. "I like when I can see all of you. All the time."

His mother raised an eyebrow when her husband returned with both his sons, who snuggled into the middle of the bed, leaving their parents balancing precariously on the edges of the mattress.

That all changed when Neil did not inherit a fire affinity, and his ears grew rounder than those of humans. His dad's attitude grew cold, and he spent more time with Albert, then no time with either of them.

They were fourteen and twelve, respectively, when their mother decided she couldn't take it anymore. She moved the three of them to an isolated town in the Allapan Mountains. The two brothers played a muddy game of marbles outside the convenience store, waiting for their mom to return with the potato chips she promised they could have if they were good the whole way there. He beat his brother and was about to claim his prize of slapping him upside the head when they were interrupted.

"You're playing wrong," a child said.

A girl a few years older than them stood above them. She was of medium build and curvy, with long, dark-blue hair. Her eyes were alight with mischief, Neil could tell, but when he turned to Albert to watch him shoo her away, as he always did with strangers, his brother's face flushed a deep red.

"We're not playing wrong," Neil responded for him.

There was the ding of a bell, and their mother left the shop. He stood and brushed off his knees, the wet mud now stuck to his fingers instead. Albert didn't stand, still gaping up at the girl. She eyed the marbles with a frown, as if she hadn't considered other kids might play entirely differently.

"How do you play?" Albert said. It stuttered out of him like a bad song, or a lie he told Mom about where he'd been all morning.

Her blue eyes twinkled, and her mouth lifted into a smile so small, Neil was sure they were the only ones who could see it.

"Boys!" their mother called them, seeing they had company. She wasn't one for strangers.

Neil walked towards her, dutifully, but paused when Albert did not follow. His eyes were stuck on the girl, who had walked towards him and leaned down to speak to him. Whatever she whispered lit his eyes up in a way that made Neil's stomach curdle in envy. He grabbed his brother's wrist.

"Albert, come on." He tugged at his moony-eyed older brother, who cursed and hissed insults as Neil pulled him towards their mom.

"What's your name?" Albert yelled before she was completely gone from sight.

She didn't reply, only waving at them with that negligible smile on her lips.

Their mother eyed the girl with the same suspicion Neil had. She placed a hand on each of her son's shoulders, and Neil could feel himself relax under her grip.

"Who's your new friend?"

"She didn't say." Albert sighed, but a smile stuck to his face all the way to their new cottage.

Sigmut was a better fit than Neil could have hoped for. Despite his dad's animosity, his absence made him feel empty. Walking through the forest tempered the empty corner of his heart his father used to live in.

One day, though, his mother wanted him and Albert to join her at home to reset the wards. So, he took the dirt road until it became brick. He was in the town center. It was a small town, mostly the wives and children of miners who worked across the ridge. The houses were wood, painted in shades of blue, silver, and green, with red-thatched roofs. The house the Leatherforths lived in was made of stone. Their whole family ran hot—Mrs. Leatherforth and Albert were both fire mages—and Neil had grown comfortable with being too warm. His body soaked in their magic like a lizard on a rock, and the smothering pressure was never too much.

His mom told him to make sure Albert was on time, but he wasn't at his usual haunts: not the bar, the grocery store, or at the shooting range. Neil bit his lip, kicking up a pebble as he walked. He crossed by the general store, where the clerk sat up front.

"Have you seen Albert?" he asked.

The old man spit his chew out onto the ground. "S'with the Aquae girl."

Neil waved in thanks and headed up the mountain, towards the river. Over the years, Paola had become part of his family. Mom never grew to like her, or trust her, but all the other teenagers in town were too boring to hang out with. Her magic wasn't hot, but there was something wild in her, something that understood Neil more than his brother and mother ever had. It was a different relationship than he had with his magic. She was drawn to the river: whispering and talking to the water and the fish like they could talk back. He was drawn to volcanoes and caves, always moving towards the earth's core, a restless search for something to finally be too hot. His excursions settled that jealous, greedy need to take his most precious people and keep them where he could watch.

Neil emerges from the tree line to see Paola looking down at Albert, who had his back turned to Neil.

"Paola, look! I'm Neil." His brother removed his shoes and placed them on his knees.

Neil put a finger to his lip, and Paola smiled when her eyes flickered back to Albert.

"Don't let Neil see you do that, Albie."

He scoffed up at her, and Neil was sure he was wearing a smug grin. "What's that weakling going to do?"

"Push you in," Neil said right into his ear.

Albert yelped and tried to shuffle away, but he moved too late, and he was pushed straight into the river.

Paola shrieked with laughter, and Neil followed suit, Albert cursing at them from the water's edge.

Many summers passed like that one. The townsfolk left them alone, save for a few young men who ventured into the forest to look for Paola, who, over the many years, had become even more beautiful. Neil did his best to throw these suitors off track. Paola was Neil's, and Albert just needed more time to realize what the fast beating of his heart really meant. No one could say Neil wasn't a devoted brother, but he would admit to that one selfish thing—if Paola and Albert could fall in love, it would keep his precious people together where he could protect them.

When he came of age, his affinity for proportion magic was disheartening. But that disadvantage sparked his obsession with potion brewing. With a right and careful mind, potioneering had infinite possibilities. To find the right ingredients, he often had to go into strange and isolated parts of the mountain, being careful of dangers both natural and magic. He'd been less inclined to be in town recently anyways. Albert had married Paola just a few seasons ago, but since then, he felt as though Paola grew more and more distant in their marriage. It seemed he was often looking for a victim to bestow his sour mood upon.

Neil cursed, drawing his hand back from the trunk of a tree and seeing a thorn stuck in it. Bad luck at the beginning of the trek was not a good sign, but as he looked back at the cottage behind him, he plucked the nuisance out of his palm and trekked onwards. The woods were dangerous, but they didn't complain about their wives.

It was on one of these excursions he saw them for the first time—the wind nymph. They were terrifyingly beautiful, impossibly tall, and hard for the eye to catch as their body changed with every change in the wind. They move erratically along the bowl-shaped glen, and Neil noticed there were words stuck to the trees, old ones in script he'd never seen.

When they saw Neil, they came right in front of him. After a moment of staring, they changed their face to look more human: two eyes, a mouth, a mockery of hair. Neil did not move, staring straight into what he knew was a wild thing, whose whims were famous for changing on a dime. They open their mouth, and a gust of wind came out, so powerful it sounded like a scream.

Neil left the glen panting and retching on dry breaths, replacing the air that was stolen from his lungs, as they pumped desperately, empty, sagging against his rib cage. It was terrifying, and he came back the next day, and the next. They couldn't speak, but they understood each other through the shape of the mountain and the sound the grass made when they breezed through it.

The nymph changed its patterns one day. It pushed and pulled at Neil's clothes, and blushing, he let it.

"What are you...?"

The breath was sucked from him as the nymph blew delightfully at his ear. So, he let it undress him. It frowned down at his member, confused. As if they were expecting something else. Wind was nothing if not adaptable, however...so then, so then, so then...

Fall came and they died. Neil knew it would happen but held out hope that the wards that captured it would somehow preserve them. Death was the nature of things, and he left for a week without a word. But he grew no closer to filling his empty ache. There was one good bit of news from that season: Paola was pregnant, and she'd begun sticking close to home and Albert. Laughter filled their house again.

So, when Elaine was born, and she looked at him with silver eyes, he knew immediately what she was. She had the eyes of the wind nymph. And instead of feeling righteous anger for his brother, and for the love he lost as soon as he had discovered it, he felt a tug on him, like he had with all his family members before.

Paola watched him regard her baby with caution. The river had given her a sense for things human mages were not usually aware of. She was wild, too, but this baby was more than that.

It was then that Neil had had the revelation that he did not love in the way that a human should—by staying, by being a source of warmth and comfort and constant protection. He loved like a dragon loves gold. He oscillated between total abandonment, needing to search the caverns of the earth's core for life to be worth living, and coming home and demanding his loved ones all reside in the same place, the same home, so he could safekeep their lives, asking for every second of their time before he abandoned them again for another several years.

"I am delighted to meet you, Elaine Aquae," he told her quite seriously, shaking her little fist in his own with one firm pump.

He decided he could be an uncle when he saw the silver babe before him. Just this once. He meant just the one time too, as the other two children, born later, were lovely, but none of his concern. And so, when his brother learned of Elaine's true paternity and rejected her, and she decided to finally leave the Allapan mountains like Neil had always known she wanted to, he just so happened to be moving to Garriver as well. He had a house with room for two, that just so happened to be equal distance between her campus and the company he'd decided to work for. Of course, he'd help her, because she was his favorite niece, and it would be no trouble at all. After all, he was already in town. What a *coincidence*, what a stroke of *luck*.

Taking care of her was like greeting an old friend.

Neil left for an impromptu visit to Sigmut after the luck mage bounty went out. Neil told Elaine it was a work trip, but he sits in his brother's kitchen, frowning at Albert sitting across from him. Initially rattled at seeing his brother at the door, Elaine's father quickly ushers him in for a cup of tea.

Albert plays with the corner of the tablecloth, eyes darting to everything in the room but his brother. Neil takes this time to observe it himself, slowly sipping from his cup as he takes in that there is still two of everything: two coats, two umbrellas, two unfinished cups of coffee on the edge of the kitchen sink.

"So, you and Paola worked it out."

Albert grunted, finally making eye contact before his eyes dart back to the closet door behind Neil.

Neil took a deep breath in. He could be reasonable. He was just her uncle.

"Elaine's been writing you."

"I haven't gotten a letter in a while." Albert sipped from his mug.

"That happens when you don't respond to the sender."

Albert places the cup down too harshly, hot tea splashing on the rim as it collides with the table. His eyes flared with anger. "Don't do this, Neil."

"I'm not doing anything."

"You don't know what it's like to learn your child isn't your own."

Neil had eyed his brother over a cup of tea. "I know what it's like to be on the other side."

"What?"

"Surely, you're not that daft." But the wide-eyed look Albert gave him was undeniably shocked. Of course, his sweet, doting, blissfully unaware brother. "Albert, did you ever wonder why Dad treated me like he did? Why he left?"

"Dad loved us both," he argued. "I—I mean, I did wonder sometimes, but Mom would never."

"She did, Albert. And Dad knew. He hated me for it, and I hated him back."

There was a silence between the brothers where the secret used to reside.

"Will you come visit, just for a weekend? She's coming back from her familiar ritual tonight."

Albert was breathing harshly, red in the face and angry. He stormed out of the house without another word, throwing a paper envelope on the table before he disappeared.

Neil had regarded the letter his brother left behind with *Elaine* scripted across the front. He knew there was something cruel inside, either intentionally or because of its distant, clinical tone. Like father like son. He placed it in the fire, watching the pale paper turn to ash as it curls and crumbles into nothing. Elaine was not a vessel to house their possessive natures, their short tempers, or their cruelest thoughts.

So, when she brought home that miscreant, that Ivan, and he betrayed them both, Neil knew he'd kill him once he was free.

A water nymph, of all people, broke him out of jail.

"Who are you?" he'd asked.

"I can answer your question or bring you to Elaine."

He was not human, no, but he could be a better uncle because he never thought to be.

30

UNFORTUNATELY, A PROPHECY

Neil punches Ivan the way you'd expect a cat to bat a bird out of the air, well-planned and merciless. A shocked look is stuck on Ivan's face, even as his hands grapple with the hard fists pummeling his chest.

"Nothing to say for yourself? I keep that bounty off yours and Nellie's backs, and you still hand deliver her to your family?"

Ivan sputters as they roll and tumble over each other, punching, biting, and thrashing as one tries to kill and the other tries to subdue.

Between the fingers shoving his face into the ground, Ivan cries out, "Elaine is safe! Someone put a bounty out on a luck mage, I thought it was you, but it was Dorian. Or Calamity, I don't know! I was wrong, but please, I never hurt Elaine. I'd rather die than betray her again."

Neil grinds his face further into the dirt.

Gasping and coughing as he breathes in moss and fumes, Ivan says, "He's going to lift my curse. All Elaine has to do is enter the fairy ring and surrender. We'll all get to live."

Neil laughs as he pulls one lanky leg at an uncomfortable

angle. "You think he's telling the truth? Like he was telling me the truth when he paid my company fee to craft him a potion for his 'sickness' when it was really to steal power, and tricked me into helping him find the entrance to Garriver's fairy ring?" Neil pulls back to point an accusing finger at Dorian. "If Elaine enters that circle, she'll die."

Ivan crawls out from under Neil, finding an exit in between the whirl of kicks and blows. He shakes his head vehemently against the thought of her passing away. It is a terrible thing to not know your father, yes, and he never expected much from him. He expected him to lie, yet the seduction of the promise of a happy life with Elaine has distracted him from the truth.

"What do I do?"

"If you really want to stop your dad before he hurts Elaine, go on and die already, curse."

Near the edge of the fairy ring, Dorian is dragging Elaine back towards its circumference. She's struggling enough to free her wrists from her constraints, but her ankles are still tied, and Dorian pulls her by her feet as she claws and throws mud and dirt at him.

"Sources of power this big always have to offer a weak point," Dorian says. "Like I said before, when you challenge me, you'll become the circle's victor. You felt the way its magic entered you when we fell."

She recalls the way her skin tinged with power when they fell into the room, and how it still fills her with a vigor she thought she'd lost when Neil was arrested. Was it the magic of Garriver's circle of power?

"Circles of power are so potent that they have a trade off: they can be challenged for control over their magic. There's an old legend that says Garriver's ring will be conquered when there's a battle between three mages. It's hidden in an old wives' tale about Garriver's mythical beginning and end saying: *One of tragedy, one of comedy, one of history. One begs, another challenges, the last accepts."*

Elaine bristles at the implication that she's a clown. "My life is anything but funny."

"What is a tragedy, if not a comedy waiting to happen? And what's a jester, if not a child painting over his frown?" He shakes his head. "You, with your hidden nature and ill-fit features, are a monster tucked inside an aspiring accountant. Is there anything funnier than sticking someone where they don't belong?"

"I'm not ashamed," she said. "I've always been me, even when I'm different from who I was yesterday." She kicks out at him. "You steal, and you take and take and take. I am a nymph, but I am not a monster."

"Oh, Elaine," Dorian says, with no small amount of pity, "you aren't very smart. Your delusions are almost endearing. But story time is over, and you're going to help me, or Ivan's going to die of the family vow."

31

THE CURSE OF IVAN GRAY

Magic came to Ivan Gray, whether he liked it or not.

The sticky summer air invaded the deserted plains of Garriver. The cows sought shade under the banyan trees to no avail. Heat stuck to them like flies, clogging the pores that so desired to cool them down. The pigs hardly noticed underneath their mud. Hiding from the sun couldn't hide you from the heat that stuck to the dirt, simmering between grasses green and bubbling with the gasses of the marsh.

Indeed, no day had been quite so hot, and the silence across trails and roads reflected the desire to hide away from the heat, within cool houses made of auburn clay. Atop the lone hill, sat a house of unreasonable size and material. Painted rotting oak bent and eroded under the pressure of the atmosphere. There was a thrum of something sickly, something dying. A lone carriage with the symbol of a staff entwined with snakes rose towards it. The wheels sunk slightly into the mud, and the horseless carriage was being sucked into the open ground. Grass evened out the road as they grew closer to the house atop the hill.

The carriage came to a rolling stop in front of the stone steps of the House of Gray. A prim flat foot stepped onto the ground, followed by a white sheath of a dress. An impressively long neck followed as Head Nurse Isabella stepped forward and out of her carriage. Several women of reasonable height followed shortly after. Isabella took confident strides towards the bent front doors. They creaked open easily but caught against a raised plank creviced within the foyer.

Isabella slammed her palm hard against the door, and when the top half ripped itself open, she entered, the other nurses a flurry of feet behind her. They made their way down the hall, following the rasped baby's cry to an in-home infirmary.

The room was hushed, save for the quiet cries of Ivan's first breaths. The small, pale windows clouded the new mother from the outside world, and kept those inside unaware of the time of day. The floorboards creaked under a nurse's foot directly to Isabela's right. The heel of the other nurse's shoe slipped into the crevice of the floor below, and she winced as it cracked off her shoe and in the rotting wood. She picked up the broken heel, shoulder bumping into the head nurse as she moved back to make space for Isabella.

In her rush, the woman clipped her shoulder on a door frame and breathed out harshly in pain. Her mouth moved to swear, but Isabella covered her mouth with a dry palm. No one could speak in the House of Gray, unless they wished to breathe in the disease, waiting to prey and latch onto their words.

Within the new mother's room, there were the shushes of Darlene Gray, mother of the baby and matron of the Cursed House. Her babe cried, unable to stop long enough to latch onto his mother's breast and eat the food of life. Instead, he wept and sobbed and wailed, sucking in the breaths of the house, each cry weakening as foreign magic relished the baby's first breath. His cries eventually weakened, and then the head nurse spoke, finally.

"Ivan Gray, five pounds, ten ounces. Born the eleventh of May, induced with the Cursed House of Gray."

Ivan was three when the house started to put itself back together. His leg had just cracked under the weight of his body, after a wild leap from the top of the swing. He had climbed higher and higher and higher, eyes horizontal to the sky. He wondered, screaming in the dirt below the swing, why his mother smiled even as she cried. He closed his eyes and breathed in, breaths growing shallower as the dirt beneath him grew green grass.

HE WAS six when the faucet water finally ran warm. It was unfortunate that it came at the cost of his right hand. Inexplicably, the fingers became painful to move, the digits curled, his ring and middle finger now almost impossible to move without the use of one another.

"Ivan." His mom smiled, hands running under steaming water. "Come and feel this—"

He saw the moment she noticed him cradling his hand, blood draining from her face.

"Oh, Ivan," she said, rushing towards him. She took his hand in hers, but he snapped away, whimpering in pain. His hand pulsed when he failed to stretch his fingers.

"Why does it hurt?" His lip trembled.

She said his name, over and over, kissing his cheeks. Ivan stood frozen, curled up against his mother, his own tears joining hers.

When he was ten, he sat alone in the library. The tomes he had picked were larger than his head, and he'd needed help from the house itself to heave them onto the reading table.

The title read: *Gray Family: A History*.

"As members of the founding families, the Gray Household has a long and honorable standing with Magical Cities. Despite the laws broken by one particular ancestor, the house lives on with high standing."

Ivan paused at the paragraph. There was no further mention of the 'laws broken', the book instead prattling on about donations and battles won. His heartbeat faster at the idea that, perhaps, he wasn't the only black sheep of the family. His family home, ever empty, suddenly feels filled to the brim with family. With *stories*. He returned to the kitchen, cheese and bread spread out for him to choose from. He spent most of his summer in the tomes of his ancestors.

It's the eleventh book that finally mentions the name he often caught his mother speaking into the walls: Dorian.

Dorian. He searched in several glossaries. But it didn't come up. His eyes wandered to the sealed doors at the end of the hall. The house had always warned him against them. His feet touched the ground, paddling towards the old doors, and the house creaked in warning.

"Please," Ivan said. "I'd rather like to learn more. There must be more about Dorian behind here."

The house became colder, and something in the back of his mind, an instinctive part of him, lit up, humming, "Run. Stop. Go back."

But when you're young, you never truly think you can die.

A thud in the distance drew his attention. A book fell from a shelf. Ivan returned to put it away. The cover was old and worn, and read *Journal of D. Gray - Life, Curse and End*

"I think I've done it," it read. "I've transferred my life to painting. My face, my body, all perfectly preserved."

Ivan rubbed his stomach, thinking of the cucumbers pickling in the fridge.

"Something has gone wrong. My portrait has become decrepit. My house, no matter how many layers of paint I coat on it, soaks itself to rot. What did I miss? What went wrong?"

Ivan was twelve when he realized his ailment was a genetic curse.

"So, what, Dorian used me as a battery?"

"Don't address him by his name," his mother hissed, eyes darting around the house.

"I can call him whatever I want, seeing as he's slowly killing me, Mom."

Her eyes watered. "You'll live a very long life, Ivan. It is an honor—"

"An honor," he scoffed. "Mom, we've never been further than the property line, and you call that an honor?"

"Every century, a new descendant is chosen to carry the burden. Without us, the family would fall destitute. Your aunts, your cousins, our wealth would dry up."

"Aunts and cousins I've never met!"

He ran a hand through his hair, the walls creaking and tightening together.

"Ivan." Her eyes grew worried, and he let hope grow in his heart. "He will be upset if he learns of your disloyalty."

"He's not *here*, Mom!" he yelled. "He's off, seeing the world and living happily with my stolen life. He's left me to rot. I'm going mad, Mom. I'm dying." His voice cracked.

His mother gathered him in her arms, shushing him. "One day, you'll understand why we have to stay."

Ivan was fifteen when he left. And the House of Gray groaned.

32

A CURSE BROKEN

Elaine can feel herself drawn towards the circle. Dorian follows after, mere feet from the fairy ring.

"Challenge me, and we can—"

"Not so fast, you fancy bastard." From the underbrush emerges Calamity. His clothes are half-burnt, as is his skin, and his eyes hold a wild gleam to them, lips pulled painfully back to show his smile. He stumbles into the circle.

"You're like a cockroach."

"I want," he pants, "my share."

Calamity, the one from tragedy lunges towards Dorian, and Elaine joins him. She throws a weak right hook, deflected by a cane, but it gives Calamity an opening blow on Dorian's stomach. The percentages whir at a speed she can't keep up with as the men continue to fight. She yelps when Dorian turns his attention back on her, lunging towards her.

Going into this fight unprepared, she's shocked when a fist meets her ear. It seems Dorian's done pretending she'll come out of this unharmed. She stumbles, holding herself as her ear rings. She can faintly recognize someone yelling, as muffled as it is. Dorian smirks in front of her, probably saying something stupid.

"Stupid." She voices the thought and nods. That'll show him.

When he winds back for another hit, she wishes he wouldn't, and the probabilities gleam yellow above his head.

Dodge—8%

She leans to the left. *16%*

Right? *82%*

The fist veers past her, but his foot soon follows and cracks against her ribs.

"Elaine!"

She wheezes, holding onto her stomach and falling to her knees. His foot is about to stomp on her spine, but she rolls to the side just in time.

"Fight back, Elaine!"

Not helpful, she thinks.

But proven true when a well-aimed foot thumps against her back.

"Pathetic."

Roll, she begs herself. *Roll!*

Her body heaves to the left, rolling her onto her stomach as his foot clips her side. The river in front of her bubbles.

"Challenge me, nymph."

Ivan pulls her out of his father's grasp, pulling the two of them farther from the ring. As he looks down at her, a strange emotion stretches across his face. He bends and fiddles with the length of rope around her ankle.

Dorian stalks towards the pair, movements slowed by the vines snapping around his ankles. Neil moves to intercept with a war cry, but Dorian whips him across the face with his cane, knocking him unconscious.

"Uncle Neil," Elaine screams.

The ring may have chosen her as its champion, but it seems

it's still fighting the threat on its own. The vines wither when they touch him, rendering them a minor nuisance. But where they fail with Dorian, they succeed with Calamity, who thrashes against the nature of the fairy ring.

"Get these things off," he yells. They wrap around his wrists and ankles. Overpowered, he lays trapped against the ground.

"You think you can protect her," Dorian says to the open air. "She is but a breeze, and I am a force of nature."

Ivan turns, grimy and tired, and smiles at Elaine. "I'm so proud of you, Elaine." He pulls her forward and kisses her on the forehead. His eyes map a path along her face, as though he's trying to memorize it. "You were my new family."

Then, with the long reach of his arms, Ivan pulls Dorian towards him and snaps his father's neck.

Both Grays fall to the ground, Dorian's neck twisted and warped, eyes wide and blank. Ivan's own face is pressed into the dirt, slack and unmoving.

Elaine scrambles up, dragging herself by her hands towards him. "No," she mutters. "Ivan, wake up." She flops down, chin clipping the ground to use both her arms to heave his body over.

"Elaine, you have to know."

"I know, I forgive you for Neil." She bites her lip, tears falling down her face. "Say you'll forgive me, please."

"Not that." He shakes his head, wincing. He smells rotten to her, like decay. Like Dorian.

"I don't need anything else in this world other than your forgiveness." She was a fool to act as though they had all the time in the world to be angry with each other.

His grip tightens on her hand against his heart. "I love you. I've known it since we were trapped underneath the rubble, at the Nygard office, but I've loved you for much longer. I thought maybe your magic was interfering with mine, and that's why the curse worsened. Convincing myself it was Neil that made my curse flair and wanted the ring's power was such a relief. It meant if I could stop him, I'd spend forever with you."

"You can," she cries. "We still have time."

His brown eyes close. "I'm afraid this time, we were a few minutes late." Ivan heaves a great big breath in, but his lungs can't handle it, and he sputters out a weak, rotten cough. His chest doesn't rise again.

"No," Elaine's voice breaks. Her hands search over his cloak, checking his still-warm breath for a sign of life. "You can't go."

Her vision worsens, no longer blurred by just tears, her magic coating everything in a layer of yellow. "Wake up," she whispers to him. In her struggle, the final rope twists off her ankle, and she scrambles up to her knees, pressing her hands to his chest in short compressions, breathing into his mouth in an attempt to revive him.

When that doesn't work, her hands spark with magic, and she presses all that she can into him. It had worked before, in the prison where he first saved her. Surely it could work again? In desperation, she kisses his lips, over and over. But with each press, he remains limp, and her touch grows violent. Soft kisses are replaced by sharp, violent punches to his chest.

"Wake up!" she rages, hair whipping wildly around her. "Wake up, you idiot!"

She wonders if she'll die like a nymph or a human. The grueling nature of a human death would not be beautiful. It would be death as she's always known it: bloating, excrement, a saddened family, food for worms, for wolves, for the blueberries. Do you feel your body decompose, she wonders, rubbing an absent hand across Ivan's neck. When do you leave your body? With the skin, with the nerves, with the muscles? Or only when the wet bones finally dry and the proteins of your marrow are sucked dry by flies?

On instinct, she rolls her neck to the left, and turns to see the attack that just missed her.

"He's dead." Dorian stands there, jaw tight and eyes glassy. It's a look Elaine is used to but seeing it on him makes something in her mind break.

Her body turns stiffly, a marionette caught on strings. *It can't be,* she thinks

But that abominable rosy hue highlights the youth of Dorian's cheeks and the twinkle to his eyes, neck crackling as the bones set themselves back in place. She stands, but his eyes are stuck on the body behind her.

"You're supposed to be dead," she hisses.

He turns his eyes towards her, malice overshadowed by the curiosity in his gaze. "He killed us, for you."

"You don't get to look at him," she snarls.

Her approach snaps him out of his shocked trance, and he easily pushes her to the ground. She immediately rises and catches him by surprise, punching him straight in the chest. He doesn't wince, but it does draw his attention back to her. He stands taller than he did before, and this time, when he swings his cane at her, he doesn't miss. The crack of it leaves a burning feeling first, then the searing pain blossoms across her jaw, and her cry of pain only exacerbates it.

"His mother will be very upset." He whips his cloak away, and the scent of mold is replaced by the scent of decay.

She gags, and the moss beneath his feet dies and withers till it's a dull brown.

He notices her disgust. "An unfortunate side effect of Ivan's little disappearing act. Rest assured, after I sacrifice you to the ring, I'll smell much—"

Elaine tackles him into the fairy ring, the garlic shining even brighter as they land in the middle. The whole cavern rumbles, the garlic spreading and multiplying outwards until they stand in a circle the length of a tennis court.

She stands up, cocks her first, and punches him so hard across the jaw that his head snaps to the side.

Punch left—82%
Duck right—91%

It stings but she hardly notices as the numbers guide her like a dance, her own feet free of the ring's ire—she is its champion.

Because when she focuses on the right parts of her magic, on what it can do instead of what it can't, she feels it like she never has before. Her stomach twists, and her head still hurts, but they fade into the background as the thrill of the fight puts her into a flow state. Every hit lands, and when she moves, it feels like flying.

Dorian is forced to stand there and take it. Vines wrap around him all the way to his thighs, and when his magic sucks them dry, three more wrap around to take their place.

"A breeze, huh," she cackles, landing another hit.

If she can knock him unconscious, force him out of the ring, she can win this. He's almost there, just a few more feet and she wins. Her eyes flicker for just a second to the blob of brown cloak strewn across the floor, and her anger falters for a moment. It's in that mistake Dorian finds his opening, punching her, then kicking, again and again until she's lost her advantage to her own mind, her thoughts entirely on Ivan Gray, dead man, and whether she can revive him. Even then, she can't stop thinking of how badly she wants him to live.

CPR - ERROR

Funny, she thinks as she looks at the yellow letters in front of her. *I've never wanted something impossible before.*

There's a flash of silver from Ivan's corpse, and hope fills her even as she lays curled up at Dorian's boot. It is the glint of a crystal hitting his silver glasses, just a trick of the light. It's why she laughs just before Dorian's boot knocks her out of her body, her mind already lost to the outside of the circle, lying next to the lump of brown they'd left behind.

33

STOLEN VALOR RETURNED

She comes to alone within the circle. She sits up and sees Dorian standing next to Ivan's body. That brings her back, and she scrambles towards them both even as her wrists throb in protest as she crawls forward, too tired to stand. Dorian kicks her forehead when she reaches them, and she's splayed on her back again.

"You're lucky your mother misses you." He sneers at the body in his grasp. "You'll be buried with the rest of the Grays despite your mutiny." He holds a cup in the air, jeweled opulence on a silver goblet. It must be the potion Neil was tricked into creating for his plan.

"With the ingredients I sourced, and the failure of the ring's mutant champion, it's complete. In my pure human form, this potion will grant me the immortality of Garriver's ring!"

As he uncorks the bottle, a shadow darts through the air above him.

"No," she breathes.

"Yes," Dorian laughs.

As he lifts the potion to his lips, something is dropped into it, and he shoots it back in one large gulp. His nose scrunches in distaste, but it's quickly replaced by a smile. The final bell sounds, announcing the end of the spring equinox.

Dorian steps into the circle. "Now, as the winner, I command the ring—give your magic to me."

There's a rumble in the earth. Garlic sprouts fill the swamp floor. Its tendrils wind around Dorian, shining silver and glowing around him.

Roger flies into Elaine's line of sight, landing on her shoulder and settling into the familiar crook of her neck.

Dorian grabs his chest, grinning. "My heart," he says. "It's beating."

That smile turns to a frown as the garlic wraps around him, joined by thorns and moss. The swamp creeps up his body, emulsifying him as it crawls upwards. and then he's choking, reaching out hands in anguish. Around him the ground opens, and he claws at the dirt, nails raking and breaking against the ground. He cries out in a mix of anger and anguish, arms failing, but with a final desperate yell, he's swallowed. It happens so quickly that it doesn't feel real. But as soon as he's swallowed, the awful stench of his magic disappears. Grief still wraps its hands around her neck, but the fear of death is gone. For a moment she worries her loss means the city will be gone when they emerge from the subterranean tunnels, but she feels the flow of the circle's magic as vividly as she did before the battle. Garriver took care of Dorian, for good.

Elaine crawls the rest of the way to Ivan. He's cold in her hands, and she tries to shake him awake.

"Ivan, please," she says. "Not now, not this time."

Roger, who she realizes was the shadow flying over Dorian while he drank the potion, descends down her arm. He makes a noise of distress when Ivan doesn't lift a hand to pet his leathery wings.

She rubs her thumb against Ivan's cheek, curling her body

over his. "You can't leave now, not when I've just found you." She cries softly, collapsing onto his still chest.

There's a twitch beneath her.

"I'm not going to lie, I'm loving the attention."

Elaine pulls away. His eyes creak open, and he grunts in pain when he rises to his palms, but he's breathing. She helps him sit up fully before collapsing forward and wrapping him in a hug, fingers pulling the thick fabric of his cloak tightly against her.

"I thought I lost you."

He places his forehead against hers and takes a moment to catch his breath. "I'm impossible to kill. Like a cockroach. Or a particularly voracious luck mage."

She laughs. "Only you could come back from the dead."

He shakes his head. "Something happened at the end. It felt like years of my life got pumped into me."

Her eyes glance to the dirt still marred with the trail left behind by Dorian's fingers.

"Your dad was taken by the ring. Maybe it restored the magic from the curse to its rightful place."

"Dead?" He repeats. "Really, truly dead?" He smiles. "Incredible."

She watches him for signs of grief, but instead, he looks relieved. Physically, he looks better too. His eyes are less shadowed, his skin a less sickly color.

"I love you," she says.

He smiles. "Say it again."

"I love you, I love you, I love you."

"Again!" he teases with a smile.

She obliges, kidding his face between every declaration. It pours out of her without reason, without a schedule or a binder, or an itinerary. It pours out like magic, like salmon up the mountains, like bears into the sea.

34

INTERLUDE: ROGER

Roger does something very brave the night Ivan dies. He creeps back into the sewers, avoiding his former family as he soars above them, higher and higher until he finds his old nesting hole. Titon opens one yellow eye, and Roger's heart beats fast. But then he looks down at the nest below him and sees no trouble (because who would look to the sky for a rat?). He goes back to sleep, and Roger continues his journey.

His rebellion under Titon consisted of a pile of stolen trinkets—left socks, loose buttons, things Titon asked for then discarded when he didn't need them anymore. They weren't allowed personal knickknacks, and this secret is entirely separate from the needs of the horde, something just for him.

He sorts through the pile with nostalgia. He doesn't need them anymore. Becoming Elaine's familiar filled that empty space previously filled by Titon. However, at the bottom, carefully hidden and preserved, is her toe. The city has been whispering to him for months now. *Follow the woman. Patience. Not just yet.* The magic is easy to hear when you cannot speak, and Roger always has his ear to the ground.

So, when the rhythm of the moss and fungi changes, his ears perk up from his seat in his old bedroom. The electricity that connects the city is not wrapped in rubber and connected through steel posts along the surface, but through the fauna that all leads back to Garriver's fairy ring.

Bring the toe, it zings. *She is in danger. Bring the toe.*

He picks the toe up delicately between two teeth. How serendipitous it is that his old masters' command, combined with his own selfish hoarding, should come back and save the other half of his heart. How grateful he is, for the chance magic has given him to absolve his sins. He loves her just as a familiar should.

Forgive me, Elaine, I did not know how much you'd come to mean to me.

He arrives with little time to spare.

You gave me wings. You taught me how to fly.

The fairy rings magic directs him to the gray cloaked corpse holding a goblet aloft.

Drop it in.

He drops the toe in just before the enemy downs his potion. Wings outstretched, Roger takes post at a shadowed cliff at the edge of the cavern. The potion shifts, he can smell it. They're particular and don't like change. But the corpse still drinks it, unaware that the drink has been changed. Elaine is injured, but alive, and Roger swings into her embrace as the corpse sinks into the ground where it belongs.

Redemption does not come to Roger in returning her toe, but in using the appendage for its original purpose: as a resource.

35

LUCK AND PROBABILITY

She's taken to the hospital by a throng of concerned medics after they follow a tunnel back into Locke, Neil and Ivan in tow in their own gurneys. She lets paramedics know Reginald Calamity is still trapped in the circle of power, but her words are slurred, and the medic is sternly asking her of any possible allergies. There's a rush of officials and nurses scurrying around her sick bed, threatening her life and fluffing her pillows intermittently. They've all been placed in separate rooms, partly because of how serious their injuries are, and partly because they are all prime suspects in a serious breach of Locke, and the city-level disaster event that almost took place. Garriver moves as quickly as usual, unmarred by what happened below the surface. On their way to the hospital, she sees the familiar explosion of the apartment across from the watchtower, and she closes her eyes, unable to fight the exhaustion blanketing her body.

She falls asleep the moment her head hits the pillow, only to be woken by the streak of sunlight entering her room from the window, and hushed voices whispering nearby. With a groan, she blinks her bleary eyes open and sees three familiar figures surrounding her. There's a squeak from the other pillow, and Roger bolts upright.

"You're awake!" her mother says.

"Thought you'd finally decided to kick the bucket." Her brother, Alan, smiles.

"Blorb," Phoebe bubbles from her tank.

"You brought Phoebe." Elaine smiles at her salmon sister, whose blank-eyed stare meets her own.

"What have you been doing, Elaine? Seventy years with no incidents, and a few months with Neil and you nearly die?"

"Oh, leave her be, Mom. We've been waiting for a little rebellion."

"Blub," her sister agrees.

Alan rubs his hands together. "Now, let's hear all about this near-death experience. Is it true you fed someone your toe and they burst into flames?"

"Alan!"

"What? My boring sister finally does something cool, and a guy can't ask a few questions?"

"My toe?"

"It seems like your familiar brought your toe, as you asked, and dropped it in that man's potion, messing up the properties and contaminating it with...non-human magic." Paola says.

"Mom!" Alan snaps.

"Oh—sorry, dear, I don't mean you're contaminated, in fact I—"

"It's alright, mom," Elaine laughs. "I know you mean there was an extra ingredient in the potion."

Paola looks to Alan with raised brows, as if to say 'see'. He rolls his eyes.

As if summoned, Roger peeks out from a pocket in Alan's cloak. When he sees Elaine awake, he rustles his wings open and jumps into her lap, scrambling up the edge of her hospital gown to sniff her face.

"My familiar, Roger," she laughs, scratching him under the chin. That's why the ritual hadn't worked all those months ago; she couldn't summon a partner she already had.

"Who told you all of that?" She asks. "Roger can't speak anything other than rat."

"A king came by to see you." Her mother shares, delighted. "What have you been up to, Elaine!"

Alan rolls his eyes. "I told you that wasn't a real king, Mom."

"Well then why was he wearing a crown?"

"Titon," she breathes out in disbelief. He must have come by and spoke with Roger.

"King Titon." Her mother corrects.

Alan makes a tired noise, as if they'd already had this conversation before, and knowing her mom, they definitely had.

He turns back to Elaine, and changing the subject, says, "They say some guy named Lord Gray was swallowed by the earth, then and there!"

Elaine winces at the volume.

"Alan!"

"Sorry, Mom."

A few more pleasantries are exchanged, but the visit tires her quickly, and her family leaves her to fall back into a deep sleep.

When she wakes next, it's to Neil and her dad arguing over her bed. She believes she's still in a dream, but then she smells her dad's magic, and not even her brain can fake the singed smell of his magic when he's in a bad mood.

"Give her space, Albert. It's been months, and her mind is scattered. Do you really think now is the time?"

"And what would you know? I'm her dad."

"Oh, are you? Then where—"

She interrupts them with a loud clearing of her throat. An inelegant coughing fit follows, her voice scratchy and weak from disuse. Her father grabs a glass of water, nearly dropping it in his haste to place it in her hands. She nods at him in thanks.

When she knows she's not about to start hacking again, she says, "I can handle it from here, Uncle."

Neil's brown eyes flit critically across his brother. He turns his attention back to her, leaning in with a twinkle to his eye. "There's one thing I still don't get. How did you live through that impossible potion?"

"I had a similar problem with my T.A. session. Ivan told me 'success isn't about getting it right', and I didn't understand what he meant at the time. If the potion was going to kill us, we'd have to make something new. The potion is only impossible if you don't use an affinity like probability magic. Since it's been dismissed as useless, they didn't prepare defenses against it when they created the trial. I made the potion right, and he combined his magic with mine to change the odds."

Neil grunts, impressed. "That's handier magic than I thought him capable of. But you, Nellie," and he smiles, proud and wide, "I knew you had it in you."

He pats her hand before standing up with the aid of his wooden staff. He stops at the edge of the curtain, which wrinkles under his grip. He turns to look Elaine in the eyes. "If the world had blessed me with a daughter like you—" he turns to Albert, "—I would have never turned you away. Blood or not."

The curtain swishes closed behind him, the air now filled with the faint beep of machines, and the mutters of hospital staff moving across linoleum tiles.

Her father shifts uncomfortably in his seat. "I'm glad you're safe."

"Mm-hm," she replies. She wishes for a cup of tea. Or an Ambien.

"Your mother and I… We wanted to tell you… *I* wanted to say I'm glad you are settling in."

It's worse than getting beat with a cane, she decides. "I think I need more pain medication."

Dad shoots up in his seat. "I'll get a nurse."

He shuffles beyond the curtain, and she's glad for the respite. Once he's gone, she lets tears fall for a myriad of reasons as aches and pains bloom across her whole body.

She spends the next few days healing, separated from her fellow inmates. She plays with Roger and fields questions politely from family and policemen alike, but her mind wanders to Ivan when she's alone. He's an unregistered, sewer-scouring mage-for-hire that probably accounts for a large number of unsolved thefts from the last few decades. If they need to, they can sneak out. They'll probably need to either way, because there's no chance Ivan Gray has health insurance.

"Good news," a nurse tells her as she drops off a pudding. "You've been cleared of all charges."

"All three of us?"

The nurse nods, never taking her eyes off the clipboard. "All three."

The nurse clears her from bedrest, and she springs from her cocoon, sheets knotting around her ankles, which she shimmies free. With Roger on her shoulder, she heads for room III, where the nurse told her Ivan is. She hesitates as her fist reaches to knock on the door.

Taking a deep breath, she enters without warning and sees Ivan doodling on a piece of paper.

"Is that connect the dots?"

His head snaps up, eyes bright. "Lainey." He moves as though to get up, wincing and grabbing his stomach, before settling back in.

"Death really did a number on you, huh."

He pouts.

Cute, she thinks.

"This is not how my neighbor's girlfriend greeted him. She brought over flowers and everything."

The word girlfriend makes her heart do strange flips in her chest. She settles into the chair next to him. His frown deepens, and he pats the spot next to him on the bed. She rolls her eyes, even as she scooches in next to him, ignoring the pleased hum that comes out of him as he wraps an arm around her waist. She leans in and listens to the rhythm of his heart.

"It's steady," she says.

"The curse is gone, at least, it better be." He kisses the top of her head. "The doctor thinks the only reason I'm alive is that Dorian had years of my life stored up inside of him, and it all returned to me when his life ended. Like a new battery."

She must have made a face because he laughs.

"You can call him names, y'know. I'm not attached to the man."

"Then I'm glad the bastard's dead. And I hope his last moments were long and painful."

A few nurses come through to check Ivan's vitals, and while they look at her position on the bed disapprovingly, none say anything.

"I'm guessing everyone knows." Elaine nods to the congenial nurses.

Ivan grins. "Yes. We are the unsung heroes of Garriver. It turns out Neil was working with the university to test and strengthen the traps around the fairy ring, but the private potion company that employed him rented him out to Dorian, who was looking for the entrance and a potion to take the ring's power. It all wrapped up nicely in a bow to blame him, but when word got out that the dungeon had been broken into *before* Neil escaped prison, they listened to his side of the story, and he's cleared of all charges."

She sighs in relief. "Attending my second year would have been difficult if the police were constantly tailing us."

"Oh?" He looks delighted. "And what are *we* getting up to in your second year?"

"Mischief, mayhem, general delinquency in the name of science."

"I'll allow the science bit, since the first part of that is so enticing."

He looks at her as though he can't believe she's real, and his lips turn down into a frown. He grabs both her hands in his, looking at her seriously. "Back when we were making the impossible potion, I need you to know that I could feel it was all going to work out. My magic told me I could have everything I wanted, but only if I listened to Dorian. There was no time to explain, and I knew you'd be mad about it."

"Nothing to apologize for," she says, rubbing a thumb across his hand. "You were right. You saved all of us."

His fingers squeeze more tightly around her own.

THEY WHISPER and laugh together for hours after that, keeping their voices low in case the charity of the nurses wears out. She places her head on his chest, warm and breathing and right. Uncle Neil is free, Roger is her familiar, and Ivan broke his curse.

"I love you," she says. "You got the chance to say it before I did, and I'm still upset you stole my thunder. So, I'm saying it first today: I love you. There. I said it first twice."

He laughs, free, like the wind. "You can say it first every day, if you like."

They whisper to each other through the night, free of burdens. There are no curses to cure, no secrets to keep, no words left unsaid; and the circle of power, Garriver's fairy ring, hums as vibrant as ever beneath the ground, singing praise to the woman who slayed a monster of old.

ABOUT THE AUTHOR

Map Feliciano is a midwestern fantasy author. In her free time, she frequents Chicago's public libraries and the Forbidden Woods hidden beneath the Sears Tower (she sneaks in when the security team isn't looking). *Luck and Probability* is her first novel.

www.ingramcontent.com/pod-product-compliance
Lightning Source LLC
LaVergne TN
LVHW100503110826
845146LV00002B/495

* 9 7 9 8 9 9 3 7 3 0 0 2 8 *